Praise for *Young Turk*

'Everyone should go out immediately and buy Moris Farhi's latest novel *Young Turk* ... Warm, witty, wise, humane, it's a delightful and moving book.'
Nicholas Murray, author of *Kafka*

'Exuberant ... a triumph of imaginative memory, on a par with WG Sebald's *The Emigrants* ... These are real stories – the type you'd stay up all night to hear.'
The Guardian

'A novel of startling integrity and beauty.'
Independent on Sunday

'Beautifully rendered, poetic and mystical ... A challenging, wry and rewarding read.'
Daily Mail

'This far-sighted novel is a pleasure to read and makes most of this year's fiction look pale and anaemic in comparison.'
Scotland on Sunday

'The novel's energy and good humour sweep the narrative along.'
TLS

'... erotic and intoxicating ... His is a quicksand sort of storytelling that sucks you in, redolent with poetry and heavy on the sex ...'
Big Issue

'*Young Turk* is infused with a passionate humanism ... Both a novel of ideas and an entertaining adventure story ... a lyrical celebration of the multicultural heritage of Turkish history.'
The Independent

'... enchanting ... a blend of memory and imagination, imbued with deep humanity and sympathy ... love in its multiple manifestations pervades this wise, generous book.'
Financial Times

'... exquisitely crafted ... With hints of Gabriel Garcia Marquez and Isabel Allende, this is evocative and enthralling; Turkey is brought to vivid life in this beautiful book.'
Good Book Guide

'A great read.'
Sunday Independent

MORIS FARHI

YOUNG TURK

TELEGRAM

London San Francisco Beirut

ISBN 10: 1-84659-028-0
ISBN 13: 978-1-84659-028-3

First published in 2004 by Saqi Books
This edition published 2007 by Telegram Books

A full CIP record for this book is available from the British Library.

Manufactured in Lebanon

TELEGRAM
26 Westbourne Grove, London W2 5RH
825 Page Street, Suite 203, Berkeley, California 94710
Tabet Building, Mneimneh Street, Hamra, Beirut
www.telegrambooks.com

For NINA
who was with me before I met her

and to my beloved friend
ASHER FRED MAYER
9 May 1934–8 May 2004

In memory of:

Anthony Masters (14 December 1940–4 April 2003)

Tomasz Mirkowicz (9 July 1953–7 May 2003)

Acknowledgments

With gratitude to my family for their love: Ceki, Viviane, Deborah, Yael Farhi; Marcelle Farhi; Nicole Farhi; Rachel Sievers and Hamish MacGillivray; Eric, Danièle, Sara, Nathaniel Gould; Phil, Rachel, Samuel, Joshua, Kezia, Joseph Gould; Jessica Gould; Emmanuel, Yael & Noam Gould; Guy and Rebecca Granot; Silvio (Jacques) Hull.

With gratitude to Barry Proner whose insights into the mysteries still sustain me.

With gratitude to my friends and mentors for their guidance: Ian Davidson; Peter Day; Anthony Dinner; Tamar Fox; Mai Ghoussoub; Saime Göksu-Timms; Robin Lloyd-Jones; David Mayall; Christopher New; Saliha Paker; Maureen Rissik; Bernice Rubens; Anthony Rudolf; Hazem Saghie; Evelyn Toynton; Vedat Türkali; Enis Üser.

With gratitude to my kindred spirits for their unflinching support: Tricia Barnett; Selim and Nadia Baruh; Erol, Eti, David Baruh; Anthea Davidson; Rio, Karen and Liam Fanning; Kağan, Yaprak and Temmuz Güner; Jennifer Kavanagh; Michael and Diana Lazarus; Julian and Karen Lewis; Robina Masters; Elizabeth Mayer; Faith Miles; Richard and Ceinwen Morgan; Christa New; Adem and Pırıl Öner; Kerim Paker; Lucy Popescu; Paul and Gabriele

Preston; Nick, Maggie and Rosa Rankin; Paula Rego; Christopher and Bridget Robbie; Hazel Robinson; Elon Salmon; Nick, Jeanine, Isabella and William Sawyer; Edward Timms; Diana Tyler; Paul and Cindy Williams.

With gratitude to my alter egos in distant lands for their solidarity: Ergun and Rengin Avunduk; Attila Çelikiz; Ayşem Çelikiz; José Çiprut; Rajko Djuric; Ahmad Ebrahimi; Bensiyon Eskenazi; Agop and Brigitte Hacikyan; Bracha Hadar; Ziv Lewis; Bill and Sue Mansill; Julita Mirkowicz; Barış Pirhasan; Donné Raffat; Ilan Stavans; Martin Tucker; Deniz Türkali; Andrew Graham-Yooll.

With gratitude to new comrades for their faith: Petra Eggers; Nina Kossman; Semra Eren-Nijar, Indirjit and Ilayda Nijar; Zbigniew and Maria Kanski; Sharon Olinka; Ros Schwartz; Osman Streater; Ateş Wise; Jessica Woollard.

With gratitude to my guardian angels at Saqi Books for their dedication: Mitch Albert; Sarah al-Hamad; André and Salwa Gaspard; Jana Gough; Anna Wilson.

Contents

A Note on Pronunciation

All Turkish letters are pronounced as in English except for the following:

c pronounced *j* as in *jam*

ç pronounced *ch* as in *child*

ğ not pronounced; lengthens the preceding vowel

ı akin to the pronunciation of *u* in *radium*

ö pronounced *ö* as in the German *König*

ş akin to the *sh* in *shark*

ü pronounced *u* as in the French *tu*

1: Rıfat

In the Beginning

In the beginning, there is Death.

All creatures meet it at birth. Animals never forget the encounter. With very few exceptions, we humans always do, even though we haggle with it several times a day. This commerce is never conducted with the brain or the heart, as we might expect, but with the genitals. The tinglings we feel between our legs are not always caused by sexual desire or fear. Mostly, they document our negotiations with the Clattering Skeleton.

These are facts. Straight from the mouth of Mahmut the Simurg. He is the Türkmen teller of tales from the circus who, true to his nickname, looks like a bird as large and dark as a rain-cloud. And though he accompanies himself on a *kemençe* that has only two strings instead of the usual four, he creates sounds that seem to come from other worlds. Those who have heard him sing the history of mankind in one thousand and one episodes will affirm that he is, as he avows, the only man of truth on this earth.

Sometimes transactions between Death and its prey get violent. When Alexander the Great, emerging from Olympias' womb, saw Death hovering about, he immediately unsheathed his sword and hurled himself at him. Death barely escaped. And he did not dare go near Alexander for thirty-three years; not until he had succeeded in bribing a Babylonian mosquito to poison the noble king.

The phenomenal and often overlooked aspect of that story, Mahmut the Simurg stresses – overlooked even in the *İskendernâme*, Nizâmi's incomparable paean to Alexander – is not that a newly born infant should have the courage to attack Death – after all, one expects such qualities from godlike heroes – but that every generation produces many ordinary individuals who are able to perceive the Keeper of the Dust. Those deathsayers with seven eyes, seven brains and the mettle to rescue Death's victims – like Hercules, Atatürk and Churchill, to name but a few – are known as *Pîr*.

(An elaboration: Death, as we all know, is an agent of Allah. But unlike Allah's other servants, he is also a fiend. Thus, whenever he can, instead of garnering souls who have lived full lives and need to transfer to a better realm, instead of choosing miscreants who deserve to die, he grabs the young, the good, the gifted, even whole races. Often he snatches, long before their rightful time, people who are heartily loved by Allah Himself. In so doing, he humiliates the Almighty. And that is iniquity beyond iniquity. Does a garden let its plants perish? *Sorry, Efendi, the roses have all died today; apologies, Hanım, tulips will be extinct by tomorrow; alas, Ağa, lilacs were exterminated yesterday!* Naturally, Allah had to intervene. So He created the *Pîr*.)

As I said, Mahmut the Simurg knows all the truths. Thus when he sang his revelations about the *Pîr*, I realized our neighbour, Gül de Taranto, was one such.

∞∞∞∞∞∞❀∞∞∞∞∞∞

Gül, approaching thirteen, was four years older than I was. Her brother Naim, leader of the neighbourhood gang, was my age. Both Gül and I were shunned by this gang as being 'of a different species'. Gül not just for being a girl, but also for being virtually an adult – she had started her bleeding. Even more unforgivably, unlike her delicate name which means 'rose', she was a tomboy: the song 'There Are No Roses without Fire' could well have been composed for her. She outshone every youngster in the district at every sport, including boxing. Her gym teacher believed that if she put her mind to it, she could make the following year's Olympics in Berlin. I, on the other hand, was fat – I had nearly died after contracting diphtheria a second time, and my mother, in an effort to build up my strength, had force-fed me as if I were a goose. Fat boys could never be gang material.

As Mahmut the Simurg would say: misfits must live,

too. So Gül and I ended up doing things together.

It all started on the day of my circumcision.

I was sitting in my room, dressed in the ceremonial white satin *camise* and hat, fighting my fear of the impending cut and wondering whether I would survive the assault on my 'key to heaven', as Mahmut the Simurg describes the penis. Suddenly, to my surprise, Gül – not her brother Naim, as I might have expected – popped in to wish me well. Then, after the briefest of pleasantries, she asked me, very businesslike, if I would show her my still-capped organ. In return, she was prepared to show me her mysterious crevice – a sight no one, apart from her brother Naim, some members of her family and Naim's lieutenant, Bilâl, had seen. She wanted to compare my 'thing' with those of Naim and Bilâl, both of which, in accordance with Jewish custom, had been decapitated eight days after birth.

Naturally, I agreed enthusiastically – ignoring, wisely I think, Mahmut the Simurg's warning that the vagina has enslaved more men than all the tyrants of history put together.

So I pulled up my *camise* and she lowered her panties.

Hesitantly, my heart pounding, I examined her cleft, even touched it.

She, on the other hand, scrutinized me casually, as if I were a medical specimen. (She had once confided to my mother, who was a nurse, that she intended to become a doctor when she grew up.) 'They say circumcised cocks are superior to uncircumcised ones. And that, therefore,

Christian women are always disadvantaged. Is that true?'

I pretended to know. 'Definitely.'

She studied my penis fastidiously. 'Not as good-looking as circumcised ones.'

'It will be. After today.'

'But it's bigger than Naim's. Bigger than Bilâl's, too.'

My spirits rose. I might have been fat and not gang material, but I was better endowed. In the male world, even at our age, that meant I was somebody. 'Oh, yes ...'

'Is it because you're Muslim and they're Jewish?'

'Probably ...'

'Though I've heard you're not a real Muslim.'

'Yes I am.'

'Aren't you Dönme?'

Dönme literally means 'turned'. As a people, it refers to the followers of Sabetay Zevi, the seventeenth-century Jewish sage who had declared himself the awaited messiah. Zevi was arrested by Sultan Mehmet IV, the Hunter, for fomenting unrest and was asked to prove his messiahship by surviving the arrows that would be shot at him by three of the realm's best archers. Zevi, sensibly refusing to submit to the test, had hastily converted to Islam. His followers, interpreting this conversion as a step towards the fulfilment of the messianic prophecy, had also converted *en masse*. However, throughout the ensuing centuries, they had remained true to their faith and practised their Jewish rites secretly.

'Who says?'

'Everybody who knows your family.'

'They've no proof …'

'They put two and two together …'

'Meaning?'

'You have lots of Jewish friends. Most of your relatives go away on Jewish holidays. And your grandparents never stop criticizing Jews – which is what many Dönme do to hide their Jewishness.'

I blushed. She was right. My grandparents, particularly my grandmother, appeared so intolerant of Jews that people accused them of anti-semitism. And, true enough, they were secret Jews who always went away mysteriously on High Holidays to an undisclosed location. And they painstakingly hid every trace of their Jewishness, particularly their Hebrew books, from all eyes, including mine.

But not so my parents. My parents were genuine converts – Muslim through and through. People could tell that just by their pietistic names: Kenan 'reserved' (my father), Mukaddes 'sacred' (my mother).

'Well, they're wrong. We may have Dönme roots, but we're true Muslims.'

Gül shrugged and laughed. 'Not that it matters. Atatürk says we're all equal.'

'Yes.'

She pointed at her vagina. 'Seen enough?'

'No …'

She pulled up her panties. 'Yes, you have!'

Ruefully I dropped my *camise*. I realized I had fallen in love with her. And I imagined that having seen each other's genitals, we could consider ourselves married – well, unofficially. I became instantly jealous. 'Why did you show yourself to Bilâl?'

She laughed. 'Because I love him.'

'Does that mean now you also love me?'

'You're too young.'

'So is Bilâl.'

'He's Jewish.'

I wished I were Jewish, too. 'Is it because I'm fat?'

She shook her head. 'No. Just too young. I'd better go. Good luck.'

'Thanks.'

At the door, she blew me a kiss. 'If you'd been Jewish you'd be laughing. You'd have been done already.'

That annoyed me. I wanted to protest. But she had gone.

So I wrote to her, explaining the many reasons that made circumcision so important for a Muslim. That it is the most momentous initiation in a boy's life and must be revered as such. That unlike Jewish boys who get chopped off when they don't know who they are or what they are – not to mention that getting cut when only eight days old makes it all too easy for them – we Muslims experience circumcision when we approach puberty, when we already have some idea of what the world is like and what we can expect from it. That whereas Jewish boys have to wait until their bar mitzvahs, when they are thirteen, before they can be considered men, we attain manhood the moment we shed our foreskin. That undertaking circumcision when we are old enough to understand the significance of the rite impels us to attain the Prophet Muhammet's perfection even though that objective is unattainable because the Prophet Muhammet, Blessed be His Name, was born perfect and was thus the only man born circumcised. That circumcision is one of the five cleansers that give us mental and moral probity; consequently, unless circumcised, we cannot pray in a mosque or perform the Haj or even marry.

Writing the letter eased my fears. When I set out for the park where the communal circumcisions and the ensuing festivities would take place, I strutted as if my silly *camise* and hat were the uniform of Mehmetcik, our indigenous soldier considered indomitable even by Tommy, his British counterpart. To keep my spirit bubbling, I envisaged Gül's downy vagina smiling at me, like two halves of a sunny peach. And I remembered the softness of her hand on my penis. My penis which, to date, could do no more than urinate and harden always at unwanted moments was, lest I forget, bigger than both Naim's and Bilâl's!

And as I lined up with my brothers-in-rite outside the circumciser's tent and received the blessing of Cemil Ağa, the rich man of the neighbourhood who was defraying the cost of the festivity as his charitable duty for the year, I shamed myself by producing an erection that no youngster of my age was supposed to have.

∞∞∞∞∞◦❀◦∞∞∞∞∞

Gül, as I have already mentioned, was a *Pîr*.

I discovered this the following summer.

We were playing football on the beach in Suadiye. (Gül was not allowed to swim. Her eyes were allergic to the iodine in the sea.)

Bilâl's mother, Ester, was swimming on her own; she was far out, halfway to Burgaz, the second of the Princes' Islands. Gül's mother Lisa, Ester's close friend, was stretched out under a parasol, reading a book. (My mother, Mukaddes, the third member of this set of Graces, had won a bursary for a midwifery course and was away in Ankara.)

Normally, Ester, Lisa and my mother swam together. Before marriage and children, they had swum to all four Princes' Islands. On a number of occasions, they had even tried to swim the length of the Bosporus, but had had to give up each time because of the shipping to and from the Black Sea. But Lisa, having been vaccinated against smallpox, had been told not to swim for a few days. (Bilâl was God knows where. Naim and he were too independent to be seen with their mothers.)

Gül was running circles round me with the ball when she suddenly stopped and pointed to the horizon. 'Ester's in trouble!'

I looked at where she was pointing. Ester – or rather her red swimming cap – was a dot on the sea.

Gül ran to the edge of the water. 'It's pulling her down!'

'What's pulling her down?'

Gül waded in and, gesticulating wildly, screeched

high-pitched sounds like a dog being tortured. 'Somebody save her!'

As Lisa jumped up, I threw off my sandals. 'I'll go! I'm a fast swimmer!'

I dived in. Ester was too far out and I had no chance of saving her, but I had to try. I swam furiously.

Then I saw another swimmer in the distance change course and strike out towards Ester.

I heard Gül shout. 'Someone's gone to help. She'll be safe now.'

The other swimmer reached Ester.

After a while, I joined them.

The other swimmer turned out to be Deniz, a relative on my father's side. One of my dream women. When she got married – I was barely four at the time – I had thrown a monstrous tantrum, calling her husband a donkey and begging her to divorce him and marry me. Deniz, sweet and good-hearted, had gently fended me off. Thereafter, I had locked her in my mind and imagined enjoying untold things with her.

Ester was suffering from stomach cramps. Women's problems, Gül told me later.

Deniz and I took turns to drag her back. It was hard work, but it had its rewards. As we toiled to control Ester, who kept flailing as if determined to drown us all, I frequently brushed against Deniz's big breasts.

On the beach, Ester, still contorted, hugged us. 'How did you know I was in trouble?'

Lisa pointed at Gül, who had picked up the ball and was practising some fancy footwork. 'She saw you.'

Deniz nodded. 'Yes, I heard Gül shout! That's what made me turn round and see Ester.'

I was amazed. 'How could you have heard her? You were too far out.'

'I don't know how. I just did.'

Gül dragged me away. 'Come on – let's play!'

Later, at siesta time, Gül and I took to our bikes. Defying the afternoon heat with strenuous activity was our way of demonstrating our toughness. We went across to the Golden Horn and, pretending we were competing in the Tour de France and climbing mountains like the Tourmalet, the Aubisque and the Izoard, rode furiously up and down the hills. Gül, being the faster rider, had long designated herself the *maillot jaune* and always wore a yellow jersey.

When we stopped to pick some figs from the trees lining the lane to the Greek patriarchate, I asked her. 'How could Deniz have heard you? You weren't even shouting!'

Gül thought for a long time. 'Strange, isn't it?'

'Telepathic, I'd say.'

'Maybe.'

'What else?'

Gül pulled me closer to her. 'Can you keep a secret?'

'You know I can.'

'Nobody must know.'

'What is it?'

'It is like telepathy, only stronger. I sense – see – things. Dangerous things. Just as they're about to happen …'

'You're kidding me …'

'I can see Death … When he gets too near …'

'That's impossible …'

She looked annoyed. 'I can! I've chased Death away many times. I chased him when he came for you …'

'For me?'

'When you had diphtheria the second time.'

'I had diphtheria the second time because they inoculated me at school before I'd recovered from the first!'

'Well, he came for you – Death … Stood around for three nights …'

I remembered those nights. My windpipe was so blocked I could barely breathe. My mother had managed to procure an oxygen cylinder from the hospital – probably the only one in Istanbul in those days – but even that hadn't helped. They had had to do a tracheotomy.

'It was the tracheotomy that saved me.'

Gül smiled smugly. 'That was my doing.'

I forced a laugh. 'Oh, sure!'

'I kept shouting at all the doctors I could think of! Inwardly – the way I shouted at Deniz this morning: Do something! Do something! Finally they performed the tracheotomy.'

I stared at her, expecting her to giggle and tell me she'd been teasing me.

She stared back defiantly. 'You don't believe me?'

I did. And I didn't. I nodded uncertainly.

'You'll keep it a secret – you promised!'

I nodded again.

She rubbed her hands. 'Right. Now, don't think Death's forgotten you. He's around somewhere. So, time to get you really strong. Turn all that fat into muscle. Do you wrestle?'

'No ...'

'Best way. Let's go!'

I gaped at her. 'Wrestle with you?'

'Why – scared I'd beat you?'

'You're a girl ...'

'I won't tell, don't worry!' We were near a plot of land awaiting builders. She dragged me there and drew a square on the earth. 'This is the mat ...'

And as we grappled, as I locked my arms around her muscular thighs and felt her buttocks, firm like flexed biceps, I decided I would definitely marry her, too young or not. I even swore I would stop being unfaithful to her in my fantasies and no longer lust after dream women like Deniz – an impossibility, as I soon found out.

<hr />

Much as I loved tumbling with her, I didn't like losing to Gül every time we wrestled. So I joined the Fenerbahçe Youth Club and began some serious training after school.

I surprised everybody, most of all myself, by showing an aptitude for sport. After about a year's weight training, I had converted most of my fat into muscle and was noticeably stronger, so much so, in fact, that I thought I might be asked to join Naim's gang. I wasn't. Prejudices die hard. Moreover, because of my association with Gül, I was seen as a girl's man.

Another year on, I finally defeated Gül. After that, I never lost to her again.

Looking back, I should confess I felt I had triumphed far too soon and too easily. With hindsight, I attribute this to the fact that, getting more and more enmeshed in her deathsayer's world, Gül was losing interest in ours.

I should also confess that, somewhere in my soul, I was aware of this dislocation. But I chose to think her detachment simply meant she no longer needed to worry about my health. As if that wasn't bad enough, I also ignored Mahmut the Simurg's cautionary tales about such oracles as Pythia and Cassandra, the Sibyl and the Sphinx. These seers, the teller of truths explained, succumbed sooner or later to a condition known as '*Pîr*'s palsy', which is a darkening of the mind that afflicts the *Pîr* after too many sightings of Death. Gül, whom I had introduced to him, was an exceptional *Pîr*, he warned me, and might yield to this palsy sooner than most.

Even more unforgivably, I didn't perceive the depth of Gül's anguish when she first confided her fears to me.

It was a national holiday, 19 May, the day celebrating Atatürk's arrival in Samsun in 1919 to launch the War of Independence. We had gone to the park where the fairground had set up shop. Though on that occasion we could have joined the gang – Naim was in bed with jaundice and Bilâl, his deputy, quite obviously had as soft a spot for Gül as she had for him – we didn't. This time Gül, stuck even deeper in her inner world, insisted that we should be on our own.

So we went round the shooting galleries, chairoplanes, carousels, acrobats, jugglers and the rest. My efforts to brighten her mood failed dismally.

But when we reached the Gypsies, she became animated. Leading me by the hand, she started surveying the booths. Then she stopped in front of one and stared at its placard. Beneath a painting of herbs and crystal balls, the legend read:

* FATMA * HEALER * MEDIUM *

'I need to go in there, Rıfat.'

I dragged her away. 'Later.'

My attention had been drawn to the enclave of a bear-leader who was challenging the onlookers for a 'brave heart' who would have the mettle to wrestle with his mammoth bear called Yavru, 'nursling'. Ten *kuruş* only – refundable if the challenger stayed on his feet for a minute.

I nudged Gül. 'Shall I?'

'Waste of money.'

'What's ten *kuruş*?'

'It's a tenth of a lira. And with a lira we can both go to the cinema.'

'But this is a challenge …'

'Oh, all right. As long as I get to see Fatma, the medium, later.'

'Sure.'

She grimaced. 'The bear stinks!'

'So? Shall I? I'm very tempted …'

'Go on, then – do it!'

I took off my shirt and paid my ten *kuruş*.

As soon as I moved into the circle, Yavru rose on his hind legs. He looked twice his huge size.

The bear-leader shook Yavru's chain.

The bear growled.

I stood transfixed, suddenly terrified.

The bear launched himself. He moved so fast that I could neither back away nor run. Seconds later, I was on the ground with his front paws triumphantly pressing on my chest.

The bear-leader whistled.

Yavru sauntered away.

I hauled myself off the ground, ashamed at having failed so pathetically.

The bear-leader shook my hand. 'At least you've got balls.' He pointed at the crowd. 'They're all chicken-hearted!'

Gül kissed me on the cheek. 'I'm proud of you!' Then she took out her handkerchief and dabbed my chest. 'He scratched you!'

I shouted in frustration. 'He could have killed me.'

'I would have been forewarned.'

'What?'

'Had you been in danger, I'd have seen it.'

'Oh, sure …'

'I see such things … I told you once … Don't you remember?'

I nodded vaguely. Still smarting from my defeat, I wasn't prepared to be convinced. I put on my shirt and started walking.

She pointed at the booth advertising Fatma, the medium. 'Wait! I need to go in there.'

I grumbled. 'Do you have to?'

'Yes. I won't be long.'

I waited, curiosity overcoming my irritation.

When she came out a few minutes later, she was smiling – for the first time that day.

That fuelled my interest. 'What do you want a medium for?'

'She's not just a medium. She's also a healer.'

'So?'

'For Naim.'

'What on earth for?'

'Let's have an ice-cream – I'll tell you.'

We bought our ice-creams and sat on a bench. Gül's smile had evaporated. She stared, seemingly nowhere, with wide-open eyes.

She looked so vulnerable that my bad humour dispersed. I ruffled her hair. 'I'm all ears.'

To my surprise, she held on to my hand. 'I'm scared.'

'Because of Naim's illness? It's only jaundice.'

'He's had it for over a month. He's very weak now. It'll get worse.'

'Come on …'

'I'm never wrong about these things. I see all the possibilities – all that might happen. All the calamities. That's what's so scary. Naim needs a healer. Fatma can make him better.'

'Would your parents agree?'

She sneered. 'My parents? Trust their son to a Gypsy? Not in this world.'

'I see.'

'It's got to be done secretly. I have to smuggle Fatma into the house.'

'That's asking for trouble!'

'I'll need your help …'

'Me? Oh, no! I mean, a healer doing things to Naim! When there are plenty of good doctors …'

'Please. You've got to help me! If Fatma doesn't treat Naim, he'll die!'

'Don't be silly!'

'I'm telling you! I can see Death! I can see how Naim will suffer! All the horrible details!' She started crying. 'Naim will die unless we intervene! Believe me!'

I remembered that time at Suadiye beach when she had somehow communicated with Deniz to save Ester. I also remembered her claiming to have saved me the second time I had diphtheria by getting the doctor to perform a tracheotomy. 'It's difficult to make sense …'

'I know. But it's true. I see these things. I see Death. That's why I'm so scared.'

I couldn't help it, I believed her. 'What will the Gypsy do?'

'What do you think? Lay hands. Give herbs. Their way ...'

'Nothing else?'

'What else? Will you help me?'

How could I refuse? 'What do I have to do?'

'Late tonight. After everybody's gone to bed. Bring Fatma to our house. I'll let you in. She said she only needs a few minutes ...'

I nodded, but remained apprehensive.

She kissed me. 'You're a true friend!'

'One thing. Do you see things about yourself?'

'Never, thank God. Why?'

'What if things go wrong tonight?'

'They won't. You'll be there. I haven't seen anything happening to you.'

∘∘∘∘∘∘∘∘∘∘∘✿∘∘∘∘∘∘∘∘∘∘∘

Gül lived in a small house by the sea at the end of a parade of taverns that catered for the staff and passengers of Haydarpaşa, the railway station that served Anatolia and the countries beyond. Thus, the neighbourhood was busy day and night, and no one – not even the night-watchman – paid any attention to Fatma and me as we made our way in the early hours of the morning.

Gül had been on the lookout at the window and opened the door the moment we arrived at the house.

Guiding us with a torch, she led us to her brother's room.

Naim, clammy with sweat, was sleeping restlessly.

Fatma lit a match, then took out a razor blade and held it to the flame.

That made me uneasy. I whispered. 'What are you doing?'

Fatma muttered. 'Sterilizing.' She directed me to the other side of the bed. 'Hold him by the shoulders. Gül – hold his head steady.'

I stammered, aghast. 'You're not going to cut him?'

Fatma growled urgently. 'Hold his shoulders!'

Gül, clutching Naim's head with both hands, hissed angrily. 'Trust her, Rıfat!'

Bewildered, I gripped Naim's shoulders.

Naim woke up with a jerk. Then, seeing us – three shadows behind the torch's faint light – he grew frightened and tried to shout.

Fatma covered his mouth with one hand. With the other, she swiftly cut three parallel lines, about half a centimetre apart and two centimetres long, on Naim's forehead.

Naim struggled violently.

Gül tried to restrain him. 'Ssshhh! It's all right! Everything will be all right!'

As he felt the blood trickling down his face, Naim's panic increased. Finding some reserves of strength, he threw us off and started screaming.

Calmly, Fatma put her blade away. 'Let's go!'

But before we could take a step, the light went on in the room and Naim's parents, Lisa and Sami, rushed in.

For a moment we stared at each other in shock.

Naim, still screaming, scrambled out of bed and rushed over to them. 'Mami! Papi!'

Noticing the blood on Naim's forehead, Lisa started shrieking.

Sami turned to us in horror. 'What have you done?'

Fatma patted his shoulder. 'He'll be all right. I took the poison out!'

Sami stared at him. 'You did – what?'

'The poison that turned him yellow. I drained it through the third eye. Your son will be fine in three days.'

Lisa, with Naim still hanging on to her, wailed. 'Fetch the police! Fetch the police!'

Gül shouted. 'No! She's just saved Naim's life!'

Lisa and Sami stared at her as if she were mad.

Gül pointed at Naim's cuts. 'Look – just three little cuts. Nothing else! The blood's drying already!'

That set Lisa off screaming again. 'Sami – the police! Get the police!'

Gül blocked her father's way. 'No, Papi! Trust me! Let me explain ...' She turned to Fatma and me. 'You two – go now! Thank you.'

We slunk off.

The next day, everybody talked about our diabolism. Only the fact that the family doctor, summoned post-haste, declared the cuts Fatma had inflicted on Naim as superficial and not at all infected prevented Lisa and Sami bringing charges against us.

On the third day, Naim's jaundice disappeared, as if angels had wiped it clean during his sleep.

In another week, as his strength began to return, he became his old cocky self again.

⚬⚬⚬⚬⚬⚬⚬⚬⚬⚬⚬⚬⚬⚬⚬⚬⚬⚬⚬⚬⚬⚬⚬⚬⚬⚬

In the ensuing months, Fatma, Gül and I – particularly Gül – came to be seen as 'different'. People who must be treated with caution.

Fatma was hardly bothered. Gypsies had always been considered different.

But I grew resentful. For a start, when I asked whether I could now join the gang, only Bilâl backed me. I confronted Naim: not only had I played an important part in saving his life, but also, thanks to having taken up wrestling seriously, I was stronger than most of the boys, including him. He agreed with me, but contrived a sly excuse: I had wrestled with a bear; that made me as filthy as any Gypsy. (I should have punched him on his third eye, but I didn't think of that. I've never been quick-witted.)

Gül fared the worst. Rather than applaud her resolve in saving Naim, people looked on her as if she had tried to murder him. Malicious tongues implied that she was a daughter of Şeytan, the Devil – even that she consorted with him. Gül ignored these rumours or laughed at them. But I could see she was much troubled by them. I could see that with each passing day the 'Pîr's palsy' was increasingly possessing her.

⚬⚬⚬⚬⚬⚬⚬⚬⚬⚬⚬⚬⚬⚬⚬⚬⚬⚬⚬⚬⚬⚬⚬⚬⚬⚬

Time passed.

We remained close, but somehow distant. I continued loving her. We met less and less. She had become a close friend of Handan Ramazan, the girl who lived next to the bakery and played the *kanun*, that magical instrument that Handan's father, our greatest player, claims can produce every sound in heaven with its seventy-two strings. They were turning into teenagers and had developed a passion for dance music and films. I had found my religion: wrestling.

∞∞∞∞∞∞◆∞∞∞∞∞∞∞

About two years later, on another national holiday – 30 August, Victory Day, we met again at the fair in the park. As if in homage to the previous occasion, we had made our way, separately, to the bear-leader's enclave.

She teased me. 'Come for a return match?'

I smiled and took my shirt off. 'Why not?'

I went into the arena. But this time I was ready for the bear. As he attacked, I jumped aside and leaped on his back. Using every skill I possessed, I tried to unbalance him. Needless to say, he eventually threw me off. But I had stood my ground much longer than the requisite minute.

After that, still nostalgically, we went to have an ice-cream. We didn't say much. I basked in my success with the bear. She stared at her hands – a sure sign that she was lost in her own world. Eventually, flustered by our silence – yet we must have had so much to tell each other – we got up to leave.

'Be well, Rıfat. And be careful.'

'Sure.'

'Terrible things are happening. In Europe. China. Worse to come.'

'You've been seeing things again?'

'Streams of them. All the time. Death everywhere. Not just for Jews. For everybody. Even for our friend …'

'What friend? Who?'

'I can't tell yet …'

'If I knew, I could try and prevent it from happening …'

She stroked my cheek. 'You're so sweet. It's very vague at the moment. And I may have got it all wrong. But confusion – uncertainty – doesn't help. Just drives me mad all the more.'

'Can't I do something? Help in some way?'

'Can you make me go to sleep? And never let me wake up?'

'If we saw each other more …'

She kissed me on my lips. 'Take care. Always.'

Then she ran off.

<hr>

Two days later, Germany invaded Poland.

<hr>

Winter set in. And it proved to be one of the coldest winters of the century. Temperatures in some parts of Anatolia dropped below minus 30 degrees centigrade.

On 26 December 1939 my mother went to Erzincan, in eastern Turkey.

As I mentioned before, my mother had trained as a midwife. She had so excelled in this specialization that she had soon surpassed most of the obstetricians who had been sent to study abroad. In 1938, following glowing recommendations, the ministry of health commissioned her to structure a nationwide training programme for midwifery.

The principal recommendation for my mother had come from none other than Professor Albert Eckstein, a German Jewish paediatrician who had been given asylum from Hitler's Germany by Atatürk himself and who, over the years, had attained the status of saint in Ankara's Nümune Hospital – the institution that serves as a model for every hospital in the country. It was through the auspices of this professor that my mother had procured the oxygen cylinder when I had contracted diphtheria for the second time and, indeed, on his advice that my doctor had performed the tracheotomy. I know this because Gül once told me he had been one of the doctors she had telepathically begged to save me.

(Atatürk's offer of refuge to those persecuted by the Nazis – an offer that not only saved countless European artists, academics and intellectuals from certain death, but also enabled them to pursue their careers – emulated the way Sultan Beyazıt had opened the empire's doors, almost 500 years earlier, to vast numbers of Jews and Moors fleeing the Spanish Inquisition. Professor Eckstein, I should add, had been initially targeted by the Third Reich more for being an anti-Nazi – which in those days was equated with communism – than for being a Jew. As my father once remarked, the fact that the good professor was greatly esteemed by a Turkish administration that had outlawed its country's own Communist Party, and imprisoned most of its members, gives an idea of the paradoxes that ruled – and still rule – Turkey.)

Inevitably, my mother had to travel a great deal. Though this was hardly to my liking, my father accepted it with equanimity. A research botanist at the Agricultural Academy in Çiftlik, on the outskirts of Ankara, he understood only too well the priorities for a nation trying to jump from the eighteenth century into the twentieth in a few decades. So the two of them turned every homecoming into a celebration and enjoyed a marriage that was the envy of their friends. (Sadly, to this day, my paternal grandparents will tell whoever chooses to listen that my mother's all too frequent absences seriously hampered my development by diverting my interest to sport instead of good old-fashioned commerce. But then they are so determined to camouflage their Dönme origins that they would criticize any act of non-conformity. And of course they have the field to themselves. My maternal grandparents, also Dönme and said to be enlightened, were killed during the battle for Izmir in 1922.)

As I said before, my mother went to Erzincan on 26 December. She arrived there at about 9 PM – a fact my father established from the log of the bus that had brought her from Erzurum. Almost immediately, she gave a lecture at the city's hospital. The next morning she was scheduled to address a group of middle-school graduates interested in a career in midwifery.

At roughly the time of her arrival in Erzincan, Gül rushed into our apartment screaming that my mother was in danger.

Weeping and agitated, she urged my father and grandparents to contact my mother immediately and tell her that she had to leave Erzincan and travel as far north as she could.

Of course, my father and grandfather knew about Gül's prophetic gifts. But they could not bring themselves to accept that my mother was in mortal danger.

I did. So did my grandmother, who believed in all things occult. And together we prevailed on my father and grandfather to try and contact my mother.

They rushed out to find a telephone – not an easy task on a bitter winter's night in Istanbul in 1939 – while we prayed that the country's antiquated telephone system would somehow defy the elements and get through to the mountainous east.

About 11 PM, while my father and grandfather were still out, Gül quietened down. She turned to us, utterly exhausted. 'It's too late now. She hasn't got time to run away.'

I tried not to believe her. But my strength drained away. I sank on to the floor and curled up.

Gül crawled to a corner and stared into the void.

After an hour of nightmarish silence, my father and grandfather returned. They had scoured all Istanbul in vain for a telephone. Finally, my grandfather had thought of going to his Masonic Lodge, which had a switchboard. They had duly woken up the night-watchman and, after what had seemed an eternity, had finally contacted my mother at her lodging. Though she had sounded fine, my father thought she had been perturbed by the call.

Gül made no comment. She withdrew further into herself.

We dragged ourselves to bed.

At about 2 AM Gül started screaming again. 'She's dead! Crushed! Dead! Dead!'

We jumped out of bed in panic.

My grandmother, always calm under pressure, switched on the radio.

And after many torturous hours of shuttling between hope and despair, we started hearing about the Erzincan earthquake. Eight on the Richter scale – a mere one degree less than the maximum. Striking at 1:57 AM. Lasting for fifty-two seconds – an eternity for those caught in it. One survivor described it as the Devil shaking the earth as if it were a die in a heated game of backgammon. All of Erzincan and many surrounding villages razed to the ground. Telephone and telegraph lines destroyed – hence the length of time for the news to get through. Regions stretching hundreds of kilometres from the epicentre also affected. (In Ankara, a relative's son, aged four, squealed with joy as his cot was shunted from wall to wall, believing that the tremors were a new game.)

The death toll reached 33,000. Approximately 120,000 homes had been destroyed.

My mother's body was never recovered. The earth where her lodging was located had opened up, swallowing all the buildings; then, as if contrite at what it had done, it had closed up again, barely showing a fissure.

I only saw Gül once in the weeks that followed. She came to show me some newspaper clippings which reported that broadcasts from Nazi Germany were calling the Erzincan disaster divine retribution; perhaps now Turkey would agree to join the Axis forces and cut off relations with Britain and France. Though I could see that Gül, as a Jew, was extremely disturbed by these demented rantings from the Nazis, I did not have the sensitivity to soothe her. I was too involved with my own grief, too much in pursuit of the desperate efforts children make in order to accept life without a parent.

Then, on Saturday 3 February 1940, I received a brief letter from Gül: '*God be praised! I know how to stop seeing.*'

I rushed to her house. Her mother told me she was

spending the weekend with her friend, Handan. They intended to go on a film binge.

I went to Handan's apartment. Gül had not spent the night there. In fact, Handan had not seen her for a couple of days.

On an impulse, I went to the park where the summer fair takes place. Like a sleepwalker I went to the bench where we had sat and had ice-creams.

Gül was there. Stretched out. Like Snow White. Peaceful. Seemingly asleep. But preserved in hoary ice. She had frozen to death.

She had died smiling. Or did I imagine that?

2: Musa

Lentils in Paradise

Paradise was Sofi's gift to Selim and me. She took us there frequently. I, Musa, was about seven; Selim a year or so older. Paradise was the women's *hamam*, or Turkish baths, in Ankara.

I can still see Sofi watching out of the corner of her eye as Selim and I surrendered to ecstasy – smiling, I'm convinced, under the scar that ran diagonally across her mouth. (Years later, Eleftheria, my Greek lover – her name means 'freedom' – who took great pride in being many women all at once, called our ecstatic state 'the sorcery of ten dances', a heavy Hellenic pun on 'decadence'.)

Sofi cherished us as if we were her own; and we loved her just as much. In fact, I can now admit, we loved her more than we loved our mothers. We reasoned that since she was under no obligation to hold us dear, the fact that she did meant we were worthy of affection. Consequently, we never believed the loose talk from parents and neighbours that, given the law of nature whereby every woman is ruled by the maternal instinct, Sofi, destined to remain unmarried and barren, needed, perforce, to treasure every child that came her way, even curs like Selim and me. (I remember a neighbour's refrain: 'A virgin she may be, but who'd take a lass with a scarred face?' And the curs, Selim and I, shouting in unison – prudently, out of earshot – 'Us! As soon as we're older!')

Sofi was one of those young women from the Anatolian backwoods who, having ended up with no relatives and no home, found salvation in domestic service in the cities. Often payment for such work amounted to no more than the person's keep and a bed in a corner of a hallway; wages, if they existed, seldom exceeded a miserable lira or two a month. But in the early 1940s, when Turkey's policy of neutrality in the Second World War had brought on severe economic problems, even this sort of employment was hard to find; the sizeable metropolises, Istanbul, Izmir, Adana and the new capital, Ankara, were rife with chilling stories of the misadventures that had befallen many maidens from the countryside who had failed to find just such a job.

My parents, I'm glad to say, paid a decent wage despite the constant struggle to make ends meet. For

Sofi was an Armenian, a member of a people that, like the Jews, had seen more than its share of troubles. Sofi herself, as her premature white hair and deep scar testified, was a survivor of the Passion suffered by the Armenians under the Ottoman regime during the First World War.

Selim and I never accepted the distinction that Sofi was a servant. With the wisdom of young minds we dismissed the term as derogatory. We called her *abla*, 'elder sister'. At first – since Selim was not my brother, but my friend who lived next door – I insisted that she should be known as *my abla*, but Sofi, who introduced us to everything that is noble in humankind, took this opportunity to teach us about true justice. Stroking my forehead gently – while Selim, recycling some doorbells we had found in a dump, rigged up a telegraph system with which we planned to disseminate her supreme message to the whole world – she impressed upon us that since Selim and I had been inseparable since our toddling days, we should have acquired the wisdom to expel from our souls such petty impulses as greed and possessiveness. She belonged to both of us, what was more natural than that? Which meant 'all for one and one for all'. So hear, hear, everybody! Follow our example! And, naturally, share all you have. Amen.

And hear, hear, everybody! Eat well, build the world and grow wings naturally, like the silkworm that feasts on mulberry leaves, weaves a cocoon and emerges as a butterfly. Amen again. 'Naturally' was her favourite word. And let the eye behold all that is good and beautiful, naturally, the way water runs. Amen.

∞∞∞∞∞∞◈∞∞∞∞∞∞

And hear, hear, in paradise our eyes did behold, naturally, the way water runs, all that was good and beautiful.

The event that paved the way to the women's baths occurred, almost as if preordained, the moment Sofi set foot in our house.

She had arrived from the eastern Anatolian province of Kars. The journey – mostly on villagers' carts; occasionally, using up her few *kuruş*, on dilapidated trucks – had taken her about a week. And for another week, until she had heard on the grapevine that she might try knocking on my mother's door, she had slept in cold cellars procured for her, often without the owners' knowledge, by sympathetic countrywomen. She had washed in the drinking fountains of the open-air market where she had gone daily in search of scraps; but, lacking any spare clothing, she had not changed her sweat-encrusted rags. So when she arrived at our flat, she had come enveloped in the pungent smell of apprehension and destitution.

My mother, seasoned in matters of disinfection – she had attended to my father whenever he had come on leave from the army – immediately gathered a change of clothes from her own wardrobe and guided Sofi to the shower, our only fixture for washing. (The shower, I should explain, though an object of pride for my father for being a modern Western appliance, was a primitive affair: rigged over the oriental toilet, it comprised a tiny rose – spurting the thinnest of sprays – crowning a couple of rickety pipes one of which always rusted in the summer because hot water was available only in winter.)

We had hardly settled in the sitting-room – I remember we had visitors at the time: my parents, Selim's parents, some neighbours and, of course, Selim and me – when we heard Sofi laughing. My mother, who had taken to Sofi instantly, looked well satisfied, no doubt interpreting the laughter as a happy omen.

Moments later, the laughter turned into high-pitched giggles. Giggles became shrieks; and shrieks escalated into screams.

As we all ran into the hallway fearing that Sofi had scalded herself – she couldn't have because it was summer and there was no hot water – the toilet door flew open and Sofi burst out, wet and naked and hysterical.

It was Selim's father who managed to contain her. While my mother asked repeatedly what had happened, he threw a raincoat over Sofi and held her in a wrestler's grip until her screams decelerated into tearful, hiccupy giggles. Eventually, after sinking to the floor and curling up, she managed to register my mother's question. As if relating an encounter with a jinn, she answered, in a hoarse whisper, 'It tickles! That water tickles!'

The ensuing laughter, expressing as much relief as mirth, should have offended her; it didn't. Sofi, as we soon learned, believed that laughter had healing qualities and revered anybody who had the gift of humour. But it had never occurred to her that she herself could be comical. The revelation thrilled her. And, as she later admitted to me, it was her ability to make us laugh that had convinced her to adopt us as her kin. Yet her decision to join our household could not have been easy. Having classified the shower as an infernal contraption, she must every day have dreaded going to the toilet and squatting, as she had to, beneath its silent and threatening head.

The afternoon ended well. When Sofi, hesitantly, asked whether she could finish washing by the kitchen tap, my mother – truly a golden-hearted person, whatever her shortcomings – promptly took her, together with the women visitors, to the *hamam*.

Thereafter Sofi became a devotee of the baths. And she used any excuse, including the grime Selim and I regularly gathered in the streets, to take us there. My mother never objected to this indulgence: entry to the *hamam* was cheap – children went free – and Sofi, Selim and I, sparkling after so much soap and water, always appeared to confirm the adage, 'Only the clean are embraced by God.'

∞∞∞∞∞❀∞∞∞∞∞

In those days, Turkish baths were seldom able to maintain their Ottoman splendour. The neglect was particularly evident in Ankara. This once humble townlet which, with the exception of an ancient castle on a hillock, had barely been touched by history, was rising fast as the symbol of the new, modern Turkey. As a result, some 'progressive' elements saw the baths as totems of oriental recidivism and sought to reduce their popularity by promoting Western-style amenities.

Yet, here and there, the mystique prevailed. After all, how could the collective memory forget that, for centuries, the Sublime Porte's spectacular baths had entranced and overawed flocks of discerning Europeans?

And so the tradition survived: discreetly in some places; openly, even defiantly, in others. And when new baths were built – as was the case with most of the establishments in Ankara – every attempt was made to adhere to the highest norms.

Two cardinal standards are worth mentioning.

The first predicates that the primary material for the inner sanctum, the washing enclave itself, must be marble, the stone which, according to legend, shelters the friendly breezes and which, for that very reason, is chosen by kings for their palaces and by gods for their temples. (There used to be a rumour in the early fifties that a particular establishment in Ankara, exclusive to diplomats and members of parliament, had, in an effort to outshine all its competitors, laid dramatic marbles ingrained with shadings of pink, blue and silver specially imported from countries with strange names.)

The second standard stipulates the following architectural features: a dome, a number of sturdy columns and a belt of high windows; for this combination will suffuse the inner sanctum with a glow suggestive of the mystic aura of a mosque. Moreover, the high windows, while distilling Apollonian light, also serve to deter voyeurs. (Despite this last provision, stories about spidermen who had scaled the heady reaches of the windows for glimpses of bathers were commonplace. I remember the gruesome tale of three *delikanlı* – the word, often used affectionately, literally means 'youths with maddened blood' – who, having climbed up, for a bet, to the windows of a *hamam* in Konya on a day when the temperature was minus 35 degrees centigrade, had stuck to the walls and frozen to death; rescuers had had to wait till spring to peel them off the dome.)

∞∞∞∞∞∞❀∞∞∞∞∞∞

Our women's *hamam*, which adhered to these standards, claimed to be one of the best in the land. For Selim and me, it was the epitome of luxury.

Let me take you in, step by step.

The entrance, its most discreet feature, is a small wrought-iron door located at the middle of a high wall like those that protect girls' colleges.

The foyer is lush. Its dark purple drapes immediately promise exquisite sensual treats. (Is my memory playing tricks? Did those purple drapes belong to the *maisons de rendezvous* I used to frequent in Istanbul years later?)

To the right of the foyer there is a low platform with a kiosk. Here sits the manageress, *Teyze Hanım*, or 'Lady Aunt', whose girth may well have coined the Turkish idiom, 'built like a government'. She collects the entrance fees and hires out such items as soap, towels, bowls and the traditional Turkish clogs, *nalıns*. (Sofi, for one who was so stoic about the vagaries of life, was fanatically fastidious about hygiene and always made sure we brought our own washing materials.)

At the far end of the foyer, a door leads into the spacious communal dressing-room. As if to prolong the anticipation, this is simply trimmed: whitewashed walls, wooden benches to sit on and large wicker baskets for stacking clothes.

Another door opens into a passageway with slatted boards on the floor. Here, as you walk, the clogs beat an exciting rhythm. Ahead is the arch that leads into the baths' marbled haven.

The next moment you feel as if you are witnessing a transfiguration. The mixture of heat and steam have created a diaphanous air; the constant sound of running water is felicitous; and the white nebulous shapes that seemingly float in space profile kaleidoscopic fantasies in your mind. This might be a prospect from the beginning of days – or from the last. In any case, if you adore women and long to entwine with every one of them, it's a vision that will stay imprinted in your eyes for the rest of your life.

Thereafter, slowly, you begin to register details.

You note that the sanctuary is round (oval, actually). You're glad. Because had it been rectangular, as some are, it would have emanated a masculine air.

You note the large marble slab that serves as a centrepiece. This is the *göbek taşı*, the 'belly stone', where the bather sits to sweat. The size of the belly stone determines the reputation of the particular establishment; a large one, such as that in the women's *hamam*, where neighbours or family groups can sit and talk – even picnic – guarantees great popularity.

You note the washing areas around the belly stone. Each is delineated by a marble tub – called *kurna* – wherein hot and cold water, served from two separate taps, are mixed. You note that the space around each *kurna* accommodates several people, invariably members of a family or a group of neighbours. These patrons sit on stocky seats, also of marble, which look like pieces of modern sculpture – Brancusi's *Table of Silence* comes to mind – and wash themselves by filling their bowls from the *kurna* and splashing the water on to their bodies. Sometimes, those who wish to have a satisfactory scrub avail themselves, for a good baksheesh, of the services of one of the attendants.

You note that, beyond the inner sanctum, there are a number of chambers which, being closer to the furnace, are warmer. These are known as *halvet*, a word that implies 'solitude', and are reserved for those who wish to bathe alone or to have a massage. For the elite customer, the latter is performed by the Lady Aunt.

This being one of the best baths in town, there are two further chambers. The first is the *Sedir*, or 'Retreat', which, as its name suggests, offers, particularly to those who come for the day, a respite from the main *hamam*. The other, the *Soğukluk*, or 'Temperate Room', serves to cool down those who have had too much heat. You note, with relief, that except for some of the older patrons, few indulge in that particular kind of masochism.

But, of course, above all, you note the bathing women, the cornucopia of breasts of every shape and size. Those for whom modesty is a virtue at all times wear *peştamals*, transparent aprons which, rather than veil the glories of their flesh, emphasize them saliently. The rest are completely naked, except for bracelets and earrings, and look as if they have been sprinkled with gold. Tall or short, young or old, they are invariably Rubenesque. Even the thin ones appear voluptuous. Covered with heavy perfumes and henna, they carry themselves boldly, at ease with their firm, soft child-bearing bodies. They are, you realize, proud of their femininity even though – or perhaps because – they live in a society where the male rules absolutely. But if they see or think someone is looking at them, they are overcome with shyness and cover their pudenda with their washing-bowls. You note little girls, too, but if you're a little boy like Selim and me, you're not interested in them. You have already seen their budding treasures in such outworn games as 'mothers and fathers', 'doctors and patients'. (Here, briefly, the gospel according to Eleftheria: the human body, at every age and in every shape and size, even in deformity, is comely. The most beautiful cock she had ever known belonged to a man with a withered arm.)

∞∞∞∞∞∞✿∞∞∞∞∞∞

I feel I have related our entry to paradise as if it were

a commonplace occurrence, as if, in the Turkey of the forties, little boys were exempt from all gender considerations. Well, that's only partly true. Certainly, over the years, I have come across many men of my generation – and from different parts of Turkey – who, as boys, had been taken to the women's baths either by their maids or nannies or grannies or other elderly female relatives – though never by their mothers; that taboo appears to have remained inviolate.

In effect, there were no concrete rules on boys' admission into women's *hamams*. The decision rested on a number of considerations: the reputation of the establishment, the status of its clientele, the regularity of a person's – or a group's – patronage, the size of the baksheesh to the personnel and, not least, the discretion of its Lady Aunt.

In our case it was the last consideration that tipped the scales in our favour. We were allowed in because the Lady Aunt who ran the establishment was well-versed in matters of puberty. She had ascertained that our testicles had not yet dropped and would convey this information to her patrons when necessary. The latter, always tittering cruelly, accepted her word. (Mercifully, dear Sofi, incensed by this artless trespass on her charges' intimate parts, would lay her hands over our ears and hustle us away.)

Selim and I, needless to say, were greatly relieved that our testicles were intact. But the prospect that they would drop off at some future date – must drop off – also plunged us into great anxiety. Thus, for a while, we would inspect each other's groins every day and reassure ourselves that our manhoods were not only still in place, but also felt as good as when we had last played with them that morning, on waking up. We would also scour the streets, even while in the company of our parents, in the hope of finding the odd fallen testicle. If we could collect a number of spare testicles, we reasoned, we might just be able to replace our own when calamity struck. The fact that, in the past, we had never seen any testicles lying around did not deter us; we simply assumed that other boys, grappling with the same predicament, had gathered them up. Eventually, our failure to find even a single testicle bred the conviction that these organs were securely attached to the body and would never fall off – surely God had made certain of that! And we decided that this macabre 'lie' had been disseminated by women who had taken exception to our precociousness in order to frighten us.

And precocious we were. We had had good teachers.

∘∘∘∘∘∘∘∘∘∘∘❀∘∘∘∘∘∘∘∘∘∘∘

Selim and I lived near the Bomonti Brewery, on the outskirts of Ankara, in a new district of concrete apartment blocks designated as the precursors of future prosperity. Beyond, stretched the southern plains, dotted here and there with Gypsy encampments.

Gypsies, needless to say, have an unenviable life wherever they happen to live. Historic prejudices disbar them from most employment. The same conditions prevailed in Ankara. Jobs, in so far as the men were concerned, were limited to seasonal fruit-picking, the husbandry of horses, road digging and the porterage of huge loads. (I once saw three men balance a grand piano on their humped backs and transport it a distance of some four kilometres.) Gypsy women fared better: they were often in demand as fortune-tellers, herbalists and faith healers; and they always took their daughters along in order to teach them, at an early age, the intricacies of divination. The occasional plenitude the Gypsies enjoyed was provided by the boys who begged at such busy centres as the market, the bus and railway stations, the stadium and the brothels.

The last was the best pitch of all. Situated in the old town, at the base of the castle, the brothels consisted of some sixty ramshackle dwellings piled on each other in a maze of narrow streets. Each house had a small window in its door for customers to look in and appraise the ladies on offer. Here, on the well-worn pavements, the beggars set up shop. They knew that, after being with a prostitute, a man, particularly if he were married, would feel unclean or sinful; and so they offered him instant redemption by urging him to drop a few *kuruş* into their palms and thus show Allah that, as the faith expected of him, he was a generous alms-giver.

Some of these wise Gypsy boys became our friends. Whenever we could – whenever, that is, they weren't out begging or hawking – we met up with them. They always welcomed us – I think, as city boys, we intrigued them – and invited us to their tents. Alas, we could never return their hospitality; our parents had forbidden us from fraternizing with 'riff-raff'.

They taught us a great deal, these friends.

Above all, relating all the intimations they had overheard from punters and prostitutes, they taught us about the strange mechanics of sex: the peculiar, not to say, funny, positions; the vagaries of the principal organs; and the countless quirks that either made little sense to anyone or remained a mystery for many years.

And this priceless knowledge served as the foundation for further research in the *hamam*.

Breasts, buttocks and pubic hair – or, as was often the case with the last, the lack of it – became the first subjects for study. Not a hard task, you will agree. Since these parts were visible to everybody, we did not have to enact the surreptitious looks so favoured by the spy films of those times; nor, mercifully, did we have to perform double-jointed contortions so as not to appear to stare.

Our Gypsy friends had instructed us that breasts determined a woman's sexuality. The aureole was the indicator for passion. Those women with large aureoles were insatiable; those with what looked like tiny birthmarks were best left alone as they would be frigid. (What, I now wonder, did frigidity mean to us in those days?) We held these myths as inalienable truths – maybe, deep down, we still do – and dismissed outright any evidence to the contrary. For the record, the woman with the largest aureoles we ever saw was, without doubt, the epitome of lethargy; nicknamed 'the milkman's horse' by Lady Aunt, she always appeared to be nodding off to sleep, even when walking. By contrast, the liveliest woman we ever observed – a widow who not only allowed us generous and lengthy views of her vagina, but also appeared to enjoy her exhibitionism – had practically no aureoles at all, just tiny, cuspidal breasts and stubby, pointed nipples like the stalks of button mushrooms.

And buttocks, we had learned, were reflectors of character. They were expressive, like faces. Stern buttocks could be recognized immediately: lean cheeks with a division thin like a strand of hair on a bald man's head signified people who had forsaken pleasure. Happy buttocks always smiled; or, as if convulsed by hysterical laughter, wobbled. Sad buttocks, even if they were shaped like heavenly orbs, looked abandoned, lonely, despairing. And there were buttocks that so loved life that they swayed like tamarind jelly and made one's mouth water.

Buttocks also farted; and the shape and tenor of the broken wind were equally indicative of character. Round, loud, odourless farts proclaimed happy extroverts; those that peeled in surprise and were shaped like question marks belonged to sensitive, insecure lovers; the screechy ones defined mean, ungenerous people.

Regarding pubic hair, there was, as I indicated above, little of it on view. In Turkey, as in most Muslim countries, the ancient bedouin tradition whereby women, upon marriage, shave their pubic hair had almost acquired the dimensions of a hygienic commandment. Since most of the women in the baths were married, the only pubic hair on view belonged to the few teenage girls or to those old women who either no longer cared for precepts or could not be bothered with the rigmarole of having to shave regularly when, but for a few thin tufts, they had shed most of their hair anyway.

Our research into pubic hair, in addition to its inherent joys, proved to be a lesson in sociology. A shaven pudendum not only declared the marital status of the particular woman, but also indicated her position in society. To wit, women who were clean-shaven all the time were women wealthy enough to have leisure – and the handmaids to assist them – therefore, they were either old aristocracy or *nouveaux riches*. Women who carried some stubble betrayed their more modest backgrounds: children or household chores or careers curtailed their time for depilation. And women who went unshaven during menstruation were often of devout background.

To our amazement – as if the chore proved less of an inconvenience if performed in company – there was a great deal of shaving going on in the baths. Eventually we found out the reason: for a small baksheesh, a woman could get an attendant to do a much better job, thus freeing herself to gossip with friends or relatives. (When Selim and I first witnessed a woman shaving herself – a clumsy effort which caused several nicks – we decided that, on our next visit, we would bring some alum and, by offering it to those who drew blood, get closer to them. We abandoned the idea after our Gypsy friends pointed out that such a move would disclose our interest in female genitalia and the ensuing complaints would prompt Lady Aunt to refuse us entry. Good advice.)

Our main study – eventually, our *raison d'être* for going to the baths – centred on the labia and the clitoris. Both these wonders, too, possessed mythologies. Our Gypsy friends apprised us.

The myths concerning the labia centred on their prominence and pensility. Broad ones, reputedly resembling the lips of African peoples, were certain to be, like all black races, uninhibited and passionate. (What did those adjectives mean to us? And what did we know of black races?) Lean labia, because they would have to be prized open, indicated thin hearts. Pendulous ones represented motherhood; Gypsy midwives, we were assured, could tell the number of children a woman had had simply by noting the labia's suspension. Those women who were childless but did possess hanging labia were to be pitied: for they found men, in general, so irresistibly attractive that they could never restrict their affections to one individual; consequently, to help them remain chaste, Allah had endowed them with labia that could be sewn together.

The perfect labia were those that not only rippled down languorously, but also tapered to a point at the centre, thus looking very much like delicate buckles. These labia had magical powers: he who could wrap his tongue with them would be able to see our twin world which lies on the other side of the sun and where life is the opposite of life here – where instead of constant war there is constant peace.

As for clitorises, it is common knowledge that, like penises, they vary in size. It is also common knowledge that the Turks, influenced by the fifth volume of Aristotle's famous opus, *The Parts of Animals*, have classified them into three distinct sizes, naming each category after a popular food. (According to Eleftheria, who was also a classicist, Aristotle's said work has only four volumes. Nevertheless, she conceded the possibilities that, one: the sage might have loaned the manuscript of the fifth to Alexander the Great so that the latter, in pursuit of his dream of marrying the East to the West, could prepare his soldiers to take to wife the women of the Hindu Kush; and two: that the manuscript might then have got lost somewhere in the Middle East and eventually been found by the Turks.)

The categories were as follows: *susam*, 'sesame', for small clitorises; *mercimek*, 'lentils' (in Turkey, these would be brown lentils), for the medium-sized ones, which, since they constituted ninety percent of the clitorises, were considered normal; and *nohut*, 'chick-peas', for those of large calibre.

Women in possession of sesames were invariably sullen. Attributing the smallness of their clitorises to a deficiency in their femininity – even though they were perfectly capable of enjoying sex – they ended up doubting their maternal feelings. Tormented by such a terrible sense of inferiority, they rebuffed children, particularly those who were admitted to the baths. Women blessed with lentils bore the characteristics of their namesake, a staple food in Turkey. Hence the 'lentilled' women's perfect roundness was not only aesthetically pleasing, but also extremely nourishing; in effect, they offered everything a man sought from a wife: love, passion, obedience and the gift of cooking. Those endowed with chick-peas were destined to ration their amorous activities since the abnormal size of their clitorises induced such intense pleasure that regular sex invariably damaged their hearts; restricted to conjoining only for purposes of conception, these women were to find solace in a spiritual life. And they would attain such heights of piety that, during labour, they would gently notch, with their chick-peas, a prayer-dent on their babies' foreheads, thus marking them for important religious duties.

Now, some of you might have begun pulling faces. (Eleftheria did when I first recounted these things to her. 'Pig', she shouted, 'clitorises have hoods. Even if you find a clitoris the size of an Easter egg, you'll have a tough time seeing it! You've got to, one: be lucky enough to have your face across your lover; two: know how to peek past the hood; three: have the sang-froid to keep your eyes open; and four: seduce the bean or the hazel nut or whatever you call it into believing that, for you, she is the only reality in life and everything else is an illusion.')

So, let me confess before you take me for a liar that, in all likelihood, neither Selim nor I ever saw a single clitoris. We just believed we did. Not only the odd one but, by that unique luck that favours curs, hundreds of them. And the more we believed, the more we contorted ourselves into weird positions, peeked and squinted from crazy angles, moved hither and thither to fetch this and that for one matron or another. We behaved, in effect, like bear cubs around a honey pot.

Of course, I admit, with hindsight, that what we kept seeing must have been beauty spots or freckles or moles or birthmarks and, no doubt, on occasion, the odd pimple or wart or razor nick.

Naturally, when we described to our friends, particularly our Gypsy friends, all that we had feasted on with our eyes, they believed us. And so we felt important. And when we went to sleep counting not sheep but clitorises, we felt sublime. And when we woke up and felt our genitals humming as happily as the night before, we basked in ultimate bliss.

An aside here, if I may. Inconceivable as it may sound, we never investigated Sofi's features. But she was, after all, family, therefore immaculate, therefore non-sexual. Now, looking back on old pictures, I note that she was rather attractive. She had the silky olive-coloured skin that makes Armenians such a handsome people. Moreover, she had not had children, hence, had not enjoyed, in *hamam* parlance, 'usage'. Consequently, though in her mid-thirties, she was still firm-fleshed and robust, still a woman in her prime.

When my family moved from Ankara, soon after my bar mitzvah, Sofi went to work as a chambermaid in a resort hotel. We kept in touch. Then, in 1976, she suddenly left her job and disappeared. Her boss, who had been very attached to her, disclosed that she had been seriously ill and presumed that she had gone to die in her birthplace, in the company of ancestral ghosts. Since neither of us knew which particular village in Kars province she had originally come from, our efforts to trace her soon foundered.

But I never gave up hope of finding her. Whenever I met Armenians, I always asked them whether they had ever come across Sofi or, better still, whether they could inquire about her within their own circles of relatives, friends and acquaintances.

Then, one day, a friend in Canada wrote to me about Kirkor Hovanesyan, a sickly sixty-year-old Armenian immigrant from Turkey who, on becoming a widower, had decided to go back to the old country and spend the remainder of his days drinking raki and eating *mezes* by the Bosporus. But no sooner had he arrived on our shores than he fell prey to our notorious bureaucracy and was conscripted into the army for the military service he had avoided as a young man. He was duly sent to the east, to Kars; but, because of his age, had served as an orderly in an officers' mess. During his time there, he had not only regained his health, but had also formed a liaison with a distant relative. After his discharge, he and this woman had married and, moving back to Istanbul, had bought and rebuilt a famous Romanian restaurant which had been destroyed in a fire.

Armed with this information, I rushed to the said restaurant.

And there, to my great joy, was Sofi.

Her husband, Kirkor, has long since died, but Sofi is still alive – though pretty old. She is well looked-after by Kirkor's children from his first marriage and, of course, by her true sons – Selim and me.

∞∞∞∞∞∞🏵∞∞∞∞∞∞

Alas, our time in paradise did not fill a year.

Expulsion, when it came, was as sudden and as unexpected as from Eden. And just as brutal.

It happened on 5 July. The date is engraved in my mind because it happens to be my birthday. In fact, the visit to the *hamam* on that occasion was meant to be Sofi's present to me. A few days earlier she had asked me what treat I would most like, meaning what special dish or cake she could cook for me, and had been amused by my resolute preference for the *hamam*. But she had readily agreed, even approved of my choice; after all, she cooked my favourite dishes all the time.

Summers in Ankara are suffocating; and that particular 5 July was exceptionally stifling; hardly the sort of day, one might think, to induce people to seek shelter in the Turkish baths. Not so. For a start, it felt fresher inside the *hamam* than anywhere else; there was, at least, refuge from a sun that seemed determined to boil people's brains. Secondly, it was in the hot season that the Temperate Room earned its keep by turning into an oasis. Thirdly, according to those who claimed to have scientific minds, a thorough scrub – so thorough that it could only be achieved after a few hours in the baths – improved a person's cooling mechanism by opening up all the body's pores.

And so, on that 5 July, the women's *hamam* was exceptionally full. (Maybe I had known or heard or intuited that it would be.) Selim and I were having an awfully hard time trying to look in many directions all at once. Such was our excitement that we never blinked once. (Today, when we concentrate on something that fascinates us, we still contort into that goggle-eyed look). It was, in effect, the most bounteous time we had ever had in the baths. (Given the fact that it was also our last, I might be exaggerating. Nostalgia does that.)

We must have been there for some time when, to our dismay, we saw one of the women grab hold of an attendant and command her, while pointing at us, to fetch Lady Aunt. It took us an eternity to realize that this nymph of strident fortissimo was the very goddess whom Selim and I adored and worshipped, whose body we had judged to be perfect and voluptuous – we never used one adjective where two could be accommodated – and whom, as a result, we had named 'Nilüfer' after the water-lily, which, in those days, we believed to be the most beautiful flower in the world.

And before we could summon the wits to direct our gaze elsewhere – or even to lower our eyes – Nilüfer and Lady Aunt were upon us, both screaming at lovely Sofi, who had been dozing by the *kurna*.

Now I should point out that Selim and I, having riveted our eyes on Nilüfer for months on end, knew very well that she was of a turbulent nature. We had seen her provoke innumerable quarrels, not only with Lady Aunt and the attendants, but also with many of the patrons. The old women, comparing her to a Barbary mare – and, given the ease with which she moved her fleshy but athletic limbs, a particularly lusty one at that – attributed her volatility to her recent marriage and summed up her caprices as the dying embers of a female surrendering her existence to her husband, as females should; one day, a week hence or months later, when she felt that sudden jolt which annunciates conception, she would become as docile as the next woman.

And on that 5 July, Selim and I had been expecting an outburst from Nilüfer – though not against us, of course. (The curious fact that she had never before turned against us – nor had ever bothered to act modestly before our eyes – meant, we had decided, that she liked us and wanted to please us.) In fact, we had noted that she was troubled the moment she arrived: she could not sit and relax with the women who had come with her, nor even stay for any length of time in the Temperate Room to which she kept going every few minutes. And she kept complaining of being pummelled by a terrible migraine, courtesy of the accursed heat outside. (The migraine, Sofi wisely informed us later, shed light on the real reasons for Nilüfer's temper: for some women migraines heralded the commencement of their flow; what might have made matters worse for Nilüfer – remember she was not long married - could have been the disappointment of having failed to conceive for yet another month.)

It took us a while to register Nilüfer's accusations. She was reproving us for playing with our genitals, touching them the way men do. (I'm sure we did, but I'm equally sure we did it surreptitiously. Had she been watching us the way we had been watching the women, seemingly through closed eyes?)

Sofi, bless her dear heart, defended us like a lioness. 'My boys', she said, 'know how to read and write. They don't need to play with themselves.'

This *non sequitur* enraged Nilüfer all the more. Stooping upon us, she took hold of our penises, one in each hand, and showed them to Lady Aunt. 'Look,' she yelled, 'they're almost hard. You can see they're almost hard!'

(Were they? I don't know. But, as Selim agreed with me later, the feeling of being tightly held by her hand was sensational.)

Lady Aunt glanced at the exhibits dubiously. 'Can't be. Their testicles haven't dropped yet ...'

'Yes. Thanks for reminding me,' howled Sofi. 'Their testicles haven't dropped yet!'

'No, they haven't!' Selim interjected bravely. 'We'd know, wouldn't we?'

Nilüfer, waving our penises, shrilled another decibel at Lady Aunt. 'See for yourself! Touch them! Touch them!'

Shrugging like a long-suffering servant, Lady Aunt knelt by our side. Nilüfer handed over our penises like batons. Lady Aunt must have had greater expertise in inspecting the male member; for as her fingers enveloped us softly and warmly and oh so amiably, we did get hard

– or felt as if we did.

We expected Lady Aunt to scream the place down. Instead, she rose from her haunches with a smile and turned to Sofi. 'They are hard. See for yourself.'

Sofi shook her head in disbelief.

Nilüfer celebrated her triumph by striding up and down the baths, shouting, 'They're not boys! They're men!'

Sofi continued to shake her head in disbelief.

Lady Aunt patted her on the shoulder, then shuffled away. 'Take them home. They shouldn't be here.'

Sofi, suddenly at a loss, stared at the bathers. She noted that some of them were already covering themselves.

Still confused, she turned round to us; then, impulsively, she held our penises. As if that had been the cue, our members shrank instantly and disappeared within their folds.

Sofi, feeling vindicated, shouted at the patrons, 'They're not hard! They're not!'

Her voice echoed from the marble walls. But no one paid her any attention.

She remained defiant even as Lady Aunt saw us off the premises. 'I'll be bringing them along – next time! We'll be back!'

Lady Aunt roared with laughter. 'Sure! Bring their fathers, too, why don't you?'

And the doors clanged shut behind us.

And though Sofi determinedly took us back several times, we were never again granted admission.

3: Robbie

A Tale of Two Cities

This July of 1942, the people of Istanbul were insisting, was the hottest in living memory. Around Sultan Ahmet Square, where the Blue Mosque and the Byzantine monuments faced each other in historical debate, the traditional *çayhanes* had appropriated every patch of shade. The patrons of these tea-houses blamed the heat on *Şeytan*: the land was fragrant with the verses and compositions of the young bards, and the Arch-demon, jealous of the Turk's ability to turn all matter into poetry or music, was venting his resentment. The narghile-smokers, mostly pious men revered as guardians of the faith, disagreed: such temperatures occurred only when sainted imams lamented the profanation of Koranic law; and, under this heathen administration called a 'republic', they had much to lament, not least the growing number of women who were securing employment – as well as equal status with men – in all walks of life. But down the hill, along the seaside *meyhanes*, where the solemn imbibing of raki engendered enlightenment far superior to that of tea or opium, the elders, veterans of the First World War, offered a more cogent reason. Pointing at the dried blood from Europe's latest battlefields settling as dust on this city, which Allah had created as a pleasure garden for every race and creed, they affirmed that man, that worshipper of desolation, was once again broiling the atmosphere with guns.

We believed the drinkers. Well, we either had just reached our teens or, like Bilâl, were at the threshold and knew, with the wisdom of that age, that old soldiers, particularly those who open their tongues with alcohol, never lie. Besides, Bilâl – actually, his mother, Ester – had kept us apprised, with first-hand information, of the carnage devastating Europe. In Greece, where she had been born, Death was reaping a bumper harvest. Letters from Fortuna, Ester's sister in Salonica, were chronicling the atrocities. Though these accounts often verged on hysteria – and tended to be dismissed as exaggerated, even by some Jews – they were corroborated, in prosaic detail, by the family's lawyer. When, about fifteen years before, Ester had left Greece to get married in Turkey, this gentleman, Sotirios Kasapoglou by name, had promised to report regularly on her family's situation.

It was in the wake of this lawyer's latest missive that - Bilâl, Naim and Can, another gang member, approached me. You may have guessed, from my references to Ester's concern for her relatives, that Bilâl – and, indeed, Naim and Can – were Jewish; and you may be intrigued by their Muslim names. There is a simple explanation: Atatürk, determined to distance the new republic from the iniquities of the Ottoman empire, had sought to instil in the people pride in their Turkishness. Consequently, by law, all minorities were obliged to give their children a Turkish name in addition to an ethnic one. Thus Benjamin had acquired Bilâl; Nehemiah, Naim; and Jacob, Can.

I remember the exact date of their visit: Monday 27 July 1942. I was with my parents in sleepy Florya, a resort some fifty kilometres west of Istanbul, on the European coast of the Sea of Marmara where, during the summer months, the British embassy maintained a spacious villa for its staff. We had just heard that the RAF had bombed Hamburg and, somehow, this news had raised the morale of the diplomatic corps much more than the month's significantly greater achievements such as holding the line at El Alamein and bombing the U-boat yards in Danzig. Suddenly the whole British legation felt convinced that we would win the war and my father, Duncan Stevenson, had seen fit to offer me my first dram of *uisge beatha*, the water of life. Though, at the time, I had already perfected the art of downing leftover drinks, these had mainly been sherry; consequently, my first taste of whisky proved a revelation – which may well be the real reason I remember the date.

My father must have come up to Istanbul for an 'appearance'. His outfit, the British-American Co-ordination Committee, set up to entice a still-neutral Turkey to join the Allies by providing its army with vital supplies, was headquartered in the capital, Ankara. To shield his activities from enemy agents, his official position had been listed as vice-consul in Istanbul. To safeguard this cover, he had to be seen living there. Thus we became prominent residents of the cosmopolitan suburb, Nişantaşı. It was there that Bilâl, Naim and Can found me drifting aimlessly in parks and playing fields. And when they discovered that I could kick a football like a budding William Shankly, they made me their friend for life.

We had changed into our bathing suits with unusual decorum. I attributed my friends' subdued spirits to the Gorgon's presence. For, throughout the time we undressed, even when we turned our backs to her to prevent our willies from turning to stone under her serpent's eyes – when, normally, like most boys celebrating puberty, we would have been comparing sizes – Mrs Meredith, the housekeeper, had not shifted her chilling scrutiny from us. This martinet, who aspired to discipline even the daisies on the lawn (the epithet 'Gorgon' had originated, some years back, from one of our senior diplomats), had a particular fetish for the parquet flooring which contributed so much to the villa's elegance; no one, certainly not four strapping boys, could shuffle or, heaven forbid, run on it without forfeiting their lives.

We reached the villa's private beach. My friends remained subdued. They should have been bubbly: this was a day stolen for fun. Normally, during the week, they helped in their fathers' shops; moreover, except for the Johnson horde, who were a jolly bunch, the beach was deserted and we could run riot. I became concerned. 'What's up?'

Bilâl, distracted by the Johnsons waving at us, spoke quietly. 'It's grim!'

Thinking that he was referring to yet another crisis with the girl who lived across the road from him and whom he audaciously worshipped from his window, I offered a sympathetic smile. 'Selma's ignoring you?'

'No. She returns my gaze. Smiles even.'

'Well then?'

'Salonica ...'

The Johnson children had risen from their chairs and were coming towards us.

I stared at Bilâl. 'What?'

Can, always the soft voice that calmed us down, whispered, 'His cousins. Difficult times for them.'

Naim, the oldest among us and hence our leader, spoke gravely. 'We must do something.'

I stared at them. Children talking like adults. 'What can we do?'

Bilâl muttered, 'We can save them. If you help us ...'

'Me? What can I do?'

Can, mindful of the Johnson brood who were almost upon us, whispered, 'Passports – we need passports.'

'What for?'

'For the family. To get them out.'

'Yes, get them out! Let's have a look!' This from Dorothy, the Johnsons' oldest. A miniature Mac West since she started growing a couple of tangerines on her chest. But a tease: she wouldn't let any boy touch her.

'We're having man-talk, Dorothy! Go away!'

She hissed. 'Men, Robbie? Where?' Then she smiled. She could be blade and balm in the same breath. 'Dad says: come and join us. Someone's sent a hamper of goodies: *lokum*, figs, halva …'

I noted my friends' reluctance, but we couldn't refuse; it wouldn't have been, in my father's parlance, diplomatic. Why do junior staff always feel obliged to pamper youngsters? Still, Dorothy had said figs and Turkish figs were worth an empire. 'Don't mind if we do, thank you.'

We followed her.

I nudged Naim. 'We'll talk later.'

Naim didn't respond. He was studying Dorothy's widening hips. Wide hips are childbearing hips, he had once told us, quoting old Kokona, our neighbourhood know-all, as an authority. Well, that formidable Greek matriarch would have known; she had given birth to fourteen children and, by all accounts, it would have taken her husband a good few minutes to run a caressing hand from one buttock to the other.

In time, both Naim and Can developed a healthy preference for wide hips. I never did. Like most northerners, I ended up thinking that ample flesh and carnal living were joys that led to immoderation. These days I ask: what's wrong with immoderation?

∞∞∞∞∞∞∞✿∞∞∞∞∞∞∞

Figs and the other treats were followed by a chess game between Mr Johnson and Can, spectacularly won by the latter who, had he not set his mind on medicine, would have become a grand master. Then a bout of jousting in the sea during which Naim had the bliss of carrying Dorothy on his shoulders – his mouth barely centimetres away from her freckled thighs – while she repeatedly unseated her four brothers despite the valiant efforts of Bilâl and Mrs Johnson, who served as their mounts. Then a couple of hours of serious swimming, an activity at which I excelled. Finally a succulent lunch, courtesy of Emine, the cook, who, except for special requests, never repeated her menus.

Thus privacy eluded us until the obligatory siesta. Because of my father's privileged status, I had managed to secure, as my retreat, the big room in the attic, which served as a dump for the villa's oddments. That's where we secreted ourselves, much to the displeasure of the Gorgon, who could not keep an eye on us in there.

Bilâl brought out the letter his mother had received from the family lawyer and translated it. His Greek was perfect. Since Ester claimed to have taught the language to Bilâl's father, Pepo, in the early years of their marriage (not true, actually; Pepo had known Greek before he met Ester, had even acted as an interpreter during the War of Independence) we used to tease Bilâl that he had learned it by listening to his parents' pre- and post-coital cooing. (A crass banter that we instantly abandoned after Bilâl confided in us that all was not well between his mum and dad.)

Much of the letter was devoted to an incident that had taken place on 11 July. On that day, a Sabbath, the *Wehrmacht* commander of northern Greece had decreed that all male Jewish citizens of Salonica between the ages of eighteen and forty-five must gather at 8 AM in Plateia Eleftherias, 'Freedom Square', to register for civilian labour. Some 10,000 men, Ester's elderly father Salvador among them, had duly reported in the hope of securing work cards. The Germans had chosen to humiliate the assemblage by keeping them standing in the blistering heat, without hats, until late afternoon. Those who had collapsed from sunstroke had been hosed down with cold water and beaten up; others, ordered to perform arduous exercises until they, too, had passed out, had received similar treatment. These horrific and arbitrary abuses, the lawyer admitted with mortification, had been witnessed, mostly with indifference, sometimes with glee, by a large number of the city's inhabitants – people who, no doubt, considered themselves good Christians. Worse still, the following day, the newspapers, brandishing photographs supplied by the German army, had praised this attitude. Perhaps even more invidious was the fact that not a single professional organization, nor any members of one, had spoken up on behalf of a Jewish colleague or in protest against the Jews' maltreatment. But what was even worse was that in Salonica – and nowhere else in the country – there had been many denunciations of Jewish neighbours by the citizens. These denunciations had much to do with Greek nationalism, which still resented the fact that throughout the centuries when Salonica had been an Ottoman city, Jews and Turks had had very harmonious relations. But it must be remembered, the lawyer bitterly lamented, that every institution in Salonica, not to say every citizen, had also worked and maintained close ties with Jews for generations. How could that tradition be forgotten? After all, history had produced only one constant in the Balkans: the Jew's word as his bond.

To date, the Germans had dispatched most of the men who had assembled on that Saturday to build roads and airfields. What the future held for other Jews, the lawyer dared not imagine. Reports from eastern Thrace and Macedonia augured the worst. The Germans had delegated the administration of these territories to their ally, the Bulgarians; but since the latter kept prevaricating on the matter of surrendering their own Jews, the Germans had decided to deal with the Jews of Thrace and Macedonia themselves. Lately there had been rumours that these unfortunates would be deported *en masse* to Occupied Poland. All of this made the lawyer look back regretfully to the time when the Italians had been the occupying power. The Italians had been humane, often in defiance of Mussolini's edicts. Throughout their occupation, they had persistently warned the Jews of the Nazis' racist policies and urged them to leave the country; on many occasions they had even granted Italian passports to those who heeded their advice. Ester might remember one Moiz Hananel, a distant cousin from Rhodes: he was now safe in Chile. But, alas, Ester's father, Salvador, disinclined to liquidate his considerable investments, had procrastinated. Now, the Italians had gone and Salvador's wealth had evaporated.

There the lawyer's letter ended.

Then Bilâl brought out another letter, the latest from Ester's sister, Fortuna. It was written in French, the lingua franca of the educated Sephardim, and he read it out loud. As might be expected of my Scottish lineage – the antithesis of the insular, monolingual English – I was quite cosmopolitan and spoke several languages fluently.

Fortuna's letter was like that of a dying person, without a trace of the billowing fury with which she normally faced adversity. Her husband, Zaharya, one of those impressed for road construction, had suffered a heart attack and died. Viktorya and Süzan, her daughters, aged eight and ten, had become the family's breadwinners. Every morning before dawn, they would leave home – which, these days, was a corner in a disused warehouse – and climb to the lower slopes of Mount Hortiatis where they would collect wild flowers. They would then run back, at breakneck speed, to reach the city by noon and sell the flowers, often in competition with equally destitute Gypsy children, to German officers relaxing at the waterfront tavernas.

Every morning, as they left, Fortuna felt sure she would never see her daughters again. Her son, David – who, like Bilâl, was nearly thirteen – fared worse. His daily task was to scour the city for scraps of food. In doing so, he had to avoid the German patrols for whom the humiliation of rabbis, women and the elderly, the beating of children and the random shooting of 'die-hard communists' – a euphemism for semitic-looking people – had become favourite pastimes.

Salvador, a man who, in his time, had never backed down from a fight, was now a ghost. Since the expropriation of his villa by the *Wehrmacht*, a few days after 11 July, he had ensconced himself in a shack, near the Eptapyrgio fortress, that terrible prison on the crest of the old upper city. Vowing that he would never again be maltreated and calling for his wife, mercifully dead for many years, to come and take him away, he had not left the shack since. Viktorya and Süzan took him food, but how long could they go on doing that?

All of this had persuaded Fortuna that she would have to learn the ways of this new world, become cunning and predatory and, abandoning all notions of decency, survive any way she could. She was still young and attractive. Greek men, everybody knew, had a fondness for Jewish flesh. The Germans, too, it was said, had a secret passion for it.

•••••••••❀•••••••••

Bilâl's relatives had to be saved. They were, to all intents and purposes, our kindred too. Bilâl, who had met them when he and his parents had visited Salonica in the summer of 1939, just before the war, had praised them to us so highly that we had adopted them unreservedly as family. Viktorya and Süzan, adorable little girls threatened by every peril under the sun, were the little sisters we all wished we had. (Naim's older sister Gül had died two years earlier.) David was our age and, on the evidence of photographs, looked like Bilâl's twin; therefore he was our twin. In Fortuna's case, the prevailing moral view that prostitution was a fate worse than death plunged us into gruesome fantasies. Thus, though we secretly felt aroused by the thought of a woman who gave herself to any man, we could not let her face perdition in a thousand and one horrific ways. We had our reservations about Salvador – he had been a veritable tyrant all his life – but we decided that abandoning him would be heinous.

Given our eventual course of action, it might be assumed that we deliberated on the matter for days. We didn't. Our decision was instant and unanimous. Such considerations as to how we would solve any problems that arose could be dealt with, we decided, in due course. We were young; and according to Plato, who had captured our imagination in those days, we were wiser than our elders. We could make the world a better place. Eradicate wars. Establish universal justice and human rights. Stop the sacrifice of millions at the altar of monomaniacs.

Bilâl presented an 'if only' scenario that had become

his mother's lament. If only we could procure five Turkish passports and deliver them to Fortuna …

He had investigated the possibilities.

As anybody who went around Istanbul with eyes and ears open knew, the black-market trade in passports was a thriving business. Those of neutral countries, like Sweden and Switzerland, or from regions outside the theatres of war, like Latin America, were worth a fortune. There were some exceptions: Turkey was neutral, yet because it was feared that Germany, seeking to destroy Soviet oilfields and refineries east of the Black Sea, would invade the country, Turkish passports were not much in demand. Basically, the market value of a passport was governed by the vagaries of war. On occasion, even passports from war-battered countries could prove a gold-mine – British passports, for instance, though they had the same modest status as Turkish ones, would fetch a fortune from Jewish refugees seeking to settle in Palestine.

In the main, Bilâl instructed us, the black market in passports was dominated by the Levantines, that tiny minority of Europeans who, enamoured of the Orient, had settled in the Ottoman empire and intermarried with its many peoples. Immensely proud of their mixed ethnicity, the Levantines had evolved, in eastern Mediterranean eyes, into 'lovable rogues'. In the new Turkey, they had perfected the highly specialized *métier* of *iş bitirici,* 'job-accomplisher'. It was said that once they accepted a commission, only death would prevent them from completing it to the client's satisfaction.

Here, Bilâl declared, luck favoured us. Naim had a perfect entrée into this community. His classmate, Tomaso (Turkish name, Turgut), was the son of 'Neptune', owner of the famous restaurant in the Golden Horn, which served the best fish in the world. Neptune was a scion of the Adriatiko, an elite strain of Levantines who were the descendants of Venetian sailors taken prisoner in the sea battles of the sixteenth and seventeenth centuries, then used as galley-slaves in Ottoman men-of-war and, eventually, set free and allowed to settle in the empire. Neptune had a horde of 'cousins' who, in pursuit of their smuggling activities, covered Turkey's four seas with a fleet of trawlers; not surprisingly, they had ended up dominating the fishing trade – which explained the excellence of his restaurant.

So, if we could get hold of five British passports, Bilâl concluded, we could approach the Adriatiko and arrange a barter for Turkish ones. The latter, he reminded us, were worth about the same but had the advantage of being bona fide for the German occupation forces because Turkey was not only a neighbouring country but also neutral. They offered the only chance of escape for Ester's family.

And this is where I came in. I was a member of the British diplomatic community. Perfectly placed to lay my hands on new passports. Fate had brought me to Istanbul for that very purpose.

❧

We wove an ingenious plan.

During the rest of the holidays I would be especially friendly with the Johnsons, particularly Mr Johnson, who was His Majesty's Consul. And I would find out, by asking the sort of casual questions that might occur to any curious youngster, how the consulate issued passports and where it stored them. Then, on my father's next trip to Istanbul, I would visit him at the consulate on some pretext and, while everybody went on with their work, slip into whichever storeroom contained the passports and pinch the five we needed. If the passports were kept under lock and key, the boys would provide me with a passe-partout. Obtaining such an item from a locksmith would be easy; having worked the markets with their fathers, they knew countless tradesmen.

Once we had the passports, Naim would prevail on Tomaso to introduce us to the Adriatiko for the exchange with Turkish ones.

The next phase, slipping into Greece, should be equally simple, we convinced ourselves. We could engineer a good excuse to leave town for a few days. Our district boy scout troop had a progressive programme of fitness and culture that included excursions to famous archaeological sites. Since our parents approved of these activities – to date we had explored several digs in Anatolia – we would 'invent' such a jaunt to, say, the Royal Hittite Archives in Boğazköy.

For entering Greece, we had two options. We could either waft into eastern Thrace by crossing the Meriç river, which ran along the Turkish-Greek frontier, or sail directly, in a hired boat, to a deserted cove.

We discounted the first as dangerous. To do that we would have to evade two armies, the German and the Bulgarian occupation forces. Moreover, despite Germany's assurances that it would not invade Turkey, the Turkish government, remembering that similar pledges had been given to the Soviets, remained alert. Consequently, the border was assiduously patrolled by a third military outfit, the Turkish army.

Naim felt sure that his friend Tomaso could be as helpful on this matter as with the passports by enabling us to hire a boat from one of his father's 'cousins' for the short hop over to Greece.

The journey to Salonica – by bus, we surmised – would be uneventful thanks to Bilâl's impeccable Greek. Once there, we would intercept Viktorya and Süzan as they went to sell flowers and would be taken to the rest of the family.

We would have a fair amount of money; we all had some savings. Moreover, because of the war, the exchange rate between the Greek drachma and the Turkish lira greatly favoured the latter. However, to be on the safe side, the best-off among us – me – would sell his bicycle and tell his parents that it had been stolen.

The journey back, we believed, would be just as easy. We would sneak back into our boat at night and reach Turkey before dawn.

Bilâl's relatives, now equipped with Turkish passports, would execute the formalities for exit visas and travel to Istanbul either by rail – directly or via Sofia – or by steamer, if services were still operational.

∞∞∞∞∞∞∞🎔∞∞∞∞∞∞∞

The first phase went perfectly smoothly.

It took me only a few days to become Mr Johnson's favourite youngster. I did so, rather cunningly, by undertaking to give daily maths lessons to his oldest son, Ernest – not the brightest of boys – who had to retake an exam in September. The fact that snooty Dorothy, after an initial bout of cold-shouldering, began to take an interest in me and contrived invitations to some of their family outings also helped. So did my mother's condition: reduced, in the space of a year, from a jolly, athletic woman to a listless, tumbledown person by the death of her younger brother in action with the Royal Navy, she had ceased engaging with the world. The Johnsons, dear people, were determined to compensate for her neglect of me by lavishing treats on me.

One such treat was a standing invitation to the consulate which, Mr Johnson must have assumed, would impress me with His Majesty's Government's delicate work and thus further justify my pride in being British. Indeed, I found the activities there – comprising, in the main, preparatory work for my father's committee – fascinating. And I discovered, to my surprise, that the passport office was seldom manned; it had never occurred to us that, in the midst of war, there would not be many travellers. As for the passports, they were stacked in neat piles, together with the consulate's stationery, in a large metal locker behind the front desk. The locker had a key, but it was always left hanging from the handle for the benefit of those who needed stationery.

I decided to take my chance straightaway and arranged another visit to the consulate, this time with Ernest and Dorothy, after having taken them to the cinema. At a convenient moment, pretending to go to the lavatory, I slipped away, stole into the passport office, filched the five passports and stuffed them in my satchel. I had brought my satchel to borrow books from the consulate library and, as might be expected of a bookworm, had made a habit of taking it with me everywhere, even to the toilet. To make sure that the numbers would not be consecutive, I picked each passport from a different pile. That was an inspired move, worthy of a seasoned agent. I am proud of it even today.

<hr />

Naim, too, had an easy time.

His friend Tomaso, envious of the adventure we had planned, went to work diligently. Arranging an exchange of passports, he told us, should be child's play. But when it came to getting in and out of Greece, he dissuaded us from approaching the old-timers. Since Germany's invasion of the Balkans, these veterans had abandoned their legendary braggadocio. They had even stopped smuggling. These swastika-Huns, they told everybody, were not like the Germans who had fought in the Great War; they were rabid dogs, just like their Führer.

However, the new generation, the *delikanlı* – those with 'crazy blood', to use that graphic Turkish expression – were itching to prove their mettle; they were particularly keen to match wits with the 'master race'. And none more so than Marko, Tomaso's mother's kid brother, not yet twenty-five, but already extolled as a Sinbad.

The exchange of passports did turn out to be child's play. Tomaso, pretending that he had undertaken a job – his first – for a Greek friend, sought advice from his father on how to arrange the exchange. Neptune, proud of the boy's initiative, supervised the transaction himself. In the true tradition of the fixer, he asked no questions. But he made sure to turn a profit of seventy-five liras.

Tomaso then introduced us to Marko.

Even today, Marko is imprinted on my mind as the manliest man I've ever met: a blend of film star, athlete and Olympian god with the thick, perfectly groomed regulation moustache of a Casanova; serene as if he had perfected the art of being a loner, yet a man always living at the peak of his spirits. We fell under his spell immediately. Even Naim, who at first perceived him as puzzlingly ingenuous, ended up mesmerized by his irrepressible confidence. But then, Marko had every reason to be confident. Since embarking on his career, he had undertaken all sorts of perilous assignments and had accomplished every one with panache, an unprecedented achievement in a very precarious profession. Moreover, he had so souped up his boat, the *Yasemin*, that he could outrun any patrol craft in the Aegean.

Marko readily agreed to help us. But he would not hire out his boat. He pointed out that we not only knew nothing about the vagaries of the Aegean Sea, but also were totally unfamiliar with the Thracian coastline. If we were chased by Turkish or German patrol boats, we would not be able to give them the slip and would either get captured or blown out of the sea.

There was only one way we could succeed: he would smuggle us in and out of Greece personally. He was an experienced sailor who knew the region like the back of his hand. He could put us ashore very close to Salonica, for instance at Acte, the easternmost promontory of the three-tongued Khalkhidiki peninsula where the monasteries of Mount Athos were situated. In fact, operating near the monasteries would be wise; in case of mishaps, the monks could be expected to provide us with food and shelter. Last but not least, he, Marko, was an irrepressible romantic who believed that saving people was a sacred duty; consequently, he would do the job for a pittance, say, a month's supply of raki.

His evaluation made good sense; his enthusiasm lifted our spirits. We could finally leave the realm of 'if only' and enter the world of action. So we agreed.

We set the date for Sunday 6 September. We would return, we calculated, a week later, on the thirteenth.

'Accounts made at home never tally in the market,' say the Turks. True enough. In no time at all, everything went wrong.

Our request to go on a week's camping with the boy scouts elicited little enthusiasm from our fathers. Naim and Can's, desperately trying to keep their businesses afloat, needed their sons for odd jobs and refused them permission outright. My father, stuck in Ankara and loath to leave my mother alone with her depression, insisted that I stay by her side. Only Bilâl's parents acquiesced – with indecent haste, according to Bilâl. Their marriage, as everybody could see, had turned sour; they welcomed the opportunity to give their son a respite from their bickering.

Two days later Marko had second thoughts. An operation that entailed the rescue of five people of different ages, he reasoned, was beyond the capabilities of youngsters, no matter how bright or brave. Moreover, we were too many – almost a crowd. We would be conspicuous. We would get caught and would probably be executed on the spot. (We hadn't told him that only Bilâl had permission to go away; we still hoped that we might prevail upon our parents to change their minds.)

Marko suggested a new plan. He would go on his own. Like every Levantine, he spoke fluent Greek. And he knew his way around Salonica: before the war, he had had a wild time there with the lusty *koritzia*. Ah, those girls – Aphrodites, all of them! Just hand over the passports and he'd be in and out in a flash. He wouldn't even ask for additional payment.

We were devastated. We asked for a day or so to reconsider. Our first thought – certainly mine – was that, all along, Marko's sole interest in our project had been the passports. I could picture him selling them to the highest bidder, making hay for a while and eventually reappearing with a cock-and-bull story about how he had very nearly succeeded but had suddenly, tragically, been struck by misfortune. But since, except for Bilâl, we had been reduced to non-participants, what counter-arguments could we offer?

At the next meeting, Bilâl confronted Marko with a sang-froid that surprised us all. 'You're right. All of us would be too many. So we'll be just two. You and I.'

Marko chuckled and ruffled Bilâl's hair. 'My little brother. Fellow spirit. Lovely boy. No.' He sipped his raki and chased it with mineral water. 'I must be alone. Only way. In and out. Finished in no time.' He flexed his biceps. 'Marko can do it. Word of honour.'

Bilâl, half-teasing Marko, flexed his own muscles. 'You and I.'

Marko stared at Bilâl's thin arms and roared with laughter. 'Oh, little brother ...'

Bilâl poured more raki into Marko's glass, then proffered his hand. 'Deal?'

Marko pushed Bilâl's hand away angrily. 'No!' He gulped down the drink, then leaned menacingly across. 'You don't trust Marko, little brother? Even when he gives his word of honour?'

'I do. But they won't.'

Marko turned to us, even more menacingly. His thick, perfectly groomed moustache bristled. 'You won't?'

Bilâl punched him on the shoulder. 'Not them, Marko. My family in Salonica.'

Marko chuckled. 'Don't worry, little brother. They will trust me. Instantly – they will love me. They will kiss my hands. They will kiss me everywhere.'

At moments like these I felt that Marko, beneath all his manliness, was a simpleton.

'They are Jews, Marko. They have to be introduced before they can kiss.'

Marko stared at him. 'You're joking …?'

Bilâl nodded. 'Yes. But it's also true. My relatives don't know you. They won't trust a stranger. Not after what's been happening to them.'

Marko shook his head mournfully. 'But I can save them, little brother! I am ready to save them!'

'They know me. They will trust me. I'm family. Then they'll kiss your hands. Kiss you everywhere.'

Marko became ebullient. 'They will?'

'Especially the women.'

Marko looked up suspiciously. 'Only one woman, little brother. Your aunt. The girls are too young.'

Bilâl smiled. 'Fine! The girls can kiss me!'

Marko grinned and clasped Bilâl's hand. 'Right! You and I then!'

✿

They left on Sunday 6 September, as scheduled, from Beşiktaş, at the mouth of the Bosporus, where Marko normally berthed his boat. Naim, Can and I sailed with them as far as Florya. We arranged to meet a week later at the same place. Did any of us believe Marko and Bilâl would succeed? I don't know. I have suppressed a great deal since then. I would say Marko, ingenuous as ever, did believe. The rest of us, I imagine, pretended.

<hr />

The day of their return, 13 September, came and went. We waited on the beach, at our rendezvous, until dawn the next day. We smoked countless cigarettes and slunk into dark corners to weep. Finally we admitted that we would never see them again. We were inconsolable.

Later all hell broke loose.

Ester, distraught at her son's failure to return home, contacted the boy scouts and was told that Bilâl could not have joined an excursion since, due to lack of funds, none had been organized.

She and Pepo then contacted our parents, who duly summoned us to an inquisition. My father managed to extricate himself from Ankara and rushed over. My mother, too distressed – she had been very fond of Bilâl – confined herself to her room.

We saw no point in hedging. Desperate to save Bilâl, if this were still possible, we told them everything.

Much to our surprise and despite harshly reprimanding us for being so immature and foolhardy, they understood us, even sympathized. Bilâl's parents, in particular, for once equable, muttered praises, in between sobs, for our compassion and courage. I believe my father, too, felt proud of me even as he told me that I must not expect him to intercede on my behalf when the legation put me on trial for stealing the passports.

Several decisions were taken. The consulate would approach the Turkish immigration authorities and ask them whether there had been entry records for the five Turkish passports – fortunately, we had noted their numbers. If, by some miracle, Ester's relatives had reached Turkey or were being held in custody at a border post, then my father, with the ambassador's blessing, would prevail on the Turkish government to grant them asylum. The parents of Naim and Can would, in turn, make inquiries in the Levantine community about Marko's fate.

∞∞∞∞∞❦∞∞∞∞∞

On Saturday 19 September Tomaso came up with some news. His father had had reports that Marko's boat, the *Yasemin*, had been seized by German patrol cutters in a cove in the bay of Kassándra, in the Khalkhidiki peninsula, on 12 September, the day before he and Bilâl were due back in Istanbul. The seizure itself, the sources insisted, was due to bad luck: a plank nailed over the *Yasemin*'s name and port of registration, Gelibolu, had worked loose and a sharp-eyed German official, intrigued at finding a vessel with Roman lettering instead of Greek, had gone to investigate.

As far as the sources could ascertain, there had been no arrests. That suggested that the boat was empty when the Germans discovered it.

It was likely, therefore, that Marko and Bilâl were lying low, conceivably with Ester's relatives – Salonica was no more than fifty kilometres from the bay of Kassándra – or somewhere on the peninsula.

We held on to this hope.

Four days later, we heard about Marko's death. He had appeared, the previous evening, inside Bulgaria, near the Svilengrad rail-bridge close to the Turkish border. He had acquired a mule and was galloping towards the Meriç river.

He had been spotted by German and Bulgarian motorcycle patrols, who had given chase. When he started scampering across the river, the Bulgarians, respecting the neutrality of no-man's-land, had stopped chasing. Not the Germans – they had opened fire. Turkish border guards, appearing on the scene, had asked the Germans to stop firing and threatened to fire back. An argument had ensued. Meanwhile, Marko had reached the bank. The Turkish soldiers, rushing to help, had found him mortally wounded. He had died shortly after, delirious and repeatedly asking after Bilâl.

<hr/>

Weeks passed.

We visited Bilâl's parents every day. We told them

we were mourners, too, that Bilâl's loss was equally unbearable for us because he was our brother in every sense of the word, except by parentage. I imagine we were insufferably insensitive. Yet Bilâl's parents, particularly Pepo, clung to our company gratefully. As if wanting to know their son all over again, they asked endless questions about him. They laughed and cried at all the crazy, boyish things he had done and begged us to repeat his more outlandish capers. We recounted as best we could, often exaggerating details, invariably glorifying the deeds. They listened avidly. They no longer quarrelled; they even held hands dumbly. As Naim bitterly commented on one occasion, Bilâl had had to sacrifice his life to reconcile his parents.

During these weeks, my father – and the Turkish authorities – continued to investigate Bilâl's fate through various channels. But all these efforts led to dead ends.

Then it was mid-November. And we, the British, were cock-a-hoop. Military analyses confirmed that, after El Alamein, Germany was no longer a threat in North Africa. The end of the Third Reich was near.

As if this were the news she had been waiting for, Ester started avoiding us. Did she, with her Jewish imagination, think that a wounded Germany would be even more ruthless towards its victims? Whenever we went to see her and Pepo, she decided either to go shopping or to drop in on a friend. Pepo, who had to receive us on his own, looked increasingly tense and apologetic.

Soon we started hearing that Ester was not going

shopping or calling on friends, but was roaming through Istanbul. Sometimes she would undertake these rambles methodically, district by district, at other times, she would move about aimlessly. Inevitably, this mysterious behaviour spawned all sorts of rumours. Some said that she had a lover, others that she had several; still others, that she could no longer bear Pepo's company; one or two implied that she was losing her mind. The grief of losing her son, the guilt from having lost him because he had tried to save his parents' marriage by rescuing her family, would be unbearable for any person, they said.

Pepo sold his business to pay the *Varlık Vergisi*, or Wealth Tax. He went to work as a caretaker in a textile factory, a job that kept him away from home at nights and much of the day. This appeared to satisfy Ester. She stopped roaming. However, she still avoided us.

Pepo continued to see us, almost daily, but in the afternoons, after school.

∞∞∞∞∞∞∞∞✿∞∞∞∞∞∞∞∞

The year 1943 arrived.

Churchill, seeking to lure Turkey into the ranks of the Allies, met with President İnönü.

February brought news of the Red Army's victory, after months of heroic resistance, at Stalingrad. Confronted by the Soviet counter-offensive and the merciless Russian winter, the Germans now faced a cataclysm similar to that suffered by Napoleon.

The economic situation deteriorated. Naim and Can, increasingly required to help their fathers, began to miss some of our meetings with Pepo. I strongly objected to their truancies, even accused them of betraying Bilâl's memory.

Pepo explained the prevailing situation. Anti-semitism had finally seeped into Turkey. Some senior politicians, still nostalgic for the Turco-German alliance of the First World War, believed that a new alliance with Germany would repair history and restore the old Ottoman glory. So they had been easily captivated by Nazi ideology. Consequently, aided and abetted by lackeys and opportunists in important government departments, they were blaming the Jews for Turkey's economic problems. Unscrupulous journalists were competing with each other to revive the hackneyed Christian lies about the Jews' time-honoured pursuits of usury, speculation, exploitation and the conspiracy for world dominion. Cartoons inspired by that Nazi publication, *Der Stürmer*, and depicting the Jews as monstrously obese, long-nosed profiteers, counterpointed these slanders. As a result, since last November, the Turkish National Assembly had levied a discriminatory tax on all Jews – and, for good measure, on certain other minorities. Known as the *Varlık Vergisi*, this tax was so inflated that few Jews could pay it. The penalties for non-payment were extremely severe. Consequently countless Jews were not only having all their possessions seized but were also being deported to labour camps where they would 'work off their debts'.

Pepo, who had sold his business in order to pay the tax, thought that sooner or later he, too, would be sent to a camp.

∞∞∞∞∞∞❀∞∞∞∞∞∞

Then it was 12 February, Bilâl's birthday. This year it was also to be his bar mitzvah, the day he would have joined his community as an adult.

We had arranged to meet Pepo in our usual *çayhane*. Instead, unexpectedly, Ester summoned us to their home.

She greeted us warmly, almost as affectionately as in the old days. But there was a strangeness to her. Despite her thick make-up, she had a neglected air. Her hair, which normally shone like ebony – and which Bilâl had inherited – had lost its lustre. And she was in an unstable mood: very excited one moment, in a trance the next. I remember feeling uneasy and looking at Pepo for reassurance. He seemed to be in a reverie, eyes fixed on his folded hands.

Hurriedly, Ester served tea and cakes. For a while, brandishing a fixed smile, she watched us eat. Then, suddenly, with a flourish, she took out a letter from her handbag and waved it at us. 'Bilâl is alive!'

I jumped up. We all did. We fired questions at her. Naim wept. Somehow Ester calmed us down. She kept on waving her letter. 'From my sister. He saved them. Bilâl saved them.' Then she placed the letter on the table. 'You can read it yourselves …'

This time we responded more coherently. One of us, noting that the letter had been written in Hellenic script, said we couldn't read Greek. Someone else urged her to tell us what had happened. I kept asking, 'Where is he? Where is he?' And wondering why Pepo kept silent.

She related the events impersonally: 'Bilâl found my sister. Gave her the passports. They're in Macedonia now. My father. Fortuna. The children. In Skopje. Safe there …'

I shouted. We all did. Skopje had a large Turkish minority. Turkey and Germany were not at war. So Turkish subjects were indeed safe. 'Is Bilâl with them? In Skopje?'

She stared at us, at first distractedly, then with an amiable smile. 'Oh, no, no, no. He and Marko were coming back. Well, you know: Marko's boat was spotted. So they had to separate. Bilâl was wise. He didn't run to the border. He decided to hide. In a monastery. On Mount Athos.'

After a very long silence, one of us managed to ask, 'How do you know?'

'Bilâl sent word with a priest. To Fortuna.' She pointed at the letter. 'It's all in there. Read it!'

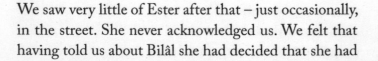

We saw very little of Ester after that – just occasionally, in the street. She never acknowledged us. We felt that having told us about Bilâl she had decided that she had discharged her last obligation to his friends and could now expunge us from her life.

Oblivious to Pepo's pain and embarrassment, we continued to pester him with the cruellest question: had Ester told us the truth?

He always gave the same answer: 'You saw the letter ...'

Then the Wealth Tax claimed Pepo. He was sent to Aşkale, an infamous labour camp in eastern Turkey, where, we later learned, some twenty middle-aged inmates, unable to withstand the heavy work and the atrocious conditions, died of heart attacks.

Pepo survived and returned to Istanbul in March 1944 after the Turkish government, finally acknowledging the iniquity of the Wealth Tax, had abolished it and pardoned all the defaulters. By then I had returned to Britain. But my last moment with him, as we embraced at Haydarpaşa railway station before he was herded on to the train to Aşkale, both of us trying to ignore the stench rising from the tattered soldier's fatigue he had been issued, will stay with me for ever.

∞∞∞∞∞∞∞❀∞∞∞∞∞∞∞∞

The sixth of June saw D-Day.

My father was transferred to European Command for the big push to Berlin. My mother, having been coaxed by a friend into helping out in a rehabilitation centre for disabled servicemen, started to return to a purposeful life. I went to Scotland, to my father's old school, to continue my studies.

Like every Briton, I lived through the last years of the war vacillating between grief and joy, anguish and hope. But every day I sojourned, sometimes briefly, sometimes at length, in my adopted Turkey, in the company of Naim, Can and Bilâl, my soul mates.

And so, no sooner had we celebrated VE-Day than I began to seek ways of tracing Bilâl.

It was a horrendous time. Every day brought further monstrous details of the extent of Nazi atrocities committed against European Jewry. People began to use a leaden word, *genocide*, oratorically, as if they had just coined it. But I think they all felt – I am sure everybody did – that they lacked the imagination to conceive of what it really meant.

Months passed.

I kept drawing blanks.

Naim and Can, with whom I was in regular contact, fared no better with their inquiries in Turkey.

Ester bombarded with petitions the various authorities who dealt with Jewish survivors and displaced people. But none of her family had been traced. It seemed probable that if Fortuna and the rest had really found asylum in Skopje, they would have been deported to extermination camps despite their Turkish passports.

Given this grim prediction, all we could do was hope that Bilâl had found sanctuary at Mount Athos. But of course we knew, deep down, that, like Ester, we were indulging in make-believe.

Eventually, we decided to direct our inquiries to Greece. But that was easier said than done. The resistance groups, the communist backed EAM-ELAS and the centrist-royalist EDES which, since the early forties, had carried out a guerrilla war against the Germans, had now turned against each other. And although British troops were trying to establish some sort of peace, chaos ruled.

Inevitably, we turned to my father for help. Since he had been very fond of Bilâl and, indeed, had admired his bravery, he promised to pull some strings.

∞∞∞∞∞∞❀∞∞∞∞∞∞

Months later, we received a comprehensive report.

According to unimpeachable sources in Greece, Bilâl and Marko had succeeded in contacting Fortuna. But they had been observed by an informer, who had duly alerted the Germans. When the Gestapo had arrived, Fortuna and her family had created a distraction to help Marko and Bilâl escape.

Marko, as we knew, had made it as far as the Turkish border.

Fortuna and her family had been arrested and deported to Auschwitz in March 1943 in one of the early transports. (There had been nineteen from Salonica, carrying almost the entire Jewish population of the city.)

Of Bilâl's fate, there were conflicting versions. One report stated that he had been shot while running away;

another, that he had been taken into custody and had either died under interrogation or been deported. But deportation could not be verified. Though the transport lists were usually compiled meticulously and included all the names of the deportees, there had been occasions when persons, either too ill or too badly tortured, were added without anybody bothering to amend the register. A third version mentioned that a youngster who fitted Bilâl's description had been spotted jumping off a precipice – the old town had numerous such drops – and had never been seen again. Curiously, the youngster's body had never been recovered. But since in those days hungry dogs scavenged like hyenas, this had not been considered unusual.

⚬⚬⚬⚬⚬⚬⚬⚬⚬❀⚬⚬⚬⚬⚬⚬⚬⚬⚬

Heart-broken, I relayed this report to Naim, Can and Pepo.

Three days later, Naim and Can telephoned to tell me that Ester had killed herself. As if re-enacting the defiance of the boy who had jumped off the precipice, she had thrown herself from Galata Tower, the Genoese edifice that dominated Istanbul and served as a fire-watch station.

A week later, I received a parcel from Pepo. It contained the copy of a text of some sixty pages written by Bilâl. Pepo and Ester had found it in Bilâl's room while clearing it out after my news about the boy who had jumped off the precipice. It was addressed to his parents and written as a valediction in case he didn't come back. He had finished writing it the day before he and Marko had left for Greece.

I read it, then immediately telephoned Pepo. One of the people he worked with told me he had left his job as well as his flat.

Alarmed, I telephoned Naim and Can. They told me they, too, had received copies of Bilâl's text and were trying to find Pepo's whereabouts. But he had disappeared.

We have never been able to trace him.

⚬⚬⚬⚬⚬⚬⚬⚬⚬✺⚬⚬⚬⚬⚬⚬⚬⚬⚬

I have a recurring dream. I meet Pepo in our regular *çayhane* in the shadow of the Blue Mosque. He tells me Bilâl is alive. Has to be. Or there is no meaning to life.

4: Selma

Half-Turk

1 January 1943

Darling Bilâl,

Everybody thinks you're dead. I don't. I did for a while. But that was because I just accepted what other people said. I don't any more. I've been thinking about it for months. How can you be dead? – you're still a boy. And we love each other. Death doesn't touch young love. Besides, there's no proof! You're on some crazy adventure, which is typical of boys your age, and that's all there is to it.

So my New Year resolution: to write to you. I need to be in touch with you. *Most of all, I need you!* Since I don't know where you happen to be, this will be one continuous letter or something like a diary. When you get back – do you realize it's almost four months since you left for Greece? – you'll know what's been happening here. And what's been happening to me.

As far as I can tell, the belief that you died spread from Handan Ramazan – that religious Muslim girl who lives next to the bakery, plays the *kanun* and was Gül's friend. Apparently she told the police – they're still investigating your disappearance – that some time in the past Gül had told her that she'd seen your death in her mind the way she'd seen Rıfat's mother die in the Erzincan earthquake. Some proof!

I still keep going to the window expecting to see you at yours. I bless the day we moved opposite you. You have such a beautiful smile. It makes the world seem safe to me. Your eyes, blue as Atatürk's, bring the sky into my heart. I so miss you these days when every minute is dark. Isn't it ridiculous we never dared say hello all that time we crossed paths going to school? Shyness is not a virtue. (Maybe in those days you had eyes only for Gül. I know from Rıfat you had a crush on her. Apparently she was fond of you, too. I should be jealous, but I'm not. You love *me* now.)

Let me bring you up to date.

Remember the new tax the government was planning? To slap on so-called black marketeers, profiteers, warmongers etc – meaning the non-Muslim minorities. Well, it's happened. It became law in November. It's called the *Varlık* and it's worse than anything anybody had imagined. It's assessed not on a person's earnings but on the wealth the assessing committee deems he has. But these committees are not made up of experts. They've been specially concocted from finance ministry officials and arriviste entrepreneurs – all of them declaring themselves 'pure' Turks – to target non-Muslim businessmen and hit them as hard as they can. Two weeks ago, they published their lists. Most of the people slated are Jews, Armenians or Greeks. My father calls this tax 'a slow death'. He says it aims to dispossess the minorities and drive them out of the Turkish economy.

And there is no right of appeal.

The sums imposed are so astronomical that only a few will be able to pay. Borrowing would be impossible – who'd have anything left to lend? Payment must be immediate – by 4 January. There's a period of grace until 20 January – that's in twenty days.

I've hesitated to mention this. But I don't want to hide things from you. In order to meet his tax demand, your father sold his shop. He received a fraction of its value.

Take care.

I love you.

See how easily I said I love you. Girls are braver than boys.

15 January 1943

Big gathering here last night.

Many Jews, Armenians and Greeks, including the

parents of Naim, Can, Selim, Musa, Zeki, Aşer, Yusuf.

Also a few Dönme. Particularly Rıfat's father, Kenan Bey. (But not Rıfat's grandparents. Unlike their son and grandson who are proper converts to Islam, they practise Judaism secretly. And though the whole world knows this, they still avoid Jewish company in the hope that everybody will think they're Muslim. But their sham hasn't helped them. The Dönme – or rather the false Dönme – have been harshly taxed, too, though not as mercilessly as other Jews. Apparently in Rıfat's grandfather's case, the fact that Kenan Bey is someone important in agriculture helped to reduce the sum the authorities had originally assessed.)

Some non-Jews were present too: Handan's parents. (And Handan.)

And a chain-smoking, curt man, Ahmet Poyraz, a professor of literature who, apparently, teaches everywhere from the university down, including the American College.

Several gentlemen whom I've never seen, whose names were barely mentioned, but who, I gather, are Masons.

Sadly, not your parents. Your mother, ever since you left, keeps to herself. Your father was working – he's taken a job as caretaker of a timber-yard. Still trying to pay off his *Varlık*.

In fact, the gathering was all about the *Varlık*. (Handan and I stayed and listened. These days we count as adults.)

Everyone agreed that the country needs to raise

money. Both the Allies and the Axis want us to join forces with them and get into the war. We have to avoid that. We can only do so if we have an army strong enough to safeguard our neutrality. Moreover, we have to tackle the food and fuel shortages – they're getting worse day by day. So we definitely need to find some money. But not by fleecing the non-Muslims!

Everyone also agreed that the *Varlık* is doomed to fail. Since only a handful can pay what's demanded of them, the nation won't be able to raise the money it needs and the problems will get worse.

Wednesday is the last day of grace. After that, properties, household goods and personal belongings of those who can't pay in full will be confiscated and sold to make up what's owed. Even then, vast sums will remain unpaid. These will have to be worked off with what they call 'corporal industry' in labour camps. For once bribes, influential friends, under-the-counter deals won't help. Nazi-lovers and their lackeys – the masterminds behind this catastrophe – want to show Hitler that Jews and 'undesirables' aren't having an easy time here.

The next problem they discussed was what would happen to the dependants of those sent to labour camps. How would their wives, children and elders survive without a breadwinner?

At that point, Handan's father, Üstat Vedat – strongly supported by his wife, Adalet Hanım – took charge. (Handan says her father likes being addressed as 'Üstat' because it's the equivalent of the European term, 'maestro', which is what the professor of music, Zuckmayer, calls him. Zuckmayer, you'll remember, is one of the many Jewish refugees from Nazi Germany given asylum in Turkey.)

Remember how the Ramazans intimidated the neighbourhood with their stern ways? How they seemed to shun fun? How Adalet Hanım – and, since Gül's death, Handan – cover their heads whenever they go out? How people mocked their piety because when surnames became obligatory they chose to call themselves 'Ramazan' after the most important Muslim holiday? And the rumours that once or twice Üstat Vedat had clashed with Atatürk on religious matters but had escaped rebuke thanks to his music?

Well, you should have heard this otherworldly Üstat Vedat. When he summed up the gathering's feelings, he spoke like a prophet. 'Racial and religious prejudices are not aspects of the Turkish character. They are European diseases. It's our sacred duty to save our minorities from this tax.'

And, in a few minutes, the gathering produced a plan.

Communities everywhere will be asked to give a portion of their food to all those left in penury by the tax. Masons and their brethren will raise money to pay for rents, heating, education, etc. There'll be hardship – for everybody – but *their* minorities will survive.

I love you.

16 January 1943

A postscript to the other day's meeting. I forgot to mention how deeply people love and respect your father. It was Pepo, Pepo, non-stop.

Üstat Vedat, it turns out, served in the War of Independence and had heard that your father did, too. (Did you know your father was at Sakarya at Atatürk's command post?) And – this will amaze you – Adalet Hanım, too, is a veteran. She was one of those legendary women who strapped shells on their backs and carried them from one battlefield to another.

That's not all. Somebody then revealed that Ahmet Poyraz was a veteran also. He was even decorated!

You should have seen how these disclosures melted the formality between Üstat Vedat and Ahmet Bey. They're so different, these two men. The first is officious, ponderous and pious; the other, impatient, fiery and irreligious. You'd never think they'd ever get beyond the basic courtesies. That said, they're also very alike. For instance, they're both very modest and get embarrassed when people praise them. Moreover, like Üstat Vedat, Ahmet Bey, too, has had clashes with Atatürk – over political matters, in his case. Yet both mourn Atatürk's early death deeply. (Strange to think there are people who didn't see eye to eye with Atatürk. Somehow that makes him more human – and more perfect.)

Here's an anecdote they told about Atatürk and your father. (Did you know Atatürk regularly employed him?)

The day before King Alexander of Yugoslavia – quite a nasty ruler, by all accounts – came on a state visit, the protocol-masters suddenly realized that they didn't have any Yugoslav flags for the bunting. So Atatürk asked your father to produce several dozen overnight. Your father gathered every adult he could find, seized every sewing machine in town and somehow procured the dyes and the necessary lengths of silk. By early morning, he had the flags ready and hanging. The king duly arrived. But, as luck would have it, no sooner had the procession left the railway station than it started to rain heavily. To your father's horror, the dyed sections of the flags began running and, within minutes, the standards were criss-crossed with coloured squiggles. Your father braced himself for Atatürk's fury. He was duly summoned. To his surprise, Atatürk greeted him warmly and congratulated him for helping heaven to deflate a despot. Thereafter he and your father indulged in some raki and praised 'perversity which, on occasions, gladly dispenses justice'.

Had you heard this story before?

Love to you.

20 January 1943

Today is the deadline for the *Varlık*. My father came home with just one doughnut. In the morning he had finalized the sale of his business and had paid whatever he had received – peanuts; that's what's happening: people are having to sell for peanuts – to the tax office.

Since all our goods are waiting to be auctioned, the doughnut, he said, was all we had – and that only because İbrahim, our street vendor, had given it to him. Then he and Mother gave the doughnut to me. I insisted we must share it. They forced me to eat half of it. The other half is for tomorrow – also for me.

I never imagined food could taste so bitter.

During the night, I heard my father cry. He kept wishing he were dead. Then, after he went to sleep, Mother started crying …

Why aren't you here? I need you! I need to be strong for Mother and Father. I need you to give me hope.

22 January 1943

Yesterday most of the Jewish men followed the old routine and went to work. Or rather, they went to the shops and offices where they used to work before they'd either sold them or where they'd been made redundant. They walked the streets in the freezing cold, shared the few cigarettes they had and watched the trams go by. Then when they would normally have finished work, they returned home.

Today they're staying in, waiting for the bailiffs or the police. No one we know has been able to pay his tax in full. So everything they own will be sold. Crowds have already gathered in prosperous neighbourhoods. Vultures! You can see them drooling. Some are acquaintances who were friendly only yesterday. Who'd have thought there'd be so many scavengers? Soon, many of them will get rich. People are now confirming what my father said from the very beginning: that the *Varlık*'s real objective is the transfer of non-Muslim wealth – what there is of it – to ethnic Turks.

In a few days the deportations to the labour camp will begin. To Aşkale, in the east, near Erzurum. A place where apparently it's harsh winter nine months of the year. Father thinks he's bound to be sent there. Mother and I are tearing out our hair. That would kill him.

I'm meeting Handan this afternoon. She's invited me to tea. She must have sensed how scared and miserable I am.

By the way, yesterday, our street – the non-Muslims in our street – received their first food parcels. Donated by Muslim neighbours, Masons and 'people who wish to remain anonymous'. Üstat Vedat, Kenan Bey and Ahmet Bey were personally in charge. That's the real Turkey, the real Turkish spirit. They're the real Turks, the true Muslims!

Love you.

26 January 1943

The bailiffs didn't come. We have to wait our turn.

As for my afternoon with Handan ... Wonderful and terrible. Wonderful because she's the most open-hearted person there is. Terrible because ...

I wasn't going to talk about it, but I must ...

You see, at some point we started talking about Gül. Handan loved Gül and still misses her a lot. In the end, she got so upset she couldn't talk any more. So she gave me her diary to read.

The diary has a section about you that made me very unhappy. So I told her about us and how we had never dared declare our love. Then I asked to borrow the diary because I wanted to re-read the section referring to you and decide what to do. Being an angel, she agreed. I'll copy the section for you. That's like betraying a secret, so don't you go and tell Handan. But then how could you? You're not …

No! I won't believe it!

Here's the section:

The day Gül was found frozen to death on a park bench as if she'd been a homeless person sleeping rough, my father told me he'd taught me everything he knew about the kanun, *that henceforth I had to play with my own heart instead of his which, though adequate, was getting barnacled, and that if my heart was as good as he and my mother believed it to be, I would surely surpass him before long. To hear from the greatest virtuoso of our time that I, barely eighteen, had mastered an instrument which, for centuries, had been kept out of women's reach, was like being told Allah was walking by my side.*

I became so ecstatic, I forgot I was the daughter of pious parents who expected decorum from their only child and retorted that I would celebrate their faith in me by playing one of Neyzen Yusuf Paşa's most difficult compositions. To my great joy, Father offered to accompany me on the oud. Mother, whose singing is compared to that of the bulbul, our people's favourite songbird, declared that she, too, would join us. (I always thought my parents would have preferred a son instead of me to carry on their musical traditions. Are they changing their minds?)

It was at that moment that Rıfat came looking for Gül.

The fact that while I was savouring the happiest moment of my life, my dearest friend, Gül, had shut her eyes for ever will always haunt me. (When I mentioned this to Rıfat as an example of life's contrariness, he quoted Mahmut the Simurg, his storyteller hero. That it's not Life that's contrary, but Death, that Life always succours life, that every time a sapling is felled, Life plants a hundred acorns ...)

It's three years since Gül died. She once told me that despite my religious upbringing – or because of it – I have a golden soul. That I know love is what clothes the living and the living are those who are about to die and, but for people like me, they would die unclothed – and nothing can be more humiliating than that. How true that is I don't know. But, certainly, I will always clothe her with my love. Yet I can't forgive her for abandoning me even though, these days, I have a better idea of the desperation that pushed her to shut her eyes.

These days I want to shut my eyes, too.

Did Gül see her own death? Did she see it as deliverance? Did it frighten her?

She wanted to save everybody. 'But', she would say, 'Death tolerates no interference.' Is that why she embraced it like a dutiful wife?

Now, all the deaths she foresaw are happening. Millions are dying everywhere in this Second World War. Millions of Jews are burning. And that nice boy, Bilâl – killed somewhere in Greece. (I never admitted this, but I think *the vision that decided Gül to kill herself was Bilâl's death. One day when we were watching Bilâl kick a ball around with her brother Naim, she turned to me and wailed, 'How many deaths can a person survive?')*

Of course, it could also have been the fate of the Jews. Because a few days before she died, she said, 'Even in Turkey, where they lived happily for centuries, my Jews will be persecuted.'

She meant the Varlık, *of course.*

Well, I want to save the world, too. Her Jews are my Jews, our Jews, the Turks' Jews. Persecution can be defeated.

It's me again: Selma.

Are you alive or dead? Do I love a boy who, like a good Jew, is trying to save lives in order to save the world? Or is there something wrong with me, as Mother thinks, because I cling to the belief that you're alive, that you're my strength, the strength I need in order not to panic? (What Mother thinks doesn't bother me. There's something wrong with everybody, we all know that.)

But the question remains: am I in love with a ghost?

1 February 1943

Still no bailiffs. They'll come on the sixth. They're waiting for a member of parliament from Ankara who wants my father's collection of Ottoman calligraphy. It's quite valuable. Mostly antique. Written on parchment, cloth, tiles and ceramic plates. Passages from the Koran, sultans' seals, verses from famous poems all expressed in wonderful geometric shapes. In fact, the MP has been trying to buy the collection for years. Now, he's sure to get it for nothing. God only knows the bribes that must have greased the bailiffs' hands. As Üstat Vedat says, the *Varlık* has brought out the worst and the best in the Turks.

15 February 1943

Sorry I haven't written for a while. I kept asking myself what is the sense in writing to someone who's gone and died?

Is death prettier than I am?

I'm a decent person, I think. At least, I try to be good. I also have a nice body. I'm not being vain. That's what girls in my class say. And boys are always eyeing me. (They hardly glance at Handan, who's very pretty, but thin as a needle and flat-chested.)

You've never seen my body. Don't you want to? Wouldn't you like to touch me? Kiss me? Do I sound like a Jezebel? Sometimes after seeing a film – I don't go to the cinema any more, we don't have the money – I used to cry because I wanted to be touched and kissed like they do on the screen. Didn't you feel like that too? Don't you want to touch and kiss me?

Is death more attractive than I am?

I'm ranting again. You're not dead.

It was your birthday the other day. So happy birthday! If you'd been here I would have given you a kiss.

The bailiffs came. Sure enough, Father's collection went for less than a glass of water. Our home is empty now. Except for one mattress – mine. That's where Mother and I sleep. They confiscated hers because the police came to take my father away just when the bailiffs were here and the bailiffs said my mother would no longer need a conjugal bed.

Father is in detention now – in a warehouse, we've been told – waiting for the train that will take him to Aşkale.

Bilâl – they've taken away my father!

God knows what they'll do to him!

Will he ever come back?

And if he doesn't – what will I do? What will Mother do? What will happen to us?

Sorry. No hysterics. I promised my father – no hysterics.

We're fine. We're all right.

Food parcels come regularly. Once a week. Incredibly generous. I think people take food out of their own mouths to give to us.

Rıfat has taken to delivering our allocation. He stays a bit and we talk about Gül and, of course, you. He's very fond of you because you're the only one in Naim's gang who was nice to him. He's grown into a hefty boy. He still wrestles. I tell him he should challenge Naim, who's a weakling by comparison, and take over the gang. 'I won't impose myself on anybody,' he says. A very decent boy.

School has turned into a pig. If I could, I'd stop

going. But I promised Father I'd be top of my class and show those who call me 'half-Turk' that when it comes to following in Atatürk's footsteps, I'm better than they are.

Were you around when these labels, 'half-Turk' or 'half-citizen', were coined for Jews and non-Muslims? Now we hear them all the time – at school, too. Not just from classmates – actually, except for a few bullies, my classmates are all right – but also from some of the teachers. The history master, Metin, for example.

Remember those caricatures that depict Jews as gigantic fat men with thick eyebrows and large hooked noses, carrying sacks of loot and mocking the poor? They started publishing them last year when you were still here. Well, this vomit, Metin, having heard that Father was going to Aşkale, showed me one of these and asked whether it looked like 'the man who sired me'. Fortunately, Father had told us what these caricatures are based on. So I told Metin, 'This is the sort of thing the Nazi paper, *Der Stürmer*, publishes to spread anti-semitism. Had Atatürk been alive, he would have smashed the hands that drew them!' Metin smiled, but he was furious. I'm sure he'll fail me next exam.

Imagine anti-semitism in Turkey … I'm so scared, Bilâl!

The Germans have surrendered in Stalingrad. Will that change things? Might it save my father?

Love is hope. My love for you is my hope.

24 February 1943

Some of the boys visited your parents on your birthday and Can told me your mother had news of you. Apparently you saved her family and smuggled them out of Salonica into Skopje, where the Turkish community is hiding you all.

I want to shout, 'My hero!' But the boys aren't totally convinced. They think someone's trying to comfort your mother. I find it difficult to believe also, I don't know why. Yes, I do know. It's the *Varlık*. We have become rudderless boats. There are no horizons left; no one can tell whether there's land anywhere.

Please be alive. For my sake. They've taken my father away. My mother looks stricken with blight. I'm like an orphan!

Love.

27 February 1943

I'm having difficulty writing. It's freezing. We have no heating. Mother and I go to bed wearing all our clothes.

I've heard some people – the neighbourhood rats – say, 'Let's burn the Jews! They're fat enough! They'll keep us warm!'

Burn the Jews, like they did during the Spanish Inquisition … Like they say the Nazis are doing …

I've even heard rumours that some municipalities here are preparing 'burning sites'. Not true, of course

– Üstat Vedat reassures us about that. Just shows how the *Varlık* chews up the mind.

Talking about Nazis. Did you know some Turkish officers have taken German officers to certain schools so that they can praise Nazism, spread anti-semitism and justify the *Varlık*?

Mother is sitting by the window, watching the street. Poor woman, what else can she do?

I'm going to bed. If I fall asleep before her, I won't have to cry with her.

I want my father back!

Why aren't you here, you pig! Why aren't you here to keep me safe? And warm.

5 March 1943

I'm sorry to tell you your father, too, has been sent to Aşkale. They picked him up yesterday, as he was about to leave for work. Apparently he told the police they should let him work so that he can pay his tax. They laughed at him. 'We don't want undesirable elements taking our jobs. Only true Turks have the right to employment,' they said.

Can you blame me for being afraid? 'Undesirable elements', 'quasi-citizens', 'half-Turks' have become today's language. Even reputable journalists are at it. You should read some of the 'unbiased' articles on Jews – poison.

Naim's father, too, has been sent to Aşkale. They came for him while the family were having lunch. On this occasion, the police had the decency to wait in another room so that they could finish eating (as if they could) and he could say goodbye.

Our world has fallen into quicksand. We can't even scream because there's mud in our mouths. Even so I keep looking at the wind in case it blows a green leaf my way.

Next week Handan will play a solo in her father's concert. You can imagine how excited she is. I'll be there to support her.

Here's the best of the latest gossip.

Aşer's aunt, aged seventy-five, has threatened to divorce her new husband (her third), aged eighty-nine, if he refuses to give up his five paramours and the seven other women who claim to be his odalisques. Though all the latter live in an old-people's home where no male, not even a tomcat, is allowed to set foot, Aşer's aunt really believes their claims. Her husband might be eighty-nine, she says, but he eats a lot of figs and consequently has the virility of ten rams.

Love is lovely.

10 March 1943

Listen to this.

We have a new Jewish boy in our class. Alev Moris. He's from Bursa. He lost his mother some years back. When the *Varlık* dispatched his father and two older brothers to Aşkale, he came here, to Istanbul, to live with his aunt. A harmless, timid boy deeply marked by his mother's death – like Rıfat. But, unlike Rıfat, not sporty. However, he reads a lot and knows all sorts of things.

The other day, Metin, the history master, confusing us with another class, started the lesson with the Age of Discoveries – a period we'll be studying next term. When we pointed this out he, being the shit he is, got angry. He started mocking our ignorance and offered a lira to anybody who could say anything meaningful about how the Age of Discoveries had affected the world. Naturally, knowing that nothing we said would be 'meaningful' to him, we kept quiet. But, Alev, being a newcomer, took him seriously and launched into an amazing monologue. Starting with the navigational advances made by Muslim mathematicians, he spoke about how the need for a sea route for the spice trade drove Columbus, Vasco da Gama and Magellan on to their historic voyages; then, describing how the lust for wealth and power had spawned the evils of colonialism and imperialism, he pronounced both the First and the Second World Wars as continuations of these pursuits.

This response – which left us gaping – inflamed Metin's anger. 'What's your name?' he shouted. Alev told him. Metin snarled, 'Moris? Moris? What sort of a name is that? All Turkish names have a meaning. Alev means "flame". My name, Metin, means "stalwart". What does Moris mean?' Well, as you know, Moris comes from the French Maurice, and is an affectation among educated Jews for Moses. So we thought Alev was cooked.

Not in the least. He thought for a few moments then

spoke slowly, as if Metin were a dimwit. 'The surname is Moriz, sir. Written with a "z". Not Moris with an "s". It was misspelled by the registrar of births, sir. As you know, *mor* means "purple", *iz* means "track". Combined, it means "purple track". This refers to the time when we Turks were trapped in a maze of mountains in Central Asia, sir. We were facing death by hunger and thirst when out of nowhere a grey wolf appeared. It laid down a track – a phosphorescent one so that it would be visible even at night, which is why it was purple – and led us to safety. As you know, sir, today many European politicians call Atatürk "the grey wolf". That's because he, too, led us out of the wilderness.'

Metin was left speechless.

God help Alev. But what courage! What imagination! What an example for the timorous like me.

Love.

16 March 1943

Yesterday, at assembly, we were told Alev had been expelled for misconduct.

Metin is a slug! Why don't you come back and step on him?

Love is hope.

24 March 1943

Handan's concert was a great success. They're already planning others.

I had never imagined the *kanun* was such a magical instrument. It has a sound like twenty string instruments played at once. I can appreciate the music now because Handan and her father have been instructing me on some famous compositions, on how they create moods and trances as pathways to love and God. Üstat Vedat defines this music as Sufism in sound. For him it's the preferred path, as opposed to poetry or whirling, for ascending the seven heavens and witnessing the Godhead. (I'm not sure I understand all that, but it has really taken hold of me.)

We have no news of my father. Is he well? Will he survive Aşkale? Mother says I should stop grieving. If anything had happened to him, we'd have heard; bad news always finds a cruel cloud to carry it. This from a woman who chains herself to the window to watch the street. I'm not that brave.

When Üstat Vedat and Handan see how little we Jews know about Turkish music, they become downhearted. 'If your people listened to classical Turkish music like they listen to Bach or Mozart,' Üstat Vedat said the other day, 'they'd soon see that Turkish composers are the equal of their European counterparts.' I'm sure he's right. Which makes me think Turks may have some justification in calling us 'half-Turks'. Surely we have the duty to immerse ourselves in our country's culture.

So that's what I've decided to do. I'll even try and learn an instrument. The *ney*, Üstat Vedat suggested. That's the reed flute. He thinks, since I can play the harmonica a bit, I should have good breath and good co-ordination.

Apropos of 'half-Turk'. At Handan's concert, I sat next to Ahmet Bey, the professor, and told him about Alev's misadventure with Metin and his subsequent expulsion. Ahmet Bey was furious. He said Metin was a disgrace to his profession and he'll make sure the turd doesn't get away with this sort of fascist behaviour.

Love you.

10 April 1943

It was Rıfat's birthday yesterday. I wanted to give him a present. He's been such a solid, reassuring presence. He won't let anybody else deliver our food. It's as if Mother and I have become his wards. And whenever he sees me at school – which is almost every day – he offers me his lunch. I refuse, of course, even when I'm hungry. After all, he wrestles and needs nourishment.

Since I didn't have any money to buy him a present, I gave him a kiss instead. I hope you don't mind.

I kiss you, too.

24 April 1943

Yesterday, my class paraded in the Children's Festival. The mayor called us 'magnificent representatives of the nation'. In our hands, he said, Turkey's future was assured.

I felt like asking him: what about the Jews' future?

Is it assured in your hands? If not – where can we run to? The Nazis are making sure there's nowhere we can escape to!

Love.

16 May 1943

Twenty-four years ago yesterday, Atatürk secretly slipped out of Istanbul. On the 19th he stepped ashore in Samsun and launched the War of Independence.

I mention this as a link to yesterday's events.

When Rıfat delivered the food, Ahmet Bey came with him. He told me he had confronted Metin and had threatened to chase him out of the educational system if he ever again discriminated against non-Muslims. Apparently, Metin got really scared. Illiberal elements in the government may hate Ahmet Bey, but he's one of the country's leading educationalists and very influential. Since he's also a war hero, he's someone to whom even fanatic nationalists defer.

Anyway, Metin has not only promised to mend his ways, but will also arrange Alev's readmission.

In the course of this conversation, Ahmet Bey also explained the ideologies behind such terms as 'Turkishness', 'Turkification', 'full Turks', 'half-Turks' and 'Kemalism'.

I'm summarizing what he said not only because it explains the present situation but also because we need to understand it for the future. As they say, 'understanding begets solutions'.

Though Turkification started as a reformist movement by the Young Turks in the last decades of the Ottoman empire, it acquired special importance when the Turkish Republic rose from its ashes. The founders of this new Turkey, proposing, almost in Marxist terms, a democratic people's state devoted to state socialism, decided that, in order to achieve this objective, the people needed a fresh identity that would shed its imperial past. An identity that would be Turkish rather than the motley of nations – *millets* – that existed before. Particularly as, following the carnage of eight years of war, the atrocities suffered by the Armenians at the hands of the Ottomans in 1915-17 and the 1923–25 population exchanges between Greece and Turkey, the ratio of non-Muslims to Muslims had fallen from one in five to one in forty. The sociologist Ziya Gökalp duly provided a new concept. He stated that a nation must be defined not by race, political system or geographical boundaries, but by a shared language, culture and traditions. What makes us human, he declared, is not our body, but our soul. (Yes, I say. Yes!) This is a definition that can embrace everybody in the land – including us, Jews.

But then certain conservative elements, noting that such Muslim minorities as Albanians, Bosnians, Circassians, Kurds and Lazes continued to preserve their own languages and cultures, decided that these diversities were a threat to Turkish nationalism. (Some traditionalists even claimed that equality for minorities contravened the principles of Islamic law.) Consequently, they expediently restructured Gökalp's definition by adding Islam as a further essential component for Turkishness. These Muslim minorities were told that they were, in reality, Turks who, over the centuries, had forgotten their Turkishness; now that they were back in the fold, they would remember their true identity and embrace it. (This would be funny if it weren't so insulting.)

Inevitably, this revised definition left the non-Muslims as outsiders, as 'non-Turks' or 'half-Turks'. At best, as 'guests in the country', at worst, as dangerous 'others'. In the hands of reactionaries, fascists, xenophobes, Nazi-lovers, it superseded the liberal, all-embracing national identity and came to be known as Kemalism. (What an insult to Atatürk's name!) And since Atatürk's death it has supported the discrimination against Jews, Armenians and Greeks – all bona fide Turks. (Atatürk must be weeping in his cloud.)

Where the future lay, Ahmet Bey could not say. But he hoped that when Germany was defeated and Turkey moved into the Allies' camp, there would be a return to the multi-ethnic national identity, the only identity that truly defined the Turk.

I wanted to ask him: we know history repeats itself. But does it ever repeat good events? Or only the disasters?

I desisted. Why should I feed my despair?

Love.

12 June 1943

Our benefactors gathered at Üstat Vedat's last night to review the situation. I never realized how difficult it is – and has been – to keep us alive. Like a child, I just took the food and hardly worried about the sacrifices that had put it in my mouth. The fact is, our neighbours and benefactors are suffering as much as we are. As if that's not bad enough, they also have the vultures to deal with. These criminals, many of them local, are constantly hovering about. They're always trying to steal the food parcels. On occasions, they succeed. Though not when Rıfat's around. They're scared of Rıfat. They went for him once and ended up with bloody noses. Even more disgustingly, they threaten our benefactors or try to blackmail them for 'aiding enemies'. Have you heard of anything more sinister? *Aiding enemies*! If anything, these attacks and thefts increase our friends' resolve. But what will happen to us when they run out of resources – as they soon will?

Both Üstat Vedat and Ahmet Bey urged them – and us – to tighten our belts and somehow hold on. Apparently some of the Allies have condemned the *Varlık* as discriminatory. There are rumours that American journalists are coming to investigate and that some people in the government are having second thoughts. Whether that includes Prime Minister Şükrü Saracoğlu is another matter. By all accounts, it was he who ordered the huge increases in the assessments.

These days, it's difficult to imagine that only three

years ago, around this time, the whole community was out in the park making rose-petal jam. Gypsies bringing in the petals they'd gathered in Thrace. Children unloading the carts. Husbands distributing the sugar – yes, sugar was available then – while grannies and grandpas stirred the cauldrons and wives filled the jars. Will those times ever return?

Which reminds me, the Gypsy children you boys used to play with bring us food, too, when they can. Often it's crusts, but considering how poor they are that's like giving us whole lambs. And they love Rıfat. A few years back, at the fair – actually Gül was with him – he wrestled with a bear. They've never forgotten that.

Next week, Handan will be playing in another concert. Rıfat and I are invited. (Handan and I have become very close. I think I've taken Gül's place.)

Love.

25 June 1943

Amazing news! We, daughters, sons and wives of deportees, have become anglers and shrimpers. You can see us casting our lines or sifting sand all along the shore. And we're not doing badly. We catch quite a few fish, mostly mackerel, and gather buckets of shrimps. (Shrimps aren't kosher, as you know, so that's for the non-observants like us.)

The idea came from Rıfat. He trains with Hacı Turgut – the famous wrestler, now retired – and he never stops talking about how wise this man is, how easily he solves life's problem. One day, Hacı Turgut told him that people who live by the sea will never go hungry because they can always fish and shrimp. So Rıfat came to us and said why don't we have a go, that anything we caught would most certainly make life easier for everybody.

That's what we're doing. And it's easing the burden on our benefactors. We even have the pleasure of treating them to fresh fish.

So, from now on, I don't have to suck pips or olive stones to fight off hunger. (I never told you this, but that's what Mother and I do when we run out of food.)

(Nor did I tell you about my recurring nightmare in which lines of people – including my father – burn at the stake while people eating pumpkin seeds drive past in tram-loads and spit the husks at them.)

Do you think I'm seeing things like Gül? Do you think the Turks will turn into Nazis? Do you think my father will die? Or is dead already?

Don't answer. Reality might be worse than nightmares.

Love.

6 July 1943

Yesterday was my birthday. I am now seventeen! A woman, Mother says. I certainly feel I am that. Ready and more than willing to be kissed. But where are you?

Mother gave me one of her old brassieres as my birthday present. I'm quite buxom, if you can still remember, and have developed more since you left, so it's just what I need.

Handan's present was a bracelet. Absolutely beautiful: filigree silver with blue and red stones.

Üstat Vedat gave me a *kaval*. And it's an authentic one – a real shepherd's pipe. He hopes, he said, that it will lead me to taking up the *ney*. So forlorn, the *kaval* sounds. Rıfat tells me there's a shepherdess in Polonezköy, the Polish village near the Black Sea, who plays it so beautifully that even the happy mimosas weep.

Ahmet Bey wanted to give me a book by Nâzım Hikmet. Instead, he made me memorize some of his verses. As you know, Hikmet's in prison for being a communist and Ahmet Bey thought that in this time of the *Varlık* it wouldn't be safe to have anything by him in the house. Apparently, your father's a Hikmet fan, too.

Rıfat has given me a ring he made out of grass. And a kiss – reciprocating the one I gave him on his birthday.

Be well.

30 August 1943

Forgive me for the very long silence.

Today we commemorate victory in the War of Independence. But we have an even greater reason to celebrate. We've just heard that several hundred inmates from Aşkale have been transferred to a camp in Eskişehir. That's almost around the corner. My father is among them. Üstat Vedat is investigating whether we can visit him. (Alas, your father is still in Aşkale.)

Rumour is, this transfer is aimed at appeasing the Allies. They've been highly critical of the *Varlık*. And since it looks like they'll win the war – they've already captured Sicily – Ahmet Bey thinks this is the beginning of the end of the *Varlık*; sooner or later all the deportees will be released.

Pray that he's right!

I was going to write about Rıfat's kiss. But maybe in my next letter.

Be well.

6 September 1943

Today is the anniversary of your departure for Greece. You've been away a whole year. Not a sign of life during all that time.

I must stop loving you.

20 September 1943

Great news!

Ahmet Bey told us that a journalist from the *New York Times* has published a series of articles denouncing the *Varlık* as a policy devised to marginalize the non-Muslims from Turkey's business life. (That's exactly what my father said, if you remember.)

The government is greatly embarrassed. The other day, the ministry of finance announced that it would pardon all those who couldn't pay their taxes in full.

That means my father should be coming home soon!

Joy! Joy! Joy!

8 October 1943

I've been procrastinating for months. I wanted to tell you about Rıfat. I just couldn't. But since I promised I'd tell you everything, I must.

Let me confess straightaway. Rıfat and I are in love.

It started with his kiss on my birthday. But, of course, we'd warmed up to each other long before that. Thanks to the food deliveries, he's been a permanent fixture in my life. Naturally, we got talking about our feelings and fears, our hopes and expectations, tragedies like Gül's death, your disappearance, the *Varlık*, etc.

I suppose it was inevitable. You being away – probably dead. He, fat-boy-turned-wrestler, growing in stature daily as he looked after our community, especially Mother and me. And I, much of the time paralysed by fear, wondering what calamities tomorrow would bring, needing solace, needing to be shielded by a man, not just any man, but a manly man, because Father was in Aşkale and we didn't know whether he was alive or dead. (There had been rumours that some deportees had died out there.)

What I mean is, I had to save myself. I had to find

a way to keep my anguish locked up in my nightmares instead of having it torment my daily dreams. And love was the way. The only way. The best way. And, mercifully, it was within reach. The distance from my lips to Rıfat's.

I must also admit – this is difficult to say because it makes me sound wanton – I have strong desires. I get aroused quickly. Often intensely. And – dare I say this? – I play with myself like you boys do. A lot, actually. It's very exciting. And almost unbearably exciting when Rıfat does it to me. I love doing it to him, too. I spend much of the day longing to be with him.

Do I shock you? I shocked myself – until I had the courage to talk to Mother. She was very understanding. She told me such desires were natural. Biologically speaking, girls mature early; they're capable of bearing children when they start menstruating, therefore, already women. (My periods started when I was twelve.)

In fact, Mother went on and on. I'm like her, apparently. An early developer. What I mustn't do is rush things. It's fine flirting with boys. But best not to go the whole way. And when it's time to get married, I must find a man who's sexually my equal – like Father is to her. That way I'll be happier than most women. (I didn't like her talking about Father and herself. So embarrassing.)

Anyway, that's me – sexual. That's what you'd have had by your side if you hadn't gone and got yourself killed.

Sorry, I shouldn't have said that. You're not dead.

Still, it's too late for us. I'm Rıfat's girl now. As you'd expect, I'll remain faithful to him.

Rıfat is also highly sexual. We're passionate about each other's bodies. We kiss a lot. When we can be alone, we lie naked and make each other come. We never feel we've had enough. But we're not having intercourse. We don't want me to get pregnant. Besides, he respects my virginity, wants me to be intact when we get married. (I can see you asking: would I marry him? The answer is: yes.)

Maybe I shouldn't have written all this. When you get back – if you get back – I'll tear off these pages to spare you reading them.

Incidentally, Rıfat knows I write to you. He doesn't mind. Isn't he wonderful?

Be well.

14 November 1943

Prejudice is not exclusive to nationalists. It exists among Jews, too. The other day, I had an argument with Rıfat's grandparents – they who pretend to be Dönme, but remain secret Jews. They're scared that Rıfat and I will marry. They don't want a Jewess putrefying – *putrefying*! – 'a sweet-smelling Dönme'. (A true convert to Islam smells of rose-water, like the Prophet – did you know that?) 'It would be criminal to think of marriage,' said Rıfat's grandpa. 'You should go out with Jewish boys,' said Rıfat's grandma. 'My grandson is Muslim, not

Jewish,' said Rıfat's grandpa. 'Find one of your own kind,' said Rıfat's grandma.

I could have argued that, Dönme or not, Rıfat was born with Jewish blood, that even if he proved to be the purest Muslim of his generation, he'd still be classified as a Jew in Nazi Germany and dealt with accordingly. But I didn't.

Instead I unleashed Ahmet Bey's views. (When you get back, I'll introduce you to Ahmet Bey. Who knows, you might end up as one of his students. He's a great man. And listen to this: apparently he has a nickname: Âşık Ahmet! Coined by his students! 'Amorous Ahmet'! It is said he's a great romantic, that he loves women and women adore him – I'm not surprised; he's a very attractive man. Had I been older, I would have fallen for him, too.)

Anyway, back to my argument with Rıfat's grandparents. 'The only quality that should be considered in judging a person', I said – I think I even sounded like Ahmet Bey – 'is whether he's good or bad, whether he obeys the directives of his soul, which are the distillations of nature's wisdom, or prefers to endorse the commands of godless power-hungry men who invent paranoid divisions like class, race, religion, nationality. Put another way,' I said, 'whether he chooses to be Nâzım Hikmet or the architect of the *Varlık*, Şükrü Saracoğlu.'

(Incidentally, Ahmet Bey suggested that we learn all of Hikmet's poetry by heart so that if one day they burn his books, we can stand up and recite his verses. You may think this is melodramatic, but as Heinrich Heine – another of Ahmet Bey's heroes – said, *where they burn books, they will also burn people*. And we Jews know how true that is.)

'Moreover', I said, 'if I marry Rıfat – and I hope I will – I'll want him to be Jewish, Muslim, Christian, Buddhist, atheist; black, white, yellow, red; Turkish, French, English, Chinese, even German.' Then I said, 'The *Varlık* and Turkification policies have shown all too clearly that the creation of a social order with separatist decrees is like inbreeding; it causes the nation to degenerate.'

Finally I said, 'Rıfat and I have decided to reject all the "nesses" and "isms". We renounce single cultures, single flags, single countries, single gods. We embrace every culture, every flag, every country, every god. We rejoice in the plurality – the infinity – of the world. In effect, we are citizens of the world.'

(Do you know, when Ahmet Bey pronounced these views at one of our gatherings, dour Üstat Vedat thanked him. 'You have given us a glimpse of the Godhead,' he said. 'Maybe that's what Turkishness really means, what Turkification should seek to achieve: to be one and everybody.')

Trump that!

11 December 1943

Father is home! What more can I say? My lovely, wonderful, beautiful father is alive and home! He arrived this afternoon from Eskişehir. He's lost a lot of weight, but is in good health.

The *Varlık* nightmare is over. We washed it away when he took his first bath in 299 days, 18 hours, 12 minutes.

1 January 1944

It's a year since I started writing to you. I'm not sure I should continue.

Father is back at work. At his old shop, believe it or not. But as an employee. He's been hired by the person who bought it from him. Having almost bankrupted the business, the man needs Father's expertise to save it. Father believes he can, and thinks in a year or so he might be offered a partnership. Whether he would accept it is another matter.

Guess what he bought me with his first pay? A *ney*. Üstat Vedat and Handan had told him I should study it.

I'll start lessons soon. Someone in Üstat Vedat's ensemble will teach me. This way I'll also see more of Handan. The last few months she was either rehearsing or playing or I was always meeting Rıfat.

Rıfat, too, will be busy this year. Recently, he became champion of his weight at a youth wrestling tournament and Hacı Turgut was very pleased with him. If Rıfat trains diligently, he says, he will stand a chance of making our Olympic team – if and when the Olympics resume, of course. Rıfat is in sixth heaven. I should be jealous, but I'm not. I give Rıfat a better heaven, the seventh heaven: my bosom.

Take care.

15 February 1944

Another anniversary. It's exactly a year since my father was taken. We commemorated that awful day with a small party. Üstat Vedat and Ahmet Bey found some sugar and we made cakes. Most of the neighbourhood came. Almost all the men are back from Aşkale. Sadly, not your father – not yet. But everyone thinks he will soon.

The Russians have broken the siege at Leningrad. No one now doubts the Allies will win. The air is full of hope. Advocate Vitali Behar, Zeki's father – the eminent lawyer, if you remember – urged us youngsters to forget the *Varlık* and carry on as before, as Atatürk's children. To this effect, he spent his first earnings on buying Zeki the ten-volume *Life Encyclopaedia*.

Looking at the future: I'm getting on with the *ney*. It's early days, but I intend to make myself a name – a Jewish name – in classical Turkish music.

Be well.

21 March 1944

The *Varlık* is officially over. Last week, on the 15th, it was rescinded by law. All those still affected were amnestied and their debts written off.

Your father is back from Aşkale. I saw him in the street the other day. He looked all right. He hasn't lost any of his charm or gentleness.

I asked him if he had news of you. He smiled and stroked my cheek. He was about to say something, but became tearful and hurried away.

He obviously knows what I have refused to know.

So maybe it's time to bid you adieu. As Rıfat says, Gül saw you die and Gül was always right. What's the point in writing to a spirit?

Indeed.

So adieu.

May whatever shrouds your remains – earth or water – be plentiful.

5: Bilâl

The Sky-Blue Monkey

There are two versions of my family's origins. Each is attested to with oaths of honour that no self-respecting Middle Easterner would ever dare to take in vain.

The first, a grandiose notion, claims that our ancestral home was founded in Toledo, Spain, in the days when the Iberian peninsula was a haven of coexistence between Jews, Moors and Christians; that the family climbed the rungs of nobility carrying the elegant name, De Flores – *perah*, the Hebrew source of our present surname, Perahya, means 'flower' – and that our direct forebears had been gallantly rescued off the Andalusian beaches on one of the few good days in the years of the Inquisition, by the Ottoman Turks, probably by the great Admiral Barbaros Hayrettin himself.

The second, an even more grandiose version, traces our lineage all the way to the first century of the Christian Era when the Romans, after decades of war, had finally conquered Judea. An extraordinary episode of those times, it will be remembered, occurred in 66 CE, during the siege of Jerusalem, when the celebrated Rabbi Yohanan ben Zakkai persuaded General Vespasian – later to be crowned emperor – to allow him to leave the doomed City of David for Yavneh on the Mediterranean coast, with a retinue of scholars, so that while the Romans did as they pleased with the Kingdom of the Lord, he, ben Zakkai, and his theologians could save Judaism by redeeming its essence for posterity – a task they accomplished, in a century or two, by compiling the Talmud. One of those exegetes, the Pharisee, Eliezer, invariably praised as 'ben Zakkai's brave and devoted companion', was, so this second version proclaims, our first known ancestor.

∞∞∞∞∞∞∞∞❈∞∞∞∞∞∞∞∞

A good start, don't you think, Mami and Papi?

You may well ask: why I am writing this? And why secretly, in the middle of the night, when you're both fast asleep?

I really don't know.

I imagine I'm writing it for you – even though it's really for me and, in any case, much of what I might write won't be unknown to you.

Then again maybe I'm writing it for my friends.

Waving them good-bye, as it were …

I have a fear that keeps tearing at my innards. I'm trying not to look at it. I don't want to recognize it. Or give it a name. The mother of my English – sorry, Scottish – friend, Robbie, a very sad woman since the death of her younger brother in the war, once told me that the moment you put a name to a fear it takes on substance.

And yet, I want to leave something like a testimonial behind me – just in case. I want to leave an impression of who we are, what we do, how our life is and has been, how blessed I am to be your son, how your love for me means everything to me, how it gives me strength, how I keep wanting to love you more, but don't know how. And, yes, also how unhappy you make me – and, of course, yourselves – when you keep quarrelling.

Anyway, I'm writing down some of the things I want to say in case they prove to be my last words.

My father, Pepo, treats both accounts of our origins deferentially. His eyes, which always reflect wonderment, shine all the more whenever elders embark on a retelling of one or the other version. But he refuses to subscribe to either – or so he admitted to me on a number of occasions when instructing me on the sensitivity one must acquire towards other people's beliefs and fantasies. Myths are fine, he says; in all likelihood, they reflect the divinity that all humankind possesses, but it is not right that existence should acquire meaning only when embedded in legends; reality, too, is meaningful; moreover, reality is immediate and demands prompt attention. (Actually, the first version, as I eventually found out, if not a fantasy, certainly lacks historical accuracy: if Barbaros Hayrettin had indeed plucked our ancestors off a beach, it would have been some forty-odd years after the Reconquista; and the beach itself would have been in North Africa, not in Andalusia.)

And so, whenever my father finds himself in less atavistic gatherings, he maintains that our family, like most families, is mongrel and that, if we think about it, this is a blessing because mongrels seldom suffer the hypersensitivity, not to mention the paranoia – indeed, the insanity – which are the bane of thoroughbreds. Moreover, since our pedigree derives from a variety of good stock – Jewish, Spanish, Turkish, Greek, Bulgarian, Gypsy, Armenian, Arab, Persian, to name but a few – we contain as much colour as the rainbow.

On the origins of the family's last two generations, however, some solid facts exist.

My great-grandfather on my father's side can be traced to Burgaz, Bulgaria. A barely legible document states that he had served there as an Ottoman functionary. Since he had also spent spells in Varna – like Burgaz, a Black Sea port – and in Rusçuk – also known as Ruse – Bulgaria's border town with Romania on the Danube, it is assumed that he had been employed by the Imperial Customs Department. Late in his life, probably around 1878, when Bulgaria became an autonomous province of the Ottoman empire, he emigrated to Izmir, the Ottoman port on the Aegean. There, he married my great-grandmother. Of her nothing is known save that, having given birth only to my father's father, she had not distinguished herself as a bounteous womb. (Nevertheless, one child was all a woman needed to produce in order to triumph, as the saying goes, over Satan.)

Since, in Ottoman times, the registration of births and deaths was an arbitrary procedure, it is assumed that my grandfather was born in the early 1880s. This date was calculated on the basis that he had sustained a disability around the turn of the century, while serving in the army, and had died in 1915, still in his thirties, leaving behind a wife and three children of whom my father, aged thirteen, was the oldest. My grandfather's death, I have often heard said, exemplified the suffering endured by countless Turkish civilians at the time of the First World War: worn out by the effort to keep his family alive during the interminable food shortages, he had been swiftly struck down by an unspecified illness. The family survived only because my father had been lucky enough to find work as a child labourer. My grandmother, by all accounts fit as ten ewes, remarried and was widowed – at least twice – and lives to this day what my parents call 'an interesting autumn in an existentialist milieu' in Alexandria, Egypt. Fatma, the Gypsy, who periodically visits our neighbourhood to read fortunes, attributes my grandmother's endless regeneration to her lustful disposition, specifically to her predilection for swarthy men. (I surmise – if I have rightly deciphered the whispers and winks – that her enviable life is that of a worldly-wise socialite popular with the non-commissioned officers of the British army.)

By contrast, my mother, Ester, a native of Salonica, the port city in Thrace, belongs to the so-called 'Jewish aristocracy'. This term, I have been told, can be traced to a tsarist monk, one of those White Russians who took refuge in Istanbul after the Bolshevik revolution. This mule, preaching in the Balkans in his acolyte years the demented message of *The Protocols of the Elders of Zion*, had observed in horror that, as a result of the education provided by the French-based Alliance Israélite Universelle, the Jews in Ottoman lands, unlike their brethren in *shtetls* beyond the Pale of Settlement, were fast attaining emancipation; that this emancipation was at its most dangerous in Salonica, where autonomy in community affairs and the pursuit of culture, wealth and cosmopolitanism had virtually transformed the city's Jews to an aristocracy; and that, therefore, the long-feared Jewish domination of the world could be expected to start in that fiendish waterhole.

At the time of my mother's birth, in 1909 – eight years before the Great Fire which, like a portent of the burnings to come, destroyed so much of the city's Jewish neighbourhoods – Salonica was still under Ottoman rule and had a population of about 180,000 souls, more than half of them Jews. In effect, as the tsarist monk had rightly stated, the Jewish majority, Europeanized in the main and economically vibrant, had earned the city the sobriquet of 'the Sephardi capital'. This situation prevailed, even after the Ottoman empire yielded Salonica to the Greeks in 1912. It is only now, in 1942, with Greece under Nazi occupation, that the Jews there face annihilation. We know this from the desperate letters my mother receives from her sister, Fortuna, who still lives in Salonica.

My mother's father, a lawyer, could trace his line – crammed with physicians, artists and merchants – to Cuenca in Castile, which, in its heyday, had competed with Toledo for the glories of the Spanish Golden Age. But during the Inquisition, between 1489 and 1492, Torquemada and his henchmen had set new standards of barbarism there. The few Jews to escape Cuenca's *autos-da-fé*, including my mother's ancestors, had adopted the name of the city, as their surname, in commemoration.

Given the differences in their backgrounds, not to mention a plethora of other considerations, I doubt whether even the Great Sybil could have foretold that my father and my mother were destined to marry each other. But then, if the books I've been reading are to be believed, marriages, in the main, are made in hell, not in heaven, and it is the demons who misdirect Cupid's arrows, not the poor little urchin himself.

Hacı Hasan, the old cobbler – according to my father, the wisest man in our part of the city – dismisses that cynical remark as unworthy of my intelligence. He tells me it has become a habit with me to muse about events as if I were a European, seeking logic in everything, even in matters where there can be none, instead of accepting, as any sensible person in the Mediterranean basin would, the laws of fate that are the primary laws of existence.

Fate is unchangeable. Hacı Hasan, who, it is said, became a dervish in the wake of his pilgrimage to Mecca soon after the Balkan wars, is unequivocal about this. What is written on a person's forehead will unfold come what may. No writing, not even a cursory scribble on the sand, can disappear, since Allah has witnessed its composition. (I wonder if Rıfat's storyteller hero, Mahmut the Simurg, knows Hacı Hasan. They seem to speak the same language.)

My Scottish friend, Robbie, finds it difficult to understand the Turkish Jews' perfunctory acceptance of Allah. He says divisions between sects, let alone religions, are so entrenched in the West that they are unassailable. I put the question to Eli, who taught me Hebrew for my bar mitzvah and who is working on his philosophy doctorate at Istanbul University under Professor Alexander Rüstow, a Jewish refugee from the Third Reich. Needless to say, Eli, who everybody says will become a professor in no time at all, rattled off the reasons without even pausing to think. In every culture where major religions rub shoulders – and, periodically, clash – the identities of the Ineffable One invariably commingle. Most Jews who have lived under Islam will admit, if they are honest, that, over the centuries, Elohim and Allah have become interchangeable – a solid journeyman who dresses now in a turban, now in a skullcap. Gods become uncompromising and merciless only when man, in pursuit of some utopia or other – like Hitler and his Nazis – alienates himself from Creation and kills the love that exists between the Creator and the Created.

Anyway, back to Fate, the irrevocable, as defined by Hacı Hasan. A strange and amazing force. It loves irony, paradox and perversity and has a great sense of the absurd. But, since it is itself a tool of Creation, it also has integrity. Thus, while it indulges in all sorts of liberties and wanders off on curious detours as it ambles its way towards its destination, it never loses sight of its position in the cosmic order. And though much of the time its meandering appears to be arbitrary, cruel, mysterious, it maintains an intimate, almost tactile relationship with the person under its charge. For most people, it has a real and continuous presence, like a once integral limb waiting, in the limbo of amputations, to reattach itself to the body.

And it is immensely inventive, immensely innovative.

And so, true to form, in June 1927, within a few days of each other, it brought two men of totally contrasting natures – one personifying sweetness, the other rage – both now my great-uncles – knocking on the door of a famous Istanbul matchmaker.

I believe the conventional image of a matchmaker, in Turkey as everywhere else, is that of a gnarled parasitic busybody. According to Uncle Jak – the good uncle

– this particular woman, bearing the evocative name, Allegra, or 'joyous', was not only an exceptional beauty, but also a student of Rousseau. She saw marriage as the only arena where women in general, and Middle Eastern women in particular, had the opportunity of defending themselves against the inequalities imposed on them by the patriarchal societies that ruled the world. Not for her the prevailing custom whereby men would discard, as and when it pleased them, their used, but perfectly adequate, not to mention well-lubricated, scabbards for new ones. Thus she always made sure that the couples, behind closed doors, at least, would have parity.

The easiest equation, in her view, was to pitch a woman who rejoiced in the blessings of her loins with a pacific man who yearned for carnal delights; thus the woman would rule benevolently, the man would be invested with a permanent beatific smile and the two would live happily ever after. Other equations included matching strong men with timorous, dependent women – or vice versa – or joining men and women who were so inanimate that they would drift through life often unaware of each other while producing children with acts akin to pollination. Most intriguingly, Allegra had scored her greatest successes when matching authoritarian men with headstrong women. Notwithstanding the sense of identity such equipoise gave the woman, the strategy also ensured that battles between husband and wife in such circumstances invariably ended in stalemate. And as stalemate after stalemate would push the contestants obsessively to further battles for at least one meaningful victory – which, of course, could never be attained – the continuation of the marriage was guaranteed. And if, as had happened on a few occasions, the battles ended in violence, the blame could always be ascribed to the stars or to the sun's spots.

Interestingly, because she had never married or been known to have liaisons with men, Allegra was often rumoured to have Sapphic tendencies. Her answer to such gossip was that in order to be clear-thinking and effective while doing God's work, matchmakers had to be celibate, like the Pope.

Anyway, as Fate would have it, the two great-uncles wended their separate ways to Allegra within a few days of each other.

Jak, my maternal grandmother's brother, waxed lyrical about Ester, aged eighteen, his beautiful and remarkably modern niece in Salonica, who not only possessed all the rubineous virtues of a Jewish woman but, as singer, pianist and painter, was also an artist thrice over. Moreover – and how marvellous that one so young should be so wise – she still saw Turkey as the spiritual home of the Jews of Salonica, and would be prepared to come and live here.

The other great-uncle, my paternal grandmother's brother-in-law Şaul, known as El Furioso, stated imperiously, as if rewarding an underling, that he had a nephew in Izmir, one Pepo, who worked in his drapery shop but who, no longer needing to look after his mother and siblings (his mother and sister had both married and settled, respectively, in Alexandria and Beirut; his brother had emigrated to Venezuela), had turned into one of those dashing, forceful young Jews and was now having ideas *au-dessus de son rang*. Moreover, Pepo, who was also a veteran of the War of Independence – and that tells one a thing or two – wanted to spread his wings, travel a bit, chase some Jezebels, even study something that would put his considerable abilities to good use – study, *nom de Dieu*, at age twenty-five! The truth was, and Şaul was loath to say it, Pepo had become indispensable to his business and had to be made to abandon all those grandiose ideas. What better than chaining him down to real life with an adamantine wife and – the things one had to do for the lesser members of one's family! – reward this loss of freedom with a minor partnership in the business?

The methodical Allegra duly visited first Salonica, then Izmir. And she contrived to meet, seemingly by chance, both Ester and Pepo. Thereafter she spent several weeks conjugating the two with various potential candidates in her books. In the end, guided by her special formula on equipollent couples, she decided that the spirited Ester and the enterprising Pepo were ideally suited to each other. For good measure – since Ester, as an aristocrat, would need something extra to consent to the proposal – Allegra concocted a variety of spells and potions. One charm, my father swears to this day, worked wonders with him: silk French knickers dusted with cinnamon powder to induce sweet turmoil in his genitals. Another, attar of roses on my mother's pillow to clear her mind of all thoughts except love for my father, was also apparently very effective.

Whether through professional acumen or through spells, Allegra's reputation for arranging an immaculate union was validated in no time at all. In a courtship that stunned even the matchmaker by its speed, my father and mother fell in love. Within weeks they were married – 'in indecent haste', according to the gossip-mongers.

On one of those luminous blue days when the gods frolic like dolphins in the sea and all barriers between parents and children crumble, I asked my father about his hasty marriage. With those eyes that look at the world in adoration, he admitted that, indeed, as the old vestals claim, he and my mother had been consumed by desire from the moment they met. But since like all good Jewish youngsters in those days, they had to observe tradition and would not have sex before matrimony, getting married as soon as possible had been their only course to satiate this hunger. So no truth in all that talk about me being conceived out of wedlock. I arrived in this world in seven months. I hope I will not leave it as prematurely.

No, I'm not afraid of the mission ahead. That will go smoothly, you'll see!

There was, however, another factor, one which proved as strong as carnal hunger, that further contributed to the hasty marriage: my mother's love for my father's stories about his adventures.

Mother, as mentioned before, was an accomplished

singer, pianist and painter. But, according to Uncle Jak, her gifts needed to be nurtured. They needed drama, strange characters and extraordinary episodes – in effect, compelling narratives. And my father who, despite his young years, had lived an eventful life and who, moreover, was a virtuoso storyteller, provided these in abundance. (Sadly, Mother abandoned her artistic aspirations soon after my birth. In the impoverished early years of the republic only the very few could pursue a career in the arts.)

By all accounts, the story that clinched the marriage was the one about the battle of Sakarya, the turning-point in the War of Independence, during which my father served as a signalman in Atatürk's command post. In my younger days, this story remained my mother's favourite. She used to make my father tell it to everybody. She even made him write it down when his memory began to blur and he had to guess details that he could not remember exactly. In later years, after the endless quarrelling had started, she stuck to her claim that he had seduced her with that story – poor, naive damsel that she had been – the way Othello had seduced Desdemona. A brutal, worldly plebeian capturing the heart of an innocent maiden with a tale of war and bravery.

Actually, since the Sakarya story is one of my favourites, too (and since this, my composition, whether it turns out valedictory or not, has evolved into a hosanna, my sentimental celebration of my mother and father – alas, no brothers or sisters: Mother thinks one child, particularly if not a girl, is more than enough), I will attach that story, as written by my father, as an appendix to this piece.

A word here about the unhappiness that rules our house. I don't know when it began. Or how serious it is. My mother and father still appear to be very close and very interested in each other. For instance, they never go their separate ways. Not for my mother, bridge parties or afternoon coffees with other women. Not for my father, the secretive world of the Freemasons or nights out at newfangled clubs with cronies.

But begin it did at some point.

Possibly, as Uncle Jak thinks, one sunless day, Mother took a look at Father and saw, in the brume, the shadow of a man who, though he had looked like a giant in yesteryears, was now impaled on a crag, unable even to defend himself against a buzzard that was tearing out his eyes. Sickened by this sight – maybe even thinking that the buzzard might well be herself and not Uncle Şaul's damned shop (which my father inherited after Uncle Şaul's death), she ran hither and thither, shouting at God, 'Did I abandon my music and paints for this?! I threw away my life for this?!' That same sunless day, Father, who was indeed a giant, who could have been a savant, a statesman, certainly a great man, if only he could have studied, but who, in order to feed the wife and child he loved, burned his bridges and boats, wept tearlessly, as the winds blew away his days, and asked in turn, 'Is this all there is to life?'

The tragedy, according to Uncle Jak, was that Mother

and Father had taken stock of their lives on the same sunless day. Had they done so on different days, one or the other would have noticed that their lives, though compromised and very much unfulfilled, were also rich beyond their imaginings: their son and their love for each other, for a start ...

After that, the unhappiness advanced with sickening speed. Now, it is a constant. Mother accuses Father of some wrongdoing – always a silly thing like not folding his napkin properly or walking home in the rain at the risk of catching a cold, to save money, instead of taking the tram. Father tries to appease her by apologizing. She responds by raising her eyes and demanding of heaven how many times a woman can forgive a man for the same stupidity. A long silence ensues. She starts again, reiterating her question. He censures her for escalating a minor disagreement into a major quarrel. That infuriates her; she starts accusing him of all sorts of misdemeanours, from being uncouth, to mocking her Greek accent (which he actually finds very endearing), to not giving her enough housekeeping money, to surreptitiously looking, maybe talking, maybe even having fun with other women. Incensed by her imputations, he protests his innocence, then retorts that she would only have herself to blame if he did go and seek the harmony and happiness he craves with another woman. This enrages her all the more: a man who can distort truth so readily, without even a twinge of conscience, is not a man, but a brute, a Nazi, a Goebbels no less. If he had his way, he would slaughter the world, starting with the wife he claims to love so much.

Last night, for instance.

It began, I'm ashamed to say, because of me.

Father was having second thoughts about my so-called boy scouts excursion to the Royal Hittite Archives at Boğazköy. The country was troubled, he said, orphaned by Atatürk's death (Father worshipped Atatürk and has not stopped mourning him), opportunist Nazi-lovers were crawling out of their holes. There was a growing economic crisis and these rats, together with right-wing elements in the government, were blaming the minorities, particularly the Jews, as its perpetrators. True patriots were either being marginalized or, as in the case of the poet, Nâzım Hikmet, were being thrown into gaol. (Father loves Hikmet's work and maintains that had Atatürk been alive, he would have come to respect Hikmet's views. I suspect, deep in his heart, Father is a socialist – or, as they call them these days, a communist.)

Anyway, Father feared that if I went on the excursion to Boğazköy, I might be harassed by ignorant fellow-scouts or scout-masters, attacked and ostracized as yet another Jew 'who drinks the nation's blood'.

As if this was the opening she had been waiting for, Mother went on the offensive. (For once, I was glad she did, because there is really no excursion to Boğazköy; that's the excuse we – my friends and I – invented so that I can go to Salonica with Marko and smuggle out my mother's family.) She accused Father of being jealous of the education I was receiving while he had had to leave school at thirteen; in effect, he was oppressing me, trying to reduce me to a nonentity like himself; any day now, he would probably start burning my books; well, she was not going to let that happen, not as long as she was alive; she was not going to let him victimize her son as well.

Here is a snippet from that quarrel. I copied it down word for word:

He: 'Victimize my son? My own flesh and blood? I'd tear myself to pieces for him!'

She: 'There you go again with your violence!'

He: 'I'd die for him as I would for you. You know that!'

She: 'You'd kill us first – that's what you'd do!'

He: 'Woman, you're mad!'

She: 'Yes, I am mad – because I'm all heart! But you? A maniac – waiting to explode!'

He: 'I'm a loving man. You took me as a loving man!'

She: 'You've changed!'

He: 'No! All these years – have I ever hurt you? Lifted a hand to you?'

She: 'You've become like the rest. A man who runs around all day. Comes home angry. Ticks away like a bomb!'

He: 'A man who is trying to put bread on the table.'

She: 'Oh, yes, never hit a hungry person. Wait for her to finish her bread, then – wham!'

And so it went on. And so it always goes on. And the horror is, she knows – as I do, as everybody we know does – that Father, despite his shortcomings, despite his frustrations, has no violence in him and is truly a loving man.

A few months ago, after an exceptionally bitter quarrel, I heard my father leave the house in a fury. There was a blizzard raging outside. Thinking that he was either going to desert us or kill himself, I went after him. I followed him down to the sea. I watched him as he sat on a capstan and started smoking. He had not taken a coat or a jacket – just a thin sweater on which the snow was settling. I remembered how Naim's sister, Gül, whom I adored and still miss very much, froze to death on a park bench like a homeless person. Afraid that my father, too, would freeze to death, I went and sat next to him and put my arms around him. He stared at me, seemingly surprised that someone still cared for him. Then he hugged me fiercely as if wanting me to become part of his body. Eventually, joking that we would soon turn into snowmen, he took me to the local *mahallebici* for some hot soup. As the warmth seeped back into us, I asked him why Mother had changed so much, why did she keep accusing him of having a brutal nature. At first, he hesitated to talk about her; then, deciding that I was old enough to know, he told me a bit about her past. He said that Mother's father had been a violent man who had, on one occasion, crippled his wife by pushing her off a balcony. He told me that, on another occasion, when my grandfather was beating up my grandmother, Mother had threatened to shoot him with a hunting rifle. According to doctors, Father explained, exposure to such violence leaves terrible scars on sensitive minds. Perhaps under different circumstances, she could have lived with those scars without much trauma, but now, with war raging all over Europe, with the Nazis in Salonica persecuting the Jews, persecuting her family, Mother could see nothing but violence and brutal death all around her. But she could be helped through this awful period. With love and patience. Then again, a single piece of good news like her family being safe would probably bring her, in no time at all, back to her old self.

It was after that conversation that I decided to find a way of saving my mother's family in Salonica.

∘∘∘∘∘∘∘∘∘◆∘∘∘∘∘∘∘∘∘

So, this is what lies ahead.

My friends, Naim, Can, Robbie and I have devised a perfect plan.

We will save all five members of my mother's family: my aunt, Fortuna; her three children, David, Süzan and Viktorya; and my grandfather, Salvador. Initially, I had been against including my grandfather in the rescue because of his violent nature, but then decided that it would be ungallant to exclude him. Sadly, Fortuna's husband, Zaharya, died a few months ago, after being sent to hard labour by the Nazis.

We have passports for them all: Turkish ones, which, we have been told, will be honoured by the German authorities because Turkey is still neutral in this war and, following the occupation of Greece, a neighbour to be wooed. We procured the passports by exchanging them with British ones. We got hold of the latter thanks to Robbie, who can go in and out of the British consulate because his father is a grandee there. The exchanges were made through the intermediacy of Naim's classmate, Tomaso, a Levantine boy whose family controls all the smuggling in this region. Tomaso also introduced us to Marko, his mother's young brother, who, although only twenty-five, has the reputation of being the best and the most daring operator in the Aegean; moreover, it is said that his boat, the *Yasemin*, can run circles round any patrol boat. So Marko will be our saviour. Originally, Naim, Can and Robbie were to have joined us. We had invented a good excuse to be away from home – the boy scouts excursion to the Hittite Archives at Boğazköy that I mentioned earlier. But, alas, Naim and Can are needed to help out in their fathers' shops and Robbie has to stay at his mother's side because she is not at all well.

So it will be just Marko and me. We will slip into Greece, make our way to Salonica, find Mother's family, hand them the passports and slip out again.

We'll be back in a week.

We sail the day after tomorrow.

∞∞∞∞∞∞✿∞∞∞∞∞∞

God, I was hoping to say much more.

Well, another time …

Oh, I nearly forgot. I had a strange dream last night. I don't normally remember dreams. Only the sexy ones that wake me up all messy.

Anyway, this dream. I was in ancient times. Watching a religious rite. People were piling their troubles and wrongdoings on to the back of a *kapora*, the traditional animal of purity, the scapegoat, in effect. But in this case the animal was a monkey, like Cheetah in the Tarzan films, only sky-blue in colour. When this monkey was so loaded that it was staggering about, they dragged it to an altar where a priest stood ready to slaughter it so that in death it would take away with it all the people's misery. As the priest prepared to cut its carotid artery, the monkey turned and looked at me.

It had my face.

Bizarre.

When I get back, I must ask Ruhiye, Uncle Jak's maid, what it means. Like most descendants of the Yürük, the original Turkish tribes from Central Asia, she is good at explaining dreams.

So ...

TO BE CONTINUED ...

WHEN I GET BACK ...

WITH GOOD NEWS, GOD WILLING!

Appendix: Herewith my father's story

Sakarya

Most historians will tell you that Mustafa Kemal Atatürk was not only a prodigious statesman, but also a soldier of genius. In support of this conclusion, they will expound on his bold and often unorthodox strategies in Tripoli, Gelibolu, Syria and the Turkish War of Independence. Some of these, I believe, are part of the curriculum in military academies across the world.

But only a historian who has survived trench warfare, who breathed the stench of decomposing bodies, who lay paralysed by fear in livid shell-craters, who, coming under fire in open terrain, ran like a headless chicken, who strove to cling to his sanity as he watched Death snatch much of his generation on fields which, only yesterday, had been adorned with poppies, daisies and marigolds, can encapsulate the qualities that made Mustafa Kemal indomitable in warfare.

I met such a man. Nikos Vassilikos. At the time, a Greek colonel. We captured him in August 1921, during the battle of Sakarya when the Hellenes were pushing towards Ankara.

As I was the only one in the regiment who spoke some Greek, my Paşa had asked me to conduct the interrogation.

If I may, I will refer to Mustafa Kemal as my Paşa. That is how he lives in my heart. Paşa, incidentally, is the rank of seraskier; its European equivalent is Field Marshal.

During the interrogation, Vassilikos repeatedly informed me that, in his efforts to become a diligent officer, he had applied himself to analysing my Paşa's strategies in previous campaigns; consequently, he could construe why – and how – my Paşa invariably obtained the advantage over his adversaries. In fact, Vassilikos had sent a detailed report to his General Staff on my Paşa's martial acumen, but they had dismissed it as a defeatist tract – a stupidity that had confirmed Vassilikos' conviction that most General Staff officers were textbook soldiers, therefore buffoons. (Vassilikos is now a respected historian. His even-handed study of the Turkish–Greek conflict has become a standard work – except for the die-hard xenophobes of his country.)

Vassilikos maintained that what the High Command could not see – or did not want to see – was that my Paşa was, quite simply, way ahead of his time. Like Alexander the Great. Tomorrow's man today. An astute rationalist who had soon perceived that accurate information on the enemy's morale, disposition, capabilities and the manner of its deployment was the principal weapon for victory rather than, as his peers obdurately claimed, a standard item of an army's ordnance. My Paşa was a visionary who saw the military potential, particularly for gathering intelligence, of every new invention, long before the desk runners in any defence establishment.

Vassilikos supported this assertion with numerous examples. Not being of a military mind, I have forgotten most of them. But I can never forget a specific strategy because, as Fate decreed it, I had been a cog in the wheel.

One of the innovations that my Paşa had speedily espoused was the field telephone. According to Vassilikos, the Gelibolu victory could be attributed, in the main, to my Paşa's exceptional use of this device. Today, many military historians agree with this appraisal.

By deploying countless look-outs on and in the periphery of the battleground, with emphatic orders that they should provide continuous reports, my Paşa could not only determine the foe's weak positions and strike accordingly, but also ascertain, often far better than the enemy's own officers, the state and morale of its troops. He was particularly interested in what most commanders-in-chief would have dismissed as irrelevant. How well turned-out was the adversary? What was the state of their uniforms and boots? How often did the soldiers eat? What did they eat? How often were they given a break? Did they smoke heavily? Did they sing? If so, what sort of songs – sad or rousing? How regularly did they wash and shave? How often did they relieve themselves? And so on …

My Paşa drummed it into us that very important deductions could be made from these seemingly unimportant details. How well the soldiers were turned out, the state of their uniforms and boots and what they ate would give an indication of how well the enemy was supplied. How often they ate and smoked, the kind of songs they sang and how frequently they washed and shaved would be excellent pointers to their morale. Moreover, a detail as banal as the number of times they relieved themselves could make the difference between victory and defeat. Too many men relieving themselves too many times would suggest that the enemy had been stricken with diarrhoea, maybe even dysentery, and that it was likely to be too weak or too exhausted to defend itself against a full-scale attack.

In 1921 I was one of the signalmen who gathered these reports for my Paşa.

How come?

Well, a number of recruits from the minorities – Jews like myself, Armenians, Levantines, Pontos, etc – had been chosen for the Signals Corps and speedily trained. We had been favoured because the Ottoman authorities' negligence of their people, particularly in terms of education, had been so ignominious that a large percentage of our comrades-in-arms had remained illiterate. Against that, most of the minorities – allowed to have their own schools and maintain their own cultures or, should they wish it, to undertake a European education in one of a number of foreign schools that had opened in the principal cities – had attained high levels of literacy. The majority of these schools had sprouted in the 19th century as an extension of the Capitulations that had been granted to some European nations by the Ottoman empire. Since literacy and the ability to speak languages were of primary importance in intelligence work, most of the conscripts from the minorities had been assigned to that corps.

Given the atrocities suffered by the Armenians at the hands of Enver and Talat Paşas, given also the Armenian nationalist movement that led to the creation, under the treaty of Sèvres, of an Armenian Socialist Republic in August 1920, you may well be surprised to hear that there were some Armenian recruits in the Turkish army during the War of Independence – as, indeed, there had been during the First World War. Notwithstanding the fact that the Armenian Socialist Republic collapsed within months of its birth and was subsumed by the Russians, the presence of Armenian soldiers in the Turkish army is a clear example of the paradox that was the Ottoman empire and, to a lesser extent, the paradox that is the new Turkey. It is also an indication of my Paşa's esteem for non-Muslim minorities.

Back to my story. Me, Pepo, as the terminal for vital intelligence reports.

There I was, barely nineteen, a city boy with some education who, inspired by my Paşa's call to join the struggle for Turkey's very existence, had readily volunteered. A boy who had never seen a weapon in his life, let alone used one. A boy as enthusiastic as a boy can be, but also scared out of his wits. A boy who, no sooner had he reached the Turkish lines – an arduous trek for those, like me, coming from Izmir or the Aegean provinces which, at the time, were under Greek occupation – finds himself in the Gehenna of war. A boy either petrified as he relaid countless metres of telephone lines under intense artillery fire or frantic as he manned, a breath away from the front, both the telegraph receiver and the cumbersome switchboards connected to look-outs with field telephones. A boy with more lives than a thousand cats, particularly when mending the communication wires that had been either clipped by enemy scouts or blown out of existence by the relentless bombardment. A boy who, instead of day-dreaming about girls or masturbating spiritedly as if aiming for a world record, had to learn not only the Morse code but all the advances in cryptography.

I am embarrassed – but also proud – to admit it, but I became an expert – the best, according to my instructors. I could receive and speedily transcribe several messages at the same time. I even managed to become ambidextrous. Consequently, I was sent from one battlefield to another until I ended up at my Paşa's command post, at Sakarya, in centre-west Anatolia.

The battle of Sakarya, as we all know, became a turning-point in the War of Independence. It lasted some twenty-one days and saw fierce fighting on both sides. The front, sometimes twenty kilometres deep, stretched over 100 kilometres, almost the full length of the terrain where the Sakarya river forms a wide loop before snaking its way north to the Black Sea. The Greek army, well equipped and well provisioned from the Aegean, had started its offensive on 14 August from its positions around Eskişehir and Kütahya, which it had conquered in July. Its main objective was to push towards Ankara, the seat of the Turkish Nationalists, and thus put an end to my Paşa's dreams of creating a new Turkey from the ruins of the Ottoman empire. Following the Greek gains in July, İsmet Paşa, my Paşa's ablest commander – and now, since my Paşa's death, president of Turkey – had pulled the Turkish army back to the Haymana plateau, east of the Sakarya river, where the terrain, about 900 metres high, was not only easier to defend but also provided unimpeded views of the Greek forces from a number of hills. Beyond lay the portals of Ankara, destined to be the nation's capital.

On 17 August my Paşa, just five days after having broken a rib during the preparations for battle, took overall command of the Turkish forces and set up his headquarters at Alagöz.

The Greek army, positioning one corps at the confluence of the Sakarya and its tributary, the Ilıca, unleashed its main assault from the south, skirting round the river's loop. By so doing, it not only avoided the tribulations of a river crossing, but also sought to strike at the Turkish army's soft underbelly.

Bitter and relentless fighting ensued. The Greeks advanced forcefully and captured a few hills. Some Turkish commanders advised a retreat towards Ankara, but my Paşa forbade it. This battle was not one where we were defending an expendable military position; here we were defending the very heart of the Motherland. Consequently, not even a millimetre of the battlefield could be yielded to the enemy. 'Make your peace with your God,' my Paşa exhorted us, 'for here we might be judged by Him.'

On 2 September the Greeks captured Mount Çal, the most strategic position on the battlefield. The road to Ankara beckoned. But by then, they had suffered terrible losses and their supplies had been severely depleted. Consequently, much of their resolve had foundered. Those who had survived felt they had no cause to celebrate. Realizing that the next offensive would prove even bloodier, they had begun to despair of victory. They yearned to return home.

We, too, had suffered terrible losses. We, too, were very short of supplies. But we were on our homeland. We could not let it be plundered. We had accepted the command to defend it to the last man. So we dug ourselves in wherever we stood.

And the fighting continued. Blood ran like floodwater and carried heads, limbs, torsos as if it were the quartermaster of an insatiable war god.

My Paşa, looking like an avenging spirit in his simple, unranked uniform of Mehmetcik – the generic name for the ordinary Turkish soldier – ran from unit to unit ordering the men to hold their positions, insisting that the Greeks would soon capitulate, that, in fact, one could hear them cracking up, even through the thunder of the guns.

Just hang on for another day.

And Mehmetcik believed him. For my Paşa was not only one of them, but in his unranked kit, he looked like any of them.

And hung on yet another day ...

Which dawned on 4 September.

I have it etched in my mind. Etched somewhat dreamily, I must admit; but then, I had been on duty, night and day, since before the commencement of hostilities and sorely lacked sleep.

According to scouts and look-outs, there had been frantic goings-on throughout the night in the Greek camp. We could not assess the exact nature of this activity; the aridity of the region cocooned every movement with clouds of dust. My Paşa was convinced that the Greeks were preparing to strike camp. Yet we had intercepted messages from the Greek High Command stating that fresh supplies and heavy armour were on their way under cover of night – though none of our scouts could confirm these.

Round about first light, when I had just closed my eyes for all of two minutes, my Paşa shook me awake. 'Don't fall asleep on me, Pepo! Not now! Not today!'

I shook my head and tried to keep my eyes open. 'I won't, sir!'

He hauled me up from my console. 'Come on! We'll walk a bit!'

Feebly pointing at my instruments, I protested. 'What about ...?'

'We'll keep our ears open. Come on! Quick march!'

'Yes, sir. Quick march!'

My Paşa had not slept for over a month – he never did on the field of battle – yet he looked as fresh as if he had just returned from an early morning swim. Moreover, his chest was strapped up; his broken rib had still not mended; yet, apart from the scabrous respiration that identified a heavy smoker, he did not seem to have any difficulty breathing; and his grip, as ever, was like a wrestler's.

Goaded by the superhuman qualities of the man, I propelled my legs forward.

We strode up and down in the wooden hut that perched precariously on the crest of Alagöz. A few of my Paşa's bodyguards – sinewy Laz braves known as yiğits, from the Black Sea regions, dramatically clad, as always, in dark clothes – kept pace with us. The hut groaned and shook under our feet as if it were about to snap off its stilts. The scene struck me as so bizarre – exhaustion has a wicked sense of humour – that I giggled.

My Paşa patted me on the shoulder. 'Find me a man who

laughs at adversity and I'll show you a Jew!'

'I'm a Jew, my Paşa ...'

'Which is why I've commissioned you to be my eyes and ears!'

'Allah be praised!'

'Are you religious, Pepo?'

'No, my Paşa ...'

'Good. Keep it that way.'

'But I believe in God ...'

'We all do. Otherwise we wouldn't be fighting this war.'

I looked up surreptitiously, thinking he was being sarcastic. But no, the freshness in his face had faded. He appeared haunted and hollowed-out. The eyes, normally lit by the famous sardonic smile that had intimidated even the German High Command, seemed dimmed by torturous thoughts.

I wondered whether this impression was caused by his simple uniform, which had begun to look like a shroud. Why had the Nationalist Assembly in Ankara not yet invested him with a rank – particularly as they had already appointed him commander-in-chief? Had they expected him to parade himself in his Ottoman army rank? Surely everyone knew by now that since the new sultan had so callously surrendered his people to the British, my Paşa had turned his back on everything Ottoman. Turks in a free country, in republican Turkey – that was what he was fighting for, that was why the sultanate had sentenced him to death.

'The enemy, too, thinks God is on his side, my Paşa.'

'Sure, he does. The Greeks love God. And God loves the

Greeks. I should know. I was born in Salonica.'

'Which makes this a funny war ...'

'That's right, son. Funny for God. Life and death for us mortals.'

Passing by the hut's crumbling window, I felt the morning air still smouldering on my face, but with a hint of coolness, which only shows that September is a month that enjoys teasing people. I took a deep breath and surrendered to the rhythmic sound of our footsteps. Within moments, I felt as if I were being rocked to sleep, or rather as if I was travelling on a train somewhere; and a woman – my mother? – was singing a lullaby.

My Paşa pulled me up. 'You're falling asleep!'

I tried to straighten up. 'No! I mean, I'm trying not to ...'

'Good!'

'Only I haven't slept for God knows how long ...'

'You'll probably have to stay awake just as long again.'

I started laughing. 'What bliss ...'

My Paşa laughed too and proffered his gold cigarette case. 'Have a smoke.'

I took one.

He lit our cigarettes, then turned to his bodyguards. 'Fetch him some coffee!'

As the Laz yiğits raced to carry out the order, I inhaled deeply. The strong tobacco made me cough. The paroxysm dispersed some of my sleepiness.

My Paşa smiled. 'I should have thought of cigarettes before.' He led me back to my console. 'Enough marching.'

I collapsed on to my chair, then stared at him in awe.

'How do you do it, sir? Never sleep, I mean.'

He strode to the window, cleared a few cobwebs, then gazed out at the river down on the plains. He pointed at a stretch of gorges – shallow at this time of the year. 'Somewhere beyond Sakarya – there are a couple of maidens ... I want them ...'

I looked at him, puzzled. 'Maidens, my Paşa?'

'One is called Victory. The other, History. I need them to save the country ...'

'I see.'

'Do you like maidens, Pepo?'

I grinned. 'I'm mad about them. Especially if they're round and rosy everywhere.'

'Good man. What else do you like?'

'Food – plenty of it.'

'Rakı?'

'Sure. But I can't hold it down very well.'

'Anything else?'

'Life – I like that best.'

'Ah ... Not the stuff of martyrs, eh?'

'No, my Paşa. I'd kill myself if I got killed!'

My Paşa chuckled. 'So stay awake ... and you won't get killed.'

Then everything happened at once. A yiğit rushed in with a mug of coffee and plonked it on my console. Another yiğit, almost tongue-tied, grabbed my Paşa by the sleeve and dragged him to the window. Other yiğits rushed around trying to get a better focus on the binoculars that had been placed along the hut's windows. And my switchboard and receivers started crackling away like a conference of birds.

I gulped down my coffee and grappled with the incoming messages.

Behind me, my Paşa, scanning the battlefield, shouted jubilantly, 'They're retreating! They are retreating! Didn't I say they would? Didn't I?'

I was getting the same message from all the look-outs. I turned round and shouted, 'They are retreating! They are!'

My Paşa had burst into a Laz song and was performing some steps with his yiğits.

I kept shouting, 'They're retreating! They're retreating!'

'Yes, Pepo, my son! They're retreating!' Unceremoniously he pulled me off my chair. 'Come! Dance!'

I did – a few steps. But the crackle of my receivers summoned me back. Every look-out was sending in the same report. The entire Greek army was withdrawing.

My Paşa allowed himself another moment's joy, then regained his full stature. He turned to the yiğits. 'Summon my officers!'

He came and sat by my side. 'Right, Pepo, this is it. The most momentous time of your whole life.'

'Yes, my Paşa.'

'Time to pursue them! I'll be sending out orders by the minute. I want you fully alert.'

I was fully alert. Fatigue and sleeplessness had vanished. The magic of imminent victory. 'I am, my Paşa. I will be.'

'This will have been the Greeks' last offensive. This is the beginning of the end. From now on and until we send the Greeks packing in their boats, you and I will be like Siamese twins.'

'Yes, my Paşa.'

And so we were. The Greeks withdrew to their old positions by Eskişehir and Afyon Karahisar. As my Paşa had predicted, Sakarya proved to be their last offensive. Throughout winter and the next spring, we prepared for victory.

On 25 August 1922 we engaged the Greeks again.

On 30 August we defeated them at Dumlupınar and inflicted heavy casualties. They ran towards the Aegean, burning and destroying every field and village in their path, butchering the peasants they came across – mostly the elderly or children, the rest were in the army.

On 9 September the Turkish troops liberated Izmir.

On 10 September my Paşa entered the city.

On 13 September, as the Greeks started taking to their boats in the Urla peninsula, a terrible bloodbath ensued in Izmir. Set on fire by some of its inhabitants, the city witnessed the slaughter of many of its Greek citizens at the hands of the avenging Turks. The city's military commander just stood by and watched.

By 16 September, when all the Greek forces had left the Turkish mainland – many of them literally having had to swim to their ships – three-quarters of Izmir had burned down and tens of thousands of refugees had either taken refuge in foreign battleships or been evacuated by the Turkish army.

Throughout all those times, I handled the intelligence for my Paşa and sent out his orders. I also conveyed his messages both to the Nationalist parliament in Ankara and to the officials of the foreign powers with whom he had begun to negotiate Turkey's future.

Then I had an accident. I had been given leave, on the very day that the great fire of Izmir started, so that I could reacquaint myself with my native city and look up relatives and friends. I was in an old residential district, trying to locate a school chum, when the fire, spreading at speed, engulfed the neighbourhood. I joined the people trying to save those trapped in burning houses. We were directed to a Greek orphanage. We went in and brought the children out. As we were guiding them to safety, to the sea front, an explosion occurred. The fire had blown up an ammunition dump nearby. To my right, a wall burst. I was holding a child with each hand. I don't know what made me do it but I pushed the children to the ground and threw myself on top of them. Chunks of the wall fell on me and crushed my legs. But the children were unharmed.

It took me almost three years to recover.

By then, my Paşa had exchanged his soldier's uniform for the garb of a statesman. He had declared Turkey a republic and had become its first president.

But he kept in touch with me. He made sure I was well looked after. He sent me provisions, clothes, books. It was he who introduced me to Nâzım Hikmet's poetry. 'A madman,' he said, 'but our kind of madman because he loves Turkey as much as we do.' He even called me to see him now and again. And after I started work – and until he became ill – he got me to do odd jobs for him.

A final word.

From Sakarya onwards, as I manned the communications for my Paşa day by day, I could see victory ahead. And the growing conviction that Turkey would be saved produced such excitement in me that I never again felt like sleeping.

Nor did I manage to sleep for years afterwards. The horrors of the Greeks' scorched-earth policy and the revenge taken on them in Izmir and in the Urla peninsula continued to haunt me.

They still do.

6: Yusuf

And His Fruit Was Sweet to My Taste

Sunken boats were a common sight for me. I had seen ranks of them in marinas along the Bosporus, purposefully immersed, 'having a bath', as Kaptan Ali, the retired seaman maintained, because boats are flesh and blood, too, and need to keep their planks healthy and stretched.

But the slain ships in Piraeus harbour, jutting out of the water with mangled hulks, reminded me of Mahmut the Simurg's tale about leviathans dying in abandoned seas because human beings no longer respected life.

It was a balmy day. Mid-June. The third-class deck that we steerage passengers were permitted to use was a sun-trap, yet I felt chilled to the bone.

I began to sob.

To my astonishment, someone clasped me. I turned round.

It was the woman who had been staring at me ever since we had embarked in Istanbul. 'What's wrong?'

I pointed at the dead ships. 'All this destruction ...'

She drew my head to her chest. 'Poor boy ...'

I wept freely as if tears could express the anguish of being young and alone in a world that cared little for the weak or the innocent.

The ship approached the quay. The port had been reduced to rubble. The passenger terminal, eyeless with its burnt windows, stood as if it were its own shadow. Another victim.

I asked her the question that would not stop tormenting me. 'Do wars ever end?'

She stared at me; her eyes grew moist. She stroked my hair. 'What a question!'

I stopped crying. Her tenderness was a balm. 'Do they?'

She thought for a moment. 'Sometimes – for some people. For others, never.' Her voice seemed to carry a mountain of sadness. Was she one of the latter?

'I don't think they ever do ...'

Again her eyes moistened. 'You may be right. But we need to hope.' She stroked my cheek. 'You're on your own, aren't you?'

'Yes.'

'We're stopping for the day. There's an excursion. To the Acropolis. Want to come along?'

At thirteen – the only youngster travelling alone – I

had become the ship's mascot. But Old Fuat, the purser in charge of third class and steerage, had told me that the crew would be too busy during the stopover to pay me much attention. Sure, they'd allow me to roam the first class, raid the kitchen that reputedly served food fit for sultans, but much of the time I would be alone. I was too unsettled to be by myself. And too distressed by the sunken ships.

I had readily agreed to my parents' suggestion that I was old enough to travel on my own – after all, I had just had my bar mitzvah and was, formally, a man. But I had not imagined that there would be such ruin everywhere and that I would feel so desolate. (The damage in Piraeus was insignificant compared to the devastation in Europe, Old Fuat had said.)

'I don't have much money.'

'Don't worry about that. I'll get you some cigarettes from the ship's store. These days – in Europe – cigarettes are worth more than gold.'

'Oh, I have enough for that.'

'Good. Let's go then. I'm Saadet.'

She was about my mother's age. But she was strongly built, like those Anatolian women who had carried ammunition on their shoulders in the War of Independence. However, unlike my mother, who saw the world as a wild mongrel that had to be trained and disciplined, she poured out kindness. Saadet means 'happiness' and she looked as if, given the chance, she could make the whole world happy, certainly every child in it.

I took her hand. 'Yusuf.'

∞∞∞∞∞∞❀∞∞∞∞∞∞

There were a lot of us on that excursion to the Acropolis. Propriety having consigned steerage passengers – even husbands and wives – to male and female dormitories, the outing enabled families to spend some time together.

In 1947, two years after the end of the Second World War, there were still numerous Turkish families anxious either to visit relatives who had survived the hostilities in Europe or to search for those listed as missing or displaced. Consequently, ships to Marseilles, via Naples and Piraeus, like ours, were packed to bursting. (The prevailing chaos in Europe, the newspapers pointedly reminded us, confirmed just how phenomenal our president's statesmanship had been. By joining the war only at the very end of it, in February 1945 – despite years of intense pressure from the Allies – the sagacious leader, İsmet İnönü, Atatürk's friend, comrade-in-arms, disciple and successor, had not only saved the country from destruction, but had also aligned Turkey as a founder member of the United Nations.)

During the excursion, several boys asked me to join them.

But I preferred to stay with Saadet. For one thing, she kept on telling me how impressed she was by my courage in travelling alone. She made me feel exceptional – indeed very much like a 'young Odysseus', as she called me. For another, when I told her that I was on my own only because my parents had been unable to find tickets that would have allowed us to travel together, she applauded me for accepting abandonment so unselfishly and letting them go ahead of me.

(Much as I felt flattered at being called a young Odysseus, I resisted Saadet's notion that my parents were insensitive to my needs. I certainly didn't see myself as 'abandoned' – even if I felt like it. Surely there was nothing phenomenal about a young boy travelling alone! My father had already started work when he was my age. More to the point, despite my 'delicate age', as Saadet put it, I was pretty mature for my years. Everybody said so. Being an only child, I had spent all my puppy years in adult company: aunts, uncles, grandparents and their even older aunts, uncles and grandparents; I had heard – if not seen – a great deal about life. So no question about being 'neglected'. I just didn't like being separated from my parents – which is only natural for a loving boy.)

I think the real reason I became attached to Saadet was that she was a troubled person. As I was. And as my mother was. But she was not unapproachable – 'armoured', my father would say – like my mother. I only had to look at the way her hands trembled – when she lit a cigarette, for instance – to know that beneath her docility she was, like me, often in tears. And, no doubt, when she had found me crying on deck, she had seen that we were of the same mould. Perhaps like a son might be. Saadet had married late – in her forties.

And since she had not mentioned having children, I assumed she was childless.

A word about my melancholy. My parents, teachers, even some friends attributed it either to puberty or to some sort of *fin de siècle* romanticism I had contracted from poetry. (I was passionate about poetry. Still am.) But those were explanations that they had expediently contrived to avert their own eyes from the truth which was right in front of them, visible even to the blind. And it was this: all the beauty, joy and happiness this world offers constitute a mirage. The real landscape is worms and maggots, slaughter and destruction. Like the unknown grave of Bilâl who perished in Greece and whom his friends – particularly my cousin, Can – still mourn bitterly.

Actually, Saadet did not hide the fact that she was troubled. She was on a journey of uncertainty, to a destination where, in all likelihood, bitter disappointment awaited her. She was going to find out whether the Displaced Persons agencies had located an old friend, a Jew, she had known in Paris before the war. She would not allow herself to be hopeful, though she did feel encouraged by the fact that my father's relatives, also Jewish, had managed to survive the war and were all waiting for me to join them to celebrate properly.

Saadet seemed to know everything. She had toured Europe extensively before the war with the friend she had been trying to locate. Whenever she told me something, she did so unaffectedly as if we were the same age. Declaring the Acropolis to be one of the wonders of the world, she made me see, better than any teacher, the differences between the classical columns. How the Doric, 'virile, severe and absolute, like indefectible power', conveyed ancient Athens' prominence through the Parthenon's majesty. How the Ionic, 'delicate, feminine and sensuous', provided an enticing welcome to the Erechtheum, Athena's temple. She so fired my imagination that, at the Propylaea, the entrance to the Acropolis, where both Doric and Ionic columns complemented each other, I decided to become an architect.

∞∞∞∞∞⊛∞∞∞∞∞

Late that night, I woke up shaking. I was being tossed about violently. But for the wall on one side and the bunk-barrier on the other, I would have been thrown out of my berth.

I managed to look around. My fellow passengers were also struggling to keep to their beds.

I thought we were about to sink. I decided to go up on deck so that I could jump clear. I was well built and a powerful swimmer. I would stand a chance of being rescued.

I tried to get up. But a heavy pulse was hammering in my head. I started vomiting. I wailed. 'Mother ... Mother ...'

Old Fuat heard me and rushed over. 'It's all right ... It's all right ...'

'Are we going to sink?'

Old Fuat had adopted me because I reminded him of his young grandson, who, he said, had my dark complexion – supposedly a sign of hardiness. He chuckled and ruffled my hair. 'We'll pitch about for some hours. In this stretch of the Mediterranean the mermaids are hungry for men. They try to catch us with undercurrents and swells.'

I looked at my bunk in disgust. 'I've been sick.'

'I'll clear it up.'

I started vomiting again. 'I can't hold my head up.'

'Go up on deck. You'll feel better. Fresh air.'

'I was trying to …'

'I'll help you.' He handed me my sweater. 'Windy up there.'

I suddenly remembered. At night the deck was off limits to youngsters. Not because it was dangerous, but because its secluded corners offered some privacy to husbands and wives who had to sleep apart. 'But the deck is out of bounds …'

Old Fuat smiled. 'There won't be any lovers tonight – believe me.'

He dragged me out. Most of the people in the dormitory were vomiting. The stench made me retch even more. I began to bring up bile.

Old Fuat left me at the steps. 'Go on. I'll see you later.'

I climbed up, panting and dribbling like a dog.

The night was mournfully dark; the ship's lights failed to dent it. There must have been thick cloud cover; I couldn't see any stars. Panic seized me. My head was spinning and I could barely keep my balance. In a desperate effort to steady myself, I tried to focus on the ship's funnel. But that proved all the more frightening. It emphasized how severely the ship dipped and rose, not just from prow to stern, but also from port to starboard.

Despite my terror, the oscillation captivated me. The sea, luminous with spume where the bows hit the swell, beckoned me. Water and sky became an infinity. I felt I was the only person left on earth.

Infinity opened up. It spoke to me. It said I would be welcome in its depths. I had a place there.

I edged forward. I no longer cared that I was the last person on earth. And no longer feared. I had a place. My very own place. In a universe that had opened up just for me. An important place. There, I would heal the universe. Within it, I would unite earth, water and sky. Shelter children and families, the dispossessed and the privileged, the missing and the living.

I walked towards the Infinity. I trod a spongy seabed as if the waters had parted as when Moses divided the Red Sea to save the Israelites from the Egyptians.

I ascended to the deck's pinnacle. I saw the stern of the ship break surface. I took a deep breath and waited for it to plummet and lay me on the water. I seized the sky. I prepared to join it with the sea.

Someone pulled me down by my legs.

I fell and hurt my arm. I howled.

'Are you mad?'

I looked up, disorientated. I was spread-eagled on

the deck. Saadet was kneeling by my side and shaking me.

I stared at her, confused. 'Why …?'

'You were going to jump!'

She made no sense. 'No, I wasn't!'

'You were on the top rail …'

I laughed, but remembered being high up and watching the ship's stern rise out of the water. 'Not to jump!'

'What then?'

'I … I was … drawn to it …'

'Drawn to it?'

'I was on my way to … I had a place …'

'You have a place here. Home. Parents. Friends.'

'This was different … This was my place … My place … My very own … Where I held everything together …'

She calmed down. 'You were suffering from vertigo …'

'It was wonderful …'

She nodded. 'Still dizzy?'

I had forgotten about my head. It didn't feel too heavy. 'Not much.'

'Still feeling sick?'

'A bit.'

'Take some deep breaths. Old Fuat recommends fresh air …'

'Did he send you?'

'He said you weren't feeling well.' She sat on the deck and pulled my head on to her lap. 'Rest a while …'

Her thighs felt strong, yet soft. I became excited. Not the sort of vapid excitement I got when Mother's friends clasped me to their breasts, but a deeper one. An excitement I shouldn't have enjoyed? The forbidden excitement?

I felt I had done something wrong. I tried to straighten up. 'I'd better go to the dorm ...'

'Not tonight ...'

'I can't sleep here ...'

'Why not?'

'It's cold ...'

'I brought a blanket.'

'You'll need that ...'

'Don't worry about me.'

∞∞∞∞∞∞∞❀∞∞∞∞∞∞∞

I spent that night and all next day on deck. Whenever I went to the toilet or to wash, I became bilious. The deck was the only place where I felt relatively well.

To the relief of Old Fuat, who had countless sick people to attend to, Saadet stayed by my side much of the time. She made sure I took in some liquid and kept me clean. Often, but particularly when she stroked my forehead to make me sleep, the deep excitement swelled up in me. I suppressed it as best I could. I didn't want to offend her, particularly as I couldn't tell whether her touch – always tentative – was because she didn't want to get too close to me – my mother was like that – or because she didn't want to encourage my desires.

The night before we reached Naples, the sea calmed down. My stomach settled. The world retrieved its colours. Couples started coming up on to the deck again. Those of us who had taken refuge there were urged to return to our dormitories.

I felt sad leaving Saadet. As we made our way to the hold, I clung to her hand.

Suddenly, someone shouted, 'Hey, you! Enough! Enough!'

I turned round. It was Mueller Hanım, the elderly woman who kept picking arguments with people. She was neither highborn nor Turkish, but had insisted on being called *Hanım*, 'Lady', instead of the prosaic *Bayan*, 'Madam', as if, Old Fuat had remarked, the title would lighten her evident anguish.

I looked about wondering whom she was addressing.

Saadet had also turned round. 'Talking to me?'

Mueller Hanım mimicked Saadet. 'Talking to me?'

She was a German musician who had been given asylum in Turkey – and a teaching post in the Conservatoire – in the thirties, when Atatürk had opened our doors to the intellectuals hounded by the Nazis – so Old Fuat had informed us. She was not Jewish, but a Catholic who had opposed Hitler's racist laws. She was returning to Germany, via Italy, to find out whether any relatives had survived. Like many people on a similar quest, she was not very hopeful.

Saadet decided to ignore her and walked away.

Mueller Hanım screeched, 'Don't you turn your back on me! Pawing the boy for days! Have you no shame? Let go now!'

Saadet faced her, flustered. 'Now, just a minute ...'

Mueller Hanım strode over to us. 'Up here like couples for conjugals! Smell of death still in the air – and all you think of is fornication! And with a child!'

Incensed, Saadet slapped Mueller Hanım. 'You poisonous ...'

Mueller Hanım started hitting out. 'You think copulation is the antidote to death? An affirmation of life? A lotus you eat to forget those brutally slaughtered?'

Saadet tried to ward off Mueller Hanım's blows. 'He's poorly! All alone!'

Some passengers rushed to separate them.

Mueller Hanım flailed uncontrollably. 'You think life is worth something? It's worth nothing! Nothing!'

Some men pulled Mueller Hanım away. A couple of others held Saadet.

Mueller Hanım went on shouting. 'Forget life! Join the dead!'

Saadet shouted back. 'This boy needs looking after!'

'He could be your son!'

'Yes! He could be ...'

'Then let him be! Go look after your own!'

'I can't!'

'Evil, you are! Like the rest!'

Saadet's voice broke as she retorted, 'My son is dead!'

Mueller Hanım froze. She stared at Saadet in horror. 'Dead?' Her body appeared to drain away. She folded into herself. 'Oh, God, no!' Her legs splayed and she collapsed. 'Sweet Jesus, no ...' She grabbed Saadet's arm. 'Oh, I'm sorry ... Forgive me ... Please ...'

Saadet, confused by Mueller Hanım's sudden disintegration, tried to extricate herself from her grip.

But Mueller Hanım clung to her arm. 'Is that why ...? Are you going where ... your son ... How did he die ...? Where were you ...?'

Saadet wailed, 'Does it matter?'

Mueller Hanım sobbed. 'I had a son, too ... I ran away ... I thought he'd be safe ... without a communist for a mother ... Is that what you did – run away also?'

Tears began to run down Saadet's face. 'I was careless ...'

Mueller Hanım stared at her, puzzled. 'Careless ...?'

Saadet repeated the word bitterly. 'Careless.'

She turned to me. Hurriedly, she kissed me on the forehead. 'Excursion tomorrow. See you in the morning.'

Then she ran off.

Mueller Hanım, curling like a hedgehog, wept unrestrainedly.

I walked away.

I was shocked. Saadet had had a son. I felt jealous, though he was dead.

He had died because she had been careless.

That shocked me even more. How could a parent be careless?

oooooooooo🦪oooooooooo

Naples harbour was an even larger cemetery for ships than Piraeus. The city itself, still in the throes of clearing up its bomb damage, was like a vast building site. Consequently, we could visit only a few of the sights. To assuage our frustration, the guide decided to take us to Pompeii.

At first, Saadet did not want to go. She felt I would be all right because Old Fuat, having managed to take the day off, had joined the excursion and would look after me. But then, mindful of my disappointment, she came along.

oooooooooo🦪oooooooooo

The areas where archaeological work had been interrupted because of the war had been cordoned off. Moreover, as there was still a shortage of qualified attendants, only some sectors were open to visitors. The same applied to the museum.

Yet, as I walked through Pompeii's ancient streets, I had the feeling that I was in a living city – and, strangely, one that I knew well, as if I had visited it recently. Old Fuat was not surprised; he had heard that in some people, past and present desolations commingle. Thus I felt that the inhabitants were only temporarily absent, perhaps on an outing or having their siesta, and that, in a few moments, they would emerge and go about their daily business, paying little attention to Mount

Vesuvius above them, which was busily preparing their deaths.

So I roamed the ruins as if expecting a recurrence of that eruption on 24 August 79 CE, when ash and pyroclastic rubble engulfed the city in a matter of hours. I registered only odd details, like the distortions in a road or the shape of the amphitheatre uncannily mirroring the volcano's crater, or the colonnade in the Forum that looked as if it had been built only yesterday. And wherever I stood, Vesuvius, snorting and blowing smoke like an Edward G. Robinson of volcanoes, kept warning me that it had last erupted just three years before, in 1944, and might do so again on a whim.

Then Saadet screamed.

An interminable scream.

It was the scream, I imagined, of a person set on fire. The scream that persists until the blaze vaporizes the victim's saliva. The scream Pompeii had left behind for posterity. The scream the martyrs of the Spanish Inquisition tried to raise in *autos-da-fé* when they were unable to beat down the flames consuming their bodies with hands that had been tied to redemptive crucifixes. The scream of countless innocents reduced to ash in extermination camps.

I spun round.

Saadet was running – away from the museum. She looked panic-stricken. Every few strides, she changed direction as if only by fleeing nowhere could she feel safe.

I had been in the museum shortly before, but had

seen nothing unusual: some pottery, some artefacts, a man and a child preserved by petrified ash.

Old Fuat, who had been smoking outside the museum, chased after Saadet.

I followed.

When we caught up with her, she flailed and screamed in frenzy.

Old Fuat, locking his arms around her, whispered soothingly, 'Sssshhh … Sssshhh …'

Gradually she calmed down. She began to cry.

Old Fuat lowered her on to the grass. He folded his jacket into a pillow and made her lie down. 'Cry, dear heart. As much as you need. We're here.'

I sat down, too, and held Saadet's hand. She didn't pull away.

We stayed like that for some time. Saadet dozed off. Now and again, she shivered.

Then our group began to assemble.

Saadet stirred. She kissed Old Fuat's hand and hugged me; then, seeing that we still looked worried, she tried to explain. 'The figure of the boy … preserved in ash … I couldn't help it … I thought of my son …'

<hr />

The next day, Saadet kept to herself.

I invented countless excuses to get up to the third-class deck where she had withdrawn, to keep an eye on her. Much of the time, she sat on a bollard and stared into herself. She had not spoken since Pompeii.

I felt bereft. We were on our penultimate day. In less than forty hours, we would reach Marseilles and go our different ways. In all probability, I would never see her again, never enjoy the feeling of being like a son to her.

But the next morning, she called me over. Though still strained, she looked more composed. We spent the day playing cards and dominoes, chatting, sunbathing and snoozing.

Then, after dinner, when people had vacated the refectory, she asked Old Fuat to join us. She had brought a notebook and a pencil. 'Let's keep in touch. Give me your addresses.'

Old Fuat and I did so eagerly.

Saadet handed us slips of paper where she had written down hers.

Old Fuat noted that Saadet's address carried another name. 'Won't your husband let you receive letters?'

'Why shouldn't he?'

'This is care of somebody. Advocate Vitali Behar.'

It was a name I knew well. 'You mean the lawyer? He lives near us ... He has a son, Zeki ...'

Saadet nodded. 'He's an old friend of the family ... Let me explain ...' She brought out a bottle of Greek brandy and took a large gulp. 'I've been meaning to ... I don't want you to think I'm mad ...' She offered the bottle to us. 'When you need it – nothing better than brandy ...'

Old Fuat took a sip. So did I, manfully.

'He's a very decent person, Abdülkerim, my husband. He was a widower. A lot older than me. But I do love him. And I get on well with his sons and daughters. They're all married. With children of their own. Seven, to date. I look upon them as my own grandchildren. Especially the very young ones – born after I came on the scene … We married only recently, you see. Two years ago …'

Old Fuat tried to make a joke. 'Still the blushing bride, eh?'

Saadet gave a gentle smile. 'Abdülkerim is my second husband. My first marriage was in Paris. In '28. To a Turkish Jew. I had a son. Born in '35.' She stroked my cheek. 'He'd be almost your age now – maybe just as handsome …'

I interjected without thinking, 'The son you lost because you were careless …?'

Saadet's eyes clouded. Hurriedly, she took another sip of brandy. 'Yes …'

I bit my lip. I felt troubled. I didn't want to hear her story. But I had to.

'I was mad about my first husband, Efraim Pesah. As *The Song of Songs* says, "His fruit was sweet to my taste." I've never loved anybody the way I loved him. Not even, I'm ashamed to say, my son, İshak. Efraim loved me just as much. Probably more. He had an immense capacity for love …

'He was from a poor family. But he was bright. He received a scholarship from the Alliance Israélite and learned perfect French. In the early years of the republic, when unemployment was rife, he emigrated to France. Took any job that came his way. But kept his eyes open.

Eventually, he saw there was a market for oriental carpets and *objets d'art*. So he went into partnership with a cousin in Edirne and began importing. It proved a great success.

'That's how we met. I had just graduated from the Academy of Fine Arts and was working for an auctioneer in Istanbul. Efraim came to one of our sales and bought several items. I helped him with the export formalities. We took to each other instantly. He asked me whether, occasionally, he could consult me about Ottoman antiques. I had some expertise in that field. I was flattered and, naturally, said yes.

'A couple of months later, he invited me to Paris. He was furnishing an apartment for a wealthy Egyptian and wanted ideas. I suggested a few items. The Egyptian loved them. Efraim took me to Biarritz in celebration ...

'Two weeks later we married.

'I moved to Paris.

'The business flourished. Became international. We went all over Europe. And America. We became rich ... And carefree because Vitali Behar – whom Efraim had befriended when Vitali was studying law in Paris – was managing our affairs perfectly.

'Then we decided to crown our happiness with a child.

'We had İshak ...

'That's when I started worrying. We were so happy. And we had everything. I began to fear: this can't last. Fate is seldom generous. When it floods you with blessings, that's a warning that years of tribulation lie ahead …

'I was right, needless to say.

'Suddenly, the war.

'What appals me is we knew what Hitler was up to. During trips to Germany, we saw how the Nazis were treating the Jews. We ignored it. We should have packed our bags and run back to Turkey, as Vitali kept begging us to do. But we were so bound up in each other we didn't pause to think.

'And, unforgivably, we had brought İshak into the world. One more Jew for Hitler. Though, strictly speaking, he was not a Jew because I, his mother, was a Muslim. But try and tell that to the Gestapo …

'Before we knew it, Paris was occupied.

'The French authorities, co-operating with the Nazis, began to round up the Jews. When they confiscated our apartment, we came to our senses. We ran from one dark corner to another. Everywhere we faced blackmail, denunciation, arrest, deportation.

'Then Efraim heard that the Turkish government was saving Jews – particularly Jews of Turkish origin. Repatriating them. Hiring trains because the seas were unsafe. So we rushed to the consulate.

'They welcomed us. Efraim – who had allowed his Turkish passport to lapse – and İshak – whom we hadn't bothered to register – were given new passports. Mine, though still valid, was renewed for good measure. And they booked us on the next train: 14 March 1943.

'It was a Sunday. A day when the Gestapo and the

police were doubly alert because on Sundays people took to the streets and Jews seeking hideouts tried to blend with the crowds.

'Departure was at seven in the evening. We set out in the late afternoon, hoping that, by that time, surveillance would have slackened. But as we approached the Gare de l'Est, we saw it was teeming with Gestapo and police. It hadn't occurred to us that departures to Turkey would be strictly checked for stowaways.

'Efraim urged us on. We had nothing to fear. Our passports were genuine and we were on the consulate's passenger list.

'İshak clung to my hand.

'As we approached the checkpoint, a German sentry smiled at İshak. It was a pleasant smile – the sort you get from someone who likes children. But it frightened İshak. 'He thinks I'm Jewish,' he said.

'Wanting to calm him down with a cuddle – he loved being cuddled – I let go of his hand.

'That's all I did. I let go of his hand. For a fraction of a second. To cuddle him.

'That was my mistake. That's how I was careless.

'I don't know whether he thought by releasing his hand I was telling him to run away. But that's what he did. He ran off.

'Efraim ran after him.

'And so, of course, did the sentries.

'By the time I collected myself, Efraim and İshak had been bundled into a van and driven away.

'I rushed at the sentries. I shouted dementedly. Tried

to hit them. They responded brutally. Punched me. Hit me with their rifles. I thought they'd kill me. I wanted them to kill me.

'The Turkish consul saved me. He had recognized me and rushed over to help. The Turks were determined no harm would come to their Jews. So they supervised the departures. Even stationed officials all along the route to make sure no one would be taken off the trains.

'The consul took charge. The authorities insisted I board the train. I refused. I was going nowhere without my family. The consul was sympathetic. He asked where Efraim and İshak had been taken. They told him it would be Drancy – just outside Paris, where the Nazis had set up a transit camp. The consul summoned his car. We would go there and he would personally secure their release.

'But Efraim and İshak had not been taken to Drancy.

'We spent weeks searching for them. Went back and forth to Drancy – just in case they had been sent there later. On two occasions, we saw Jews being loaded into cattle-trucks for dispatch to concentration camps.

'Some two months later, the consul was informed that, immediately after their arrest, Efraim and İshak had been rushed to the border and put on a transport on its way to a camp. There was nothing the Turkish authorities could do except protest vehemently.

'The consul tried to console me. Advised me to wait for the war to end. Told me the concentration camps could not be as bad as they were said to be. Both

Efraim and İshak were healthy and should survive their incarceration.

'So I went back to Turkey and waited for the war to end. When it did, I learned the truth about the camps. Though I felt sure Efraim and İshak had perished, I still registered their names with Displaced Persons agencies.

'Then in December 1945 I received notification that, according to a Gestapo document, both Efraim and İshak had died while being transported from one camp to another. A death march, by all accounts …

'By then, I was working for Abdülkerim. He runs an antique business. We had become good friends. He was kind, caring, understanding. And lonely. A widower, as I mentioned before. When I told him Efraim was dead, he proposed marriage.

'I accepted. What else could I do? I had no strength left. My spirit had wasted away. I was all alone. Worse, I had no one to love. Or care for. Or to look after. I might as well have been dead. Yet somewhere a part of me insisted that I live.

'Abdülkerim and Vitali dealt with the formalities. I became a widow – officially. Then we got married.

'Then, last month, Displaced Persons contacted me. They had found a man in a mental institution in Colmar, in Alsace, who spoke Turkish and fitted Efraim's description. Despite his darkened mind, they had established that he had been in a concentration camp and somehow survived. Could I come and check?

'You can imagine my shock …

'And my confusion ... What was I to do?

'Abdülkerim decided for me. See this man, he said. Otherwise he'll haunt us for the rest of our lives ...

'That's what I'm doing ...

'And I'm terrified ...

'I keep imagining I'll find a man – like the dead in Pompeii – fossilized by ash ...'

<hr />

Next morning Saadet and I met early so that, on Old Fuat's recommendation, we could enjoy the magnificent sight of entering Marseilles harbour.

Her disclosure – 'confession', she called it – had revitalized us. Particularly me, though I hadn't wanted to hear it. It had, in fact, brought us closer. As she later told me, she could express her feelings for me without the fear that she was betraying her son's memory. And I could adopt her as the mother I would have loved to have by accepting that some mothers, like my own mother, find parenthood difficult because of their own histories and upbringing.

And so we felt stronger and, therefore, more able to live with unhappiness. Marseilles, we kept telling each other, would open a new page for us. She would ascertain that the man in the mental institution was not her first husband – how could he be? – and go back to Abdülkerim with a clear conscience. I, young Odysseus, would complete my rite of passage and emerge as a person everybody, not least myself, would be proud to know.

I noted, as we entered the harbour, that there were no sunken ships. I took that as a good omen.

But the dock was still in ruins. People who had come to meet passengers thronged the rubble in ragged lines.

Then I saw my uncle. I recognized him by his bushy hair, a family trait. I waved wildly. He spotted me, dived into the throng and surfaced with my father. They both shouted, 'We've got passes. We'll come up ...'

Something – maybe my joy at seeing my father – upset Saadet. She squeezed my hand, then ran off.

Hours later, after the passengers had disembarked and the crew had begun preparations for the return journey, we were still aboard. Saadet had locked herself in a toilet and would not come out until the ship set sail back to Turkey.

Old Fuat and I sat on the floor, sharing her anguish. The captain, a couple of his officers, my father and my uncle paced the corridor. Having heard Saadet's story, they, too, were sympathetic – particularly my uncle, who, having spent the war years hiding in monasteries, was a survivor himself. Nonetheless, as men who prided themselves on being practical, they tried hard to resolve her problem.

But Saadet's conflict was beyond them – even I understood that. She had not, as they thought, simply lost her courage. Knowing all that she knew about concentration camps, she could not, she felt, summon the strength to meet someone who had survived them. And if, by some twist of fate, the survivor did turn out to be Efraim – what then? How could she, who had not shared his horrors, face him? And even if she did face him, what could she do? Could she touch him? Look after him? Where could she take him? Home? Which one? The one in Paris – if, that is, they could reclaim it? Or to Abdülkerim's? And what about Abdülkerim? What would she do about him? And about their marriage? Where would they stand legally?

So she had decided to leave things as they were. And go back to Abdülkerim. To live a sort of life – with fewer and fewer memories, if lucky; and if not, by returning to that inner sanctum where she kept herself locked up with the ghosts of Efraim and İshak.

In the end, it was I who offered a solution. I suggested that we all go with her. That way she would not have to face her ordeal on her own; she would feel more confident.

Both my father and my uncle thought it a sensible suggestion, but they were unable to comply. My uncle had to get back to work. My father had to take me to Paris, where my mother and our relatives were waiting. We were due to return to Turkey soon and we needed to devote all our time to the family.

I proposed a compromise: my father and uncle could

leave and I would accompany Saadet. I would rejoin the family when her crisis was over – all being well, in a day or so.

We argued for a while. I suddenly realized that I had developed the will to stand up for myself. So I prevailed. I even obtained the satisfaction of having my father, who normally just kissed and hugged me, shake my hand.

An hour later, Saadet, having equally failed to convince me to leave with my father, emerged from the toilet. She gazed at me for a long time, then kissed my hand. I felt I had become not only a son to her, but also a guardian.

∞∞∞∞∞∞❀∞∞∞∞∞∞

The moment we entered the ward, the patients grew distressed. Some screamed abuse and tried to chase us out. Others begged us to claim them as brothers, fathers, sons. Yet others, exposing their genitals, importuned us.

The doctor pointed at an emaciated figure on a bed at the far end.

Earlier, he had told us to brace ourselves. We would meet a person who was very frail and immensely disturbed, whose eyes, in so far as it could be ascertained, had turned permanently inward. In all likelihood, it was that inner world – miasmic or paradisal, unfathomable as yet – that somehow had kept him alive.

He further warned us that the patient rambled much of the time – with varying degrees of coherence.

Continuous and dissociated monologues were symptomatic of his condition.

Saadet moved – shuffled – in that direction.

I followed – just as nervously.

I stared at the patient. He was talking solemnly, in Turkish, towards points ahead of him, as if giving a lecture. I tried to understand what he was saying. In vain. He kept jumbling up the words. Yet his body was completely still. But for the cacophony of his voice, he lay like an animal playing dead.

Saadet mumbled, 'He's so thin ...'

The doctor sighed. 'He won't eat. He hoards his food. We have to feed him intravenously.'

'Hoards his food?'

'Many from the camps do. A hidden crust meant surviving another day.'

Saadet faltered and held on to the doctor. 'Oh, God ...'

The patient caught Saadet's movement and cast a furtive look in our direction. About to avert his gaze, he stopped; then he turned to look at us again. This time, he focused – first on Saadet, then on me. I felt unsteady, thinking he had recognized her. Also, it suddenly occurred to me that he might think I was İshak. Then he blinked as if to brush our presence off his eyes and went back to his rambling.

Saadet reached his bed.

He did not look at her, but fixed his gaze on the window facing him. By doing so, he presented a full view of his face – as if he wanted her to recognize him.

I managed to catch something of his gibberish. He was listing the ingredients he needed for preparing Circassian chicken.

Saadet stifled a cry. 'That's his favourite dish.'

Inexplicably, I felt shocked. 'What?'

Saadet turned to the doctor and nodded sorrowfully. 'It's him. It's Efraim.'

The doctor was elated. 'Are you sure?'

'His mouth …'

Whatever Efraim's condition, she had said, while showing me some photographs she had brought along, she would recognize him by his mouth. Nothing could change the full lips gently curving towards the ears and seemingly about to laugh or say something loving.

She wept silently, as if directing the tears into her inner self. 'The mouth – it's him. Not the rest. The rest is not him at all.'

That was her anguish reacting. Because I could see, despite the flow of words, despite his opaque, unseeing eyes, that this Efraim still possessed something of the aura of the athletic, debonair Efraim of the photographs. Like an olive tree seen through a smudged lens, he was lustreless, but recognizable.

I felt miserable. I had hoped he would have proved to be someone else. Then Saadet could have gone back to Turkey less troubled. And I could have had a second mother, one less formal, more affectionate, more intimate.

Tentatively, Saadet embraced Efraim. 'Dear heart … It's me! Saadet …'

Efraim, still staring at the window, shuddered as if a current was going through him. He spoke faster, raising his voice; the words became lost within each other.

Saadet held on to him. 'It's me, Efraim … It's me, my heart …'

Efraim's words became an incomprehensible screech. He still lay inert with his fixed gaze. A lifeless Pinocchio except for wildly fluttering, fleshless cheeks.

Saadet turned to the doctor and me. 'Leave me with him …'

∞∞∞∞∞∞✿∞∞∞∞∞∞

That evening, we ate at a small bistro near the hospital. We hardly touched our food and much of the time – except when she thanked me for 'being family', for 'saving her sanity, indeed, her soul' – Saadet remained silent. I kept wanting to engage her, ask what she intended to do, but managed to hold my tongue.

Then, on the way back to our *pension*, she stopped in front of a farm outhouse that had been converted into a cottage. 'Pretty place, wouldn't you say?'

I shrugged. 'Yes.'

'My new home. I rented it this afternoon.'

I was stunned. 'What?'

'I'm staying here.'

I yelped. 'No! Why?!'

She held my hand. 'Because Efraim is my husband.'

'So is Abdülkerim.'

'Not any more.'

'Did you talk to him – to Abdülkerim? Did he say that?'

'Abdülkerim is a good man. He will understand. Efraim is my life. My fate. I can live again.' She took a small box from her pocket and handed it to me. 'My wedding ring. Can you give it to Abdülkerim – when you get back?'

I took the box hesitantly. 'But Efraim is ...'

Saadet caressed my cheek. 'In some impenetrable world? Yes, he is ... Then again, maybe not – entirely ... Sometimes I can see him, behind his ramblings – playing hide-and-seek, as we used to ... So I'll try and catch him ...' She held my hands. 'Also, sometimes, I feel my son is there with him – in his being ... Which strikes me as reasonable ... I mean, İshak is dead – killed during the death march. I made enough sense of Efraim's monologues to know that. But he has kept İshak alive – inside his sunken world ... I imagine that's how he survived ... That's how I'd like to think he survived – by keeping our son alive. For himself as well as for me.'

I tried to respond like an adult, to look as if I understood her reasoning. Instead I wailed, 'What about me?'

'You, young Odysseus, believe it or not, put life into my son ... There he was, barely alive, inside Efraim ... I took him from Efraim. Put him inside me. But you, you breathed life into him. You gave İshak your face, your mind, your deep feelings ... I feel as if I'm betraying İshak by saying this, but every time I think of him, I'll think of you. Every time I try to picture him, it will be your face I'll see ...'

I wanted to cry, but controlled myself. 'If you ever need me ...'

She embraced me. 'I know, my Yusuf ... I know, my dear, dear Yusuf ...'

There was nothing more to say. Or rather there was, but I couldn't bring myself to say it.

Saadet smiled, held my hand. 'There's something else on your mind.'

I nodded.

'What is it?'

'If ... If Efraim ...'

Saadet's eyes clouded. 'Dies?'

'Or doesn't recover?'

She looked at the night sky. 'I'll thank God for having given me such a man. Like you Jews at Passover, I'll say, *Dayyenu* – it's enough ...'

7: Havva

A Wrestling Man

Mahmut the Simurg knows everything. He is the storyteller who goes round the neighbourhoods during the day and performs as our fire-eater at night. He says every happening has a cause and a consequence and the cause always starts in the celestial bodies. If, for instance, a flea lands on the Dog Star, its weight, though minimal, still affects the star's pull on us and alters the course of our lives.

I imagine that's how my life and the lives of those around me changed when the comet that passed by recently breathed upon the earth.

I felt the beginnings of this change the night we went to Sulukule looking for the drunkard Babacık, my father, had been asked to help. But no doubt, as

Mahmut the Simurg would say, it had started before that with a death because there can be no beginning without Death.

Babacık led the way. Mama Meryem and I followed.

Sulukule is one of Istanbul's poorest neighbourhoods. A maze of narrow streets nuzzles the Byzantine ruins. Every pothole is a pool of sewage. In the rubbish heaps that are everywhere, anything edible – even rotting food – is instantly snatched by hungry mouths. The houses lean on each other for support and many doorways lead to cheap drinking houses. I overheard Hacı Turgut – he's the one who asked Babacık to help the mysterious drunkard – say that men come to these places to kill themselves – either with raki or by surrendering what little money they have to opium-smoking belly-dancers who pick up the coins with their privates.

Not a place for Mama Meryem, who looks and is as Italian as Anna Magnani, and a slip of a girl like me. But not even a gang would dare molest us with Babacık at our side.

Here and there Babacık paused to scrutinize some drops of fluid on the cobblestones. When we looked puzzled, he explained. 'Drunkards are like wounded animals. You can track them by their bleeding. Only they don't bleed blood – they bleed the sap of their soul.'

We nodded. When Babacık speaks, we all prick up our ears.

'What colour is the soul's sap, Babacık? Red too?'

Mama Meryem smiled. She likes it when I ask questions because she never does. Babacık is head of the family and Mama Meryem observes the conventions. Whereas I – I'm a foundling. I'm not expected to behave like everybody else. I can be the urchin I am.

'Depends who's bleeding.'

Babacık likes me being an urchin because urchins, he thinks, are smart or they would have perished when their poor, misguided begetters abandoned them. So he always answers my questions. Yet he distrusts words. Words are mirages, he says. They delude people, particularly the young, and fog their minds. He believes people should be judged only by what they do.

I make him sound severe. But he's as gentle as a butterfly. The only person in the world who takes people as they are. That's why the whole troupe loves him. Why they come to relax around our tent before a performance. Sure, they also love him because he makes everybody laugh, but that's because those who can make the world laugh have souls that glow. That's a gift from Allah. We circus people know that. Babacık – he's the giant clown who tumbles all over the ring – can make even *jinns* piss in their pants. (You may think my nickname for him, 'little father', is funny, too. Well, when I was a toddler and couldn't tell the difference between big and small, I once called him that. He found it very amusing. So I stuck to it.)

I looked around with greater determination. I was curious about the sap. I have perfect vision – essential for a juggler. That's what I'm training to be. Juggling ten rings and six clubs, that's my target.

Several men, holding on to each other, came out of a drinking house.

Babacık stepped forward to shield us. He's an old wrestler, Babacık is. The greatest there's ever been. Unbeaten in all official competitions. That makes him even better than Hacı Turgut, who won several gold medals in the Olympic Games and now coaches the national team. In fact, Hacı Turgut always defers to Babacık as 'master' though they're about the same age. That's because, during the few years when they were on the mat together, Hacı Turgut never defeated Babacık. Babacık always won by a *tuş* – by pinning down Hacı Turgut's shoulders. We heard that from Hacı Turgut himself; Babacık never boasts.

The drunken men ignored us and staggered towards the ramparts. They tried to piss, but collapsed. As the urine trickled out of their trousers, they wept.

Babacık looked as if he might weep, too. 'These are men who can't find work. That's their sap, Girl: tears.'

Mama Meryem caressed Babacık's face. Allah's compassionate servants have wives who suffer twice as much as they do.

The reason why Babacık is not as famous as Hacı Turgut and won't even be asked to coach our wrestlers is because one dark day he lost his amateur status. Amateur status is very important to sports people. Without it they can't compete in the Olympic Games. Babacık turned professional when he signed up with a Hungarian promoter for some exhibition contests in

Europe. That was before the war. He was the oldest son in a large family and had to provide for them. Mama Meryem told me those years were a time of humiliation for him; occasionally, to draw in the crowds, he was ordered to lose to lesser wrestlers.

But Babacık's woes led to my happiness. When he was able to give up his 'enslavement', as he calls it, he joined the circus. And when Mama Meryem discovered me in the refectory tent, nameless, wrapped in bloody rags, a baby abandoned at birth, Babacık took me instantly to his heart. And in no time at all he convinced the company that rather than hand me over to the police, who would put me in an orphanage, they would adopt me and, when I grew up, train me for an act.

I heard the sound of glass breaking. I turned round and saw a man leaning against some crates of empty bottles. He was grinning and squinting at his hands. A broken bottle lay by his feet. A strapping man, despite his condition. I knew instantly he was the one we had come to find. 'Over there!'

Babacık had seen him, too. 'Yes, Girl.'

When I was a child, I used to be called 'Emanet', which means 'held in trust'. Now that I'm older, they call me 'Girl' or 'My Lamb' or, when they get angry with me, 'Kerata', which is one of those vulgarities that means anything from 'cuckold' to 'little devil'. In my case, it must mean 'little devil' because only men can be cuckolded; besides, I'm just sixteen and not married – and don't intend to be since that means having children and I don't want children. Anyway, Girl or Kerata are hardly names that light up people's eyes. As for Emanet – held in trust for whom? For parents who didn't want me? For one of Mahmut the Simurg's heroes who just by looking at a girl makes her as beautiful as the moon? I can wait for ever for that, can't I?

No, one day I will choose a name for myself, myself – a name that will take everybody's breath away.

Babacık addressed the man. 'Good evening.'

The man ignored him. Maybe he hadn't seen us. He picked up another bottle and threw it in the air. As it dropped he tried to catch it, but failed. The bottle smashed into pieces. The man glared at his hands – which were huge – and laughed bitterly.

Babacık approached him. 'What's funny?'

The man snarled. 'On your way, old man!'

Mama Meryem moved forward, ready to protect her husband. 'I le ask question: what's funny?'

I managed to keep a straight face. Dear Mama Meryem – whenever she gets excited, her accent gets thicker and she sounds like our comedian, Kadir, imitating foreign politicians.

The man hesitated. I could see his temper rising, but obviously he was not someone who yelled at women. That earned him a good mark from me. 'If you must know, Grandma, I can't catch. Not a thing. Not even death – which is said to be the easiest thing to catch. That's what's funny.'

Babacık nodded sympathetically. 'Born like that, were you?'

The man snorted. 'Now that's even funnier! Actually,

I was a catcher. A real-life catcher. The best, I'd like you to know! I could catch the sky if I had to.'

'What's changed?'

'Piss off, you old fart! Get going!'

'I'm Kudret. I'll take you home. You'll be my guest.'

'What?'

'My wife, Meryem. My daughter.'

I grimaced. No name. Just 'daughter'. I must definitely choose a name for myself. Everybody should. That would be a truer way of describing a person. After all, who knows a person better than the person herself? Some mothers say they do, but I don't believe it. And not because I was abandoned by my mother. I've really thought about it. We're all as different as the knots on olive trees. Only the person herself sees her true self. Only she knows whether she's a killer or a life-giver or a bit of both or many things in between. But then truth needs courage – which I have. Many don't. So they keep the names of greatness or goodness chosen by their parents even though such names hang on them like the oversize coats of clowns. (But there are exceptions. Babacık's father got his own son's name right: Kudret means 'strength'.)

The man started laughing again. 'Are you crazy?'

'Come along ...'

The man lurched forward. 'Get lost before ...' Seized by a spasm, he sank to his knees and started throwing up.

Babacık sighed. 'That's his sap, Girl – vomit. Lost soul's sap.'

The man puked out his innards. Then, trying to straighten up, he passed out.

Babacık picked him up.

I rushed forward. 'Let me help.'

Babacık nodded. 'Carefully. Let him know we care.'

Mama Meryem laughed. 'He dead to world!'

Babacık shook his head. 'He'll feel the touch. He'll know.'

We carried the man as if he were made of ancient glass.

<hr />

We took Adem to our tent. That's his name, Adem. He slept all night and most of the next day. He moaned and wept a lot. Alcoholic poisoning, Babacık declared.

When Hacı Turgut received word that Babacık had found Adem, he immediately came over. And he brought with him his nephew, Osman, and Osman's wife, Hatice.

Hacı Turgut didn't stay long – just the prescribed time to pay his respects and kiss Babacık's feet for taking charge of Adem. But Osman and Hatice erected their tent within the circus campsite as if they had joined the troupe. Osman is a trapeze artist – what we call a flyer – and has been looking for a partner, a catcher. Hatice – who is a big woman – watches over him like Mahmut the Simurg's creature with the hundred eyes; if she could, circus people say, she'd put a ring round Osman's nose and rule him like a Gypsy's bear.

All night and most of the next day, we watched over Adem. Or rather Osman watched over him and Hatice and I watched Osman watching him. We could see he was taking Adem into his heart, limb by limb, like an ant carrying a beetle to its nest bit by bit. And all that time, his eyes never strayed from Adem's hands. I had sensed this would happen. For a flyer the sight of a good pair of hands, old-timers say, is like the vision that sends a dervish into a trance; he's likely to whirl straight into the presence of the Godhead.

I felt jealous. Adem had captivated me, too. When he woke up, it would be Osman's face he would see first. I know how it is with some men: one look and they become soul mates. I may be just sixteen and set on remaining unmarried, but that doesn't mean I'm not interested in men. Otherwise I wouldn't bother about my appearance. People say I look and smell like orange blossom – not an easy feat in a place like a circus, where even make-up smells of animals.

So I also kept watching Adem until I, too, took him into my heart limb by limb. He was a stocky fellow. Yet his face was so delicate, it could have been embroidered by a lace-maker. And, yes, his hands, as if magnified several sizes by a distorting mirror, kept filling my eyes. I thought they could hold not only the sky but the whole earth as well. No wonder Osman drooled over him. A trapeze partnership must be like walnuts and dried figs, a near-perfect pairing. The best pairings are made in heaven.

Mama Meryem told us what Hacı Turgut had said about Adem.

He was from the Caucasus, an Abkhaz. Not Muslim, but Christian. Many of them are. His father, a beekeeper in Sukhumi, had been so overjoyed to be blessed with a son that he had become a man of the church in thanksgiving. In Stalin's godless USSR that had been a foolish act; both he and his wife had been executed.

Close relatives had somehow managed to save the child – christened Vladislav. They had smuggled him into Turkey and entrusted him to an Abkhaz family in Rize who owed them a debt of honour. But this family had played false and had worked the boy like a slave on their tea-plantation instead of treating him as one of their own.

The boy had eventually run away. After countless menial jobs, he had reached Istanbul. There he had found employment as a groom in Sirk Karelya, a circus owned by a White Russian refugee, Pyotr Nadolski. At some point, this Nadolski, having noticed the size of Vladislav's hands – beekeeper's hands like his father's – had tried him on the trapeze. The youth had proved to be a natural. Thereafter, Nadolski, changing Vladislav's name to Adem – a good Turkish name that also conjured strength – had trained him until he became an outstanding catcher.

But since to attain his full potential a catcher needs

an equally gifted flyer, Nadolski had started searching for such a prodigy. Adem's growing reputation had brought many hopefuls to his door, but they had all been either average or past their prime.

Then one day, a Greek youth called Yorgo, from a small Aegean circus, had walked in and asked for an audition. Something about the youth's blend of shyness and eagerness, doubt and certainty had appealed to Nadolski. He had tried him out. Old-timers who had witnessed that trial swear that when Adem and Yorgo had locked hands, there had been a sound like Allah taking to nature's breast.

Thereafter the two men, calling themselves Kartallar, 'The Eagles', had perfected not only the triple somersault, an act achieved by only a handful of trapezists, but also proceeded to train for the quadruple – a feat believed to be impossible.

Then tragedy had struck.

During one performance, Yorgo had mistimed his take-off and had dropped towards his partner a moment too early. The two had brushed fingers but could not lock hands. Yorgo had plummeted down, crashed on to the side of the safety net, bounced off it, fallen into the ring and broken his neck. He had died instantly.

Though all the witnesses at the inquest had attributed Yorgo's mistiming to his indulgence in opium the night before, Adem had refused to believe it. Instead he had blamed himself, claiming that having brushed fingers with Yorgo, he should have been able to hold him; he had failed because his hands had failed. And so, immediately after Yorgo's funeral, he had left Nadolski's circus and has been drifting ever since.

∞∞∞∞∞∞∞🪷∞∞∞∞∞∞∞

When Adem stirred and seemed to be waking up, Babacık sent us out. People should emerge from their nightmares alone, he said. That pleased me. It wouldn't be Osman that Adem noticed first.

We brewed some tea and sat outside the tent. We had a couple of hours before the evening performance. That's a magical time in a circus. We had watered the ring, cleaned up the seats and the bandstand and checked that all our gear was securely fastened. Except for those who had to groom the animals, it was the time to unknot muscles, have a smoke, catch up on our lives, hear the latest gossip, smooth out any butterflies in the stomach and think of new feats. We're a good outfit even if we don't have a high rating. (For that we need a trapeze act. Easier said than done when good trapezists are like snowdrops in a desert.)

Babacık put on his costume and make-up then indulged in a narghile with our neighbour, Fevzi, the Syrian acrobat and father of The Ziggurats. Then the 'little people', Ekrem and Esin, came and passed round the pastries Esin had baked that day. (Had she not been a midget Esin would surely have been a famous cook.) Before long, as they did every evening, the whole troupe gathered round and all, except Mahmut the Simurg – who always stayed silent to keep his throat well lubricated for his fire-eating act – babbled away.

(Osman, I observed, drank in the atmosphere enviously. And I realized how difficult life must be for a flyer without a partner.)

Then, just as everybody started leaving to get ready for the show, Adem stumbled out of the tent. He looked bewildered. 'Where ... is this ...'

Osman went up to him. 'Circus – where Kudret Reis works ...' He extended his arms, hands down, as trapeze artistes do. 'Welcome ...'

Adem stared at Osman, then at Osman's hands. His voice cracked. 'Yorgo ...?'

'Osman.'

The two men could not shift their eyes from each other. Though they had only just met, they looked as if they felt compelled to create something together – were creating it. I used to think that was how people made babies, by making love with their eyes.

My jealousy took over. I jumped up. 'I'm ...' I tried to think of a good name, then decided on the old one. 'Emanet ...'

That broke the spell. Adem turned round. 'You ... I remember ... The old man – your father ...'

I pointed at Babacık who was drawing on his narghile and gazing at him.

Adem stared at Babacık's costume. 'A clown?'

Babacık waved a hand. 'How are you feeling?'

Adem, recognizing Babacık by his size, snarled. 'Why did you bring me here?'

'This is where I live.'

'Why me?'

'You need help.'

'From you?'

Babacık's arm encompassed the circus. 'From all of us.' He indicated the spectators who were trickling in. 'From the punters.' Then he pointed at Osman. 'Mainly from him.'

'Who's he?'

Again Osman proffered his hands. 'Osman. I'm a flyer.'

Adem started shuddering. Then suddenly he punched Osman viciously. 'Bastard!' He turned on us. 'Bastards! Bastards!'

And he ran off.

A long time ago, when Babacık was a lad in his village, a man called Veysi, who was blessed with a good wife, several children and a fertile plot of land, suddenly disappeared. Since he was much liked and since, in those days, people never disappeared – even when they got killed in an accident or by brigands or wolves, some remains were always found – villagers from all over the region went searching for him. To no avail. Then one of the old women remembered that Veysi was of Armenian descent, that he had a twin brother and that, being born in 1896, at the height of Sultan Abdülhamit II's brutal persecution of the Armenians, both he and his twin brother had been given up for adoption to different Muslim families. On hearing this they started searching for this sibling; for ancient wisdom says that if we know where a person wants to return to dust, then we will know where to find him. Ancient wisdom also says that twins, even if separated at birth, communicate with each other in inexplicable ways. And so, after much searching, they found Veysi's twin in Kastamonu. He had been buried a short time ago. When they visited his grave, they discovered that Veysi was buried next to him. And the story unfolded: Veysi, having had a premonition that his twin was ill, had somehow traced his brother and appeared at his side. In the excitement of the reunion both had suffered heart failure and died.

So, with this story in my mind, I went searching for Adem at railway stations. I quickly scoured Sirkeci. Since that station serves only Thrace and Europe and since Adem had had no links with those lands, I did not expect to find him there.

Then I went to Haydarpaşa, the mainline station to Anatolia and on to Asia and Arabia.

And there he was, swaying because he had been drinking again, and trying to read the timetables.

I went up to him. 'Come back.'

He stared at me, his surprise mixed with hatred. 'Who sent you? The old man? Or that squirt who calls himself a flyer?'

'I came on my own.'

'And they let you – a child – run around in this merciless world by herself?'

'I'm not a child. I'm sixteen. I can look after myself!'

'Then go look after yourself somewhere else!'

'Where is Yorgo buried?'

He raised his hand, ready to hit me.

I stood my ground. 'Tell me.'

He snarled. 'You look like a tart!'

'What?'

'All that make-up ...'

'It's not make-up. It's henna.'

'What for?'

'To look good.'

'For me?'

I saw no point in denying it. I was trying to look 'feminine', as the contortionist sisters, Halide and Pınar, would say. 'Yes.'

He sniggered. 'You're crazy.'

'Where is Yorgo buried?'

'I told you to shut up about that!'

'Where? Tell me!'

He tried to move away from me, but collapsed on a bench. 'Konya ...'

'What will you do when you get to Konya?'

He stared at his hands, then at his wrists. 'Oh, I'll ...'

'Cut your veins?'

He started weeping. 'You don't understand ... He was my soul ... Two wombs, from two different peoples – one Greek, one Abkhaz – produced one whole man. One whole body and soul ... That was the miracle. I was he and he was me ... Together we were one ... We completed ourselves and each other ... When we entered the ring, God came to watch us …'

I sat next to him. 'You and Osman could be the same …'

'You're talking shit!'

'Why?'

'As Nadolski said – we've run out of lions.'

'What's that mean?'

'The sun has died. The lions have stopped performing. They've left to find another planet.'

'The sun will come up again. It always does.'

'You still don't understand! The lions performed because Yorgo and I were perfect. They copied us. Took pride in that. Then I dropped him. And they realized we were not perfect – body and soul not entirely together. Just another couple of useless humans. They decided they must be useless, too. Not the kings of the beasts they thought they were – just oversized cats. So they left …'

'They can come back …'

'How?'

'I don't know. Ask Babacık. I'm sure he can make them come back.'

'You're really crazy. So is he! Must run in the family …'

'Give it a try … What can you lose?'

He stood up hesitantly. Then he started laughing.

'What's so funny?'

'You mean death can wait. I can always die tomorrow – or the day after. It doesn't have to be today.'

'Something like that …'

He shook his head. 'Crazier still …'

I tried to hold his hand. 'Come …'

He recoiled from my touch and shoved his hands into his pockets. But he followed me.

As we descended the steps from the station to the landing stage, I caught sight of Osman and Hatice. They were trying to keep out of sight. Obviously, Babacık had sent Osman to make sure I would come to no harm. And Hatice had tagged along. Protecting her man was Hatice's aim in life.

We boarded the boat to Karaköy. No sooner had we sat down than Adem fell asleep.

I caught another glimpse of Osman and Hatice. This time, I also noticed Hacı Turgut. He was with a band of his trainees, including that nice young man, Rıfat, who has become one of our regular patrons because he loves Mahmut the Simurg's stories. All there to protect me?

Osman, I noted, was smiling, mouthing congratulations. Hatice was as sombre as a grey day.

<hr />

Adem refused to lodge with anyone. He wanted his own place. So Babacık found him a corner in the stables. Adem welcomed that. Stables were where he had started his circus life. He and horses got on well. They even talked. I heard them: he told them stories about hidden prairies where horses lived free because humans couldn't get there.

And every night, during the performance, I saw him

standing in the dark, as far away from the Big Top as he could get, listening to the excitement of the audience, breathing in the gasps, the sighs and the applause as act after act rose to its climax. And some nights, I saw his eyes twinkle and knew that he was crying.

For several weeks, he kept away from the ring. That was where Osman was training and he didn't want to see what Osman could do.

Osman was tireless. Hour after hour, he swung on his trapeze, performed twists, turns and somersaults. Every week he rigged his platform higher up the cone to give himself more space and more time in the air. He was training for the quadruple – 'the impossible'. That had become his obsession since he had heard that Adem and Yorgo had been trying for it. He believed he would be the one to do it – providing he and Adem teamed up and providing also that he had a high enough Big Top to give himself sufficient space to execute the somersaults.

Though I feared that if he and Adem teamed up, I'd take second place, I had to admit Osman was truly astonishing. He had the grace and agility of a falcon in full flight.

During those weeks, Adem spent much of his time with Babacık. I would watch him trying to keep away by busying himself in the stables or helping out with other animals, or even going to town. But he would soon trail back, sit down with us and help sandpaper the chess pieces Babacık carved out of wood for a souvenir shop that specialized in reproductions of Ottoman sets

– painstaking work given that the pieces comprised miniature sculptures of janissaries, siege towers, viziers, sultans and sultanas.

I relished those times because, except when I had to practise my juggling, I could sit with them. Mama Meryem, however, wasn't happy to have me around. She had grown to dislike Adem. I'd heard her say several times that people who burdened others with their problems were tapeworms.

And she feared I would fall for him. I heard her say this also: 'Women's brains between their legs! They drop skirts for any ram!'

Me, fall in love? What next? And at sixteen? No. Infatuation – maybe! Just to make the blood run faster.

Fortunately, Babacık did not take Mama Meryem seriously. And since she never disputes his wishes, she put up with my presence.

Adem did get talking about Yorgo. Often repeated the same things. How Yorgo was the greatest flyer of all time. How they had fused their bodies and souls. How they had joined the supreme band of entertainers that stretched all the way back to ancient Egypt. How they had perfected the triple somersault and were working towards the three-and-a-half and then the quadruple ...

Invariably, after all this anguish, he would wail, 'Why couldn't I catch him, Grandad?'

That's what he called Babacık – Grandad. (Did he foresee something I didn't know?)

And Babacık would say, 'Why do children die?'

And Adem would always miss the real meaning of that answer. So he would wail even more. 'Spread out like a broken doll, he was ... Blood – red like I've never seen, Grandad – trickling out of his mouth ...'

And Babacık would try to console him. 'We are weak. But we are also noble. We do what we must do – and do it always chest out, never by turning our backs ...'

And Adem would weep. 'Why me, Grandad? Why did it have to be me?'

And Babacık would look at him sternly. 'Why not you? Why should you be spared? What's so special about you?'

At this, Adem would stride off. I'd want to go after him, but I'd restrain myself. I'm not one to knife Mama Meryem's trembling heart, particularly when it trembles for me.

∞∞∞∞∞✿∞∞∞∞∞

'I'm a killer,' Adem declared solemnly in his usual sunless way one Monday, our rest day.

This outraged Mama Meryem. 'What nonsense you talk!'

We were having a picnic at Çamlıca, the pine wood on the Asian side of the Bosporus, the beauty spot nearest to our circus.

Adem held up his hands. 'Look! Killer's hands.'

'I know killers. You not one of them ...'

Mama Meryem was sewing – a new outfit for Vahit, the tightrope walker. She made all the troupe's costumes.

Babacık was carving his chess pieces. They were never idle – not even during a picnic.

I started laying out the food. 'I hope everybody's hungry. I'm starving.'

Adem dropped his hands on to his lap and stared at them. 'What's terrible is – it's so easy ... to be a killer ...'

Mama Meryem cast a quick glance at Babacık as if seeking his permission to speak. When he showed no sign of displeasure, she erupted. 'You listen! Killers I know! That's how met Kudret, our Baba! Like everything in world, they come two kinds: the mad and the not mad. The mad kill to cure some pain they have or because maniacs have poisoned them; and they kill until they dead themselves. Those not mad kill because guardian angels take eyes off them a moment; then rest of life they try repair world in atonement. Baba is second kind. You neither.'

Adem looked at me as if I shouldn't have heard any of this. I smiled at him sweetly and continued sorting out the food. I knew the story – Babacık won't permit secrets in the family. Also I was enjoying Mama Meryem's outburst. Her accent was so thick she sounded as if she was singing one of her favourite arias.

Adem asked Babacık in awe. 'You killed, Grandad?'

Babacık's eyes clouded as they always do when he's reminded of the bad times. 'Yes.'

'How?'

Mama Meryem replied instead. 'He hit man! One blow!'

I nudged Adem. 'Ask why!'

'Why?'

'He was still wrestler then. His outfit had engagement in Italy. Trieste. His boss make deal with gamblers. Kudret to lose match. But Kudret's opponent useless. When Kudret touch him, he crumble. So gamblers go for Kudret. With iron bars. Kudret fight them. When he kill one, others run. But not before they shoot Kudret. Luckily police come. Kudret rushed hospital.'

I interjected proudly. 'He had five wounds. Mama Meryem saved him. She was his nurse.'

Mama Meryem chuckled. 'I to be nun. Nurse to serve God. But when I see Kudret I forget religion. When he recover, I decide I be Kudret's, not Jesus' bride. No Sister Maria. Mama Meryem.'

'But didn't they charge him with murder?'

'Sure. But obvious self-defence. Get two years.'

'That was lucky.'

I interrupted again. 'It still took them six years to get married.'

'Why?'

Mama Meryem sighed. 'Because suddenly war. Kudret to labour camp. I to field hospital. Then Americans capture me. I nurse for them. When war end Kudret and I have no contact.'

'But Babacık found her.'

Babacık shook his head. 'No, the Gypsy clairvoyant, Fatma, found her. They had sent me back to Turkey. I'd found work in a circus. I consulted Fatma at a fair. She told me Meryem was working in a hospital in Genoa. I went to a scribe – got him to write her a letter ...'

I concluded proudly. 'She was here within the month.'

Mama Meryem nodded sentimentally. 'Twenty-one days, four hours, eight minutes.'

Adem was moved. His voice became sad and wistful. 'And you've lived happily ever after ...'

Babacık scrutinized the chess piece he had just carved. 'Yes. And no.'

'Why "no"?'

'Because I've lived with the fear I might kill again.'

'Why should you?'

'If someone hurt Girl or my Meryem ...'

Mama Meryem muttered in trepidation. 'And I – that someone might kill Baba ...'

'Who would? Everybody loves him!'

'But will they protect him?'

'From whom?'

Mama Meryem faced Adem. 'From himself – mostly.'

Adem averted his gaze and turned to me. 'What do you fear?'

I laughed. 'Nothing. I fear nothing.' I pointed at the food. 'Lunch!'

⚬⚬⚬⚬⚬⚬⚬⚬⚬❀⚬⚬⚬⚬⚬⚬⚬⚬⚬

One day, Babacık was going through his wrestling exercises in the meadow. He still did them every day. I always went with him. That's when I practised my juggling.

As he formed the defensive move where the wrestler anchors himself with his head and legs – like an upside-down 'U' – in order to keep his shoulders from touching the ground, Adem appeared.

(I should confess: since Adem's arrival, I often imagined that I was using him as my juggling prop, throwing him up in the air, then catching him as he flew into my hands!)

'That looks difficult, Grandad. Where do you go from there?'

'It's a bridge. Defensive move. To stop your opponent pinning down your shoulders.'

'Looks pretty indestructible.'

'I've seen better.'

Babacık was being humble. We know from Hacı Turgut that no one has ever broken Babacık's bridge. I also remember that, when I was younger, all the children in the troupe used to climb on him and his bridge wouldn't even shake.

'I hear you were the best, Grandad.'

Babacık straightened up. 'I was all right.'

'Glad to have retired?'

'Who likes retirement?'

'I do.'

'You expect me to believe that?'

'Well ...'

'Have you ever wrestled, Adem?'

'No.'

Babacık offered his hand. 'Try it. Work the muscles we've been given. Understand what it means ...'

Adem shunned Babacık's hand. 'What what means?'

'Wrestling.'

'Wrestling is wrestling ...'

'It's much more than that. It's love – to put it simply. We wrestle because we love. We look at a man and see he's beautiful, inside and out. This creates respect, admiration. We want to touch him – love him. So we wrestle.'

Adem cast an embarrassed look at me. 'Sounds great, Grandad. But surely, when all's said and done, it's just a contest. Win or lose.'

'Not for the wrestler. Never a contest. More a celebration. You wrestle to the best of your ability. You honour Creation. Who wins when you make love? Both partners. And by their example – everybody else.'

'That's the strangest rule I've ever heard!'

'Rules, you learn in five minutes. I'm talking about classic wrestling. About what makes a man fight fair, what makes him see his opponent as his equal.'

'What about hate? What happens when you hate your partner – I mean, opponent?'

'No room for hate. That belongs to fist-men, pretenders, cheats. Not for us.'

'Us?'

'When you and Yorgo performed magic in the air – what was it like?'

'I don't know, Grandad ...'

'I do. I saw you. Union. Simple. Natural. Perfect union.'

'Maybe ... I mean yes, often it was as if we breathed at the same time ... Like when we did the triple ... When he let go of his trapeze on the last swing – so high he could have touched the cone – I felt him stop breathing, same time as I did. And as he performed the somersaults, as I swung to meet him, we held that breath. And he fell into my hands like a feather. And you heard our hands lock – clack! Perfect grip. Clean as anything you'll ever see. And we breathed out – same time, as if we had the same lungs ...'

'That's what I'm trying to say, Adem. When flesh touches flesh lovingly, there is beauty. There is union.'

Adem smiled.

Babacık stretched out his hand again. 'Come. Let's wrestle ...'

Again Adem shrunk away. 'Another time, Grandad ...'

And he walked off.

<hr />

Some weeks later, Adem finally dared enter the Big Top.

Babacık took that as a sign that Adem was feeling better in himself. He went into the Big Top, too.

Mama Meryem and I followed.

We found Adem watching Osman on the trapeze.

Osman, obviously inspired by our presence, performed magnificently.

Hatice, I noted, kept looking uneasily at Adem.

Like Mama Meryem who worried that Adem was bewitching me, Hatice feared that Osman, too, was falling under Adem's spell. Perhaps Mama Meryem should have told Hatice, as she told every woman who asked her advice, that providing she had made a home for Osman between her legs, she would have nothing to worry about.

Osman finished his exercises and jumped off the bar. He ran straight to Adem. 'Was I good?'

Adem nodded graciously. 'Yes.'

'Might we try …?'

Adem shook his head curtly. 'No.' Then he softened his tone. 'Sorry …'

Osman tried to hide his disappointment. 'Another time …'

Hatice, who had been towelling off Osman's sweat, dragged him away. 'Come, you mustn't catch cold …'

Mama Meryem, taking advantage of their departure, pushed me forward. 'Let's go. Nothing will happen today.'

I followed her out, then telling her that I had promised to help out in the menagerie, slipped back in.

Babacık and Adem were squatting in the ring and talking. I stayed in the shadows and listened.

Babacık asked, man to man, 'Is he good – Osman?'

Adem nodded grudgingly. 'Yes.'

'As good as Yorgo?'

'No!'

'Could he be?'

Again Adem nodded dismissively. 'Maybe …'

'Let's hope he doesn't get a liking for opium ...'

Adem's anger rose. 'What's that supposed to mean ...?'

'Not what a flyer needs – opium ...'

'Is that what they've been saying? That Yorgo was an addict?'

'Was he?'

'He smoked the odd one. We all indulge now and again!'

'I don't. Meryem and Girl don't. I've never seen you use it ...'

'So what? No harm if it's the occasional one ...'

'Why?'

'Why what?'

'Why did he smoke – the occasional one?'

'To relax. To get out of his skin.'

'Wasn't he happy in his skin?'

'Sure, he was. Like everybody else.'

'Most people are not.'

Adem laughed nervously. 'So sometimes he got depressed. It's natural.'

'What about?'

'How should I know? People get depressed! Something – out of the blue – upsets them!'

'He never told you about the things that upset him?'

'No.'

'The night he fell – had he been smoking?'

Adem sneered. 'You can't smoke when you're on the trapeze!'

'What about before the performance?'

'Grandad, I don't know what you're getting at, but ...'

'Was he depressed – before the performance?'

'Who knows ...?'

'Can you think what might have depressed him?'

Adem protested. 'I didn't say he was depressed!' He stared at his hands wearily. 'If he was, I don't know why! I never knew what was in his mind!'

'But you were so close ...'

'Even so ...'

Babacık shook his head. 'I think you know what depressed him.'

'I'm telling you, I don't!'

'Your eyes are telling me you do ...'

'To hell with my eyes!'

'They're saying there's a weight around your neck – and you're sinking ...'

Adem wailed. 'Grandad!'

'Talk about it. Throw off the burden. Free yourself.'

Adem sighed heavily. 'It was nothing. Stupid, in fact! We – had an argument ...'

'What about?'

'Something he did – I didn't like ... I told you – it was silly ...'

'Silly enough to want to die?'

'He didn't want to die! I dropped him!'

'On purpose?'

'No!' Adem started to shake. 'Is that what you think? That I killed him?'

'No. That's your fear. I know – everybody knows
– that he fell because he mistimed his take-off.'

'No! He was too good for that!'

Babacık nodded pensively. 'What was it he did – you
didn't like?'

'I told you – nothing ... He ...'

'What?'

'He – kept ... watching me ...'

'How do you mean?'

'When I slept ... We lived in the same caravan ...'

'Sure ...'

'And he also ...'

'Yes ...'

'Stroked me – as if I were a ... child ...'

'I see ... And you wanted to be stroked like an
adult?'

'Yes! No! I didn't want to be – touched!'

'Did you tell him that?'

'Yes ...'

'You must have hurt him ... The man who shared his
breathing – not wanting to be touched ...'

'Oh, I hurt him all right ...' He sprang up. 'Sorry,
Grandad. Too painful to talk ...'

He rushed out.

Adem was going to run away again. We knew –
even I did – that we would not be able to find him this
time.

But Babacık was not one to leave a conversation
unfinished. He charged out of the Big Top and
confronted Adem, who had gathered from our tent the

few clothes he had acquired during his stay.

'Before you go, Adem!' This was the first time I had heard Babacık shout. Such was the power of his voice that he must have sounded like one of Mama Meryem's formidable prophets. 'I told you about touching! I'll tell you again!'

Adem stopped as if held by an invisible harness.

All the members of the troupe rushed out, wondering what was happening.

Babacık raised his hands as if preparing to worship. 'Look! Our hands! Allah created them to do three things.' He opened up his hands. 'One: to be palms – to touch, stroke, create, love.' Then he clenched them. 'Two: to be fists – to strike, hurt, destroy, kill!' Then he put them in his pockets. 'Three: to hide – to run away, to do nothing.'

Adem pleaded. 'Let me go, Grandad!'

Babacık faced him. 'Everything that's good in this world comes from touch, when hands are palms. Everything bad happens for lack of touch, when palms turn into fists. We must touch as if we're mothers giving suck, with smiles and sighs and blessings to Allah for having created touch.'

Adem was becoming agitated. 'Grandad, please let me go!'

Babacık moved closer to him. 'When men and women wrap themselves around each other, they're in heaven. When people like you and me lock hands, we're in heaven. All those who hold daughters and sons to their chests, they're in heaven. Because touch creates love. Makes male and female jump like dolphins. Makes men like us feel the miracle of our bodies, admire the grace of muscles flexing, the honest way we share our strength. Makes us fulfil Allah's will!'

Adem yelled, 'And if the touch is not entirely honest?'

Babacık thundered, 'If the touch is given with love, it's always honest!'

Adem bellowed, 'You don't understand!'

Babacık outshouted him. 'I do!'

Enraged, Adem tried to punch Babacık.

Babacık seized Adem's fist and held it in his palm.

For what seemed an eternity, they stood, eyes locked, gauging each other's strength.

Then Adem unclenched his fist, pulled his hand out of Babacık's grip and strode away.

This time Babacık did not stop him.

Sadly, the troupe made way for him.

Both Osman and I shot forward to stop him.

Babacık held us back. 'Let him go. If he's worthy of you, he'll come back.'

<hr />

He came back weeks later, when Osman and I – though not Babacık – had given up hope.

I had expected him to look weak and haggard from too much drinking and maybe even on opium, like Yorgo. Instead, he looked like a film star, like Errol Flynn who saved England for Richard the Lionheart.

He arrived by taxi. When he got out, he did not salute those members of the troupe who came out to welcome him. Barely nodding, once to Babacık and Mama Meryem and once to me, he proceeded to the Big Top, dragging a trunk.

Osman, as usual, was training. When he saw Adem, he scrambled down to greet him. He, too, received a cursory nod.

Adem took off his jacket, shirt and trousers. Underneath he was wearing the white vest and tights of a trapezist.

By now the whole troupe had heard of his arrival and had rushed into the Big Top. As they settled around the ring, they made happy sounds like animals coming to feed.

Adem unlocked the trunk and brought out his trapeze gear. He started rigging it in the catcher's corner.

I gaped at his torso. Not even Babacık possessed such powerful shoulders.

Babacık noted my wonderment. 'He's been getting into shape.'

'He looks so strong.'

'Has to be. When a flyer drops for the catch, he falls like a meteor – at great speed. That makes him much heavier than his weight. If you don't have the strength to arrest such a fall, you'll tear off your shoulders or get pulled off your perch.'

His trapeze now secured, Adem sat on the bar. He began swinging, slowly at first, then faster and faster.

Had he not been in costume, he would have looked like a giant child in a playground.

Babacık looked pleased. 'Wise man …'

'Yes?'

'He's coming back from the depths – maybe from the edges of life. He's coming up slowly – trying to keep his mind clear.'

Adem seemed set to swing for hours. Some of the troupe got bored, urged him to show them what he could do.

He ignored them.

Babacık chased us out. 'He's not ready yet! Let him be!'

∞∞∞∞∞❀∞∞∞∞∞

Thereafter Adem went into the Big Top every day. Week after week, he sat on his trapeze and worked on his swing. Then he practised swinging in the catcher's position, hanging upside down while he gripped the bar with the insides of his knees.

Babacık left him to find himself.

Occasionally, Osman offered to exercise together. Adem refused – delicately, in order not to offend him.

But he allowed me to stay and watch.

And I did. I devoured Adem – every part of him – with my eyes and relished the moist warmth in my crotch. I even began to think I might like motherhood.

Adem pretended to ignore me. I knew he was pretending because every time I left the ring – either to have a pee or change my rags during my monthlies or, if there was a commotion outside, go and see what it was about – he would watch me leave. And often, when I returned, I'd find him down from his trapeze, seemingly towelling himself, but actually looking for me.

One such day, Mama Meryem had got there before me. Adem had come down from his trapeze and she was talking to him.

I hid so that I could listen.

Mama Meryem had put on what Babacık called her Catholic voice. 'You had women, Adem?'

Adem looked like a cornered animal. 'A few …'

'What happened? You loved and left?'

'No … They were … in brothels …'

'Ahh … Ever love somebody?'

'Why do you ask …?'

'No. You not have. You not loving kind …'

Adem became defiant. 'I did – love.'

'What happened her?'

'He died.'

Mama Meryem was left temporarily speechless. 'You telling you don't like women?'

'No …'

'What then?'

'I can love.'

'What about my girl?'

'I haven't touched her.'

'I know. If you had, I see it the way she walks.'

'Then why do you ask?'

'Listen, I'm no Muslim. No even Catholic any more.

Just mother wants Girl happy. I give camel's turd about virginity. My girl will break hymen one day. Soon the better, I say. Best life for woman when her legs open. But *how* Girl break hymen what concern me! Will be bang-bang? Or will be kiss-kiss everywhere?'

'You needn't worry about me.'

Mama Meryem forced a smile. 'If you no can love her … Spare her … Please …'

◦◦◦◦◦◦◦◦◦◦❦◦◦◦◦◦◦◦◦◦◦◦

Then on 10 June – which happened to be his birthday – Adem asked Babacık, Mama Meryem, Osman, Hatice and me to meet him in the Big Top.

He was standing by his trapeze. He had washed and ironed his vest and tights as if for a performance and looked illuminated. I was reminded of Mahmut the Simurg's description of Eternity, the Beneficent Immortal whom the god Ahura Mazda baked from russet Samarkand clay.

He had rigged up the safety net. 'I'm twenty-five today. I'll try and start a new life.'

Babacık ruffled his hair. 'Good man!'

Adem put his arm on Osman's shoulders. 'Still want me as partner?'

Osman beamed. 'Yes!'

'Let's have a go. A few passes first. Then maybe some twist-and-turns. I'll signal – clap my hands! All right?'

'Great!' Osman ran to his rope ladder on the flyer's side of the ring and climbed up to his trapeze.

Adem climbed on to his.

We sat down.

I was excited, but also nervous. Babacık looked confident. Mama Meryem was expressionless. Hatice's teeth clattered.

Adem and Osman started swinging. As they gathered speed, they settled into their positions: Adem, hanging upside down, arms and hands loose and ready to catch; Osman holding the trapeze like a gymnast on a fixed bar.

Minutes seemed to pass. We could have had our eyes closed but we would still have known by the swishing sound they made that they were swinging in perfect rhythm.

But no signal from Adem. We could see him rubbing his hands, trying to summon up courage.

We grew anxious, fearful.

Hatice shut her eyes and started mumbling a prayer.

Finally Adem clapped his hands.

We held our breath.

Osman let go of his trapeze just as Adem swung to meet him.

He floated down perfectly into Adem's hands.

Adem caught him. And held him.

We clapped as they swung back.

Babacık silenced us. 'Sssshhhh!'

We looked up.

A terrible grimace distorted Adem's face. Osman was slipping through his hands.

Adem managed to hold Osman until they were above the centre of the safety net. Then he dropped him. A moment later, he regained his perch, tied up his trapeze and scrambled down.

Osman ran to him. 'Adem, it was perfect!'

Adem brushed him aside. 'Sorry, can't do it!' He went up to Babacık. 'I tried, Grandad! You saw how hard I tried! I even believed I could do it. But I can't!'

Babacık held him to his chest. 'Try again, son! Try again.'

Adem kissed Babacık's hands. 'No!' Then he broke free and ran out.

Babacık shouted at Osman. 'Take the safety net down! Immediately!' He turned to me. 'Girl, get him before he disappears! Tell him I need his help! Tell him it's life or death! My life or my death!'

I ran out, so scared that my legs shook.

I heard Mama Meryem wail. 'What you do, Baba? What you up to?'

I caught up with Adem at the gate. Osman joined us moments later. Adem refused to believe that Babacık needed his help. Or that it was a matter of life or death. Not until Mama Meryem and Hatice came out screaming, calling everybody to come and save Babacık.

We ran back to the Big Top.

Babacık had taken Osman's trapeze up to the highest perch and was now swinging from it.

The safety net was down. The drop beneath him was over twenty metres. If he fell he would be killed.

Some of the troupe had rushed to the safety net, but Babacık had forbidden them to rig it up. If they refused to do as he asked, he had threatened, he would drop – head first.

Adem climbed the rope ladder to Babacık's height. 'Grandad! What are you up to?'

'I'm waiting. For you.'

'For me?'

'To catch me.'

Adem bellowed, 'Grandad, I can't catch! You've seen with your own eyes, I can't!'

'You caught Osman beautifully.'

'I couldn't hold him!'

'Sure you could. But something inside you didn't want to.'

'What?'

'Fear.'

'Sure – I was afraid I'd kill Osman!'

'And Yorgo? Were you afraid for him, too?'

'No! I don't know! I dropped him because ...'

'You didn't drop him. He mistimed ...'

'No, Grandad, no! He ... He ...'

'Unless you mean you dropped him because he touched you ...'

'No!'

'He loved you ...'

'Grandad! Please!'

'I love you, too. So does Girl! So does Osman! And Mama Meryem and Hatice! Everybody! So now you have to be afraid for all of us!'

'No! To hell with you all! You mean nothing to me!'

'We'll see about that.'

Down from the ring Mama Meryem wailed. 'Baba, I no love him! Nobody love him! He not lovable! He afraid of love! He run away from love! Please, please no do what you thinking doing!'

'I won't do anything, my Meryem. I'll just hang here. Until Adem catches me.'

Mama Meryem screamed. 'Kudret! Please!'

I screamed also. 'Please, Babacık!'

Everybody started pleading.

Babacık thundered, 'Quiet! All of you!'

Adem was near to tears. 'Grandad, I can't catch! Why won't you understand?'

'I'm quite strong, Adem. I can hang on, ten, twenty minutes, half an hour. Maybe even an hour. After that, I'll drop. Sooner or later you'll have to catch me.'

'Why are you doing this, Grandad? What do you want from me?'

'To beat your fear. Of the hands. Of the heart. I want you to fulfil your destiny. Become the great catcher you are!'

'What for?"

'For you. For Girl. For Osman. For me. For my Meryem. For everybody! Or for nothing! Must you measure everything?'

Adem looked desperate. 'Grandad, I'm not worth it!'

Mama Meryem ran over to his rope ladder and started shaking it. 'Go! Go! Catch him! What you wait for? You want him die? You want kill only angel in world?'

'No, Mama Mer ...'

'Save him! Save before he falls!'

Osman shouted at him, 'Go on, brother. You can do it ...'

Tears started running down Adem's cheeks. I could see: another moment – and he would run away.

I climbed up the rope ladder to his level. I grabbed his hands, kissed them. And then – even though my parents could see – I pulled his hands to my breasts. I whispered, 'You have great hands. Hands born to catch. Hands that can hold the sky.'

He tried to pull his hands away.

But I wouldn't let him. I held on to them, pressed them to my breasts. 'Hands born to touch ...'

For the first time Adem looked at me as if I was a person and not a scrag-end in a circus. And I could see that the way he breathed, sighed, the way his eyes ran in every direction, he was fighting himself. Fighting not to run away.

I pressed his hands harder to my breasts, this time trying to tell him I was a woman and not a girl, that if he saved Babacık, everything would be his, including me. I whispered again, 'Catch him. You have great hands! Catch him! You can do it!'

His eyes sparked as if he had read my thoughts. 'And if I can't?'

I shouted at him with all the voice I could muster, 'Then fall with him! Die with him!'

Suddenly he relaxed. He smiled. 'Yes. I can always do that.'

He kissed my hand – gently – then slipped out of my grasp and scrambled down the rope ladder. 'All right, Grandad! I'm coming! Do exactly what I tell you!'

Babacık smiled. 'Of course.'

Adem climbed the other rope ladder to the catcher's perch.

We watched him in silence. Allah only knows how our legs managed to keep us upright.

Adem settled on his trapeze. 'All right, Grandad?'

'Yes.'

'Now, start swinging. Higher and higher. You have to get to a point almost above me, then drop. You understand?'

'Sure. I've seen many trapeze acts in my time.'

'Right. Go!'

Babacık started swinging.

Adem started swinging, too. Then as he gained speed, he took up the catcher's position. 'Keep swinging, Grandad.'

We watched, our hearts in our mouths.

Babacık swung higher and higher.

Adem shook his arms, rubbed his hands together. 'Grandad, when I clap, let go of the bar and drop. Exactly when I clap. Not a second before or after. Got it?'

'Yes.'

Babacık and Adem swung towards each other.

They swung for what felt like an age.

No one breathed.

Adem clapped his hands.

Babacık dropped.

Mama Meryem buried her face on my chest.

Babacık fell. He looked as if he would fall for ever.

Then a sound, like a thunderclap, rang in the ring.

I saw, barely, between my tears, Babacık swinging with Adem. Safely – oh, so safely – held by his hands.

A huge shout rose in the ring.

Mama Meryem collapsed, laughing and crying and thanking the Virgin Mary.

Osman grabbed Hatice and started dancing with her.

And Adem and Babacık yelled loud enough to wake the gods.

I was the first to return to reality. 'Put up the safety net! Let's get them down!'

Within seconds, Osman and several men had rigged up the safety net.

Adem dropped Babacık on to the net; then, performing a somersault, he dropped down, too.

Babacık, somehow able to stand up on the wobbling net, pulled Adem to his chest. As they hugged, they lost their balance. Entwined like that, they looked as if they were wrestling.

∞∞∞∞∞∞∞∞∞∞

Adem and Osman are now a team. They call themselves The Twin Peacocks on Mahmut the Simurg's suggestion. It's the Arabic representation of the Gemini in the Zodiac.

They spend most of their time together, practising, talking, planning and day-dreaming. They raced through one, two and two-and-a-half somersaults in a few weeks. They are now perfecting the three – they have performed it regularly in practice. And they feel confident that soon they will be working on the three-and-a-half and, indeed, the four. I have even heard Adem tell Babacık that, like Archimedes who could move the earth if he were given a long enough pole, he and Osman could perform five or even six somersaults if they were given a high enough Big Top.

Sometimes when I watch them practise, when I see how perfectly they lock hands, how lovingly they put their arms around each other, I get jealous. In that I have become like Hatice. But then what else can I do? – as soon as I reach my seventeenth birthday, I will be Adem's wife.

I know Adem and Osman will love each other more than they will love us, their wives. But at least Osman will sleep with Hatice and Adem will sleep with me. And Babacık says that there is nothing in the world that conjures paradise better than man and woman sleeping together. And every time he says that, Mama Meryem smiles knowingly.

Incidentally, I now have a proper name. I chose it myself as I said I would. It's Havva. The name of the first woman. Adem, who is named after the first man, thinks I have chosen well. Osman likes it, too, but thinks it's a bit too bold. I don't care. It declares my right to Adem. It's time we women had a say in our affairs, too.

8: Mustafa

Rose-Petal Jam

Our beloved ...

She gave us a taste of the Seventh Heaven. And because that taste is as rare as the Anka bird, reason insists it should last a lifetime. But reason has no sway below the umbilicus. And a taste is never enough when the hunger is insatiable.

Love goddess to thirteen boys ...

She never divulged her name. When she disappeared, we inquired about her. At first secretly, each boy on his own. Then, after we discovered that we had all been her lovers, collectively. We found out she was called Suna Azade.

Suna ...

She had rented her apartment in Bebek on a short lease. And she came there only at weekends. Her car's number-plates indicated she was a resident of Edirne, the ancient Adrianople. That disconcerted us. What was a divinity doing in that dead-end city? (As elitist Istanbul citizens, we looked down on Edirne; yet it had been the Ottoman capital before the conquest of Istanbul and is a city with a rich heritage.) Takis, the Greek, claiming to know the Balkans well, decided that Suna was a spy assigned to keep Turkey safe from communism; her mission was to infiltrate the neighbouring countries – often risking her life as she slunk past dangerous borders – and seduce senior politicians and generals like a modern Catherine the Great. A ridiculous conjecture, without doubt. Yet it made us suicidal.

Our beautiful lady ...

I had my own name for her: 'rose-petal jam'. When she had found out that that was my favourite preserve, she had promptly served it to me smeared on her clean-shaven vagina. Its nectarous taste as it blended with her prodigious love-dew was and is and will be one of life's greatest gifts to me. Did any of the other boys enjoy the same treat? I don't know. But I choose to believe that no one in the dormitory liked rose-petal jam as much as I did.

Our dormitory's beloved ...

In later years, when her dalliance with us became part of college mythology, she acquired the sobriquet Aphrocirce. It described her perfectly: salvation in one breast; perdition in the other.

But we should have known. As the storyteller Mahmut the Simurg says, whenever divinities visit our world, their aura scorches the earth. And though our beloved, our Suna, our beautiful lady, our belladonna, did bestow salvation upon us, it can be said that she also destroyed our greatest achievement, our perfect society, our dormitory.

Our dormitory ...

The epitome of Turkishness as created by our teacher, Âşık Ahmet ...

∞∞∞∞∞∞⚜∞∞∞∞∞∞

Our dormitory came to be known as 'Gelibolu'. The name implied that we, its residents, were of the same mettle as Atatürk's troops at Gallipoli. It was coined not by us, but by rival dormitories.

We deserved the sobriquet. Though we were a small band, both in numbers and in age, we had never been defeated in inter-dormitory battles during the two years we were together. This achievement still stands as a college record. Considering that, in those days, dormitories usually accommodated boys of diverse ages – even some over-twenties from the Anatolian hinterland, while ours housed, as customarily, only fourteen- and fifteen- year-olds – the record is unlikely to be broken.

In retrospect, I can say without hesitation that the quality that made us formidable was our multi-ethnic composition. In effect, we twenty-four boys represented almost the full spectrum of Turkey's demographic cocktail: Abkhaz, Albanian, Âlevi, Armenian, Azeri,

Bosnian, Circassian, Dönme, Georgian, Greek Catholic, Greek Orthodox, Jewish, Karait, Kurd, Laz, Levantine, Nusairi Arab, Pomak, Pontos, Russian (White Russian, to give their preferred appellation), Süryâni (also known as Assyrians), Tatar, Turk and Yezidi. Thus no single *millet* – the Ottoman word for 'ethnic peoples' that our teacher had rescued from history – could form a majority in order to dominate or claim superiority, as had been the norm and was still the case with some of the other dormitories. (One incident that has been mothballed and hidden away depicts perfectly the extremes to which such divisions can lead. One year in the late twenties, the college governors, adopting the strategy of 'divide and rule', had split the dormitories into Muslim and Christian entities. Consequently, every time an issue affecting the two religions had arisen, these dormitories had found themselves in grave dispute. Such had been the ensuing attrition that, by the end of the semester, several dormitories had been smashed up and numerous students injured.)

Admittedly, when our dormitory had first been assembled, there had been attempts by some of the boys to form cabals with co-religionists but these moves instantly expired in the wake of the first raid on our dormitory. As we fought our attackers, we quickly realized that had we splintered into factions, we would have met with swift defeat. And defeat meant performing the victors' daily chores: making their beds, cleaning their lavatories, sorting out their laundry, laying their refectory tables, serving them meals and washing up their dishes. And so, when we had put our adversaries to flight and strode about savouring our victory, savouring particularly the bruises that provided proof of victory, we felt transformed. (I had someone's tooth embedded in my knuckle; I still bear the scar.) Cengiz, the Tatar, was the first to shout the catechism with which Atatürk had sought to unite Turkey's minorities: 'Blessed is he who can say I am a Turk.' Then Agop, the Armenian, a passionate romantic since reading *The Three Musketeers*, bellowed his favourite slogan, 'All for one and one for all!' At which Zeki, the Jew, clamoured, '*No pasarán*', that famous Republican exhortation from the Spanish Civil War, in which one of his father's French cousins had lost his life.

Thus, drunk with the joys of our plurality, we, the hybrids, bonded, seemingly for life. We never suffered a betrayal in our ranks. No matter how severe the teachers' interrogation, not a single person snitched on such peccadilloes as who pissed on the radiator and stank the place out, or who dressed up in a sheet and frightened the night matron by pretending to be a ghost, or who opened the gate to Memduh when he came back from the brothels that he frequented at least twice a week. (Memduh, the Süryâni, a latecomer to education, was twenty-one, came from Diyarbakır, slept in a rival dormitory and always tipped generously whosoever opened the gate for him. Hooked on sex, he refused to get involved in dormitory battles.) Since the college's long-established punishment for betrayal was the insertion of chilli paste into the offender's anus – an infliction that, burning the victims' innards for days on end, all but drove him mad – our dormitory had the distinction of remaining 'virgin in the arse' throughout our years together. That, too, is a record unlikely to be beaten.

∞∞∞∞∞∞∞∞⚜∞∞∞∞∞∞∞∞

As mentioned before, the multi-ethnic constitution of our dormitory had been forged by our literature teacher, Professor Ahmet Poyraz – nicknamed Âşık Ahmet, 'Amorous Ahmet', for reasons I will shortly explain.

Âşık Ahmet, who has remained an inspired mentor to most of his students, has been the most vociferous defender of the Ottoman empire's immense contribution to civilization. More to the point, he took this stand at a time when the luminaries of modern Turkey were competing with each other to denigrate the accomplishments of their predecessors in order to ingratiate themselves with the so-called 'civilized West'. His contempt for the cupidity of the Occidental powers, who claim to be paragons of morality while happily killing millions in wars and in pursuit of colonial possessions, has become legendary. Treasuring the Ottoman empire's *millet* policy – a policy that had ensured tolerance towards its many peoples – as a great leap forward in political philosophy, Âşık Ahmet had progressed to Rousseau and to the need to unify humankind in brotherhood. Naturally enough, the concept of the United Nations had also affected him profoundly even though the first attempt at such an organization, the League of Nations, had foundered so disastrously.

Consequently, in support of the evolution of a 'world nation', he set out to restore what he called 'real Turkishness', a multi-*millet* community. Our dormitory was to be the prototype. We would demonstrate, not only to our government but also to the world, that chauvinist policies seeking to impose unity in a country of diverse peoples and religions were doomed to failure because they specifically sought to reduce plurality to singularity. If such an objective were to be achieved, society would become monolithic and ultimately perish as a result of inbreeding. Our dormitory, by contrast, would demonstrate that harmony could only exist through the preservation of plurality, that only a multi-*millet* policy could elevate Turkey to greatness whereas rabid nationalism – always camouflaged by such emotive terms as Turkification or Kemalism – would blight it irredeemably. We would prove, with our prototype 'world nation', that, in an unfettered crucible, different races and religions would create an ethos of mutual respect where all individuals would be equal and free. We would prove that our achievements in microcosm could also be achieved in macrocosm.

(The experiment, I should declare promptly, proved immensely successful. But then, pluralism always does – until, of course, Fate tampers with Pandora's box and releases shoals of politicians who behave like sharks at mob-feeding time. Or, as in our dormitory's case, it delivers Pandora herself ...)

Âşık Ahmet was a tall, craggy, athletic man with impeccably coifed hair and moustache. He was always sombrely dressed in a dark suit and polished black shoes. The girls in our sister college found him very attractive – a cross between Errol Flynn and Boris Karloff. But since he never taught them, they never had to face his fierce temper or run for cover as he stormed through the corridors like his surname, the north wind. He was a hero of the War of Independence and a visiting professor at various universities – and, as a result, his status among the teaching staff was above even that of the Regional Inspector of Schools. He was, in effect, a law unto himself, unchallengeable, beyond criticism.

For Âşık Ahmet, education started with poetry. Unless anointed by a balm of sublime verse, he claimed, we would turn into soulless bodies, lives devoid of life.

He was a formidable champion of Nâzım Hikmet. The latter, indisputably one of the greatest poets of the twentieth century and, for many of us, the most immaculate Turkish soul, had been convicted and imprisoned for preaching communism; calumnied by the Establishment, most of his writings had been banned. Despite that, Âşık Ahmet not only openly lectured on his poetry, but also led a samizdat network for disseminating his works. (Such devotion to justice was typical of Âşık Ahmet. For instance, at the time of the Second World War, he had been very active in helping Jews and other minorities who had been crushed by the *Varlık*, the infamous Wealth Tax. Some of the sons of those he had helped had become his students – like Zeki, a member of our dormitory, and Musa and Naim, two years ahead of us.)

For those students averse to poetry, Âşık Ahmet had devised an assortment of punishments. A rap on the knuckles for anyone who dared yawn while he recited – which he did beautifully and sonorously. Ear-twisting for those who failed to fathom the stylized delicacy of the courtly *Divan* literature or who complained about learning the Arabic and Farsi words with which the verses were suffused. Same punishment for those who failed to appreciate the simplicity and immediacy of folk literature, which always ran a rival course to *Divan*. A kick to the bottom for those who sniggered when he waxed lyrical about Hikmet. Masses of weekend homework for those who missed one of his classes. And, in the belief that prevention is better than cure, a slap on the neck for those caught in the corridors without a book of poetry in their hands. The last occurred rarely: Âşık Ahmet was a chain-smoker and emanated a pungent scent that was a mixture of tobacco and his lemon-scented cologne; thus we could always sniff his presence and get out of the way.

Though we were willing guinea-pigs in his dormitory project, he never treated us preferentially. Paradoxically for someone so liberal, he stuck to the ancient tenet that the relationship between teacher and student was like that between a sultan and a humble subject. On the other hand, fearsome as he was, he was not unaffectionate. Those students, myself included, who had ingested the joys of poetry would regularly get a pat on the shoulder or have their hair ruffled or, if the encounter took place outside the college precincts, be offered, man to man, a cigarette.

Yet I think that during the course of the semester chronicled by this retrospection he did come to perceive us not as adolescents frothy like fresh sheep's milk, but as young adults with the solid texture of mountain yoghurt.

Most people at the college and just about everybody down the hill, in Bebek, knew that Âşık Ahmet was having a passionate affair with a widow called Leylâ. Unable to marry her because she had a young son and risked losing custody of the boy to her in-laws, he was fanatically discreet about this romance and went to great lengths not to be seen in her company. However, on one occasion we – the whole dormitory – caught them in a most compromising situation. We had just won another battle, one that had broken a couple of our adversaries' noses; knowing that we faced a heavy punishment – no weekend leave, at the very least – we decided to console ourselves, at the risk of further punishment, by cutting classes that day and drinking to our victory in a sea-front *meyhane*. When we finally decided to return to school late that afternoon, we chose to climb our hill's 'wild flank' – so called because, given its craggy topography, it did not have a road serving the college – in order not to be caught by the caretakers. Suddenly, in a secluded copse halfway up the hill, we spotted Âşık Ahmet and Leylâ in an embrace.

When we finally managed to shake off our shock, we scampered away as quietly as we could, restraining ourselves from exchanging lewd looks and, indeed, pretending that we had not even seen them. Though, in the weeks that followed, we could not tell by Âşık Ahmet's behaviour whether he himself had spotted us, we maintained a diligent discretion. I imagine those who never got to know Suna did so in fear of his fury. But the rest of us, having just experienced both the apogee and the nadir of love with our beloved Suna, found a new solidarity with Âşık Ahmet. Manliness resides in silence – so our beloved had instructed us when she had made us promise to keep our trysts secret. Those who babble away, be it to boast or to groan, are creatures of indeterminate sex.

∞∞∞∞∞∞∞✿∞∞∞∞∞∞∞

Our beloved …

She appeared outside the college gates, at the beginning of our second semester.

I believe we all noticed her immediately. Standing by her Studebaker convertible and smoking, she looked like something out of the American magazine, *Esquire*. At first, since she always came on Saturdays, the day our weekend leave started, I thought she was a mother who came to collect her son. As I watched her draw on her cigarette like Rita Hayworth, I felt sorry for the boy: fantasies about voluptuous mothers were our staple for masturbation. (Why do sensual women always smoke?

Is it to warn us, men, that we're only good for a few
puffs before being stubbed out?)

She had shining auburn hair that matched – as I
eventually found out – the magenta of her vulva. She
had inherited her dark-shaded sex, she told me quite
seriously, from a Sudanese ancestor who had been a
eunuch in one of the sultan's harems, but who, obviously,
had not been a de facto castrato. In contrast, she had
such white skin that had she lain naked on the snow she
would have been invisible save for her hair, eyes, mouth
and nipples.

Soon her presence became intriguing. She had
claimed no one as her son. She would just stand near the
gates and watch us disgorge from school like prisoners
liberated from the Bastille. It was as if she had reserved
Saturday mornings for an outing on Bebek's promenade,
where the sea breeze and the view were heavenly and
where, for good measure, she could be amused by
the wild antics of robust youngsters. Inevitably, I was
reminded of stories about perverts who loitered outside
girls' schools and wondered whether she was a female
counterpart. After all, perverts were reputedly old and
this woman was undoubtedly of a certain age.

(I doubt whether she was older than thirty-five,
but for a boy of fourteen, hurrying to be fifteen, every
woman about his mother's age is old.)

And little did I know that I would end up adoring
women of a certain age because only they, given their
maturity, can provide sexual miracles. After all, to
evolve as a sexual miracle a woman needs many years

of zealous couplings – and a fair percentage of failure. The failures are particularly important, for without the knowledge of ineptitude, there can be no knowledge of ecstasy. Âşık Ahmet, who was much taken with Sufism, would often say, 'Witness how success and failure, joy and grief, birth and death have the same gossamer texture.'

Anyway, our beloved …

There soon occurred a series of strange happenings; happenings not necessarily puzzling in themselves but, given the adamantine bonds that held our dormitory together, quite unexpected and inexplicable.

For instance: a dark cloud, after a particular weekend, on the shoulders of Kâzım, the Azeri, which left him staring disconsolately into space for days on end; whereas normally he would have had us roaring with laughter as he recounted the exasperation his outlandish capers induced in his parents, brothers, sisters and tribe. Or the fanatical refusal of Cengiz, the rock-like Tatar, to sacrifice a weekend leave and partake in a do-or-die football match with a rival dormitory, when at any other time he would have considered such an abandonment sheer betrayal. Or Laz İsmail's sudden reluctance to allow us to re-examine his single testicle for any signs of change and to discuss yet again whether it was the missing testicle's length that had been added on to his penis to make it hang, even in detumescence, like that of a horse. Or the tribulations of Eşber, the gentle gargantuan Turk, who, hopeless with words but determined to shower his paramour with poems, terrorized our bard, Zeki, the Jew – acclaimed as a poet of promise by no less an authority than Âşık Ahmet – to act as his Cyrano.

∞∞∞∞∞∞❀∞∞∞∞∞∞

And then it was my turn.

It was one of those April weekends when crotchety forty-eight-hour drizzles chase away the balmy spring days. The air was palpable with the frustration of people who scanned the hills for a hint of strawberry shoots.

Like most Pomaks, I am an amphibian myself and, by that winter's end, I was impatient to join the dolphins in their games. Consequently, as I came out of school, I decided to ignore the rain and walk along the promenade. My friends, not so motivated, hurried off to Bebek to pick up buses, trams or the collective taxis, *dolmuş*.

I had stopped to gaze at a Chris-Craft, attached to a buoy some twenty metres out. This was a boat I had been coveting for months; the boat, I had promised myself, I would one day own. (Don't ask me how I would have achieved that when, in pursuit of the idealism inculcated in us by Âşık Ahmet, I had decided to take up teaching as a career.)

Then I heard her calling.

'Young man!'

She was driving her Studebaker and had stopped by the kerb. She might have sounded brusque, but so alluring was she that I stared, bewildered.

'Yes?'

'Are you deaf?'

'Sorry …?'

'I've been calling you …'

'Oh … Forgive me … I – was day-dreaming …'

She smiled. 'About mermaids?'

'No …'

'Make sure they have legs. Those with fins aren't much fun …'

'What …? Oh …'

She laughed heartily at my discomfort. She sounded like one of those society ladies who consider themselves more equal than men. 'Bebek – how far is Bebek?'

I pointed at the village, barely half a kilometre away. 'Just there.'

She consulted a piece of paper. 'I'm looking for a street – Yeni Sokak. It's where I live. Can you help me find it?'

'There's a newsagent at the corner. He would know.'

She opened the passenger door. 'Get in.' Seeing me hesitate, she beckoned me over. 'Come on, come on. I need help. I've only just moved here.'

I got in like an automaton. I wanted to say how surprised I was that she couldn't find her home. After all, Bebek was a tiny village; not even a blind person could get lost in it. But I was tongue-tied.

She sped off like a racing driver. I looked at her with a mixture of admiration and apprehension. And I registered her clothes: black shoes, black stockings, black skirt, black sweater, black scarf and black leather jacket. It suddenly struck me. Here was an existentialist. A Juliette Gréco; an icon of my generation. A symbol of turpitude to the Establishment and our parents. Here was rebellion incarnate.

She prodded me. 'Newsagent, you said. Where?'

I pointed at the shop.

And almost at the same time, I caught a glimpse of Dimitri and İsmail, standing on either side of the road, watching me. I waved at them; they didn't wave back.

Then a moment later, I saw Cengiz, then Eşber, then Agop and Kâzım, all within a small radius of the newsagent. They were drenched, yet were hanging around for no apparent reason. I waved at them too. They didn't return my greeting either.

As we came up to the newsagent, she pointed at a road on the right. 'That looks familiar. Shall I give it a try?'

I read the street-sign: Yeni Sokak. 'That's it!'

She turned into it, cooing happily. 'I must have the makings of an explorer! Mrs Magellan! Sounds good, don't you think?'

I smiled and made a faint acknowledging sound.

'We need number thirty-eight.'

I had been staring at her hair: a dark shade of auburn, as I mentioned, but loose and billowing in the wind like a weeping willow. Definitely an existentialist. But she was about my mother's age. Were there existentialists as old as that?

She caught my stare. 'Something wrong?'

'No. No ... I'm looking for number thirty-eight.'

'Good boy.'

Number thirty-eight turned out to be half-way down the street. And it proved to be one of those beautiful wooden buildings that are relics of Ottoman Istanbul. 'There!'

She stopped the car outside the house, switched off the engine and sighed with relief. 'Made it!'

I managed to nod.

She patted my shoulder. 'Thank you. You've been wonderful. I'd never have found it without you.'

I smiled shyly. Then, feeling that I might be imposing on her, I clambered out of the car.

She got out, too, and started rummaging in her handbag for her house keys.

I started walking away. 'Bye ...'

She found her keys. 'Don't just go like that! You've been so nice! Come in and have a drink! Show me how you young braves imbibe raki!'

'What's there to show?'

'All the mystique.'

I stared at her, puzzled.

'Do you water it down or just use ice? And what do you chase it with?'

I nodded lamely. 'Oh, I see what you mean ...' I tried to sound worldly. 'Whatever you prefer?'

By now she had opened the front door. 'Come on, show me! Ooooh! Nice and warm in here!'

I stood at the doorway, hesitant, yet honoured that such an old – mature – person should deign to invite me for a drink.

She pulled at my sleeve. 'Come on, let's get out of this rain!'

As I stood in the ornate hallway, I became aware of the perfume that permeated the house. *Her* perfume. It would linger in my nostrils for years.

She kicked off her shoes and pointed at the front room. 'In there! The raki's out. There's ice and mineral water. Pour generously. Nothing like a long drink. I'll be back in a second.' And she soared up the stairs.

I hung my coat and satchel on the portmanteau. Then I took off my shoes and put on the guest slippers. They could have been magical slippers transporting me from reality into illusion.

The front room enhanced this feeling with its quiet opulence. I could have been in one of those Ottoman inner sanctums that I had read about, seen pictures of, but which, according to Âşık Ahmet, had ceased to exist, except possibly in very conservative homes, because Western trends, in the wake of Atatürk's reforms, had taken possession of the country. The room was crammed with low sofas, soft cushions, ivory-inlaid coffee tables, arrays of exquisite bibelots and ornamental İznik plates, yet it emanated a sense of spaciousness. The original bright colours of the furnishings, particularly of the antique carpet, permeated a genteel glow. I imagined, as I threaded my way to the cabinet where various bottles stood on a tray, that if I clapped my hands a bevy of odalisques would appear to do my bidding.

To my surprise, I felt aroused. Since, given my hostess' age, I had not entertained any thoughts of sex with her – such thoughts occurred only in fantasies – I can only assume I had sensed what was to come. But then, as Âşık Ahmet would say, the body is wiser than the mind.

I filled two glasses with ice-cubes and poured large measures of raki. Then I prepared two glasses of mineral water, also with ice, and arranged the dishes of nuts, dried fruits and sweets, as best I could, on one of the coffee tables.

∞∞∞∞∞∞✿∞∞∞∞∞∞

When she returned, the ice in the raki glasses had melted. Throughout that time, I had fidgeted indecisively, thinking I ought just to shout goodbye and leave, yet wanting to stay, if only to keep inhaling her perfume, which had lingered in the room and was sustaining my arousal.

She came in bearing more fragrance. This time, musk soap. Which, while it literally arrested my breath, also announced that she had just bathed. The realization that she had actually undressed, walked about in the nude, washed and soaped her private parts when I was in the house, no more than a ceiling, a wall and a staircase away, so overcharged my imagination that my mind ceased functioning.

She had changed into a peignoir – black, like her clothes, and gleaming. She was barefoot, her toes unpainted. She had let her hair cascade down on to her shoulders. It was quite curly; splashed against her black dressing-gown, it emanated a dusky sheen. The rest of her hair, having fallen forward, framed a cleavage that struck me as incomparably generous even though she did not have large breasts. She was not wearing a bra.

I forgot her age instantly.

I offered her the raki.

She examined it as if it were an exotic brew. 'You drink it with water, I see ...'

'No. With ice. It's melted. But only just. It's all right to drink.'

She nodded. 'And the mineral water? A chaser? Right?'

'That's how I like it.'

'Which is good enough for me.' She pointed at the titbits on the coffee table. 'Help yourself.' She indicated a sofa. 'Sit down.'

Immensely aroused – and embarrassed as well as ashamed for being so – I slumped on to it. Then, in the hope that munching might prove a distraction, I grabbed a handful of nuts. My heart was running so fast I thought it would burst out of my mouth and stop only when it hit the Byzantine city walls.

She sat opposite me on a cushion on the floor. 'What's your name?'

Her peignoir had parted, revealing one of her thighs. Fleshy, but muscular.

My mouth dried up and my voice squeezed forth as a hoarse whisper. 'Mustafa.'

She smiled. 'Named after Atatürk. I approve.'

I could not move my eyes from her thigh. Desperately, I gulped down a few mouthfuls of my raki. I was aware that she was watching me gaping at her. I forced myself to speak, say anything. 'I'm what they call a Pomak. We're originally from Bulgaria.'

'Circumcised?'

'What?'

'Pomaks are circumcised, aren't they?'

'Of course. We're Muslims.'

She crossed her legs. 'Better-looking – circumcised cocks. Aesthetically speaking. More elegant.'

My heartbeats became uncontrollable. As she had crossed her legs, her peignoir had parted even more; now both her thighs were exposed. And above them, I could see the curvature of one of her buttocks and also, unless I was dreaming, a glimpse of her vaginal divide.

'Don't you agree?'

'What?'

'Circumcision. Gives a refined mien. Foreskins look so ugly.'

I forced myself to gaze at my drink. 'I – I wouldn't know.'

'Haven't you seen uncircumcised boys? I thought you had just about every race in your school. Surely you had a look. In the dormitory. Or in the shower.'

'Yes ... But ...'

This time, as she uncrossed her legs and exposed more of her thighs, I caught a perfect view of her crotch. Smooth. Shaven. Not a trace of hair. I then thought maybe she was not an existentialist, not another Juliette Gréco. After all, women who shave their pubic hair – and armpits – are supposed to be devout Muslims.

Depilation is a sign of personal cleanliness. It reflects mental and moral health.

I erupted in cold sweat. I could feel my hands shaking. I looked at her. She smiled.

Again, I felt I had to say something. 'What's yours – name, I mean?'

She waved a dismissive hand. 'Oh, ugliest name in the world. I never use it. I prefer the names my friends give me. What do you think I should be called?'

I couldn't think of a woman's name – except my mother's. 'İpek.'

She nodded appreciatively, then raised her glass. 'Excellent. Do you think I fit the name?'

She certainly did. İpek means 'silk'. 'Oh, definitely …'

She stretched to pick up her cigarette case and lighter. 'You're so gallant …'

This time I saw the full contours of her buttocks. I was so aroused I had visions of ejaculating into my pants.

She lit a cigarette as if performing a ritual.

I suddenly thought a cigarette might help my condition. 'Can I – can I have one, too?'

'Of course.'

She craned forward, proffering me her case. As I took a cigarette, I saw her breasts. As I had first observed, not very large. But mouth-wateringly pendulous. Dark aureoles. Pointed nipples.

I caught her watching me. Again, hastily, I looked away.

She lit my cigarette. Her hand brushed against mine. 'Oh, dear. Your hands are wet.'

My hands were sopping – clammy with the sweat of excitement. 'I …'

She jumped up. 'Here you are drenched by the rain and I'm jabbering away.' She yanked my sweater off me before I could move. 'Right, let's take this off!' She clutched my shirt. 'And that!'

'It's all right.'

'No, it's not. It's soaked. Off with it!' Quickly, she undid the buttons and pulled the shirt off too.

I sat, turned into stone, unable to move.

'The vest. Wet also.' She pulled that off too. 'They'll dry in no time.'

I thought I should try and cover up my naked chest. But I couldn't move.

She ran her hands across my shoulders. 'Strong boy, aren't you? Do a lot of sport, I bet.'

'Yes.'

'Like what?'

'Swimming. Weight-lifting. Wrestling.'

'A wrestling Pomak! Imagine that!'

I looked up sharply. 'What's wrong with that?'

'Nothing. It's great. Time the Pomaks showed how strong they are.'

'Are you Pomak, too?'

'No.'

'What then?'

'A bit of everything. Must be so exciting – wrestling. Body entwined with body … Like sex, I should think …'

'I – I wouldn't know ...'

'No? Surely, you do ...'

'It's hard work, wrestling is ... Also you've got to think – the moves ahead. Like a chess player ...'

'Like a chess player? Even more exciting. Constantly changing positions. One minute on top. The next, underneath ...'

'Not quite ...'

'I bet you're good at it?'

'No. I don't think fast enough. I'm good at weight-lifting ...'

'You're so modest. Ever wrestled with a woman?'

My erection had begun to throb. 'I ... How ...?'

She chuckled. 'But you'd like to, right? You've got a lecherous mind, my boy. I can see it in your eyes ...'

I was on the verge of ejaculation. 'You can ...?'

'But that's good. That's how it should be.'

'Yes?'

She smiled and nodded, then she felt my trousers. 'What about these? They're wet, too.'

'They're all right.'

'Take them off!'

'No, please ... I'm all right ...'

'You're not shy, are you?'

'No, but ...'

She hauled me up. 'Come on, come on. No need to be coy with me.' She pulled down my trousers and saw my bulging pants. 'Oh ... Oh dear ...'

I must have blushed the colour of a sunset. But where was the darkness to rescue me? I tried to cover

my erection with my hands, but had forgotten that I
was still holding my glass. So I spilt my raki on the
carpet. I was near to tears. 'I – I'm – I'm sorry ...'

She relieved me of my cigarette. 'Lift your foot.'

I did so and she pulled off one trouser leg.

I continued mumbling. 'I'm sorry ...'

She stubbed out the cigarette. 'The other foot.'

I lifted that, too.

She pulled off the rest of my trousers.

'I'm really sorry ...'

'Don't worry. Carpets love raki.'

This time I managed to cover my erection with my
hands. 'I – I don't know what to say. I – I couldn't – can't
help ...'

She looked at my erection and burst out laughing.
'Oh, you mean that ...' She patted it. 'No need to
apologize. I'm flattered.' She collected my clothes. 'I'll
hang these up to dry. Won't be a moment ...'

I realized I was going to ejaculate. I had passed the
point of no return and was rising fast. I bit my lip in a
desperate effort to stop the eruption.

She paused by the door. 'Actually, these are so wet
they could do with a wash, too.'

'Please – no need to do anything ...'

'On the other hand, do you have to go home this
weekend?'

I started shaking. 'What?'

'You could stay here. Then I can iron them ...'

I sank on to the sofa. I was ejaculating. 'But I ...'

'You boys don't always go home at weekends, do

you? I've heard sometimes you're punished and have to stay in …'

I was coming in torrents, messing my pants. 'Yes, but …'

'Good idea, don't you think? I can ring your parents. Pretend I'm the matron. Tell them you've been detained for some misdemeanour. Easy …'

I was coming so beautifully. Yet I couldn't enjoy it. Instead of shouting deliriously I had to be quiet, feign that nothing was happening. 'I – I …'

'It'll be fun. Think about it.' She waved my clothes like a banner. 'I'll get these dry while you decide. In the meantime, fix us another drink!'

She came back a moment later. Seeing that the glasses were still empty, she gave me a quizzical look. 'No drinks?'

I had forgotten about the drinks. Perched on the edge of the sofa with my hands covering my pants, I was trying to figure out how I could leave the room and go and wash without her noticing that I had soiled myself and, once washed, how I could ask to have my clothes back. 'I – I'm sorry …'

She noticed my discomfort. 'Are you all right?'

'Yes. Yes. I – I just – need to – go to the bathroom.'

'Upstairs. Door facing you.'

I hauled myself up, still trying to cover my pants with my hands; all uncomfortably sticky.

She laughed. 'Aren't you a bashful boy!'

'I'm …'

Then she noticed. 'Oh, I see …'

'I'm sorry …'

She came up to me, pulled my hands away and inspected my pants. 'And so much of it …'

'I – I couldn't hold …'

She pulled my pants down. 'What a compliment! What an acclamation! I'm honoured …'

I tried to edge away. 'Please … I must wash …'

'And waste all this delicious cream?'

'What?'

She pushed me down on to the sofa. 'Lie down.' She pulled off my pants. 'What a feast!'

I watched in horror as I became erect again. 'What?'

She held my penis, smiling. 'Oh, what a virile boy …'

I protested meekly. 'I need to wash …'

She started caressing me. 'I'll tell you what. When I've gorged myself, I'll ring your parents. I'll tell them you're being kept in. And then …' She took me into her mouth.

I moaned and surrendered to a softness that can never be imagined, only experienced.

And in no time at all, I climaxed again.

∞∞∞∞∞∞∞∞✿∞∞∞∞∞∞∞∞

She dropped me back at school on Monday morning. We had made love all through the weekend and, by way of goodbye, just before leaving her house. She had proven to be one of those women – a rarity, as I was to discover in later years – who became aroused at the merest touch and who made love unceasingly as if born to do just that. But that morning, when, if anything, she had been even more ardent and had clung to me during her intense and repeated orgasms and had described these, using my own favourite Sufi metaphor, as 'witnessing the deity', I had begged her not to let me go. I had told her I would give up school, run away from home, beg, steal, murder, if need be, in order to remain welded to her. She had refused: that way, we would be each other's slaves, she had said; no amount of joy would compensate for the loss of freedom.

Desperately, I had changed my plea. I had promised her all the freedom in the world. I would respect her independence with devotion and patience. I would ask nothing in return except to be with her a few hours a week.

Again, she had refused, this time telling me to be true to my political beliefs. It was all very well claiming to be a devotee of Nâzım Hikmet's poetry, but I should also prove myself a practising socialist, an egalitarian who would share with his comrades anything and everything life had given him, including the woman he loved – particularly the woman he loved. After all, my chums from my dormitory – well, those she had known to date – had shown their valour by agreeing to this. More to the point, they had honoured her trust in them – as she expected I would – by maintaining complete silence about their association with her.

It was then that I had discerned the cause of the

melancholy that had devastated Agop, Cengiz, Dimitri, Eşber, İsmail and Kâzım. She had soon admitted, gently but candidly, that I was number seven out of my dormitory's complement of twenty-four. This did not indicate, she had reassured me, that I was a middle-rung lover, simply that, in the alphabetical order of first names, mine came seventh. (Even so, I agonized for years – and even quite frequently in adulthood – that being number seven was not as good as being number one, that maybe Agop, who had been number one, had surpassed us all by wresting from her a superior 'witnessing of the deity'.)

And so, that Monday morning, she dropped me at school, or, rather, at the newsagent.

The rain had cleared. And the bright sun appeared to have set aflame, as in Nâmık Kemal's famous poem, all the windows in Kandilli, across the Bosporus. The air, having acquired substance from the soft wind and sweetness from the budding flowers on the hills, felt edible. The sea was like mercury: placid, unmarked, but intimating viscid density and unyielding depths. I registered these impressions purposefully, as if taking an inventory, with the thought that this Monday morning might be – should be – my last morning on earth.

Then I saw Dimitri, Eşber, İsmail and Kâzım, respectively numbers three to six, clustered by the gate, watching me. Behind them lurked the other two: Agop, number one; Cengiz, number two. (How lucky my name didn't begin with an 'S' or a 'T' or, worse, with a 'Z' like poor Zeki – he would have been number twenty-four

– because, for one thing, cancellation of leave kept us in at school some weekends and, for another, our semester comprised eighteen weeks, which meant that even if we had not had some leave cancelled, the last six in the alphabetical order would have had to wait for the next semester …)

I approached the boys, hating them, wanting to tear them apart. I could see they were trying to read from my expression whether our beloved had discarded me as she had discarded them or had chosen to continue with me. I thought, villainously, that I would pretend I had done better than they, but I could neither find the will to break my promise to her about keeping our tryst a secret nor, had I been inclined to be so treacherous, find the energy to do so. Energy for any activity, even for a romantic suicide, I soon discovered, had deserted me. Today I am very thankful for that. Imagine how many of life's miracles I would have missed had I had the nerve to kill myself.

As I carried on walking, the boys fell in behind me. We climbed the hill without exchanging a word. We checked in at the dormitory, then went to our classes.

Thereafter, as, in the following weeks, numbers eight to thirteen joined our ranks, we maintained an obdurate silence.

Then the summer holidays arrived.

∞∞∞∞∞∞∞∞✿∞∞∞∞∞∞∞∞

When we returned in the autumn, we found out that,

to Âşık Ahmet's great fury, our dormitory had been disbanded.

That might have been bearable. But we had also lost our beloved.

We never saw Suna again.

Of course, we thirteen who had been her lovers inquired about her in the village, even shared the meagre information we received. She had left in mid-summer, suddenly and surprisingly. (According to her landlord she had more than a year to run on her tenancy.) She had not left a forwarding address.

Some of us came to believe she had left because she had met a real man and found him preferable to us boys.

Then we started hearing gossip about our 'depravity'. At first we thought Âşık Ahmet's fury had more to do with our assignations than having our dormitory disbanded. Then we reasoned that since he had tried to keep the dormitory intact, he could not have been too outraged by our activities. We further argued that, given his radical principles and his belief in the benedictions of carnal love, he might even have approved of the manner of our initiation. Therefore, we postulated, it had been other factors that had forced our beloved to leave.

Fortunately, gossip is never selective. Details of secret machinations started leaking out. And we were proven right.

A neighbour of our beloved's, having observed her weekend dalliances, had informed on her to a college teacher living in Bebek. (A denunciation borne out of spite, the gossip intimated. The neighbour, a middle-aged man who fancied himself as a Don Juan, had tried to seduce our beloved and had been rebuffed.)

The teacher, a pious American widow, alarmed that we, young and impressionable boys, would be traumatized for life with nightmares of being cooked and eaten up by a witch, had duly alerted the college governors.

Only Âşık Ahmet had defended our beloved. Ridiculing the teacher's hysteria as a hangover from the Brothers Grimm, he had argued that nasty witches were an importation that never concerned Turkish children because for them women, all women, represented love, tenderness and paradisal pleasures.

The teacher, even more shocked by Âşık Ahmet's liberalism, had then recruited a cabal of clerics of various faiths. These eminences, professional bigots all, had not only agreed with the teacher that we boys had been irreparably damaged psychologically, but also had rued the fact that, because of Turkey's secular constitution, the harlot could not be stoned to death as religious law stipulated.

Again Âşık Ahmet had risen to defend our beloved. Claiming to know her – we never found out how – he had presented her as a moral pioneer, a disciple of the philosopher Sartre and his companion, Simone de Beauvoir, who, by personal example, pointed the path to a new, tolerant and sexually liberated Europe. She was the sort of feminist modern Turkey needed in order to free our women from the taboos, inequalities and injustices by which, despite all efforts at emancipation, they were still ruled.

But the governors had refused to heed his arguments. Those who glibly take the names of Allah, Jesus and Yahweh in vain still win every disputation. Not just in Turkey, but everywhere in the world.

And so, the governors had ordered our beloved to leave Bebek; should she refuse, they had threatened, she would be handed over to the police.

∞∞∞∞∞∞⚙∞∞∞∞∞∞

One last word about our dormitory. At first those of us who had known our beloved felt relieved that the dormitory had disbanded. We had spent the summer wondering whether we could ever reforge the bonds we had had before our beloved had come into our lives or, indeed, whether we wished to do so. But after hearing the way Âşık Ahmet had defended her, we felt bereft. I am sure we still believe that if our dormitory had been left intact, we would have reclaimed the harmony we had created – if only for Âşık Ahmet's sake.

If a school dormitory can do that for one individual, couldn't the United Nations do it for all humankind?

∞∞∞∞∞∞⚙∞∞∞∞∞∞

Thus my first, my unforgettable love ended, like most loves, in dreadful heartache. I felt inconsolable, damaged beyond repair, cursed for ever.

But then, like all damaged goods, like those cracked urns of antiquity, I became an object that had been well used. I attained the wisdom of experience and developed a heart where every visitor could sign his or her name.

Above all, I learned about love, particularly about carnal love. I learned that it is a hunger which, if not fed, emaciates and kills just as mercilessly as the hunger for food and water. And I learned to thank God for instilling in us such a hunger.

I learned that no joy on earth compares with the joy two people experience as they lie naked and awash with bodily fluids. Feeling alive can mean only that.

I learned that there is no holier creation than the human body.

I learned that slow movements are beautiful, that gently humming interlocked bodies generate the sort of sublime electricity that the world needs, but which it rejects because it believes in perpetual activity which, invariably, means perpetual conflict.

I learned that there are as many love games as stars in heaven, that one can conjoin with one's partner like a centipede or like a bull and that, mercifully, there are still free-spirited men and women who are trying to find new ways of making love.

Let me leave you with this vision: I am stretched out on a sofa. My beloved is determined to assess my age. She has an infallible method for doing so: the way they ascertain a tree's age: by counting the rings in its trunk. Consequently, she has my member in her mouth.

Her lips are thick with lipstick. Starting from the base of my penis, her mouth ambles upwards. At each half-centimetre, her lips imprint a red ring around the shaft. She continues until she runs out of length. She counts the rings. On this occasion they add up to thirty-six. (An hour ago, the number had been forty-one.) She cuddles up to me. She coos. 'Thirty-odd rings. What a mature oak in one so young!'

We embrace. She smears her breasts and vagina with rose-petal jam. She squats above my face so that I can imbibe her splendour. She lowers herself on to my mouth and lets me lap up every bit of the rose-petal jam. Then she mounts me and, as she begins to rock, she rubs her breasts all over my face. I am in such ecstasy that I am ready to die. In fact, I want to die, because I know I shall never again find this heaven, the Seventh Heaven.

9: Attila

Cracked Vessels from the Same Ruin

Orhan arrived at Konstantin Efendi's *lokanta* early one Sunday morning, long before the old Romanian or any member of his extended family had come down from their flat above the restaurant to start preparations for the day. Squatting by the main entrance and barely moving a muscle, he waited – almost two hours – until Ebony Nermin had the wits to bang on Konstantin Efendi's door and shout that he had a visitor. By that time, most of the neighbourhood – and certainly, we youngsters – had gathered in the square and were offering opinions about who the stranger was and where he might have come from. Many, judging by the way the man could sit on his haunches seemingly for ever, maintained he was from eastern Anatolia, probably a labourer who had come to Istanbul in search of work. Others, struck by his high Asiatic cheekbones, suggested he was a Kurd from Persia or Azerbaijan. Yet others, pointing at the stranger's grey Hollywood-style suit with broad white stripes like lanes on a running track, at his azure tie hanging loosely on his cream shirt – the shirt itself wide open to display the thick fleece of black hair on his chest – at his patent shoes shining like metallic roofs on sunny days, and at his thickly brilliantined hair, contended he was a gangster, probably a member of the Cossack mafia. Surely, he had come to demand protection money from Konstantin Efendi. After all, the old Romanian, whose Balkan cuisine had become popular with the smart clique, was minting it. Not to mention the fact that Cossacks could never stomach Romanians because the latter maintained that their religious truth, specially blessed by the patriarchate of Constantinople, the bedrock of Holy Roman orthodoxy, was Absolutely Immaculate, whereas the Cossack – and other Slavic orthodoxies – had been defiled over many centuries by countless depraved heretics.

Eventually, Konstantin Efendi, still in his pyjamas and escorted by his sons, nephews and mammoth wife, Liliana, came down.

Towering over the stranger, their voices deepened by some decibels for effect, they fired their questions.

'Who are you?'

'What do you want?'

The stranger, languidly smoothing his robust, bull's-horns moustache, pulled himself up and smiled like earth after rain.

The fluidity of his movements induced Ebony Nermin to volunteer her opinion. 'Clark Gable. But with a real moustache. Not a piddling eyebrow over the lips.'

The stranger, broadening his smile, proffered his hand to Konstantin Efendi. 'Orhan.'

Konstantin Efendi, not much thinner than his wife, ignored the gesture and pushed closer to him. 'Family name?'

Orhan, unperturbed by Konstantin Efendi's effort to intimidate, shrugged. 'Just that. Orhan. Never had another name.'

A quiver of pity streaked across Konstantin Efendi's face. He was sensible enough to know that, even these days, there were still people bereft of lineage – and not just in Turkey. 'What do you want, Orhan?'

'I have a proposition.'

'Oh, yes?!'

Orhan turned to Konstantin Efendi's eldest son, who was carrying a bunch of keys. 'Open up. Let's escape the heat.'

The latter responded as if to a command and unlocked the *lokanta*'s door.

Orhan sauntered in and picked a table at the back of the dining area.

Konstantin Efendi and his clan followed as if Orhan were an inspector from the municipality.

The rest of us, led by Ebony Nermin – always the impetuous one for having a mind that lagged marginally behind ours – piled in behind them.

Two men placed Orhan's accent as north-east Anatolian. They were wrong. It was southern, from the Toros mountains, but from an isolated community. I knew about accents. I had spent half my life listening to comedy sketches on the radio.

Orhan sat down, pulled the chairs on his flanks closer to himself and rested his arms on them. He beckoned us as if we were long-lost friends. 'Konstantin Efendi – let's have some raki. To sprinkle my proposition.'

This time Liliana towered over him with all her 140 kilos. 'First – the proposition.'

Orhan beamed at her. '*Madamitza* – you have a beautiful voice ...'

'Do I?'

Orhan, smiling, took out his cigarettes and offered her one. 'And powerful. Have you ever thought of singing, *Madamitza*? You'd have the nation at your feet ...'

Liliana, who normally treated strangers as if her father owned the mountains and she the hills, relished the compliment. She refused the cigarette with a coquettish shake of the head. 'The proposition ...'

Orhan lit his cigarette. 'Of course, *Madamitza*. But please forgive me if, the next second, I die of thirst.'

Liliana, now smiling, gestured impatiently at her younger son. 'Get some raki!'

Konstantin Efendi, disconcerted by his wife's docility, barked. 'On the double!'

The youth fetched a bottle of raki, a glass and some ice.

Orhan wetted his mouth with an ice-cube, then dropped it in the glass. He poured himself a large measure and drank it in one go. He refilled his glass – this time, with the normal quantity. 'I am a *kabadayı*, Konstantin Efendi. *Madamitza* ...'

Kabadayı, literally 'rough uncle', has many connotations; but, give or take a nuance, they all mean 'lout', 'tough guy' and similar species.

Konstantin Efendi nodded. 'So I see.'

'To be precise: I am a *kabadayı* of the old school. In the classical mould, you understand. Nothing like the ruffians, hooligans and villains who have stolen our good name.'

'I didn't know there was an old school of *kabadayı*.'

'Sadly, dying out. But not quite yet. I'm one of the best, if I may be permitted to boast. A professional, in today's parlance ...'

Konstantin Efendi smiled derisively. 'A professional?'

Orhan sipped his drink. 'I have come to offer my services.'

Konstantin Efendi started laughing. 'That's very considerate ...'

Orhan ignored the derision. 'You have a classy establishment. You might need a strong arm ...'

Konstantin Efendi pointed at his sons and nephews. 'I have all the strong arms I need.'

Orhan sipped his drink. 'I've heard talk of Cossack gangs ...'

Konstantin Efendi scoffed. 'And you think you can

deal with them? On your own?'

Orhan put his glass down, then abruptly – without even getting up – struck the chair to his right with the side of his hand.

The chair, made of wood, but sturdy, broke into pieces.

Orhan smiled. 'Yes.'

A silence ensued.

We were all stunned. Though our neighbourhood was not a particularly rough one, we had had our share of brawls, even witnessed the spillage of blood. But we had never seen such strength and authority, such a spontaneous and casual explosion of power.

Orhan resumed drinking. 'For your peace of mind – I'm cheap as *kabadayı* go. I don't ask for wages. Nor a cut from the takings. Just my daily bread – melon, cheese, olives, a piece of fish or meat now and again. And raki. My portion is a bottle a day. I don't need lodgings either. I'll sleep in a corner. I got used to that in the army ...'

Konstantin Efendi found his voice. 'I don't understand...'

'Money's never interested me, Konstantin Efendi. I'm happy without it.'

'But why – such a job?'

'It's my vocation. Where I come from, being *kabadayı* is considered an art. Like playing the *kanun*. That's good enough for me.'

'Where do you come from?'

'Here and there. And everywhere. Prison even.'

'Prison?'

Orhan smiled sadly. 'Compulsory – in this country. Like primary school.'

'What were you in for?'

'Matter of honour. What else?'

Another silence ensued. Serving a prison sentence, in Turkey, on a matter of honour – which invariably meant avenging insults, rapes and wrongs committed against family members – made a person special. He joined the elite – like poets, artists and leftists.

Konstantin Efendi faced him solemnly. 'If I refuse? Call the police?'

Again, without any warning, Orhan struck at the chair to his left. That, too, smashed into pieces. 'It's your prerogative …'

Konstantin Efendi bellowed, 'That's two you've broken!'

Orhan sipped his drink. 'I'll repair them. I'm good at that, too.'

Konstantin Efendi looked at his wife, hoping she might have something to say.

Orhan got up, fetched another glass, filled it with ice and raki, waited for the drink to turn cloudy and luminously white, then handed it to the old Romanian. 'Here, some lion's spunk! Let's seal the deal.' Suddenly abashed, he turned to Liliana. 'Forgive me, *Madamitza* … I meant angel's milk …'

Liliana waved her hand flirtatiously. 'I prefer lion's spunk.'

Orhan nodded courteously. 'Spoken like a true

lioness, *Madamitza* ... May Allah be praised for creating the likes of you ...'

Noticing that Konstantin Efendi had been listening to the exchange with disapproval, Orhan winked at him.

Even more confused, Konstantin Efendi winked back.

Orhan turned to us. 'Everybody – drink up! Only make sure you pay!'

∞∞∞∞∞∞⊛∞∞∞∞∞∞

To give Konstantin Efendi his due, he not only refused payment for the drinks, but also closed the restaurant for lunch – a very lucrative time for business. When some of the neighbours, happily afloat on raki, teased him about his generosity and asked him why he had decided to pamper the stranger he, too, looked puzzled. One son, trying to answer for him, declared that he had a big heart – as everybody knew. Another argued that his father had admired Orhan's audacity, a quality that he had been trying to inculcate, not very successfully, into the men in his family. A third son, much the wiliest, contended that his father must have engaged Orhan as a warden; talk of gangs – and not just Cossacks, but also Albanians and others – extorting money from businesses were not idle rumours; the protection racket was becoming a growing industry. Conceivably, the presence of a *kabadayı* might deter some of these gangs or, at least, in the event of an attack, give Konstantin

Efendi enough time to alert the authorities.

But only Ebony Nermin appeared to have fathomed the real reason. 'Because the Efendi likes him. That's why he's hired him.'

Big Liliana, perplexed as ever – though not as furious as she had been when her husband had closed the restaurant for lunch – turned to her as to an oracle. 'But he's only just met him!'

Ebony Nermin nodded ingenuously. 'So have I! And I adore him!'

No one dared challenge that. Ebony Nermin might be slow in thought but, like the tortoise who raced the hare, she always got to the finishing line first. According to her only relative – an old aunt who had recently died – this was a gift she had inherited from her Nubian great-grandmother, who had been a famous oracle in her time and had saved the lives of at least three sultans from Seraglio intrigues. (As it happened, Mahmut the Simurg, the storyteller, had based one of his prophetesses on this great-grandmother.)

'I will be his wife,' concluded Ebony Nermin.

I, Attila, heard her and felt very jealous. Like every lad in the neighbourhood, I loved Ebony Nermin, even though, at almost nineteen, she was a few years older than I was. I loved her not because she was beautiful – there were other beautiful girls around. Nor because she had contours like Ava Gardner – though that delighted me, too. But because she was good through and through. A child spirit, as it is said. The only person who believed everything she was told and trusted everybody who crossed her path. She always smiled, always had something nice to say to everybody, always touched your hand gently when she greeted you, always showed her private parts on request (and never asked for money like some of the other girls). And she never ever snitched on you.

So, forlorn, I hung around Orhan. I had intended to be rude to him – maybe even glare at him and warn him that, in a few years, I would be his adversary.

To my surprise, soon after he settled in, he regaled people by reciting poetry to them. And he recited well – even shed tears now and again. He seemed to know every line written by Orhan Veli as well as many poems by Nâmık Kemal, Fâzıl Hüsnü Dağlarca and lots of others. When people asked how he came to know these verses, he said he had learned them in the army, where the government had finally done its duty and taught him how to read and write. In fact, it was his love for Orhan Veli, he confessed, that had made him take the poet's name as his own. This statement, contradicting his earlier contention that Orhan was the only name he had ever had, elicited a barrage of questions about his real identity.

Which just made him laugh. 'Orhan is what I answer to!' he avowed repeatedly.

That merely increased his mystery.

And soon, inevitably, we boys, graciously gave up on

Ebony Nermin. We saw, within days, that she truly adored Orhan. She would get up at the crack of dawn, wash quickly, run to the *lokanta*, find him wherever he had chosen to sleep – the yard in the summer, the kitchen in the winter – and gently wake him up. As he performed his ablutions, she would prepare his breakfast. He was a frugal eater – some bread, cheese, olives and onions. Then she would line up two glasses of raki – raki got a person going much better than coffee, he claimed – and three cigarettes which he smoked one after another to open up his chest. After that, he would move to his table which was at the back of the restaurant, near the kitchen, but with a clear view of the dining area, and set up his stall for the day. He would put a stool – he once explained that people got up faster from a stool than from a chair – at the head of the table, then place two chairs – chairs that he might have to smash up as a warning to disputants – on either side. Thereafter, he would line up two empty raki bottles on the table, each within easy reach of a hand. (He would keep the bottle he was drinking from underneath the table, in an ice bucket.) Finally, he would strap his stiletto on to his left calf – he was left-handed – then, almost ceremoniously, perch on the stool. Thereafter, he would shut his eyes and meditate, for a quarter of an hour or so, to attain the *kabadayı* spirit. Ebony Nermin would sit on the floor by his legs and spend the time until nine o'clock either staring at him in adoration or telling him things in her candid way that would make him smile with a tenderness I have never seen in another man.

Around nine o'clock, Liliana and her sons and nephews would come down to clean up the place and set the tables. (Orhan was never involved in the running of the restaurant; that was not part of a *kabadayı*'s duties.) At ten Konstantin Efendi would bring in fresh produce from the market and the whole family would start cooking for lunch. At this juncture, Orhan would go out into the yard and train. And we boys, or rather those of us whose families could not pay the fees for secondary school, would watch him. At midday, Ebony Nermin would go to work – she cleaned people's houses – and Orhan would return to his table and sit there until four in the afternoon, when the restaurant closed for a couple of hours to prepare for the evening trade. During this interlude, he and Ebony Nermin would retire to their quarters – which Konstantin Efendi had provided for them by allowing Orhan to partition the storeroom – and talk about babies and the future. (Yes, within three months, they had married. The wedding reception given by Konstantin Efendi and Liliana, to which all the friends and regulars of the restaurant had been invited, is now part of the neighbourhood's folklore.)

On the dot at seven in the evening, Orhan, like a genial janissary officer, would take up his post again and, sipping his raki, would keep falcon eyes, until closing time – around midnight – on customers and swarms of itinerant vendors selling flowers, lottery tickets, prints of the Exordium and beads against the evil eye. He would be particularly vigilant when the Gypsy belly-dancers put on their show. These artists, shuttling between all the restaurants in the vicinity, were constantly pestered by lewd, drunken men.

At about ten, Ebony Nermin, having finished work, would return to the *lokanta* , where she hung around until closing time. Konstantin Efendi always offered her food, but she never ate until after midnight, when Orhan took his second meal of the day. (To keep lithe and alert, he never ate on duty.)

Their love, as Liliana told everybody, was more miraculous than the virgin birth. Where or when had anybody seen a man devote himself to a woman as if she held in her person all the blessings of the world? Where or when had anybody seen a man caress his woman's face and kiss her spontaneously, every other minute? And not just her cheeks, but her lips, arms, hands, fingers, knees, even feet? Even more to the point, where or when had anybody seen a man have his woman walk by his side, index fingers locked tightly, instead of a pace or two behind him? And in public! In front of everybody! Even in front of the imams! Not to mention the police, gendarmes and government officials!

∞∞∞∞∞∞∞❈∞∞∞∞∞∞∞

A year passed.

Long before then Orhan had ceased to be an outsider. One of Konstantin Efendi's sons and two of his nephews had emigrated to America to make what they called 'real money'. (By all accounts, they were well on their way to achieving their objective with a chain of hamburger parlours.) This made many in our community assume that, when Konstantin Efendi and Liliana decided to retire, they would offer Orhan a partnership with their remaining sons and nephews. Indeed, they had grown so attached to him that they treated him as a member of the family. Most of the neighbourhood would be hard put to remember that Orhan was still an employee, still the Romanian's *kabadayı*.

By then also, Orhan and Ebony Nermin had crowned their marriage with a baby daughter and were keen to have more children. (After her marriage, by Liliana's edict, Ebony Nermin was called simply Nermin.)

Orhan and Nermin proved a perfect couple – certainly the happiest the old-timers had ever seen. But neither his love for Nermin nor his responsibilities as a father slackened Orhan's devotion to his job. In fact, he manned his post with even greater vigilance. For in those days we kept hearing that a consortium of gangs, lusting after the protection racket's easy loot, was parcelling out Istanbul into exclusive territories.

<hr/>

Some hours after his daughter was born, Orhan came to the damp basement that my father called home. Orhan had just closed the *lokanta*, but knew I always stayed up late, listening to the radio. (In those days I wanted to be an actor, better still, a comedian, and was trying to learn the various regional accents as well as the grandiose

Turkish of the newscasters.)

He had brought a couple of bottles of raki and carried an endless smile such as Allah must have worn after creating the universe. He announced that the world was blessed with a new bloom. Both Nermin and Çiçek – 'flower', that was the name they had given the baby – were doing fine. We had cause for celebration. Moreover, by sunrise, I would have learned an important lesson: how to drink without getting drunk.

So we went to the beach, sat by the water and, watching the constant traffic of ships through the straits, imbibed the lion's spunk.

When I got drunk without being drunk, I plucked up the courage to ask him why he had chosen me, of all people, to join him in such an important celebration. I was a reticent person; though I was a fixture in the neighbourhood, I was a stray; much of the time, I kept to myself, watched and observed. Some people thought I was the possessor of an evil eye and asked me what sort of thoughts I manufactured behind my eyes – which left me all the more mute. Even my father wouldn't have anything to do with me.

To my surprise, Orhan said he and I were kindred spirits. Cracked vessels from a ruin somewhere out there. Trying to carry water for good people. Dripping from every fracture, but still able to offer mouthfuls to the thirsty. Then, before we could quench one soul: bang, pulverized by villains. Reduced to useless dust in the wind. In one word: *kabadayı*.

I asked him to elaborate on that. Then I passed out.

And elaborate he did, over several weeks, as he continued teaching me how to drink and keep upright.

The *kabadayı* are not villains. They are like the outlaws of bygone times – like Pîr Sultan Abdal, Köroğlu, Karacaoğlan and Şeyh Bedreddin – who defended the people against cruel rulers, corrupt officials and rapacious landowners. In our times, of course, services such as the police, the gendarmerie and the night *bekçi* should be performing these duties. But no matter how diligent these forces are, they are not effective enough to deter the wicked. Moreover, they are riddled with corruption. So people still suffer, whether they are peasants or fishermen, poets or musicians, employees or shopkeepers. The real outlaws, it should not be forgotten, are still the Establishment, still the cruel leaders, corrupt officials and rapacious landowners. While the poor lose their last rags, these either put on new tuxedos, uniforms and turbans or change names.

So, to address these injustices, the *kabadayı* have to continue to exist.

The *kabadayı* have commandments just like in the Sacred Books. But this Rule has not been written down. Since blind obeisance to canon has always led to oppression, the *kabadayı* have chosen to keep their tenets hidden in their hearts.

It could be said that the *kabadayı* are born with their special talents; they can't be formed or trained like people in other trades. In this they are like master poets and musicians. Many become aware of their gifts early on in life. Others are so humble that they choose to disbelieve their intuition. (Orhan affirmed I was one such.) Fortunately, the master *kabadayı* are constantly on the look-out for new blood and soon gather these self-effacing men to the fraternity. Needless to say, talent does not always fulfil its promise. Thus, before declaring that a candidate possesses the *kabadayı* spirit, a master oversees him for a time; hasty judgements always carry seeds from the Devil. Since, like countless false men of God, there are countless false *kabadayı* also – all of them self-declared, of course – a lengthy examination of the candidate's soul is imperative. In the main, allowing for the usual beginner's strains of shyness and humility, it takes a master some six months before he can be sure that his candidate has the makings of a *kabadayı*. After that, the master imparts the *Kabadayı* Rule and the initiate takes it into his heart.

And Orhan chose none other than me, Attila, as his candidate – me, nobody else, not even Tarzan Hamdi, the local daredevil.

And over many glasses of raki, as I finally learned how to drink and keep upright, I received the *Kabadayı* Rule.

'First and foremost, believe in Allah – even when, because evil fares better than good, it is impossible to believe in Him. The alternative, moaning and cursing, is a waste of energy. *Kabadayı* never squander energy.

'Therefore, always shun money. It rots the mind.

'Be tranquil. Perfect the art of sitting alone peacefully.

But keep watch always. Observe people's every move and consider the purpose behind it. You will realize everyone is searching for something.

'Train every day.'

'Never start a fight. Try to avoid them as best as you can. Offer your adversaries raki and, to pacify them, serve a portion larger than yours. Always pay for the drinks; but when such a gesture might be considered an insult, allow your opponents the privilege of that civility. If these courtesies fail, tell them you still wish to be friends, that you are even prepared to entrust your throat to them by allowing them to shave you. If that, too, fails, change tack, warn your opponents you are likely to cause them serious injury. As proof, smash a chair. Or bend iron bars. Or lift cars. Or catch wasps with your mouth. As a last resort, play the fool, pull faces, act the madman.

'However, if these warnings also go unheeded and you are forced to fight, fight like a demon.

'Occasionally, you will meet adversaries whose souls have turned to stone. You'll know the moment you see them that you will have to fight them. Tackle these people by fuelling their anger first. Mock them, insult them, offer them dribbles of raki instead of generous portions. When blood rushes to a man's head, it veils his eyes and he charges in different directions.

'Never run away, never ask for mercy.

'But always grant mercy. Mercy is the *kabadayı*'s only currency. Be extravagant with it as if you have only a day to live because usually there isn't a tomorrow.

'Never be timid about weeping in public when affected by people's joy or misfortune or by their songs and poems or by their workmanship and art. A *kabadayı* is not *kabadayı* unless he lets his emotions flow.

'Never hurt women, children, old people or animals.

'Be clean and dress well at all times.

'Grow a big moustache. Moustaches reflect integrity. But make sure you always trim it. Like circumcision and paring the nails, that is part of the Prophet Muhammet's prescription for personal cleanliness and for mental and moral health.

'Show the hair on your chest. In summer it will glisten with sweat and dazzle the enemy. In winter it will gather icicles and its din, like cymbals announcing the last judgement, will make them turn tail.

'Never masturbate. That offends Allah and women.

'Eat frugally. A bloated bear cannot dance. Drink raki, never wine. Wine muddies the mind. Raki clears it. But make sure it's pure. Lion's spunk or tiger's milk. Not ass's piss.

'Never carry firearms. They are cowards' weapons.

'But strap a knife to your calf and always have empty bottles within reach. Use the knife only when you must.

'Never kill. Not even if you're dying. Why go to the other world carrying the additional burden of your enemy's miserable soul?'

Nearly another year passed.

Nermin was pregnant again.

By then, I looked upon Orhan as my only family – as the mother, brothers and sisters, yes, even the father, I had always longed for. In fact, I had a father, Ragıp. I also had a couple of uncles, Cemal and Bahadur. Good men, all of them. But I had always felt I was of no interest to them. Cemal and Bahadur, my mother's brothers, were mariners and, consequently, always away on one ship or another. On the occasions they happened to wash ashore in Istanbul, they spent their time either looking for another ship or gambling. My father, originally from eastern Turkey, had lost all his relatives in the Erzincan earthquake of '39. But he had kept faith with life and had felt saved when he had married my mother, a native of neighbouring İzmit who had found work in a shoe factory in Istanbul. According to Uncle Bahadur, my birth had been touch-and-go for my mother and, thereafter, she had been unable to hold a foetus. Then, one dreadful winter, tuberculosis had carried her off. I was six at the time, an only child.

After her death, my father more or less gave up. He had been a public scribe during his married years, but abandoned that as too harrowing because most of the letters he was asked to write imparted terrible news like dire poverty, hunger, eviction, deaths, particularly children's deaths. (They still remember him around the Yeni Cami, the mosque at the end of Galata Bridge, as having a special flair for phrasing condolences.) Eventually, he found a job as a caretaker in a block of flats – the one where that famous *kanun*-player, Handan Ramazan, lives. So he would come home once a week, on Fridays, after prayers. He would make me a meal – very lovingly, as if to tell me that this was the only treat he could give me – then go out. First to a licensed brothel – they were relatively cheap – then to a *meyhane* to get drunk. (His weekly visits to the brothels, people told me, were his attempt at preserving his sanity. There was no other way a man who could not find a wife or bring himself to marry again could survive.) Late in the night, he would return – tottering. He would allow me to undress him and put him to bed. But I don't think he ever slept. Then, at dawn, he would slip out quietly and go back to being a caretaker. So we hardly talked. Or shook hands. He never patted me on the back or ruffled my hair or pinched my cheek as fathers do. The only time we touched was when I helped him to bed. Then, as I undressed him, he would put his head on my shoulder and weep silently. I hesitate to admit it, but I loved those moments. Not only because they gave me a sense of his warmth and love, but also because I knew he was trying to say things to me, like maybe he was sorry for being such a wreck, or that maybe if I stuck by him, he might change, might manage to crawl out from under the weight of all those he had buried.

And then Orhan appeared. And filled my life. And told me we were alike.

Not just a man who was clear water all the way down to his innards and all the way up to his very soul. But also a loving man. A man who hugged me like a mother

– who hugged everybody like a mother. A man who treated his woman as his greatest treasure, as his equal, as the meaning of life, as someone more sacred than the deity. A man who taught me the *Kabadayı* Rule and how to stand on my own and everything else I wanted to know. Who listened to the radio with me, took an interest in my dreams of becoming a comedian, heard me practising accents, praised me when I did well. Who patted me on the back, ruffled my hair, pinched and kissed my cheek – often for no reason, but just because he liked me. Who asked me if I had tumbled with a woman yet or whether I was carrying a torch for some *houri*. In short, a parent such as we imagine Allah to be.

And so he became my mother and father, my sisters and brothers, and all the countless relatives who had spent an eternity clinging to a cloud, fretting over me.

He even became my son and my daughter. The children I will never have. That's how well he taught me how to love.

⚬⚬⚬⚬⚬⚬⚬⚬❀⚬⚬⚬⚬⚬⚬⚬⚬

Then darkness came.

It was a balmy Saturday night in July, soon after eleven, when the late diners were eagerly awaiting their *Bela Rugosi* – the *lokanta*'s special dessert, which, Konstantin Efendi swore, had been created by a French chef for Vlad the Impaler, alias Count Dracula.

I was working in the restaurant. On Orhan's

recommendation, Konstantin Efendi had hired me part-time. I did menial tasks: clearing dishes, laying tables, serving drinks. And I loved doing it because I was in Orhan's orbit.

To add to my happiness, Nermin, too, helped out in the restaurant. I was thus able to drool over Çiçek as she slept or played her strange infant's games. Nermin had become like an elder sister. And Çiçek, who seldom cried, but busily observed the world around her – and smiled whenever she caught sight of someone – had become as precious to me as if she were my own flesh and blood.

They sauntered in, as if they owned the sky. Five fellows, one with his head shaven, like a corsair from bygone times. Hefty bruisers. Not Cossacks, as I had first thought. Real gangsters. Ready to gouge out a man's eyes for nothing.

They sat at a table near the entrance.

I glanced at Orhan.

He had seen them, of course, and was scrutinizing them. Then he nodded imperceptibly, indicating that I should attend to them.

I approached their table. 'Good evening, gentlemen. The kitchen is about to close. But if you order quickly ...'

The shaven-headed man, obviously the leader, barked. 'Get Konstantin Efendi!'

'Sir?'

'Get him, you little bastard! Tell him Octopus wants to see him.'

As I backed away towards the kitchen, Orhan whispered. 'Ease everybody into the kitchen. Tell them to stay there!'

I nodded.

'Then serve those pigs raki. A droplet. No more. Tell them it's from me.'

'But that would be insulting …'

'That's the idea.'

'Men with stone hearts – right?'

'Right.'

'That's what I thought. Soon as I saw them.'

'Go on – move! Then get into the kitchen, too.'

'I can help you …'

'You are. Do as I say!'

I gathered everybody and pushed them into the kitchen. They stood there, huddled by the door.

The men watched, amused.

I poured the raki as Orhan had instructed me and served the men.

The one calling himself Octopus stared at the drinks. 'What's this?'

'For you.' I pointed at Orhan. 'From him.'

Octopus looked at Orhan, then began laughing.

Orhan, sipping his raki, smiled back, then gestured at me to go into the kitchen.

I did so, reluctantly.

Octopus stood up and poured the drinks on the floor. 'Sense of humour – I like that.'

The patrons, sniffing trouble, shifted about uneasily. Some half rose, ready to leave.

Octopus addressed them. 'Off you go, people! We have some business here. If you haven't paid, don't worry. Konstantin Efendi can afford it.'

The patrons stared at each other, unable to decide.

Orhan addressed them. 'Good patrons, take a breather by the sea. Then come back. Say, in a quarter of an hour.'

The patrons, mostly regulars and chummy with Orhan, left in an orderly stampede.

Octopus turned to his companions and pointed at Orhan. 'This must be the *kabadayı* we heard about …'

The men sniggered.

Octopus, assuming a mocking tone, addressed Orhan. 'Honourable sir, we've come to collect from the Romanian shit-face. Insurance premium. He pays up, we protect this place. We see to it that not even a toothpick is broken. With your permission, naturally …'

Orhan pursed his lips as if trying to think up an answer; then, shrugging his shoulders, he started pulling faces and blabbering.

Infuriated, Octopus bellowed, 'Hey, vomit of a syphilitic cunt! I'm talking to you!'

Orhan gabbled and prattled even more dementedly.

Octopus nudged one of his companions. 'Shut the fucker!' He turned to the others and indicated the kitchen. 'Bring the old snot!'

As the men moved forwards, Orhan eased himself off the stool and roared, 'That's far enough!'

Surprised by the unexpected authority in his voice, the men stopped.

Orhan waved them away. 'Get back slowly. Collect your Octopus. And goodbye ...'

The men, hesitating, looked at each other, then at Octopus.

The latter screeched, 'Cut the catamite's balls off!'

They launched themselves forwards.

Then everything happened so quickly that I almost missed it.

Orhan kicked his stool in the direction of the three men moving towards the kitchen, tripping them up. Almost at the same time, he lashed out at the fourth man, striking him on the bridge of his nose and felling him. Still in the same movement, he grabbed the empty bottles on his table and shattered them on the heads of two of the assailants he had tripped up. As the latter passed out, he seized them by their hair and smashed their faces on the head of the man he had knocked over with the stool.

When he straightened up a moment later, he had unsheathed his knife and was pointing it at Octopus.

Octopus stood frozen, staring incredulously at his prostrate companions.

Orhan, drawing circles in the air with his knife, addressed Octopus. 'I could carve my name on your chest. But that would be foolish. The police would get involved. Konstantin Efendi would have all sorts of problems.'

Octopus hissed, 'I'll get you!'

Orhan grinned. 'Ssshhhh. I'll shit in my pants ...'

Some of the men, groaning, were trying to lift

themselves off the floor.

Orhan prodded them with his foot. 'Come on, pick up your men! And out!'

It took Octopus several minutes to drag out his companions. As they piled into the Pontiac parked by the restaurant's entrance, he turned round and, putting thumb to teeth, mimed the 'revenge' sign.

By then, we had all burst out of the kitchen and surrounded Orhan. But he was pushing us away, trying to get to a bucket of sawdust.

Reading his mind, I grabbed the bucket and spread the sawdust thickly on the floor where the men had bled.

And just in time, too. Because a moment later, several police from the local station burst in.

Some patrons, who had obviously called them, followed.

The detective in charge barked, 'What's going on?'

Konstantin Efendi pushed forward. 'Ah, Detective Dursun ...'

'What's all this commotion?'

Konstantin Efendi stared at him innocently. 'What commotion?'

Detective Dursun, uttering the sigh of the long-suffering policeman, started looking around, searching, no doubt, for some evidence of trouble. 'The commotion they could hear even in Romania, Konstantin Efendi ...'

Konstantin Efendi put his hand to his forehead, as if suddenly remembering. 'Oh, you mean the drunkards.

Ah, yes – a noisy lot! I told them what's what and they left.'

Detective Dursun turned towards Orhan.

Suddenly I noticed Orhan was trying to hide his knife in the small of his back. Realizing that if the police found the knife on him, he could be arrested for carrying a weapon, I stepped forward as if to clear the way for the detective. Then I tripped myself up and as I stumbled forward I shunted one of the policemen on to the detective. As the latter tried to keep his balance, I took the knife from Orhan and put it in my apron pocket.

I turned to Detective Dursun, looking as contrite as I could. 'Sorry, sir ...'

He glared at me disdainfully.

I backed into the kitchen, still apologizing. Keeping a distracted mien, I went to the sink and put the knife on the pile of cutlery waiting to be washed.

Detective Dursun stopped by the upturned stool and the broken bottles. 'What's all this?'

Orhan picked up the stool. 'Someone must have knocked it over, sir.'

'The broken bottles?'

Liliana came forward, giggling. 'Those drunks. They were playing at being Russian. Drinking, then smashing bottles ...'

'They drank only two bottles?'

Liliana turned to him indignantly. 'I stopped them smashing others. Two bottles is two too many.'

Detective Dursun did not look convinced. He turned

to Orhan again. 'Did you use them in a fight?'

'Me, sir? No, sir!'

'*Kabadayı* – isn't that what they call you?'

'They tease me, sir.'

'Tease you?'

'I'm the night-watchman ... So people poke fun ...'

'What's your name?'

'Orhan, sir.'

'Orhan what?'

'Orhan Veli. Like the poet.'

Detective Dursun smiled derisively. 'Really?'

'That's why I know all his works by heart. Many others, too ...'

'Trying to be funny?'

'No, sir. Listen ... *"The things we have done for our country, some of us died and some of us declaimed ..."*[1] Beautiful, isn't it?'

'Do you have a gun? A knife?'

'Me, sir? Never, sir.'

Detective Dursun turned to one of his men. 'Search him.'

The latter did so. Orhan co-operated fully.

The policeman shook his head. 'Clean, sir.'

Detective Dursun, still dissatisfied but unable to find anything incriminating, turned to Konstantin Efendi. 'Something happened here. I smell it. So be warned. I'll be watching ...'

He gathered his men and left.

The patrons settled down.

Others, who had been lingering outside, wafted in.

Konstantin Efendi, almost in tears with relief, hugged Orhan. Then he and Liliana went round the tables, offering sparkling wine on the house.

On his way back to his table to resume his watch, Orhan clasped me to his chest. 'Thank you, brother ...'

I tried to shrug, but I felt so gratified that I froze.

Then Nermin kissed me on the cheek. 'Dear, dear Attila ...'

Even more flustered, I hurried into the kitchen and looked for something to do.

⁂

The *lokanta* burned down in the early hours of the following Saturday. I wasn't working there that night – Friday is my father's night off – so I can't say I could have prevented the fire if I'd been there. Yet I knew, all that Friday – sensed it – that something terrible was going to happen. But I thought it would happen to my father. He would be hit by a bus or suffer a heart attack. He had become a heavy drinker and there seemed nothing I – or anybody else – could do to dissuade him from killing himself.

Those who saw the blaze said how quickly it had consumed the *lokanta*. The time it takes a match to burn out. Or a star to fall. Or a pan of oil to burst into flames.

A pan of oil that caught fire was assumed to be the cause. Somebody left it on the cooker, forgot to turn off the gas – and boom! Even though Konstantin Efendi and all the staff swore that this sort of negligence could never occur. No restaurateur would close up before all the cookers were turned off and the cooking utensils washed up and stored away. That's rule number one. Even beginners know that, let alone old hands like Konstantin Efendi.

I knew Konstantin Efendi was right. But maybe … So I cursed Providence for not working that night. Had I been there, I would have checked the cookers – several times. I always did.

Moreover, had I been working that night, I might have spotted something else, maybe even what caused the fire. I might have spotted, for instance, a car driving away, the very Pontiac a courting couple claimed to have seen parked by Lovers' Lane – the secluded footpath, not far from the restaurant. If it had been Octopus's Pontiac, I would have known. I had memorized its number when I watched the gang pile into it after the trouncing Orhan had given them.

At the very least, if I had been working that night, I might have seen the fire on my way home and rushed back. I might have got there in time to save Orhan and Nermin … and the child who would have been born in a few months.

But as they burnt to death, I was putting my father to bed and listening to his silent weeping.

✺

This is how they died.

The fire started around 1:30 AM, supposedly in the kitchen area.

Liliana, being an insomniac, had not fallen asleep and noticed smoke wafting through the floorboards of her bedroom, which was just above the kitchen. She alerted her husband and the rest of the family and they all managed to get out of the place – without mishap.

They rushed to the back, to the storeroom where Orhan, Nermin and little Çiçek slept.

By then the storeroom, which was adjacent to the kitchen, was ablaze, burning more fiercely than the *lokanta* itself.

Almost immediately, they saw Orhan emerge from the flames with Çiçek in his arms. And they saw him look back, expecting Nermin to be behind. But she wasn't there. Then he looked around quickly, no doubt wondering whether she had come out from somewhere else. He shouted her name, desperately, several times. Then, handing Çiçek to Konstantin Efendi, he ran back into the storeroom.

Just then, there was a series of blasts – according to Konstantin Efendi, wines, spirits, oils and paraffin exploding. Moments later, the roof collapsed. Then the walls.

Eventually, when they had put out the blaze, the firemen found Orhan and Nermin's remains. Incinerated beyond recognition, but still holding each other.

Detective Dursun took charge of the investigation. He refused to consider the possibility that the fire might have been caused by something other than a pan of oil combusting. He dismissed outright the possibility of arson, perhaps perpetrated by the gang who had paid a visit to Konstantin Efendi the previous week. In the first instance, Konstantin Efendi had not reported such a visit the night he, Detective Dursun, had come to check on the disturbance. Such an allegation now might be seen as a ruse to extract more money from the insurers – particularly as, sadly, the other key witness, Orhan, could not corroborate the story. Alternatively, and more likely, Konstantin Efendi was having delusions. A common occurrence in cases of shock.

As for the courting couple and the parked Pontiac by Lovers' Lane, no one could take that statement seriously. For a start, like all love-smitten couples, they would have been in their own impenetrable world. More to the point, whatever they claimed to have seen – if, that is, they had seen anything – they had seen it in the middle of the night, in a place so dark that even lips eager to kiss struggled to find their partners.

Then Detective Dursun dropped his bombshell.

'Following my encounter with Orhan last week, I thought I should check up on him. He was an arrogant fellow – and arrogance always covers up hidden dirt.

'Well, I amassed quite a dossier. He had several aliases. Poets' names, all of them. He wasn't lying when he said he loved poetry.

'Crime-wise: nothing very gory. A born drifter.

Some altercations – he won most of them. Resisting arrest – always put up a fight. Petty theft – invariably, food – when on the run.

'Then something totally unexpected. Unusual for a drifter. A ladies' man. Bigamist. At least two wives in different places. Maybe two others, but I don't have all the facts on those yet.

'And some children. Not surprising, I'd say. Which makes Nermin his third or fifth wife and Çiçek his seventh child. Not bad for a man in his mid-thirties.

'You wouldn't believe this, all the wives still love him. Apparently, he was very good to them. Treated them tenderly …'

That's when I walked away.

○○○○○○○○○○○●❀●○○○○○○○○○○○

I packed the few clothes I had. And took the little money I had saved. I left a note for my father. Told him I'd go where the bus took me and find some work. I added I would miss him. And now that I wouldn't be around to remind him of my mother, I expected him to find some happiness. I don't know why I wrote that last bit. Grief, I suppose. I had to take it out on someone.

Then I went back to the *lokanta*. Detective Dursun had left. But Konstantin Efendi and Liliana were there, sitting on the pavement by the charred remains, waiting for the loss assessors. Konstantin Efendi was holding Çiçek, so he couldn't discharge his fury. Liliana did it for him.

They hadn't believed a word Dursun had said. I was glad of that. They wouldn't have understood that the *kabadayı* must drift, move from place to place in order to help people. That this is part of their calling. Of course, their women aren't happy about that, but they understand it. And accept it as Allah's will. Which is why they continue loving their *kabadayı* even after they've gone.

Dursun was a man with a sewer mind. The sort who shares a lamb with the wolf and laments its loss with the shepherd. His crude parting shot to Konstantin Efendi and Liliana had been that they should consider themselves lucky for being delivered from Orhan and doubly lucky for the hefty insurance they would receive. Now they could either retire or build a bigger and better place.

Dursun was also a crook. There were already rumours that the reason he had declared the fire in the *lokanta* an open-and-shut case was because his palm was being greased by Octopus.

I told Konstantin Efendi and Liliana that I was leaving. I asked whether I could take Çiçek with me. I tried to convince them that I would look after her well, give my life for her.

We argued for the rest of the day, the whole night and the whole of the next day.

Finally, they convinced me. I was a good lad, but still very young – only fifteen. A baby needed special care all the time. Try as I would, I would never be able to provide that.

Then they made me a promise. They would not abandon her to an orphanage. They would take care of her themselves. In fact, adopt her. But, of course, they would raise her as a Muslim.

Then one day, when I returned, there she would be. A young woman. Old enough to marry. Maybe my bride – why not?

∞∞∞∞∞∞❀∞∞∞∞∞∞

I am thirty-three now.

Çiçek must be eighteen. I imagine she is still with Konstantin Efendi and Liliana.

I often fantasize about going back. We recognize each other immediately. And join our lives as if we had not spent all these years apart.

But I won't go back. I made sure of that by destroying Konstantin Efendi's new address after he sold the site of the *lokanta* to an elderly Armenian who had returned after many years in Canada and decided to build a new restaurant there. The Armenian is dead now, but his wife still runs the place, and I am often tempted to go and ask her for Konstantin Efendi's address. But only tempted. As I said, I won't go back.

I am a *kabadayı* now – have been for some ten years. A good one. Orhan would be proud of me. I am emulating his life. Except I don't set up house with women. Not because they don't like me. I have had several proposals through matchmakers. In this respect, I am also mimicking my father. A man paralysed by too many deaths. (I heard that my father had died a few years back. Cirrhosis. Nothing had changed in his life.)

Now and again, I visit prostitutes.

I have come to cherish prostitutes. They understand pain. They give you the courage to go on a bit more, round another corner.

I really wish I could go back.

But no sense in that.

I won't leave orphans behind me.

I'll stay a *kabadayı*. As Orhan could see, we are a dying breed – that appeals to me. Maybe we are also a breed that wishes to die. That's appealing, too.

I'll go on until someone torches my room. Or shoots me in the back. Or runs me down with a car.

And if, in the next world, there is a place for the *kabadayı*, Orhan will be there. And I'll join him.

10: Zeki

When a Writer Is Killed

My exile started when I was twelve, seven years before my actual expatriation.

On 31 December 1947 we – the academy's first-year students – had been offered the traditional end-of-semester treat: a jovial afternoon in the Emirgân *çayhane*, for centuries one of Istanbul's favourite tea-houses by the Bosporus, as guests of our quixotic professor of literature, Âşık Ahmet.

One objective of this outing was to welcome the New Year with readings of sublime poetry; another was to obtain from us, students on the threshold of adulthood, the pledge to pursue Atatürk's cherished dream of transforming Turkey into one of the world's most advanced nations. For, as we had been instructed often enough, the Father of the Turks, having restored a terminally sick country to resurgent health, had spawned us, in the last years of his life, as his successors; it was our duty to consolidate his miracle.

The third objective was Âşık Ahmet's improvisation on the second. On this day, every student would select his future profession, then take an oath that he would never renege on his decision. Moreover, he would make his choice not in the expectation of financial rewards but because that particular career would provide one of the many skills the country needed for its development. Only through such unselfish dedication would we be able to reclaim the paradise the latter Ottoman sultans had so heinously despoiled.

It was one of those translucent winter days when Istanbul unseals her occult colours. Snow and sun either conjoined passionately or chased each other flirtatiously; and the windows of the ancient wooden mansions along the Bosporus turned into mirrors to reflect them. The breeze wore the city's unique fragrance of sea, pine, honey and rose-water. The giant plane tree that canopied the tables of the tea-house susurrated its timeless wisdom. And Âşık Ahmet, zestfully smoking a chain of cigarettes, strutted at his charming best.

The tea flowed like a stream, as tea always does everywhere in Turkey. *Mezes* and the speciality of the house, aubergines prepared in ninety-nine different ways, arrived on a succession of vast copper trays. (According to Turkish folklore, mankind's limit for aubergine recipes is ninety-nine; it is presumed that there are at least another ninety-nine, but these are only known to

Allah.) Important subjects such as sport, girls, puberty, masturbation, wet dreams and the myriad mysteries of the vagina that awaited us were freely aired.

When we were all happily languid and looked upon Âşık Ahmet as to a prophet, he rose and addressed us. It was time, he said, that we – the chrysalises of the greatest nation on earth – emerged from the pupal stage and entered the future. Here and now, each one of us had to stand up, in alphabetical order, and declare the career he would pursue. There would be five minutes allowed for deliberation. Except for such professions as medicine, engineering and business administration, of which there was a great shortage in the country, nobody was allowed to pick an occupation that had already been chosen by one of his peers. Swapping, being the indulgence of irresolute people, was prohibited. No doubt, some boys at the tail end of the alphabetical order would be disappointed because the career they would have wanted would not be available to them. But that in itself would be an invaluable lesson, an introduction to life's first axiom that human existence, even for the luckiest, is persistently unjust.

And so, one by one, my classmates declared their choices: careers from doctor to engineer, chemist to accountant, merchant to banker, geologist to metallurgist, soldier to aviator, hotelier to farmer were pronounced. When a boy floundered either because the profession he wanted had already been taken or because he could not think clearly, Âşık Ahmet – or some of us – suggested alternatives.

I was the last. I stood up, tense and shaking. I had decided on my profession the moment Âşık Ahmet had announced the outing. It had been an impulsive decision, aimed, I must admit, at impressing him. But it had taken hold of me and I had been praying that no one else would choose it.

Âşık Ahmet turned to me. 'And you, my young Jew, what will you be?'

I announced happily. 'A professor, sir. Of humanities.'

'A professor of humanities?'

'Yes, sir.'

'What decided you on this, Zeki?'

'Sir?'

'Hero-worship? A desire to emulate me?'

I squirmed. It was obvious I worshipped him. We all did. But I had additional reasons. Firstly, he was one of the people who had saved my mother and myself from starvation at the time of the *Varlık*, the nefarious Wealth Tax imposed on the minorities. Secondly, he was a champion of every just cause; indeed, in some quarters he was known as 'the great democrat'. Thirdly, he knew all there was to know about world literature. Fourthly, wanting to impart this knowledge to the whole country, he taught right through the educational spectrum from university to primary school. Fifthly, he was so manly that all the women, even girls our age, were attracted to him.

'Well, Zeki?'

'I – I … Maybe, sir …'

'Waste of time. You can't be like me!'

'I know, sir. But I'd like to try, sir …'

'And should you succeed, what would that make you?'

'A noble person, sir.'

'No, sir! You'd be an imitation.'

'Oh.'

'Is that what you think you should offer our country? A mimetic chimpanzee? A suicidal parrot?'

'No, sir.'

'Then think again. What are you good at?'

'Not much, sir. Running, maybe. I have good lungs.'

'Running is hardly a career. An Olympic medal, at the most. What about literature?'

'That's why I want to be a teacher, sir. I love literature, sir.'

'You're good at it, I'll grant you. You can tell what's prose and what's poetry. You have a feel for language and you write good essays. I wager you'll be my best student yet! For a Jew, that's phenomenal!'

'Is it, sir?'

'You also have an oversize dome – plenty of space there for words.'

I blushed. I'd taken a lot of teasing from my peers about my large head. Then I'd come to realize that though tall and thin, I was not necessarily weak. So one day I'd stood up to a bully and gone on to beat the shit out him; I had never looked back. I retorted angrily, 'I can't help the size of my head, sir. I was born that way.'

Âşık Ahmet grinned. 'And for a very good reason.

You have a writer's head. And that's what you should be! A writer.'

'Me, sir? A writer?'

'It's in your bones! Can't you sense it?'

'I don't know, sir ...'

'Damn it, boy! Don't be a dunce! Touch your feelings!'

'I – I don't know how, sir.'

'Don't be coy with me!'

'I'm not, sir.'

'Now, repeat after me: I'm a writer. I know it in my bones. Come on!'

'I'm a writer. I know it in my bones.'

'And that's what I'll be. Novelist. Poet. Playwright. Essayist.'

'Oh.'

'Let's hear it!'

'That's what I'll be. Novelist ... Poet ... Playwright ... Essayist ...'

Âşık Ahmet clapped his hands. 'That's settled, then!' He shouted at the waiter. 'Bring this boy some raki! Bring several bottles! We have cause for celebration.'

I stared at my friends, quite dumbstruck, as they cheered and applauded. Somewhere in my mind, I wondered whether they were acclaiming my choice or the prospect of getting drunk.

Âşık Ahmet took to the floor and started dancing. Then he started reciting Nâzım Hikmet:

Imagine TARANTA-BABU
How sublime life is
To understand it like reading a masterly book
To hear it like a love song
To live
In wonderment like a child
Oh, how sublime living is
TARANTA-BABU …[2]

Later, Âşık Ahmet, inebriated yet solemn, came and sat beside me and replenished my glass. 'How goes it, my young Jew?'

Drunk and emboldened by the raki, I quipped, '*Oh, how sublime living is …*'

'You like the poem?'

'Yes, sir.'

'Know what it's about?'

'Denounces fascism, sir. Written when Italy was preparing to invade Abyssinia. Composed as letters from an Ethiopian student in Rome to his wife, back home.'

'A Hikmet *aficionado!*'

'*Aficionado*' was that year's catchword. Âşık Ahmet had borrowed it from Hemingway, whose rakish masculinity, he maintained, made him the most Turkish of foreign writers.

I nodded proudly. 'I've only read what's around, sir. Most of his works are banned.'

'So is *Taranta-Babu*.'

'My father has a copy, sir. He got it when it was first published.'

'Your father ... Of course ... Vitali Behar, the lawyer. The one who defends the defenceless – right? I must meet him.'

'Actually, you saved his life, sir.'

'Did I? How come?'

'By feeding my mother and me during the *Varlık* ... Father had been sent to Aşkale labour camp ...'

'Hold on – is he the man who bought his son an encyclopaedia with his first earnings? When he came back from the camp?'

'Yes, sir.'

'And you were the son?'

'Yes, sir.'

'No wonder you turned out as you are. And he loves Hikmet.'

'Jews know about fascism, sir.'

'I remember something else. One of your family dying in the Spanish Civil War ...'

'Father's French cousin, sir. Yes.'

'A family of lefties. All the more reason to meet him. We'll have a conference of lefties.'

'Yes, sir.'

'On second thoughts, maybe he shouldn't be seen with me. For some people, I'm even worse than a lefty ...'

'Even worse, sir ...?'

'Like a sewer-rat – meaning "pluralist", therefore, ravisher of nationalism. Or socialist pig – meaning enemy of capitalism and all good things. And, of course, communist vermin – the maggot that's trying to eat the country's heart.'

'How dare they, sir?'

'When mindless people   opportunists, reactionaries, religious zealots – get to power, they try to hold on to it any way they can. And the best way they can do that is by feeding our paranoia. Like this anti-communist hysteria we're now having. And we become the scapegoats ...'

'But you're a great patriot, sir. A war hero ...'

'Yes, that's a bit of luck. It deters some of them. On the other hand, I'm small fry. They want Turkey's very soul. And they've got him. And they've put him in chains ...'

You mean Hikmet, sir?'

'Yes.'

'Did you know him, sir?'

'Met him a few times.'

'What's he like?'

'Orpheus reincarnated.'

'I'd love to meet him ...'

'One day – all being well. There's a campaign for his release.'

'In the meantime, I can't read many of his works!'

'You can if you join a samizdat network.'

'How?'

'I run one. We mimeograph all his banned works and distribute them where we can.'

'Oh, I'd be very keen to join!'

'I should warn you. You could get into trouble ...'

'I realize that, sir.'

'Is this raki-brave? Or are you naturally so?'

'I don't know, sir. Maybe both ...'

Âşık Ahmet lit yet another cigarette, then offered me one.

'I suppose I should have asked this before you took your decision, Zeki ...'

I took the cigarette.

He lit it for me. 'If – when you become a writer – if they started banning your works ...?'

'I can't imagine them being interested in me, sir ...'

'For much of the world, the freedom to write is a luxury. All the more so, if you care about humanity. If you defend freedom and democracy. If you criticize rulers, governments, institutions. If, like Hikmet, you preach equality, an end to wars, universal peace ... For some regimes these themes constitute grave crimes ...'

I looked at him in perturbation. 'I see ...'

'Being a Jew, I suspect you'd be writing in that vein. So you'd be branded a subversive. They'll set the Furies on you. What then?'

'I don't know, sir ... What do you think, sir?'

'The risk of persecution – and gaol – go with the writer's job ...'

'Then maybe I shouldn't be a writer, sir ...'

'And renege on your oath ...?'

'But prison ...'

'Can be very beneficial. Builds up a person in many ways.' He replenished my glass. 'What do you say?'

I gulped down my drink. 'Do I have a choice, sir?'

To my great surprise – and I think, everybody else's – he hugged me. 'You devil Jew – God help you!'

That night I told my parents of my decision.

My mother, who was blessed with an artistic disposition – she was a very gifted miniaturist – immediately burst into tears. But then she burst into tears whatever the news, good or bad. (To my great embarrassment, I take after her.) When she eventually composed herself, she turned to my father – who had not said a word – and listed a million reasons why I should be a writer. 'Doubt not,' she told him, 'our son will be a Tolstoy, a Rabelais, a Cervantes, a Shakespeare, maybe even a Homer or a Rûmi or, who knows, maybe even better than all of them.'

My father remained silent.

Later, when people dropped in for coffee, my choice became one of the subjects of conversation. I was doing my homework, but I sneaked out several times to eavesdrop.

On one occasion, I heard my great-uncle, Lazar, trying to comfort my father by telling him that my so-called career choice was merely an adolescent fantasy, that it would soon fade into oblivion and that, within a few months, I would happily decide, like every good Jewish boy, to take up medicine or dentistry or accountancy or, best of all, commerce.

(Not a loveable person, my great-uncle Lazar. A book-keeper in a public company, he was an opinionated man with a violent temper and a veritable bully towards children. Indeed, he so disliked children that each time he heard the muezzin call the faithful to prayer, he was reminded to thank Elohim for making his wife barren – or so he boasted. However, according to the old folks' gossip, this boast was self-protective; in effect, it was he who was sterile, since my poor, sweet great-aunt had given birth to a boy when she was a mere sap of a girl, during the War of Independence. Tragically, after her lover had been killed at the battle of İnönü, she had had to give the baby up for adoption.)

To my surprise, my father affirmed that he would be very proud to have his son become a writer. What concerned him was the sad reality that writers seldom made a decent living and were always at the mercy of self-aggrandizing publishers, reviewers, columnists, pundits, not to mention rulers and politicians. He would be more than happy to support me for as long as he lived, but who would take care of me after his death?

On hearing this, my mother, needless to say, burst into tears. (Actually, so did I!)

The next day, as I left for school, I caught special smiles on my parents' faces. Obviously, in celebration of my choice, they had made each other exceptionally happy during the night. If there had been any thoughts in my mind of reneging on my literary career, those smiles banished them for ever.

Thus my fate was sealed. Unbeknown to my parents or to myself, my exile had begun.

∞∞∞∞∞∞∞✿∞∞∞∞∞∞∞

Within weeks, I had read everything by Nâzım Hikmet that was circulating clandestinely or had not been confiscated by the authorities. About the same time, I joined the ranks of the samizdat mimeographers and earned many commendations from Âşık Ahmet for spending countless weekends with a dilapidated Gestetner.

I also started trying to write poetry and published a couple of poems in the college magazine. Sadly, they turned out to be pathetic parodies of Hikmet's verses – even I could tell that. Indeed, I might well have given up poetry then, had not Âşık Ahmet pronounced that some of the metaphors had contained 'sparks of originality'.

Within a year or so, I became the principal distributor of Hikmet's poetry to all the secondary-school students along the Bosporus' European shore. On two occasions, I was caught red-handed and arrested – denounced, according to Âşık Ahmet, by some retrograde teachers from those schools. The first time, I ended up at the local police station and the duty officer released me with a caution. The second time, I was taken to the district station, where the chief of police decided that I needed to be taught a lesson. So I was roughed up a bit. The blows, threats and insults barely hurt, but the state of fear, which carries with it a taste like rotten meat, induced in me a paralysis that still afflicts me today. I was also warned that I now possessed a dossier, entirely allocated to my august little self, prominently placed in the 'pending' tray of the National Security Organization;

a third offence would see me looking at the sun from behind bars.

∞∞∞∞∞∞✿∞∞∞∞∞∞

Then, in no time at all, it was 1950.

May brought Adnan Menderes and his Democratic Party to power. Those of us who swaggered as Hikmet's *aficionados* felt our spirits rise. There would be an amnesty; the gaols would be emptied; that was the convention after elections. And since, for some time, influential groups and student organizations had been campaigning for Hikmet's release, we believed the new government would disregard its abhorrence of communism and free him forthwith. We held on to these expectations even when old-timers warned us that the growing paranoia against any leftist views, churned up by the US's mighty propaganda machine – and pushed into a frenzy after the outbreak of the Korean war – was even more virulent than the one that had led to Hikmet's imprisonment.

Matching this hysteria with fulminous ire, we mimeographed even more fervently.

July came. Reports that Turkey had been invited to join NATO began to fuel further anti-communist delirium. Those who cautioned that the price of admission to that 'elite organization' would be countless soldiers' lives because Turkey would be coerced into participating in the Korean war were hounded and, in some cases, prosecuted and gaoled.

Then, on 15 July, as we began to despair of an amnesty for Hikmet, he was released.

Our joy was unsurpassable. It made us believe that defenders of the word could never be defeated, that Fate somehow contrived to protect them, sometimes even used, paradoxically, repressive regimes like that of Menderes, to give them back their pens.

I spent the rest of the summer mimeographing. Some weeks I barely slept. But I didn't care. I was permanently euphoric. My hero was free; even more importantly, so were hitherto unknown batches of his work. Hikmet, anxious to publish again, was collecting the poems he had written in prison from those relatives and friends to whom he had given them for safekeeping. Many of these found their way to Âşık Ahmet. He, in turn, passed them on to us, the mimeographers. Soon, people heard of these poems and inundated us with requests for copies. This provoked the ever-active reactionary worms to defame Hikmet even more savagely; we, his devotees, were branded as his '*moujiks*, odalisques and catamites'.

But we, his *moujiks*, odalisques and catamites, laughed at them. We bared our chests and challenged them to engage us. We told them they were a dying breed; that we had no sympathy for their death throes; we were Atatürk's children engaged in important work. We even claimed that Atatürk had dearly loved Hikmet and that, but for his death, he would have protected him from the fascists who had gaoled him. And we proclaimed Hikmet's famous poem from prison to his first wife, Piyale, as our anthem:

They are the enemies of hope, my love,
enemies of running water
of trees fruiting in their season
of life spreading itself and maturing.
Because death has stamped their foreheads –
the rotting teeth, the flaking flesh.
And certainly, my darling, absolutely certainly,
freedom
will roam this beautiful country
swinging its arms
dressed in its most glorious habit,
its workers' dungarees.[3]

Would youth of such calibre give a fuck about armoured generals, bloated politicians and godless men of god?

∞∞∞∞∞∞❀∞∞∞∞∞∞

The rest of the year streaked away in a gallop.

My devotion to our clandestine press soon propelled me into Hikmet's orbit. Here and there, I attended the readings he gave for his friends. Occasionally, I even spoke to him; or rather he spoke to me and I stared at him in awe. As Âşık Ahmet had described him, he was Orpheus reincarnated.

Once, in the grounds of an admirer's villa, he put his arm around me as if I were his compeer and suggested, as we walked around the orchard, that we free-associate with the feelings that the various fruit trees elicited from us. I stammered some inanities like the mulberry being a nipple that gushed answers to life's mysteries, the peach a symbol of the perfection of the world and the fig a depository of seeds capable of repopulating the earth. He generously praised these pretentious associations and then remarked that while a fruit was a miracle in itself, the tree that bore it was an even greater miracle. And pointing at the trees around us, he showed me how each one with its singular strength and beauty stood witness to the great, but mysterious design of Creation. His praise of the trees reminded me of the famous lines from *Kuvâyi Milliye*, his epic about the War of Independence:

> *To live like a tree single and free*
> *And in brotherhood like a forest*
> *That is our aspiration ...*[4]

Physically, too, he was the most striking man I have ever met: tall, lively, with a large elongated head, thick Titian hair like a perpetual sunrise and a natural elegance. An ever-present pipe that he either sucked with relish or used like a conductor's baton enhanced his authority. For me, the trait that really summed him up was the way his eyes constantly smiled – as if he were witnessing a new miracle every time he looked at something. How had the clear blue depths of those eyes withstood, one wondered, the desolation of long years in prison. (A joke doing the rounds at the time thanked Providence for keeping Hikmet and Atatürk apart even though they had been forged in the same crucible, Salonica. For both were so dazzling in appearance that anybody seeing them together would have been confused as to whom to worship.)

Soon, however, we began to be concerned about his future. He had a heart condition and needed to avoid stress. But, short of funds, and unable to find employment within an Establishment that treated him like a pariah, he and his second wife, Münevver, had had to accept hospitality first from a close comrade, then from his mother. Eventually an old friend had offered him work in a film studio and the Hikmets had moved in to a basement flat.

Our greatest fear was the constant threat that he might be rearrested and sent to prison again. The government saw his popularity, particularly among intellectuals, left-wing organizations and students, as a likely source of opposition. Consequently, the police kept him under permanent surveillance and, to emphasize the menace, did so openly. Moreover, the fact that he had become an international celebrity – the 2nd World Peace Congress in Warsaw had just awarded him, together with Pablo Neruda, Pablo Picasso, Wanda Jakubowska and Paul Robeson, its peace prize – made him an even more charismatic adversary. (Needless to say, because of the government's anti-communist stand, he could not travel to Poland to collect the award. Neruda had accepted it on his behalf.)

By spring 1951, which should have been an exceptionally happy time because his wife had just given birth to their son, Memed, we were at our wits' end. We kept hearing, on the grapevine, that in defiance of international opprobrium, the authorities were seeking new ways to indict him.

In response to this threat, some of Hikmet's closest friends began investigating the possibility of smuggling him out of the country. The USSR was mooted as the most likely country to offer him asylum.

Then, early in June, the government struck. Hikmet received call-up papers informing him that since his years in prison had interrupted his military service, he was now required to complete that obligation at a posting in eastern Anatolia.

∞∞∞∞∞∞∞🌼∞∞∞∞∞∞∞

A day or so later, Âşık Ahmet summoned me to his office. He related all the events leading to Hikmet's conscription: how the poet's earlier efforts to secure exemption from military service on the grounds of ill health had failed; and how a specially appointed, and therefore skewed, medical committee had found him fully fit. We all knew that eastern Anatolia, where he had to serve, was a mountainous region with extremely harsh winters. Given Hikmet's heart condition, the posting was a death sentence. He would be dead within six months.

Then, swearing me to absolute secrecy, Âşık Ahmet informed me that he and his friends had devised a plan to whisk Hikmet to the USSR. Bearing in mind the round-the-clock surveillance on the poet, the plan was quite convoluted and required a few auxiliaries to act as decoys. Since these auxiliaries would not be involved with the actual escape, they would not, in all likelihood, face any danger. However, every covert operation, by its very nature, carried a degree of risk and the same held true of this one. If by some mischance something went wrong and the decoys were spotted, they might be arrested, even maltreated.

There he paused and scrutinized me.

I engaged his eyes. I had read the question he had left hanging in the air. My heart began to beat frantically. 'You want me to be one of the decoys?'

He smiled. 'You lovely Jew, you!'

He had addressed me in this manner God only knows how many times. But, on this occasion, it riled me. 'Why do you always call me that?'

He stared at me in surprise. 'Call you what?'

'Jew.'

'Does it offend you?'

'Sometimes.'

'Why?'

'It sounds anti-semitic. Coming from someone like you, it doesn't make sense. You don't address any of the other boys by their race. You don't call Agop "you lovely Armenian", or Takis "my devilish Greek" ...'

'I do.'

'I've never heard you.'

'Haven't you? I'm sure I do. I certainly do in my mind.'

'In your mind …?'

He became as passionate as when reciting a poem. 'I do it in celebration. I swear to you. Because it's like being in a beautiful garden and calling every flower by its name. The joy of pluralism. Of difference. Of diversity.'

'I see.'

'You don't look too convinced. And you have a valid point. Why do I call you "Jew" out loud – often without even realizing I'm doing it – and address the others only in my mind?'

'It's all right, sir. It doesn't matter …'

'Matters to me. I'm not anti-semitic. Or am I? I mean, I'm sure I take a person for what he is. And you – I love you like a son. Surely you know that. I've watched you develop and guided you with great pride.'

'I know, sir.'

'But … still, the question remains. Why do I call you "Jew"? Is it in my nature? Am I anti-semitic deep down?'

I shrugged sadly.

He nodded solemnly. 'I'll think about it. I might have to revise my opinion of myself. And if I have to, I'll change, I promise you.'

I perked up. 'So what do I do?'

'You, nothing. It's me …'

'I mean, as a decoy.'

'Oh, that.' He looked concerned. 'You're sure you want to?'

'Yes.'

He beamed. 'You lovely J …' He paused. 'I don't know what to call you now …'

'"Zeki"? Or "young Turk" …?'

'Right, you lovely young Turk. Are you really sure about this? Things might go wrong. You might get into trouble …'

'I'm sure.'

'If you're arrested, they'll interrogate you. They'll want to know about me, about the press, the mimeographers, whoever supported Nâzım … They might even get rough …'

'I'll try and hold out … But what if they break me …?'

'We'll repair you.'

'And if I tell them about you? The others?'

'We'll suffer the consequences. We're resigned to that. By then, hopefully, Nâzım should be safe.'

I shivered with excitement and trepidation. 'That's all that matters.'

He got up and slapped me on the shoulder. 'Let's get moving!'

As we moved towards the door, he stopped me. 'One thing, young Turk: don't lose the young Jew. Cherish everybody's difference. If we all become the same, we're bound to perish.'

The next day, at Âşık Ahmet's house, I met the team. (We had finished our exams and were just two days away from the summer break; consequently, attendance at college, both by teachers and students, had become irrelevant.)

There were two 'magicians' – Âşık Ahmet's designation for the people who would whisk Hikmet away – and fifteen decoys, including myself.

Âşık Ahmet had made certain that we, the decoys, came from all walks of life. Symbolically, we represented the diverse peoples of the country to whom Hikmet had given a strong communal voice. Apart from me, there were four other students, all from Istanbul University's various faculties.

The 'magicians' – Yannis Karolidis, a reputable undertaker said to be rich as Croesus, and Aybek, a Circassian from Trabzon, both middle-aged – were men of such contrasting appearance that, in less momentous circumstances, I would have perceived them as Laurel and Hardy.

Immediately after the requisite proprieties, Yannis – he was the large man – took the floor. As he strode up and down, collecting his thoughts, I realized how deceptive my first impression of him had been. This was not a flabby Oliver Hardy, but a monolith of solid muscle.

He introduced himself as one of Âşık Ahmet's old students; one who, though crimped by circumstances into the ranks of mercantile life had, nonetheless, remained faithful to his first love, poetry. Consequently, he considered it a matter of honour to help Hikmet – in his estimation, the greatest poet of our times.

To this effect – and to his great joy – he would, for once, apply his professional skills to providing an extension to a person's life instead of returning him to dust. He would arrange a lavish 'funeral', ostensibly for a Pontos *ağa* who had 'died' in Istanbul and whose last testament had stated that he should be buried in Çoruk, his place of birth, a village near the Black Sea town of Trabzon.

Yannis, who was a Pontos himself, reminded us that his people were descended from the kingdom of Trebizond which, after the fall of Constantinople, had stood as the last outpost of the eastern Roman empire for eight more years before it, too, had succumbed to the Ottomans. Yet a sizeable number of these people had remained in the Black Sea area, preserving assiduously both the traditions of the Greek Orthodox Church and the Hellenic vernacular of Byzantium. This was true, in many syncretic ways, even of those offshoots, like his own, that had eventually converted to Islam. Hence the transportation of the remains of a Pontos man, even of the Christian persuasion, to his native village would not be considered inordinate by the authorities.

And, of course, instead of this fictitious *ağa*, it would be Hikmet who would be conveyed to within a stone's throw of Turkey's north-eastern border with the USSR. Needless to say, the coffin itself would be specially crafted to be airy, easy to get in and out of and comfortable like a bed in a harem. Because of Hikmet's heart condition, it would not be entrusted to the vagaries of provincial roads. Instead it would be transported, with due pomp and circumstance, by sea. No one would question these arrangements or check the coffin; Yannis' lavish gratuities to everybody from officials to grave-diggers would make sure of that. On the prescribed day, while Hikmet was well on his way to the USSR, the burial of the empty coffin would take place with due solemnity. And that would be that.

Then Aybek, the Circassian, took the floor.

As I watched this man, thin as a rake, present himself as an *iş bitirici*, a 'fixer' of all things impossible, who, to date, had never failed a commission, I also had to revise my first impression of him. Despite his pencil-thin moustache, he seemed to gain weight each time I looked at him. His eyes, almost mauve, like the waters of the Black Sea itself, hypnotized the beholder.

He spoke briefly. He explained that he ran, among other things, a very profitable contraband racket in the Black Sea area with a select band of Turkish and Soviet border officials. In Trabzon, Yannis would hand Hikmet over to him. And he would duly smuggle him, by car, into the USSR via a road specially built for their trade and omitted from all maps.

Âşık Ahmet concluded. Preparations would take about ten days. Nothing would be left to chance. Aybek would provide the documentation for the 'deceased'. Yannis would attend to all the formalities; such was the potency of his reputation and purse that he would not even have to find a corpse. For good measure, the 'funeral' procession would start as far away from Hikmet's neighbourhood as possible.

All the moves would be rehearsed until perfected.

The first imperative would be to smuggle Hikmet out of his home without alerting the police. This would be executed late at night when, in all likelihood, his surveillants would be either too lethargic or snoozing. However, during the five or six days it would take to transport him to Trabzon and thence to the USSR, Hikmet would have to be seen to be 'in the house'.

This is where we, the decoys, were to play our part.

First and foremost, one of us would have to impersonate Hikmet. His surveillants would need to have frequent glimpses of him playing with his baby son or talking to his wife through the window. And since it was Münevver, with Memed in tow in a pram, who went shopping, Hikmet had also to be seen waving them off and welcoming them back.

Other decoys would be deployed as admirers. Such was Hikmet's popularity that there was always a stream of students, writers, poets and film people visiting him. A sudden cessation of this flow would immediately arouse suspicion.

To my great surprise – and concern – I was the one chosen to impersonate Hikmet. Like him, I was tall, slim and had a large head. I also had a pale complexion. Equipped with an auburn wig and mimicking the poet's particular stride, I could look, certainly from a distance, very much like him.

We set the date of the 'funeral' for Saturday 26 June, a few days before Hikmet was due to report for military service.

We, the decoys, spent the next week or so rehearsing our moves.

My routine was as follows: I would sneak into Hikmet's apartment, early in the morning, just before the surveillance teams changed shifts, when those on night duty, impatient to be relieved, would be watching the road instead of the gardens at the back. Once inside, I would put on an auburn wig, don one of Hikmet's shirts and occasionally appear either at the door to welcome visitors or at the windows, in various moods, but mostly distracted as if in the throes of composing verse.

After a few days, we noted that my impersonation drew no suspicion from the surveillance teams; they maintained their bored or cursory looks. (This attitude so increased my confidence that, in no time at all, I began to fantasize that I really was Nâzım Hikmet.)

Simultaneously, those decoys designated as visitors made regular calls on the apartment. The surveillants duly noted their arrival and departure and, no doubt, filed their descriptions, too.

We also verified that, as we had expected, those surveillants on night shifts invariably dived into stupor. Most dozed right through the night; a few chain-smoked or stealthily got drunk; some sang softly – always sad songs; and one, a young man, kept going behind a hedge – to masturbate, we presumed.

On Sunday 17 June, just as I was about to leave for Hikmet's apartment, Âşık Ahmet came round. He looked pale and tense; his nicotine-stained fingers, for once devoid of a cigarette, trembled.

Standing at the top of the stairs, as if ready to run away, he whispered harshly, 'Don't go to Nâzım's place today.'

I became alarmed. 'Why?'

'Stay in – all day. I'll explain later.' And he rushed off.

He rang soon afterwards. And several times during the day. Each time, he repeated that I was to stay in. As time went on, his tension increased; on a couple of occasions, I thought he was going to break down.

Around midnight, he rang again. This time he sounded relieved and close to tears. 'All's well.'

'What's been going on?'

'Stay put. Pretend you're ill. I'll come over when the time's right.'

He came over on Thursday 21 June.

I received him in a state of shock. I had just read in *Cumhuriyet* that Nâzım Hikmet had escaped to Bucharest, Romania.

I waved the newspaper at him. 'Is this true?'

He couldn't stop smiling. 'Yes.'

'How?'

'Never mind how.'

'When?'

'I don't know exactly. But, in case we're questioned, he was still here two days ago. He left home that morning to go to Ankara to appeal against his call-up.'

'His escape – was it a sudden whim?'

'Does it matter?'

'Sure, it matters! Didn't he trust us?'

'Of course he did. But there might have been an emergency. Or suddenly he saw the perfect opportunity ...'

'We had a foolproof plan!'

'His wasn't bad either, was it? He grabbed his chance! Can you blame him? He's safe! That's what matters!'

I nodded, then started laughing. 'Yes! That's what matters!'

He took me by the arm. 'Time for a celebration! Let's get the gang!'

I followed happily, feeling weightless and unco-ordinated. 'In a way – it's a relief! I couldn't stop worrying. We – I – might have botched it!'

'We wouldn't have botched it. But there might have been mayhem. Now we should be spared that ...'

⋯⋯⋯⋯⋯❀⋯⋯⋯⋯⋯

Nâzım Hikmet arrived in Moscow on 29 June 1951, to

a tumultuous welcome.

I was spared the mayhem. So were the other decoys. But not Âşık Ahmet.

The authorities reacted to Hikmet's escape with fury. First, by ministerial decree, they divested him of his citizenship. Then, raiding the homes of his close friends and supporters, they destroyed everything in print, every scrap of paper that might have contained a fragment of his work. No one knows how much of Hikmet's writing was thus lost for ever.

Eventually, some of these friends and supporters managed to flee the country and settle abroad. Many others were arrested, tried and sentenced to lengthy prison terms. Some, like Âşık Ahmet, were also harshly treated.

Hikmet's wife, Münevver, and his young son, Memed, who could not have accompanied him without jeopardizing his escape, were put under even closer surveillance and had their passports confiscated. (This harassment continued for some ten years; in the end, they, too, were smuggled out of Turkey by friends. They were given refuge in Poland.)

As I mentioned, we, the decoys, were spared the mayhem. True, all the decoys, myself included, were taken in for questioning. Though they never discovered that I had acted as Hikmet's impersonator, I still qualified as a suspect for having distributed his works. After all, Hikmet's surveillants had photographed us regularly. But, miraculously, our age saved us. We were classified as confused, impressionable youths who had been proselytized by the USSR's universal Fifth Column of 'megalomaniac intellectuals, vainglorious writers and subversive ethnic minorities'. We were admonished to come to our senses. And for good measure, we were marked down, as and when we would be called up for military service, for the Turkish expeditionary force to Korea. Out there, in that God-forsaken place, we would see for ourselves the shit that was the communist dream.

I resumed 'normal life'. The fact that I could do so convinced me that Fate had her eye on me. Apart from Âşık Ahmet's ongoing trial, life spared me from worries.

Moreover, I was left with a priceless possession: one of Hikmet's shirts. A day or so before his escape, I had spilled some coffee on it and had taken it home to be washed. After his escape, it became too dangerous to take it back.

I still have the shirt, made of cheesecloth in Şile, Istanbul's resort on the Black Sea. I wear it, when I dabble in poetry, in the hope that grains of Hikmet's genius will osmose into me. Writers will do anything for art: some will imitate, others will try primitive magic.

In 1954, in my final year at college, Âşık Ahmet's

trial came to an end. He was sentenced to four years' imprisonment.

On the first occasion when he was allowed visitors, I went to see him.

It was the end of February and freezing cold – so cold, in fact, that for the first time in some 200 years, the Bosporus had frozen over – yet I found him sitting on a bench in the prison quadrangle, chain-smoking as ever.

He had shrunk to a fraction of his normal size. Except for the eyes, where thunder and lightning conducted business as usual, that once ramrod, heroic body had been reduced to ungainly bones, lumpy flesh and loose skin.

'What have they done to you, sir?'

'Nothing. Nothing …'

'How could they?'

He pointed at the parcels I had brought. 'Cigarettes and books?'

'Yes.'

'Thanks. Have you been writing, my lovely Jew?'

'A few poems.'

'Recite them.'

'Here? Now?'

'Yes.'

I recited a couple.

'Not bad. You're getting better.'

Listening to his trembling voice, I felt like crying. 'What's the good of that?'

He looked up at me sharply. 'You're going to be a

writer! You're getting there …'

'But look at what they've done to you!'

'To hell with that.'

'I might end up here, too!'

'Occupational hazard. So what?'

'I don't think I can take it, sir.'

'Sure, you can.'

'I've been offered a scholarship. Oxford or Cambridge.'

He looked up, quite tremulously. 'Sensible of Oxford or Cambridge.'

'I'm thinking of taking it up.'

He forced a smile. 'Absolutely right! Grab it.'

I forced myself to look into his eyes. 'I – I might not … come back. I can't write with the fear of prison behind me …'

He unleashed his fury. 'You think you can write in exile?'

'Why not?'

'You're rooted here, you bastard! That's why! You're a Turk! Not an Englishman!'

'I'm a Jew – remember?'

'So what? You're still a Turk – through and through! You've proved that with every breath you've taken!'

'But prison … I'm terrified …'

'So was Nâzım.'

'He escaped.'

Âşık Ahmet pulled me closer to him. 'Listen to me, you creep! He escaped because otherwise he would have died. But in Russia, cut off from his beloved Turkey, he's dying another death. A worse death! His spirit is dying. All that great poetry that won't see the light of day! Don't you understand, Zeki? Your country is your soil! Her traditions, her peoples are the seeds and the rain you need! Without them you are barren earth where nothing germinates. And the writer in you dies! That means you also die! A slow, merciless death!'

'If Turkey treats her great men the way they treat you, then Turkey doesn't deserve them.'

'Oh, she deserves them, my young Jew! She certainly deserves them! What she doesn't deserve is our power-mad fascists, our reactionaries and our religious fanatics! But they come and go! Who remembers them afterwards? They disappear – without a trace!'

I nodded.

'Now read me some more of your poems …'

'I haven't got any more.'

'Then go and write some!'

I saw Âşık Ahmet a few more times. On each occasion he asked me for my poems, but I had none to recite. He asked me why I wasn't writing. I lied, telling him that I was working hard for my final exams. He smiled as if he believed me. But he didn't hide his disappointment.

A few days before I left for Oxford, I visited him for the last time. We hugged, quite desperately. We both knew that I might not come back, that I might be yet another member of my generation who would renege on his word and abandon his country, that I might well be starting my exile.

No, not my exile. My death. My spiritual death safe from fear in a safe corner of the world.

As I was about to leave, he gave me a folded piece of paper. 'I've written a poem. For you.'

Surprised, I started unfolding the paper.

He waved me away. 'Read it on the plane.'

I read it outside the gaol:

when a writer is killed
language
loses one of its words
when all writers are killed
there will be
no words left
no language

only
dictators
racists
nationalists
whores of war
false prophets

only
the worship of death

(The details of Nâzım Hikmet's escape became known some twenty-five years later. In a simple but daring manoeuvre, one of his great admirers, Refik Erduran, had smuggled him in a powerful motorboat out of Istanbul into the Black Sea on Sunday 17 June 1951. There, they had intercepted a Romanian ship, the *Plekhanov*. Hikmet had promptly requested asylum. His request had been granted only after the Romanian authorities had received the USSR's approval. Erduran, his saviour, had slipped back into Istanbul that same night.)

11: Aslan

Madam Ruj

Haydar Koyunlu's interment should have been symbolic; more like a memorial. There should not have been any remains to bury. Haydar had converted to Buddhism. His body should have been left on a mountainside to be consumed by vultures and wild beasts or, failing that, cremated. But in Turkey, in the early fifties, organizing such rites was as unprecedented as finding a politician who loved his country more than his own ambition. So Haydar had the conventional Muslim funeral.

But since he had prepared his suicide in true platonic spirit, as a brave and laudable deed when life turns unacceptable, we, his friends, decided to honour his death with due celebration. We considered his failure to have his body dematerialized by the elements inconsequential. After all, he had often maintained that accomplishment belonged to the gods; whereas failure measured the man.

He had known about failure more than most people. He had been an indefatigable champion of lost causes. It was even suggested that the cancer that had killed him had been spawned by the tribulations of his last campaign, the imperative to abolish borders in order to create a world government. Except for some support from such fervent democrats as Professor Ahmet Poyraz, alias Âşık Ahmet, his efforts had met with nothing but ridicule. Not surprisingly, the precept of abandoning national interests in favour of global welfare as the path to universal peace had proved anathema to Kemalists, irredentists and Islamists. Indeed, some of these factions made sure that Haydar was regularly arrested and, sometimes, imprisoned.

The obsequies, we agreed, would be a pluralistic affair. We were a motley crowd and, like Haydar, we had declared ourselves 'citizens of the world'.

Immediately after the burial, at the suggestion of his Jewish friends, we declared a *shivah*. However, we didn't sit and mourn for seven days. Instead, recalling the scene in *The Iliad* where old Priam goes to Achilles and, kissing the hands that had slain his son, obtains permission to arrange funeral games in honour of Hector, we devised contests in Haydar's memory. In deference to his adopted religion, we called these the Karma Games. We would hold them over all Istanbul so that the world's most beautiful city would also pay homage to him. To preside over the proceedings, we hired Zahir, the Afghan rug-dealer from the Grand Bazaar who, Haydar had once informed us, had been a shaman.

Buddhism and *The Iliad* might sound a strange duality, but it summed up Haydar perfectly. He had embraced Buddhism during the Korean war while serving in the Turkish expeditionary force. Having been an atheist all his adult life – and a virulent foe of all religious institutions – his submission to a faith, let alone Buddhism, had surprised all his friends. He himself, however, had been expecting such a reversal. Having believed in God – or rather, in a god infinitely more humane than the ones preached by our monotheisms – he had known all along that sooner or later he would bump into Him somewhere. That somewhere happened to be Korea. And he did not attain enlightenment just from witnessing the daily carnage that is the fare of all wars. He also acquired a greater insight about himself and thence about humanity, as he put it, 'simply by reading *The Iliad* – the first anti-war novel'. He understood that, individually or collectively, we always have the choice between war and peace, but that being demented admirers of Ares rather than wise followers of Aphrodite, we always choose war. For who, in his right mind, would prefer making war to making love? Even Ares, in his moments of sanity, rushed to entwine limbs with Aphrodite.

Homer, whom Haydar had discovered in a military library, had been, he would quip, the first of the three Purple Hearts he had acquired in Korea. The second had been his conversion to Buddhism. And he had received the third, the actual US military medal, after the battle of Kunuri. (Since Turkey's sole honour for valour, the *İstiklâl Madalyası*, had been created by a special law in 1923 for those who had fought in the War of Independence, those who had distinguished themselves fighting in Korea had ended up receiving US decorations.)

∞∞∞∞∞✿∞∞∞∞∞

On the first day of Haydar's funeral games we ran the cross-country course from the Upper Bosporus to Belgrad Ormanı, a forest created in commemoration of Süleyman the Magnificent's conquest of Belgrade in 1521.

On day two, we rode our bikes, against the clock, for ten circuits of Büyükada, the biggest of the Princes' Islands.

On the third day, we raced dinghies from Florya to Yalova, some sixty kilometres across the Sea of Marmara.

The next day, we competed in a tug of war in Üsküdar, the first village on the Asiatic side of the Bosporus and a great favourite with Eartha Kitt.

The day after that, we shot arrows from one shore of the Golden Horn to the other.

On the sixth day, we wrestled at At Meydanı, the site of the Byzantine Hippodrome, near the Blue Mosque.

And on the last day, as the games' crowning event, we

swam across the Bosporus from Anadolu Hisarı, Yıldırım
Beyazıt's fort on the Asian side, to Rumeli Hisarı,
Mehmet the Conqueror's fortress on the European
side – at barely 700 metres, the strait's narrowest point.
(Given the currents that charge through that narrow
reach, this is a tougher undertaking than swimming the
wider stretches.)

We reserved the evenings for prayers. Following
Haydar's conviction that every place of worship
– provided that it did not have a minister officiating
– revered Creation because it expressed man's yearnings
for the original, tender, motherly deity – the deity
that phallus-oriented religions never understood – we
shuttled between mosque, church and synagogue. Since,
in those days, Istanbul lacked a stupa, we improvised
a Buddhist ritual by burning oil and incense beneath
the great architect Sinan's aqueduct in Kâğıthane and
chanting, under Zahir's guidance, the mantra *Om-
Mani-Padme-Hum.*

The nights were a mystical interlude. This is the time,
a dervish had told us, when a being communes with his
deity and, in so doing, recreates beauty. Beauty that is
sometimes ephemeral, like the sudden nearness of the
Milky Way, or solid, like the body of a loved one.

And at night I became Orpheus. I picked up my saz
and mesmerized both the first and the second coterie.
No mean achievement, this. The first coterie was reserved
for Haydar's peers, men and women he had gathered,
like a latter-day Socrates, from school, army and work.
The second, to which I belonged, comprised the *talebe*,

'students', the initiates from whom no contribution other than blind loyalty was expected. Naturally, the paternalism in the Turkish character imposed strict boundaries between the coteries; but my virtuosity with stringed instruments had elevated me, a callow eighteen-year-old, to the company of adults twice my age.

Thus while the first coterie, recounting Haydar's countless deeds, declared that he would most certainly reincarnate in some glorious form, I put the sentiments into words and music.

Then we wept.

∞∞∞∞∞❁∞∞∞∞∞

The morning of the last game dawned ...

I had been at my most inspired throughout the night. I was also quite drunk. And I found myself straggling into Haydar's cemetery, high above Rumeli Hisarı. I think I wanted to thank him with a special song I had written for him. For Haydar had not only repaired my saz when I had damaged it at a party, but had also imbued it with such mellifluous tones that he might well have been Stradivari reincarnated. (Repairing things – anything, from broken hearts to broken vessels, from mechanical failures to minds confounded by maths – had been yet another of Haydar's miraculous gifts.)

As I approached his grave, I saw a woman kneeling by it ...

I thought I had taken a wrong path. Then I recognized

her; she had been at the funeral: Mazal Levi, known as 'Madam Ruj', the famous – and, for someone in her profession, surprisingly young – matchmaker. (At the time, she had just turned thirty.)

Seeing me, she jumped up.

I mumbled. 'I'm – sorry … I've … intruded …'

She regained her composure. 'It's all right.'

'I'm … a friend of … Haydar …'

She wiped her tears with a handkerchief. 'Me, too …'

'Great man. The perfect man.'

She shook her head vehemently. 'No. Not perfect.'

I grew indignant. 'How can you say that? He was a man who gave meaning to existence.'

She faced me, eyes blazing. 'If he was so perfect, why did he die?'

Her beauty, particularly her incandescent sable hair, captivated me. 'He … was … ill …'

'He should have recovered!'

'How? Who can beat cancer? But the way he died – so brave … Proof of his perfection …'

'Only those who defeat death are perfect!'

I turned away. I didn't want her to see me cry. 'He was a hero … unique …'

She touched my arm. 'I'm sorry … Forgive me … Grief makes one say all sorts of things … He was unique, yes …' Gently, she caressed my cheek. 'I'll leave you with him …'

I wanted to hold on to her and weep my heart out. Instead, clumsily, I held up my saz. 'I wrote a song for him … I was going to play it …'

She smiled. 'He'd love that. He played the saz, too …'

'I know.'

She started walking away, then stopped. 'Do you think …? Could I stay … and listen? I'll keep my distance …'

I shook my head. 'Don't! I mean, yes. I mean don't keep your distance … Stay …'

'Thank you.' She moved to the other side of the grave.

I tuned up, then sang:

in Rumeli's shadow
death
voluptuous
waylaid me

she held me by the hand
my eyes scared lambkins
I pleaded

she whispered in my ear
my heart a humming-bird
I consented

she rubbed her breasts on my face
my mouth insatiable
I suckled

she opened her legs
my manhood a dolphin
I plunged

there in her well
I found
the only true water

I ended up weeping uncontrollably and, surprisingly, didn't feel embarrassed.

She came across and kissed my hand. 'May your heart be always full of love.'

I couldn't speak. Afraid of becoming hysterical, I staggered away.

At the top of the slope, I composed myself and looked back.

The sun was rising over the Anatolian shore; a roseate tide was engulfing the cemetery.

Madam Ruj had sat down again. She was bathed in a glow that could have emanated only from Haydar's soul. She had taken out her lipstick and was putting it on.

The constant application of lipstick, I remembered, was one of her idiosyncrasies. All Istanbul knew that. Her cigarette case and lighter and her lipstick were part of her accoutrements. Wherever she sat down, she lined them up in front of her with the intensity of a chessmaster setting up his pieces.

I watched her.

She looked like a somnambulist: uncontrolled yet

constrained. She didn't seem to need a mirror. And the way she applied the lipstick, she could have been painting a portrait. Or obliterating it.

∞∞∞∞∞∞🐚∞∞∞∞∞∞

We met again six years later.

I had just returned from England. I would stay a year, shuttling between Istanbul and Ankara – with occasional visits to my supervisor in Oxford – researching my doctoral thesis. Determined to revive a fatigued mind with a good holiday, I had headed for Büyükada. To my parents' disappointment, I had declared full independence by spurning the family villa and renting a room.

Hooked on rugby, I had become a hefty youth. And I considered myself rather experienced in sex – if, that is, one can call rushed couplings in digs, bedsits, the last row of a cinema or the back seat of someone's car, experience. (I deserved little credit for all that sensualism; in those days, a Turkish male in England was still a rare, if not exotic, dessert for debutantes voraciously feasting on Oxbridge fare before their demure ascent up the social ladder.)

I was ready for Istanbul's sun, sea and passionate naiads. And, in pursuit of these, I had begun looking up old flames.

I was not being very successful. Passionate naiads in my age group were not interested in a summer affair with a dusty scholar who was going to spend several years working on a thesis and then end up teaching at some dreary university for a risible salary. They were looking for men who had graduated as engineers, architects, lawyers, doctors or who were on the way to becoming grandees of industry or commerce. Indeed, passionate naiads in my age group were dousing their passion lest they be perceived as wanton women unfit for marriage; they were determined to usher autumn in with an engagement ring so that next summer they could compare fur coats, limousines, months spent skiing in Switzerland and, not least, pregnancies.

I had had dinner at a fashionable restaurant with Emine, with whom I had had a spirited flirtation before going to Oxford. Having set her sights on one Bülent, a graduate of Harvard Business School, she had eaten and drunk lustily, for old times' sake, then had dismissed me with a peck on the cheek and a perfunctory 'good luck'.

So I had caught the last ferry to Büyükada and, to repair my pride in seclusion, had settled in the first-class enclosure.

As the ferry's horn announced its departure, I spotted a woman sprint down Galata Bridge and scamper over the gangway.

She was followed, seconds later, by a bony middle-aged man whom I had noticed lurking on the pier.

As she entered the first class, I recognized her: Madam Ruj.

Though the enclosure was empty, she came over and sat at my table. 'If I may ...'

I nodded. 'Sure.'

She took out her lipstick, cigarette case and lighter and lined them up on the table. 'I'd feel safer.'

The bony, middle-aged man, I observed, had taken a seat on the deck and was watching her. 'Is he bothering you?'

She looked at the man and chuckled. 'Dan Weiss? Couldn't hurt a mosquito.'

'What's wrong, then?'

She lit a cigarette. 'Demons.'

'Demons?'

She started freshening up her lipstick. 'Inside. Don't you have demons?'

'Many.'

'Tiresome things – but what can you do?'

'Madam Ruj … Right?'

'Who else?'

'You don't recognize me?'

She smiled. 'Sure, I do. I'm not in the habit of plonking myself at a man's table without knowing who he is. It's names that get cloud-hidden sometimes.'

'Aslan. Aslan Erdoğan.'

'Of course. I have a big file on you.'

'You don't have to humour me. I'm not offended.'

'I'm doing nothing of the sort! We met – at Haydar's grave. You sang a song.'

'You do remember …'

She put her lipstick back on the table. 'I have a tape – where you sing that song …'

I looked at her in surprise. 'Really? I only made a few

copies – for friends.'

'Yes, well, I managed to get a copy of a copy … Do you still compose?'

'Sometimes.'

'Only sometimes? Why?'

'Lost the urge. Then studies … I've been away …'

'Six years.'

'How did you know that?'

She smiled, dragging heavily on her cigarette. 'It's my job to know. As I said, I have a file on you. I'm a matchmaker.'

'Yes, but … I mean, how could I be of interest?'

'You're a bachelor. A good catch in many ways …'

'Me?' I laughed. 'Marriage is the last thing on my mind. I have a thesis to write!'

'When you finish. People would be prepared to wait …'

'What people?'

'Interested parties …'

'Who, for instance?'

She shrugged. 'All sorts.'

'You don't mean my parents?'

She chuckled. 'No. Your parents wouldn't employ me. I'm Jewish. They'd find someone Muslim. But your grandmother …'

'My grandmother?'

'She's from Salonica. A very Jewish city until the war. She feels close to the Jews.'

I was baffled. 'My grandmother – approached you? You're joking …'

'I never joke about business.' She picked up her lipstick and retouched her rouge. 'There are people of other denominations also ... You see, we're improving. As a society, I mean. Burying prejudices. Intermarrying. Excellent for my business ...'

'I don't believe this ...'

She looked at me – pityingly, I thought. 'I have at least eight parents of teenagers interested in you. Their daughters will ripen just when you finish your doctorate ...

I started laughing. 'But me, of all people ...?'

She put her lipstick back on the table and picked up her cigarette. 'Gilt-edged. Well-educated. An English university – and not just any university, but the best. Enlightened, in all probability. Therefore made to measure for intermarriage. You're peerless!'

'Well, I'm amazed, Madam Ruj ...'

'Call me Mazal. Madam Ruj is for clients.' She stubbed out her cigarette and lit a new one. 'Did you write other songs about Haydar?'

'Yes. At the time. A few.'

'Could I hear them one day?"

'Sure.'

She gave me her card. 'Come to lunch – before you go back to Oxford.'

I read the card. 'You live on the island – nice ...'

'Yes – though not all that nice in the summer. Half of Istanbul descends on it. But in winter – it's heavenly. Which is perfect for me. That's when I take my holidays.'

'Don't people arrange marriages in winter?'

'Not unless they're desperate. You can't exhibit merchandise all that well in winter. Whereas in the summer, in a bathing suit by the sea, even Dan can look captivating.'

I laughed and glanced at the bony man. 'Hard to imagine that.'

'Don't be fooled by appearances. He's a rock. Looks after me like a father.'

'He doesn't look that old ...'

'He's not. But he's made it his business to keep an eye on me ...'

'Why?'

'In case I go Haydar's way ...'

'How do you mean?'

'Do myself in ...'

I stared at her, suddenly chilled to the bone. 'Why should you?'

'Good question ...' She put her head on my shoulder. 'Can I doze a bit? I'm exhausted ...'

'Of course.'

She shut her eyes. 'I've just completed a *shiddach* – made a match. It was hard work. But I'll earn a fortune ...'

'Congratulations.'

She muttered drowsily. 'Want to know how much?'

'It's none of my ...'

'I'll tell you anyway ...'

She fell asleep.

She was still holding her cigarette. Carefully, making

sure I didn't burn her, I extricated it from her fingers. Then I put an arm around her and, impulsively, to spite Dan, kissed her cheek.

I turned towards him to catch his reaction, but he had stopped watching us and was reading a newspaper.

※

When we reached Büyükada, I nudged her gently.

She stood up, somewhat confused and embarrassed.

Hastily she touched up her lipstick.

She collected her cigarette case and lighter, then, just as she had done at Haydar's graveside, she kissed my hand. 'Thank you.'

She hurried away.

As I disembarked, I saw her settle in a landau and reapply her lipstick. I watched the carriage trot into the night.

Dan Weiss followed her in another landau.

※

Haydar had planned his suicide meticulously. He had swum out from Bodrum, the ancient Halikarnassus, on 20 May at 5:28 PM and had expected to expire 'as fish-fodder' at around midnight, just outside Turkish waters, off the Greek island of Kos.

He had worked this out, in several notebooks, by computing the speed of the currents, their seasonal anomalies and the ebb and flow of the Mediterranean's negligible tides. But he had either miscalculated or had tired too soon. (During his last weeks, his energy had been fast diminishing.) Consequently, his body had washed ashore the following morning at the tip of Bodrum's peninsula, bloated but untouched by the fish.

In other notebooks, he had discoursed on death's holy role in life, the blessings of the return to primary matter and the even greater blessings of reincarnation. ('How can we attain Nirvana if we do not experience the states of being and non-being of every organism?')

His last notebook, scrawled with barely legible handwriting, expounded on the benedictions of terminal illnesses, particularly those that inflict intolerable pain. Partly the ramblings of a man shuttling between the euphoria of morphine relief and the torment of morphine deprivation, partly an espousal of redemption through suffering – that effluvium of monotheism which, though he had passionately rejected it, kept resurfacing to poison his consciousness – and partly a manly stand against unendurable adversity, the discourse revolted me. I saw it as the sentimental vacuity of a man terrified by death. Whereas I had wanted him to bellow his wrath at being cut down in his prime so that those who faced untimely and humiliating quietus – all humankind, in effect – could use that wrath as an anthem. What's the use of our religions if they keep worshipping Death?

These and Haydar's other papers – poems, letters received, copies of letters sent, pamphlets seeking equality for the Kurds and the rehabilitation of their language and culture, articles condemning the Menderes regime's corrupt and paternalist rule, indictments of the Soviet bloc's homicidal treatment of dissenters, panegyrics on the Universal Declaration of Human Rights, treatises on steering humankind to peace through a world government – indeed, just about everything he had owned, written or been associated with, including the tape of the song I had sung by his grave – had been kept by Madam Ruj in her Büyükada villa, in a blue room seemingly blending with the sea that she called 'the shrine'.

I became a devotee of this temple of love and catalogued every document. (This devotion set back my thesis by several months. On the other hand, I did manage to get Haydar's poems published as a collection and to favourable reviews.)

My involvement started after I visited Madam Ruj, as I had promised, to play the songs I had composed for Haydar – five in all – all that time ago. She liked them and insisted on giving them their rightful place in the shrine.

Thereafter, she summoned Dan – 'bony Dan' – to record them, assuring me that, coincidentally, like Haydar, he was an accomplished jack-of-all-trades.

My initial response to Dan had been one of deep antipathy. This most adroit father figure, I had decided, was an opportunist – even though I had known that it had been Madam Ruj who had cast him in that role. (She had been quite frank on that point, admitting that, having lost both parents when still an infant, she had wanted some form of parenting.) However, within a short time, Dan's natural dignity and genuine decency dispelled my prejudices and we became close friends.

Dan had never met Haydar.

He was an Ashkenazi Jew whose father and mother, academics in Berlin, had been confrères of Erich Auerbach, the author of *Mimesis*. When, in the wake of the Nuremberg Laws, Atatürk had offered sanctuary to the Jews of the Third Reich, Auerbach and, in his wake, Dan's family, had accepted the invitation and emigrated to Turkey. Auerbach, duly appointed director of Istanbul University's School of Foreign Languages, had, in turn, installed Dan's parents in the faculty. When, at the end of the war, the full dimensions of the Holocaust had emerged, Dan had embraced Zionism and run off to Palestine. He had fought in the Arab-Israeli war of 1948-49, then settled in a kibbutz established by Turkish Jews. About three years back, Madam Ruj had visited that very kibbutz in search of a widow for an elderly client; Dan, assigned as her guide, had instantly fallen for her. Thereafter, abandoning his Zionist ideals, he had followed her to Istanbul. Since then, despite her repeated declarations that she had sworn never to marry again because she would never love a man as she had loved Haydar, he had orbited her patiently.

Yes, she and Haydar had married.

Secretly. Soon after they had met at the wedding of one of Haydar's army friends where both had been guests of honour: Madam Ruj because she had brokered the marriage – the bride, being a Karaite Jew, had come under her constituency – and Haydar because he had saved the bridegroom's life by carrying his wounded body through the Chinese lines during the battle of Kunuri, despite being hit himself. (In military terms, Kunuri has become a legend: the Turkish contingent, surrounded while collecting shell-cases that could be sold as scrap, had had to break the encirclement with a bayonet charge. This astounding feat had left them with heavy casualties. The fact that the shell-cases were being collected for a fund for the families of fallen comrades had compounded the tragedy.)

The wedding had captured Istanbul's imagination. Celâl, the bridegroom, had ended up a paraplegic; his bride, Sara – four years older and so plain as to be considered unmarriageable – had lived a reclusive life working in an old-people's home. Yet, within days, the couple had fallen deeply in love. In a letter, Haydar had described the fairy-tale atmosphere thus: 'This wedding is a portent for a better future, both for the country and the world. I now know Mazal is my destiny.' (There is a haunting double entendre here. *Mazal* means 'luck' in Hebrew.)

And so they, too, had married. In Las Vegas, of all places. During Haydar's tour of the United States, as a hero of the Korean war, to promulgate the importance of NATO. Haydar, who hated such jingoistic razzmatazz, would not have gone but for Madam Ruj's categorical refusal to marry openly in Turkey.

The secrecy, I immediately assumed, had been to protect Madam Ruj's career. For that was the time when Haydar's campaigns for a world government were being severely censured; matchmaking and politics were hardly compatible bedfellows.

But Dan, reassuring me that the people, stirred by Haydar's integrity, would have taken the couple to their hearts, divulged the real reason: her obsession with the need for celibacy.

The orphaned Mazal had been brought up by her great-aunt, the legendary matchmaker, Allegra. Groomed to follow in her guardian's footsteps, Mazal had sought to emulate her. What better way to thank Allegra for all the years of nurturing? However, to achieve success, matchmakers needed to be unattached – like monks. That was the rule. Haydar, of course, had derided this perverse logic. If matchmakers really wanted to have an insight into their clients, he contended, they should do the opposite: throw themselves into the fray and experience the tribulations of connubiality. But Madam Ruj, forever intoning Allegra's indoctrination, even years after the latter's death, held that a knowledge of conjugality – be it in carnal matters or in the unabated monotony of cohabitation – distorted the matchmaker's vision of the grand design, namely, a union made in heaven. Only celibacy perceived the original perfection. The fact that most marriages turned into wars of attrition was irrelevant. When unions made in heaven foundered on earth, the fault lay neither with heaven nor with the matchmaker; it lay with human frailty.

Yet, somehow, Haydar's views on love and life had prevailed. Mazal had finally yielded to his ardour. But she had insisted not only on the secret ceremony in Las

Vegas, but also on living apart – for some years, at least – and meeting clandestinely, as they had done since starting their affair.

Eventually, she had come to find even this arrangement a burden. Haydar's growing desire for children, combined with her paranoia that someone would find out about her marriage, had compelled her, before a year had elapsed, to return to Las Vegas and divorce him.

However, despite that 'unforgivable betrayal' – so Haydar had remonstrated in numerous love letters – they had been unable to give each other up.

Naturally, at a great cost.

Haydar had grown increasingly desolate. Mazal's unequivocal refusal to have children, in particular, had felt like an immutable sentence. Many of his letters had expressed the fantasy of running to some poor country and returning with a bunch of orphans. A short prison sentence, around this time, following his defence of Kurdish culture, had virtually broken him.

One letter, written shortly before the diagnosis of his cancer, had accused her, quite blatantly, of killing him – 'slowly, but surely'.

I could not even begin to comprehend how Madam Ruj, who had loved Haydar so intensely – still did – could sacrifice their happiness in pursuit of an occupation that was not only parasitical, but anachronistic.

Dan, however, had no difficulty in understanding. The blame, he affirmed, lay with her great-aunt, Allegra. Why did this woman – by all accounts, a veritable beauty – take up a profession when, in her days, her contemporaries never even thought about working but waited to be snapped up for marriage? And why, of all pursuits, did she choose such a fatuous one as matchmaking? As for that evangelical rubbish about celibacy – what did it really signify? Matchmakers know better than anyone that reality lies in the opposite direction, that, in the main, marriages are made in hell! The reason they persevere valiantly is because they also know that living in solitude is worse than hell. So what prevented Allegra from electing the lesser evil? Why did she then go and infect Mazal with the same dread?

Well, obviously, Allegra had been quite disturbed. Maybe an abused child. Maybe simply a child who had suffered irreparable parental neglect. Maybe indoctrinated with hatred for men by a maltreated family member. Maybe even appointed the family breadwinner, therefore designated a male, therefore forbidden to marry.

∞∞∞∞∞∞❀∞∞∞∞∞∞

A word here on the imprisonment – the fourth and last – that had virtually broken Haydar. By the mid-fifties, the Menderes government had plunged Turkey into political turmoil. Any criticism of its conduct – indeed, any controversial topic – incurred for the 'offender' immediate arrest, speedy trial and gaol. Under these circumstances, the dissemination of such liberal views as a world government or the advocacy of

Kurdish rights was harshly repressed. Haydar had had the temerity to address both issues at a music festival after a Kurdish singer, trying to sing a song in Kurdish, had been bundled off the stage. Jumping on to the stage himself, Haydar had declared that as and when a world government came into being, all the suppressed languages, starting with Kurdish, would be resurrected as part of humanity's cultural heritage.

Instantly thrown off the stage in his turn, he had been duly charged with accusing Turkey of oppressing its Kurdish minority when the whole world knew that no such minority existed since all who called themselves Kurds were in reality Turks who had forgotten their Turkishness and were now coming back into the fold.

Ironically, despite the fact that he had lost many members of his family during the Kurdish revolt of 1937, Haydar had chosen to renounce his Kurdishness – as demanded by the Turkification programmes – early on in his campaign for world government. He had done so, not because he had felt cowed by the authorities, but in the naive belief that the dream of Turkicizing the country had been a temporary aberration caused by the demise of the Ottoman empire and that, as and when Turkey recovered from that grief, it would duly reclaim the pluralism of the Ottomans – perhaps even serve as a prototype for world government. But he had soon realized that societies aspiring to be monolithic could not accommodate diversity and that, therefore, they would always set out to destroy heterogeneity. The corollary to that, he had further realized, was that should a society succeed in becoming a monolith, it would have sown the seeds of its own destruction. By renouncing intercourse with other racial, national and ethnic groups, it would have forbidden itself regeneration and new blood; it would have committed, as it were, suicide by collective onanism.

Thereafter Haydar had become an ardent supporter of Kurdish rights.

∞∞∞∞∞∞◦❀◦∞∞∞∞∞∞

On one of those sunny autumn days when Büyükada, disburdened of summer folk and day-trippers, feels like a mythic realm, Dan and I, sitting on the balcony of Haydar's shrine, were exploring the limits of raki's milky way, a favourite pastime of the melancholic Turk. Madam Ruj, having donned her official mien – 'the myrmidon look', Haydar used to call it – had gone to meet a prospective client. I remember thinking, on starting our third bottle, that as long as she pursued her vacuous career, there would be no redemption for anybody, not even for me, the outsider who had soldered a wistful trio into an even more wistful quartet.

So we sat silently, bracing the wind in duffel coats, drinking, chain-smoking and watching sea and sky conceive that eternal cruel question: what if ...

As if on cue, Dan grew earnest. 'Aslan, do you love Mazal?'

I nodded sentimentally. 'I adore her!'

'And desire her? As I do?'

'Dan ...'

'Answer me! Truthfully!'

'She's very attractive ... but ...'

'That means you do. Good. Go for her!'

'What?'

'You're somewhat younger, but that shouldn't matter. She likes you. Admires you. Seduce her!'

'Dan, you're drunk ...'

'I'm serious!'

I got angry. 'What do you take me for? She's your woman! Is that how you see me – someone who'd cuckold a friend?'

'I could bear that. Besides, she's not my woman ...'

'She is – as far as I'm concerned!'

He held my hands. 'You and I – we don't count. She needs to be saved. You could save her ...'

'Save her? From what?'

'From herself. She wants to emulate Haydar. Only she wants to do it better. Disappear without trace.'

I scoffed. 'What nonsense!'

'I'm telling you!'

Suddenly I remembered my conversation with Mazal on the Büyükada boat. About going Haydar's way. And the mention of inner demons. 'How do you know?'

'I know.'

I didn't want to believe him. I wouldn't. 'How?'

'I go through her things. I'm good at that. I leave no traces. I once served in Intelligence. She's keeping a notebook, like Haydar did. Hides it in her bedroom. It's all in there ...'

'But why?'

'Guilt, I imagine. You remember Haydar's letter where he says she's killing him?'

'Yes …'

'Now she agrees with that.'

'Rubbish! She told me several times: starting with VD, soldiers pick up all sorts of diseases overseas. Haydar was unlucky. He picked up cancer.'

'She no longer believes that. It was a good palliative, she says. Now she's convinced she caused his illness – broke his heart. She contends that if they'd stayed married, lived together like an ordinary couple and had children, he'd still be alive.'

'That's ridiculous.'

'Sure, it is. But she's come to believe it.'

'And let's not forget the treatment Haydar received in police stations and in gaol. People say it was the beatings that brought on his cancer.'

'Yes, I heard that, too.'

'Well, tell her that!'

'I did. She won't hear of it. She insists she killed Haydar. She wants to atone for it.'

'Atone – how?'

'Plans to swim out – also from Bodrum. A life for a life.'

I could no longer repudiate what deep down I knew was the truth.

My despondency reanimated him. 'I've been thinking for months … How to stop her? I've even consulted experts. But no one understands her as I do. There is a way – one only. She must love again. Must want a man again – sexually. I hoped to be that man. She won't have me.'

'And you think she'd have me?'

'She might. Yes …'

'And if she does?'

'We'd have saved her.'

'And you? What would happen to you?'

'Who cares?'

'How would you feel towards me?'

'Probably hate you for ever.'

'Great!'

'Fuck our sensitivities! Don't you understand? This is our only chance to save her!'

'It's crazy …'

'Will you do it?'

'I'm not convinced …'

'Will you do it?'

'I'm writing a doctorate … I'm away a lot …'

'Will you do it?'

I leaned back, too drunk to offer another objection.

He embraced me and wept, almost happily.

The year 1958 had trampled on intellectuals and writers; 1959, we knew, would be worse. So we hoped for miracles and watched the calendar.

It was rumoured that Madam Ruj loved New Year's Eve parties. Socialites always put her first on their guest lists. She attended as many parties as she could, osmosed from one to the other, even breakfasted with the diehards, at a famous tripery in Beyoğlu. (In a letter to Haydar, she had revealed that she actually hated these parties, but attended them because the general frenzy served as a litmus test for assessing marriageable men and women.)

This year, however, she had decided to forego them. The decision had alarmed Dan, leading him to think that her 'swim' might be imminent, a New Year's resolution. He begged me to seduce her without delay.

I contacted her immediately. Much of my New Year's holiday, I claimed, would be hard grind; consequently, I was in need of a morale-boosting drink with a dear friend. Dan, whom I would have asked to join us, I lied, was involved with cousins and relatives.

Mazal, rejecting the usual haunts as too boisterous – a reaction both Dan and I had counted on – invited me instead to dinner at her house on the island. She even suggested I should stay the night as boat services from the islands to the city, on New Year's Eve, were severely reduced.

And so, bearing flowers, I went.

∞∞∞∞∞∞∞✿∞∞∞∞∞∞∞

She had prepared a feast.

I sensed she was tense. (If she gets tense, Dan had said, it's a good sign; it'll mean she's tantalized.)

She must have sensed my tension, too. (If she senses

you are tense, Dan had said, that's also a good sign; she'll know you want her.)

We ate leisurely, savouring every morsel, but drank abstemiously. (If you both drink temperately, Dan had said, that'll be the best sign; it'll mean you want to be sober in order to have sex.)

And we talked. Surprisingly, very little about Haydar. Some about Dan. Mostly about aspects of modern poetry, the subject of my doctorate. To my delight, she had kept abreast of Turkish literature.

Then it was midnight.

We kissed, formally, to welcome 1959.

I had prepared a surprise for her. 'I've written you a song.' (One of your sexy songs, especially composed for her, Dan had assured me, should prove the clincher.)

She clapped her hands, delighted like a little girl. 'Wonderful! Please play it!'

I picked up Haydar's saz and sang:

forget
romantic love
forget
traditions
principles
friends
family
beau monde

the sea is libidinous
there is madness in our blood

so come
on this carnal night
let us
lose ourselves
in
each other's
light

I put the saz away, wondering whether I had been too audacious.

She came over and kissed me, this time with some passion.

I responded with greater passion.

'How long have you wanted me?'

I dissembled. 'From the day we met.'

'Dan told me. I didn't believe him.' She pointed to her bedroom. 'Undress. Get into bed.' She went into the bathroom.

I did as told.

She returned, naked.

She lit the candle on the dresser and switched off the light.

She lined up her lipstick, cigarette case and lighter on the bedside table.

I noticed her hands were shaking and her smile was strained.

I threw off the covers.

She stared at my erection – quite sadly – then folded into herself and collapsed.

Later, we talked.

She tried to reassure me that the debacle had nothing to do with me, that she had frozen many times before. I was a very attractive man, immensely kind and gentle. Most women would walk through fire for me. But, alas, whenever she dared be with a man, she crumbled.

It wasn't as if she disliked sex. She was very keen on it. But at a safe distance. It had been so even with Haydar. Very intense, for example, after they had divorced. Which might also explain her difficulties with matrimony. Best to enjoy through other people's marriages, as her great-aunt used to say. Better still, to imagine that the marriages she had arranged were her children. Why not? Hadn't she created them in the first place?

Then she apologized again. She had used me. But, horrendous as that was, she could not have done so had I not been very dear to her. She had grown to love Dan and wanted to marry him. But she had not had the heart to subject him to the sort of fiasco I had just experienced. Yet she had kept hoping that if she could only conquer her paralysis, if she could just enjoy a man's body naturally, she could then live with Dan happily ever after.

Thereafter we sat silently and held hands.

Then morning came and she asked me to leave.

Dan had been waiting for me at the pier. We took the first boat to Istanbul.

Though he was obviously relieved that Mazal and I had not made love, my account of the night perturbed him.

It was time, he decided, he had a heart-to-heart talk with her. Time to expunge the past and start the future. They would certainly marry – even if they never ever touched. They would be together. Loving. That's all that mattered.

He returned to Büyükada on the next boat.

But he was too late.

Mazal had left.

∞∞∞∞∞∞✿●●●●●●●●●●

We spent days scouring the bay of Bodrum.

To no avail.

She had disappeared without trace.

Then a rumour appeared – by all accounts, originating from the local fishermen …

That every night from sunset until dawn, a mermaid with luminous black hair and a dolphin, rotund like a Buddha-figure, made love deliriously in the waters between Bodrum and the island of Kos.

12: Davut

He Who Returns Never Left

I couldn't decide whether I should shout for help or fall on to my knees and beg for mercy. There were four of them. Two on either side of me. I tried to walk between them, intrepidly, like a film hero being led to his execution – Ronald Colman, was it? But my legs shook and I could barely hold my urine.

True, I wasn't going to my execution; but they were going to beat the shit out of me – that's what they'd said – which was not much of a consolation.

I turned to Faruk, the fellow holding my right arm, the tallest of the four and the one with the strip of plaster on his forehead. It was he who had accused me of causing the wound on his head – actually, not a wound, but the sort of boil that afflicts men who don't have regular sex and won't masturbate. Not to mention the fact that, even if I'd wanted to hurt the turd, there was no way I could have reached his forehead since he was twice my height. Not to mention also that I'd never met him before, though I'd sometimes seen him in my reaches of the Bosporus. On this occasion he had approached me at the tram stop in Arnavutköy and, thinking that he wanted to ask directions, I had stopped to talk to him. 'You sure you're not mistaking me for someone else?'

'Positive.'

He looked at the others: Nuri, Salih and Hasan – 'brothers' who had answered his call to help him fight this superman – me – who had beaten him so mercilessly. Nothing less than family honour was at stake.

They answered in unison. 'No. You're the man.'

I turned to Faruk again. 'Would you at least agree that you're much bigger than I am? That there's no way I could have punched you on the forehead?'

'You could have – if I was asleep.'

'But you weren't. You said we got into a fight. You said that's when I hit you.'

'I often fall asleep when I fight.'

Normally I would have laughed. It's always courteous to admire wit. But how can you when you're shaking with fear? I tried another tack. 'Don't you think it's beneath you – and beneath your he-men brothers – to beat the shit out of a weakling like me?'

'No. It'll be good fun. Besides, you're not a weakling.' He pointed at the strip of plaster on his forehead. 'You hurt me.'

'I didn't touch you. I didn't even know you until you stopped me and pretended you wanted to ask me something.'

'I did ask you something. Or rather brother Hasan did. He asked you why you hit me.'

'And I told him you've got the wrong man.'

'With due respect, we don't believe you.'

Finally, I tried my best ploy in circumstances like these. 'How about if we all go to the cinema? There's a good film. Gary Cooper. I'll buy the tickets.'

'We've seen it.'

'Something you haven't seen then?'

'We've seen all the films.'

'All right – the music hall? Lots of women with bare legs …?'

'You want us to masturbate? And walk around the rest of the day in a defiled state?'

'No! No! You could – just watch.'

'And get frustrated?'

'Isn't there any way I can change your mind?'

'Look, stop all your clever stuff! We'll rough you up a bit, then let you go. You'll be good as new in three days. If you fight back, you'll be in hospital for a month.'

I sighed. Three days compared to a month wasn't too bad. But it was still three days too many. More to the point, I'd had a bellyful of these arbitrary beatings. Layabouts picking on passers-by to prove – to whom? to themselves? – that they were brave and strong. I didn't have the stomach for such foolery any more. Either battle fatigue or undergraduate years in England had softened me. I just wanted to cultivate my garden peacefully.

I looked back disconsolately towards the café where Melek was waiting for me. It was three in the afternoon, the hottest hour of the hottest month. Everybody was indoors snoring with the shutters down. Which was why Melek and I could meet and not be seen by members of our respective families – or worse, by gossip-mongers – who were already outraged by our love affair. A Muslim girl going out with a Jew! And that wasn't all: we had both moved out of the parental home and shared flats with friends – not the done thing, though we were both over twenty and I had already spent some years living alone in England. Indisputably, such independence turned us, in the minds of the elders, into the sort of degenerates whose every thought was tumescent with sex. (But then, that's how it should be!) Consequently both set of parents, suspecting – rightly, of course – that whenever we could we would run off to the hills to do what nature urged us to do, had a network of spies on surveillance duty. (Most of the time, we managed to avoid these spooks. After all, we had been suckled on Agatha Christie, Dashiell Hammett and Raymond Chandler.)

I sighed again. Not only had these villains who were bored out of their minds confiscated our blissful hours but they had also spoiled the next three days – providing, of course, they kept their word and didn't do a hospital job on me. I took another look at Faruk and his brothers; they seemed the sort who would keep their word. But then, appearances …

I would have to run for it. It wouldn't be very manly or like Ronald Colman, but there was nothing else I could do. I was an adequate runner and pretty fast. And I had noted that there were bulges of good living around the bellies of my abductors; they were bound to struggle for breath after 100 metres or so. Whereas I had plenty of stamina – as Melek was my witness.

I would have to move when they least expected it. When they became complacent. That would be when they turned chivalrous and offered each other the honour of hitting me first.

They led me into a narrow alleyway that was secluded and shaded. This is where it would happen. I braced myself to sprint away.

A voice roared from the shadows. 'Fuck off, you louts!'

I recognized the fortissimo. Ergun, the local part-time policeman. He was pissing into a drain and we had disturbed him.

He could be my deliverance. I shouted, 'Sorry, Ergun! Didn't see you! It's Davut! Hello, anyway!'

I heard Faruk and his mates greet Ergun also.

Ergun emerged out of the shade, buttoning his trousers and smiling. He looked amiable, not at all angry at having been disturbed in mid-piss. That was good news. I mean, I'd been a fine friend to him, helped him with his studies so that he would graduate to full-time policeman, advised him to wear French letters so as not to get the domestics – mostly village girls – pregnant and have their fathers come after him with knives. But a policeman is a policeman and that means their good mood can change in seconds, particularly on a hot day – or a rainy day, any day, actually. 'I didn't know you fuckers knew each other ...'

I grabbed my lifeline. 'We don't. We've just met.'

Faruk stared at Ergun. 'You know him?'

'Davut? My bosom pal! How did you meet?'

Faruk looked embarrassed. 'We didn't – actually – meet. Our paths crossed. And – well, we were going to rough him up a bit.'

'What for?'

I shrugged with bravura. 'For the fun of it.'

'That's stupid. They'd beat the shit out of you.'

I smiled. 'What's a bit of shit between friends?'

I had barely finished my sentence when Faruk lifted me off the ground and kissed me on both cheeks. 'Apologies, Davut, dear heart. Any friend of Ergun's is our brother.'

Then his other brothers kissed me.

Faruk herded us out of the alleyway. 'Come on! We'll bless this reunion. The raki's on me.'

Ergun protested. 'I've got to be on duty in a few minutes.'

Faruk grabbed his arm. 'Fuck that. Tell your chief you bumped into some villains and went after them.'

'What villains? Where?'

'Right here. We're villains, aren't we?'

'You're small-time black marketeers pushing cigarettes – Bulgarian ones, at that. Hardly worth the sweat.'

'We got hold of some whisky yesterday. From NATO. Real Scotch. We'll give you a few bottles. That should keep your chief happy.'

Ergun nodded. 'Now you're talking.'

Faruk put his arm around mine. 'No hard feelings, eh?'

'None.'

'Good man. You're my brother for life.'

He led us to the café where Melek was still waiting for me.

She watched incredulously as I sat and drank with Ergun, Faruk and the rest. I tried to signal to her that I had to be with them for a while otherwise I'd be in trouble, and that she should wait a bit. She didn't, of course. She often dismissed my point of view.

Ergun went to work after an hour or so – with four bottles of Scotch.

I went on drinking with my new brothers until late into the night. I grew to love them, all the more so after they listened attentively and sympathetically to the doctoral thesis I was working on about the contradictions in the Turkish character and how old-fashioned fascists were exploiting these in order to enslave Turkey's noble soul. As we hugged and said goodnight – actually, good morning – they swore they would protect me through thick and thin – even spring me from gaol should I be imprisoned for offending Allah knows who with my scribbles.

<hr/>

Melek was irate when we met the next day. But her priorities were right and she waited until we had regained our secluded copse on the hills above Rumeli Hisarı and made love before telling me off for ignoring her the previous day. But by then her anger, which can be as unforgiving as the glacial winds of Hakkâri, had waned to a mere breeze. There is nothing better than sex to smooth male and female brows; indeed, to bring peace upon human beings. (I should also say that Melek and I had made love even more hungrily than usual. We had to get our ration for that day, then make up for the day we'd lost thanks to Faruk and his brothers, as well as stock up for the next day when we would be travelling to Bursa to pick up my old teacher, Âşık Ahmet, who was being released from prison after having served yet another sentence for disseminating Nâzım Hikmet's work.)

Melek had grudgingly accepted that my inability to approach her the previous day was due to forces beyond my control, but she refused to be sympathetic. 'You should have yelled bloody murder!'

'There was no one about!'

'I was there. I'd have created havoc.'

I hadn't thought of that. 'I didn't want to involve you.'

'Liar! You were enjoying it.'

'Don't talk rubbish! They were going to beat me up.'

'Which would have made you the heroic victim. Everybody would have admired you. You love that!'

She knew me well, Melek. Probably better than I

knew myself. That would have been me – until recently. But not any more. Not since I'd fallen prey to fear. 'Actually, I was petrified ...'

Studentship in drab, post-war England – where people kept out of each other's way and no one hugged or kissed, let alone picked fights for fun – had softened me. Then while I was comparing the qualities of a chauvinistic, confrontational Turkey with the genteel pugnacity of England, fear, which must have been hibernating in my mind, began to stir. Thereafter, drifting here and there, stealthily feeding at sulphurous nooks and crannies, it had billowed. Now it was a massive obesity, a mound of rotting melons.

Melek opened her eyes wide, as if surprised. 'Are you telling me you're getting to be human at last?'

I smiled tentatively and nodded.

I had managed to focus on my fears only recently – to be precise, about six weeks earlier when, returning from London for the summer holidays, I had been grilled, for some two hours, first by customs officers then by plain-clothes policemen who, judging by their implacable expressions, could only have been agents of the dreaded MIT, the secret service. Though I had brought all sorts of fashionable gifts for friends and family – items that I had meticulously declared and for which I expected to pay a hefty duty – the customs officers had been more interested in the outline of my doctoral thesis and the two box-files that contained all my primary documentation. What made them look upon me as if I were a man with the heads of seven snakes was that I had actually sat down and written a sheaf of pages and annotated them with comments and references. The MIT agents were even more sophisticated; they asked what they thought were subtle questions on my political inclinations while anybody who cared to look into their eyes would have seen the phrase 'this fellow is a communist' flashing in neon lights from their irises. All of which meant I was worse than an alien from outer space.

Melek realized I had strayed into another dimension. Immediately she became maternal. She pulled me down on to her lap. 'What's wrong, my sugar?'

'Nothing ...'

'Come on ...'

'I'm wondering how many times I can make you come in a day ... Fifty?'

'You want to kill me?'

'Forty, then ...'

She slapped me playfully. 'Stop it! What's bothering you ...?'

'Nothing ...'

'Something is, I can tell ...'

'I suppose I'm scared ...'

'Uh-huh ...'

'Not a good feeling. Captain Marvel – scared ...'

'Scared of what?'

I had told her about my episode with customs and MIT. And the baleful questioning that had ensued. How the senior agent had lectured me on the true nature of printed matter, which, until proven otherwise by vigilant minds like his, was dangerous for humanity, was, in effect, a deadly mine strategically placed to blow up both the ships of state and their defenders. How another agent had mused that texts in English, like my thesis – when completed – would most certainly spawn countless other dangers. (My assurances that I intended to translate it into Turkish had alarmed him even more.) And how calamity had finally struck when they had confiscated my outline after hearing that my thesis dealt with the contradictions in the Turkish character. That its specific premise was how the Turks' innate nobility tempered with the best of Islamic teaching made them the most tolerant people in the world, while the plethora of complexes instilled by the worst of Islamic teaching could – and sometimes did – turn them into ogres. Of course, I should have lied and told them something simple and innocuous, but I am not a good liar. Besides, as Melek had remarked, it wouldn't have helped because they would have confiscated my outline even if every page had contained only verses of the national anthem.

'Scared of the authorities ...'

Melek kissed me on my forehead. 'Fuck the authorities.'

'It's the irrational. The arbitrary decisions. The injustices power condones. Not just condones, but permits, encourages, perpetrates ... That's what I fear ... It has become so much part of our daily life ...'

'That's how it has always been.'

'I didn't realize. Didn't even stop and think ... And then ...' I began to laugh. Amazing that something as stupid as escaping a beating had clarified existence for me. 'Suddenly – wham! – it hit me ...'

Melek stroked my chest. 'Sometimes it takes longer to see what's in front of our eyes ...'

'I don't like being afraid ...'

'Nothing you can do about that. The moment you put two thoughts together – you get fear ...'

'Fear of ourselves?'

'What do you mean?'

'I think that's my worst fear – myself. That I was born afraid. That I'll be ruled by fear. Which, let's face it, is not normal. Âşık Ahmet isn't afraid of himself. You're not – of yourself ...'

'I think if we were honest we'd all admit we are.'

'But I wasn't. I could have taken any amount of beating – until yesterday. And proudly act the heroic victim – as you put it. I can't any more. I've lost the courage. Worse than that, I've lost the will. Whatever it is – I've lost it. Fear has taken its place.'

Melek smiled. 'Welcome to adulthood.' She ran her hand over my groin. 'And there was me thinking that at the ripe old age of twenty-five you were already a mature man.'

'Melek, you're humouring me ...'

'Yes.'

'But I'm serious!'

She kissed me. 'Best time to humour you.'

I responded. We kissed for a while. Then I held her close to me. 'One last word on fear. The fear that makes people run. Turns them into deserters. That's the bugger

I fear most. I was ready to run yesterday …'

'Very sensible …'

'Melek, I'm trying to say something important.'

'Then say it straight.'

'I want to be someone who does good in this world. Who protests against everything that's wrong. I want to be an Emile Zola and shout: *J'accuse!* I want to be a Hikmet and tell everyone on this planet that universal peace is possible … But I don't think I can be …'

'Sure you can.'

'How?'

'By being stoic. You're a Turk. You know how to take things in your stride. Sunshine one day; hailstorm, the next. The Turk's fate.'

'What sort of a life is that?'

'Now you're asking too much.'

Melek could not understand my anguish. Only those who doubted their courage, or rather who knew that courage was deserting them, could understand. Melek's courage never faltered.

I began kissing her again. I suddenly felt I had to make love to her, enough to last me a lifetime.

∞∞∞∞∞∞✿∞∞∞∞∞∞

Âşık Ahmet looked twice his age. He had lost a lot of weight. And of his robust silvery mane that had waved greetings to the world as he strode along, only a few strands remained. He was also unsteady on his feet – according to Agop, the result of spinal damage incurred from the systematic beatings political prisoners received. Imagine torturing one of the nation's greatest sons! A hero of the War of Independence! One of Atatürk's greatest reformers!

I had expected many of his students to come to Bursa and welcome him from prison. In the event, besides Melek and myself only Agop, Musa, Naim, Zeki and Mustafa came. The rest, fearing that MIT agents who would be keeping an eye on Âşık Ahmet might decide to investigate them, too, had chosen to play safe. But who was I to judge them? Despite their fears, they had never stopped supporting our mentor, nor would they ever. And, of course, they had been right to be wary of MIT. I counted at least half a dozen men at the periphery of the prison gates watching us as we met Âşık Ahmet; two others, in an unmarked car, photographed us quite blatantly.

Agop and Mustafa had wanted to bring their wives, but had desisted, thinking that the presence of a woman might upset Âşık Ahmet. For the dear man's beloved wife, Leylâ, had committed suicide a couple of years earlier by taking an overdose. Having seen him in hospital after he had been beaten almost to the point of death, she had not expected him to recover. Perversely, her suicide had saved his life. A note she had left behind had caused such a public furore that the authorities had been forced to stop torturing him. (Actually, the note is a paean to love. Describing Âşık Ahmet as the 'Loving Man' *par excellence* and 'Turkey's greatest democrat', she declared that dying as his wife – they had finally been able to marry when her son from her previous marriage had come of age – had always been the only death she had wanted.

I, on the other hand, reversing my friends' logic, had brought Melek along. As an enlightened young intellectual, she was in many ways like Leylâ and I felt that her presence, mournful as it might make Âşık Ahmet, would nonetheless provide him with happy echoes of the passionate love he and his wife had enjoyed. (I was even toying with the idea of telling him, at an opportune moment, that the secret copse where Melek and I ran to make love was the same place where, years ago, Mustafa and members of his dormitory had stumbled upon them.)

Agop and his wife, Sabet, had cleaned up Âşık Ahmet's house, decked it with flowers and stocked it with food, books and records. What he needed most was weeks of rest. Consequently, we had planned to go to Istanbul immediately by taxi and get him settled at home. But Âşık Ahmet, hungry for fresh air after his time in gaol, insisted that we go by boat. On such a beautiful summer morning, skating over the sea would be intoxicating.

So we went to Yalova, boarded the ferry there, found a shady corner under the awning on the upper deck and crossed the Sea of Marmara.

I imprinted the day carefully on my mind. For, by then, I felt certain that the fortnight or so I still had in Istanbul before returning to London to finish my thesis would probably be the last I saw of Âşık Ahmet.

(I had another motive – an unconscious one which revealed itself years later. Istanbul is where the spirit of Turkey becomes palpable. And although there are many ways of internalizing the city – ways that need countless lifetimes – the best way to absorb her, or rather to witness her divinity, is to ingest her from the sea. Every panorama from the Bosporus or from the Sea of Marmara or from the luxurious expanses of pine and cypress woods reflects centuries of history. Hues that could only have been created on God's palette are scrolled on the huddled houses, on the majestic wooden *yalıs*, on their sun-stroked roofs, on pencil-thin minarets and their breast-shaped domes. And it is also by standing on the water that one can hear the numinous calls of Turkey's soil – calls which, streams of poetry tell us, invariably conjured visions of paradise to warriors, martyrs, bards and mystics alike. No wonder those who behold this heavenly city swear, like Jews do about Jerusalem, 'If I forget thee, O Istanbul ...')

Much of the time on the boat, Âşık Ahmet dozed, looking as if he carried the fatigue of several lifetimes. We took turns and held his hand. That – and no doubt the fragrance of the spray that the breeze occasionally sent our way – kept a smile on his face. And, as I had guessed, Melek's presence delighted him. On one occasion, when she had gone to get us some tea, he told me he could easily believe that she was the daughter Leylâ had always yearned for but had never had.

In between his naps, he chain-smoked and questioned us all. What were we doing? What were our aspirations?

And what were the chances of achieving them? He encouraged Melek, who had another year at Ankara University for her philosophy degree, to continue her studies and, like me, go for a doctorate. He discussed one or two points about my thesis; he knew a great deal about it because we had been corresponding regularly on its principal aspects. Indeed, by virtue of his network of sympathisers that covered the full spectrum of society, he had provided me with many important insights. But the fact that the authorities had confiscated my outline perturbed him. Much as I assured him that I had at least three copies tucked away in London, he kept saying we must find a way of getting it back.

Then he talked about himself. Though he was now retired – actually unemployable, particularly in education, because of his prison record – he was working harder than ever. He corresponded regularly with a number of ex-students who sought his advice not only on theses, lectures or speeches, as I did, but also on such intimate matters as marital and personal difficulties, the problems of bringing up children, the struggle to make ends meet and so on. The rest of his time – actually the bulk of his time – was taken up by his efforts to have the ongoing ban on the works of Nâzım Hikmet lifted and, just as importantly, to have Hikmet acknowledged internationally as one of the greatest poets of the twentieth century. Hikmet was still alive, still living in exile in Moscow, still writing. But he was in poor health and only Allah's grace – because Allah loved great poets as much as we did – kept his weary heart ticking. He, Âşık Ahmet, still corresponded with him through various and devious – channels, still received all that the great man produced. (During those times when he languished in prison, trusted colleagues collected these works and kept them in safekeeping.) He still disseminated a stream of Hikmet's poems, plays, letters and polemics to lycées, universities and foreign publishers. Tomorrow, he would resume these activities.

∞∞∞∞∞∞❀∞∞∞∞∞∞∞

When we had settled Âşık Ahmet in his house, Agop, Musa, Naim, Zeki and Mustafa went to their homes.

Melek and I stayed behind to cook a special dinner. Much as Âşık Ahmet wanted to praise our efforts on the delicacies we had prepared – aubergine salad, artichoke hearts in lemon and olive oil and swordfish in greengage sauce, all of which he loved – he could not manage to eat. Prison food, albeit meagre, was normally nourishing – and tasty – because, in the main, it was cooked by the prisoners with ingredients brought to them by relatives and friends. After years of maltreatment, however, Âşık Ahmet had been left with a barely functioning stomach. Thus he could only eat small portions of bread, olives and white cheese and, as a luxury, some yoghurt with molasses.

We should have left then, but couldn't bring ourselves to do so. Âşık Ahmet was far too tired and we wanted to be around just in case he needed something.

As Melek and I settled for the night in the lounge, he called us.

We went to him.

He was sitting in bed, smoking. The skin on his forehead had creased, indicating that something was troubling him. 'Davut, this thesis of yours …'

'Yes?'

'You say you have all your primary material here with you?'

'Much of it.'

'Go and get it – every scrap of it. Leave it with me.'

'Why?'

'It's best to play safe.'

'But nothing that I have is secret. Everything is declassified – available to everybody.'

'Everybody is not interested in it. You are. It's the back-up to your thesis. That makes it special.'

'I don't understand …'

'Look, if they've been holding on to your outline for this long, something is obviously rattling them. Give me all the material before they make a move.'

'What sort of a move?'

'A raid, probably. To confiscate what you have. To scuttle your work. Who knows? I'll try and find out. I still have spies in the reactionary camps. In the meantime …'

'But I'm only writing a thesis.'

'Theses contain words. That's what frightens them. And the more truthful these words are, the more they're terrified. Go on. Bring everything. I'll find a way of getting it all to you in London.'

'But … at some point – for certain parts of my thesis – I'll have to come back for further research …'

'Don't. Stay in London. Until things get better. Whatever you may need from here, I'll dig it up for you somehow.'

'And if things don't get better? Do I stay in exile?'

'Exile is too big a word. Besides, if they tie up your tongue, bury your words or put you in prison you'll be an exile in your own country. Let's say, you need to retreat a little in order to advance better later. I remember suggesting the same to Nâzım.'

I stared at him, unable to take in all the repercussions of what he had said.

He turned to Melek. 'Do you two tumble?'

Melek blushed. 'Yes.'

'Do you like it?'

Melek smiled boldly. 'Very much.'

Âşık Ahmet nodded approvingly. 'Good. If this world can be saved, it's the lusty women who'll save it. Does Davut like it, too?'

'Oh, yes.'

'Nothing to worry about then. Keep your honey sweet. He'll always come back.'

I managed to control my apprehension. 'Sir, aren't we presuming …?'

He looked at me fiercely. 'You still here? Go on, off you go! Get your fucking stuff here! Now!'

I nodded and rushed out.

When I reached home – the apartment I was sharing with some friends – there was a message for me. A couple of plain-clothes policemen had called; they had left their phone number; nothing of importance or urgency; but would I ring them as soon as possible to arrange a meeting?

Panic seized me. I couldn't think what to do. I managed to ring Âşık Ahmet.

He chuckled as soon as he heard my voice. 'Good thing you left when you did, Davut. The police came here looking for you. They obviously knew you'd been with me. Anyway, they want you to ring them and arrange a meeting.'

I spoke hoarsely, suddenly drained of all saliva. 'They called here, too.'

A pause, ominous and increasingly alarming, ensued.

I wailed anxiously, 'Sir – are you there?'

'Yes.'

'Do you think they want me because they saw me with you or because of my thesis?'

'I don't know. Because of your thesis, I'd say. Whatever the reason, I don't like it.'

'What shall I do?'

'Let me think.'

I waited. Almost an eternity.

When he spoke his voice had regained its old authority. 'No sense in being grilled by those hoodlums.

They can trick you with any number of questions and hold you in custody for ages.'

'What then?'

'You'll have to run.'

I began to shake. 'Run where?'

'This is what you do. Pack your things. Don't forget your passport. Don't take anything in writing – not even a newspaper. I'll send an old friend, Bekir – he drives a taxi. Give him your box-files. He'll bring them to me. You'll get them in London in a few days. After Bekir's gone, make straight for the airport. Take the first plane out – anywhere in Europe – and then proceed to London. I'll make all the arrangements. Melek will meet you at the check-in with your new ticket …'

'Won't you come to the airport too? I can't leave without saying goodbye.'

'You'll have to. I'm always under surveillance, so they'd spot you. In any case, I hate goodbyes. When you and Melek stop kissing a moment, give her a hug for me. I'll make sure I get it.'

'Several hugs.'

'And keep in touch.'

'Of course, sir.'

He hung up.

I started packing while panic tore at my guts.

<hr/>

The first flight out was to Vienna. I would have to spend a night there, then pick up a BEA flight to London.

No extra charge. Âşık Ahmet's contacts had rearranged things perfectly.

There had been no awkward questions at customs and immigration. Obviously, it had not occurred to the police that I might run away.

Melek had been allowed to accompany me to the departures lounge. She had approached one of the immigration officials, told them we were newly married and very sad to part even though it was only for a few days, and could we stay together until I boarded my plane. The man, looking implacably officious, just melted and waved us through. Talk about the contradictions in the Turkish character!

So we sat huddled on adjacent chairs, like mourners keeping vigil by a corpse.

Indeed, we were sitting around a corpse: our love. I knew that. Did she? I had realized, on my way to the airport, that I was about to kill the most precious thing in my life in order to save myself. I had turned – seemingly overnight – into the coward I had feared I was. The mere fear of arrest, of trials in dubious courts, of prison and torture was making me desert not only all my ideals – ideals entrusted to me by Atatürk as well as Âşık Ahmet – but also my beloved country and my equally beloved Melek. I was exchanging my full-frontal confrontational Turkey for the veiled treachery of Europe. What a paradox! And I was doing it with deliberation, with my eyes wide open. So there was no longer any sense in lying to myself. I was not coming back – certainly not in the foreseeable future. And while many would condone my desertion, would even praise me for being wise like Hikmet and many others, I knew I wasn't just another Turk forced into exile; I knew I was not withdrawing in order to fight another day. Nor was I disowning my country, as some bigots were bound to intimate, because, as a Jew, I was still considered by many as a non-Turk, or, at best a half-Turk. I was running away simply to save my skin. Decamping, like all cowards, at the first sign of trouble. I was failing myself – and everybody who had believed in me. And there was no way back, no chance of redemption, from such a failure.

I plucked up the courage to look at Melek. For a mad moment, I had the urge to seize her, tear off her clothes, run my body all over her body, make endless love to her.

I mustered all the integrity I had left and mumbled, 'I won't come back. You know that, don't you? I won't have the courage.'

She tried not to cry. 'Yes.'

'When I told you I was afraid of my fears, this is what I meant. But I never expected it would be so soon. That I'd succumb so easily. I can't tell you how ashamed I feel, if that means anything any more ...'

She nodded.

I held her hands. I asked my burning question, though I knew what her reply would be. 'There's another option. If you come to England ... I can lecture ... Turkish language, literature ... My college more or less asked me to ... We'd have enough to scrape by. And we'd be together.'

She smiled. 'It's tempting ...'

'But?'

'I can't.'

'Why not?'

'I'd wither there.'

'Nonsense.'

'I belong here, Davut. I'm not one who can be transplanted.'

'You don't know that.'

'I do. In my guts. I've thought about this more than you think ...'

'Even so ... Give England a try ...'

'No. Maybe that's the fear I have. That I might like it there. And choose to stay. I don't want that. There's much to be done here.'

'You can do it from England.'

'You can. And I'm sure you will. I can't.'

'What about our love ...?'

'It will live on.'

'Melek – it will die.'

'Does love ever die? Never! It just moves on to another plane ...'

'What good is that? If we can't feed it? If there's no touch ...?'

'It will find a way to feed itself.'

'You're only saying that to make leaving you – abandoning you – easier for me.'

A sudden anger clouded her face. 'What else can I say?'

I faced her – as bravely as I could. 'The truth.'

Only her tears moderated the fury in her voice. 'Very well. Âşık Ahmet was wrong when he said all I had to do was keep my honey sweet and you'd come back for it. You won't – ever. No matter how sweet I keep it. Your fears will send you running all over the world. Here and there you'll pick up honey and feel saved. But, sadly for you, they'll be synthetic – a semblance of sweetness at best, never pure honey. Even if you have a thousand women from every continent, you'll never find a kindred soul like me. Never find a body so welcoming. Loins made just for you. You'll be lost for ever. A wandering prick gradually putrefying.'

I began to cry. 'That's too cruel.'

She wiped her tears with her sleeve. 'You wanted the truth.'

The loudspeaker announced my flight.

The fire, barely flickering in our eyes, went out.

'One other thing. Even crueller because it concerns your soul. Wherever you go, whatever you do, you'll find you've stayed here. You'll realize you've never left our soil – neither our country's nor mine. Or if by chance you manage to transplant a limb here and there, your mind will always return. Your conscience will be more unforgiving than my body.'

Again the loudspeaker announced my flight – this time in English.

'That's your flight.' She brushed my hand with hers. 'Goodbye.'

She turned away, walked a few paces and then ran.

13: Âşık Ahmet

Go Like Water, Come Like Water

My dear child,

In the beginning, there is Death.

I'm trying to think which one of you told me that. Sadly, memory turns wayward with age. It was from a Türkmen storyteller, I remember that. Yet I have difficulty recollecting the features of all my boys and girls, even their names. Which is why this letter does not have an addressee and is written as much to you personally as to all of you. On the other hand, maybe this is a good thing. This way I can abstract all my students – particularly those I love (how many are there? One thousand? Two thousand? Five thousand?) – into one, conflate them, as it were, into a kaleidoscope so that rather than running hither and thither in my mind trying to find them, I give myself a shake and up you all come in wondrous shapes and colours.

So to the beginning.

Death is sitting opposite. And she – yes, female as you rightly intuited – is just the way you described her in a song. (Am I confusing you with one of my girls? Or my wife?)

Anyway, naked she is – Death. Voluptuous. Bountiful breasts. A perfect oval vagina, wide open like the Creator's mouth – which is what it is, of course – about to annunciate Âşık Ahmet's new beginning.

About to – not immediately. She's nice, Death is. She will let me write this valediction. I've made her tea and put a fresh packet of cigarettes on the table. She's even stroking my feet – bliss. My soles never recovered from the *falaka* lashes in prison.

As you know, my child, I'm not a religious man. But looking at Death, so desirable, so eager to bring me to life again, I now hope that my new beginning will be an extension of my old life, but with more, much more time with my Leylâ.

(Come to think of it, there must be another Death – the male one. He who wreaks havoc and deluges the world with rivers of blood. But no matter how hard he pursues us or breaks us, she – our beautiful Death – saves us. And makes sure we live again. And love again.)

Imagine: a new time with Leylâ … How long is it since she died? Was it only yesterday? Fifteen years? No matter. She left me her aura. So, in effect, she never died, never abandoned me.

You don't really know about Leylâ and me, my child.

Nobody does. Discretion became such a set pattern in our lives that we kept everything about our relationship secret. These days, I keep thinking maybe we were too evasive, maybe we should have told our story. Maybe, for once, life should contradict Shakespeare's Antony and not inter a person's goodness with her bones.

So here goes ...

I am from peasant stock. Born with the twentieth century. In Amasya. The family had some land and an apple orchard. Big family. Grandparents, uncles, aunts, the lot. Which meant we just about scraped a living.

Like most boys, I went to the *medrese*. Unlike most boys, I got to love learning. So the *hoca* recommended me to the local *ağa*. The latter, unlike most of the rich, was a charitable man and agreed to pay for my schooling. I was sent to Sıvas. I left home just as a widower uncle brought his new wife, Zeynep, all the way from Yozgat. She was hunchbacked. 'A hard worker', he boasted, to make it clear that he wasn't interested in her otherwise. I hated him thereafter.

I did well at school. I had an inspirational teacher, Vartabed Uncuyan, an Armenian. He opened my heart to poetry. I loved him.

Then the First World War came. And with it, the Armenian Passion. Sıvas, with its considerable Armenian population, suffered the worst. My wonderful teacher, Vartabed Uncuyan – and his family – were among the first to be killed; and his school was smashed up.

Somehow evading troops, brigands, deserters, refugees and the killings, I made my way back home.

I was as near mad as a boy of fifteen who has seen unspeakable horrors can be. Mercifully, little had changed in our backwoods. A few deaths from age or illness – including the uncle who had married Zeynep.

The family had allowed Zeynep to stay. For she truly was a phenomenal worker. Worth three men at least. And a gentle, caring person to boot. She transformed our home into a haven. And with so much love pouring out of her, she looked beautiful. Despite her deformity. Beautiful in non-specific ways just as a day remains beautiful no matter how hard man tries to despoil it.

I witnessed this beauty in all its aspects. I looked into her soul. Something about me, perhaps the fact that I still mourned my Armenian teacher, made her regard me as a kindred spirit. So she kept an eye on me. Helped me in the orchards, saved me extra portions of food, filched cigarettes from the men. Always very discreetly, needless to say. After all, she was still a young woman – barely thirty years old – and I was fast moving to a marriageable age and you know how we all think that if a man and a woman are within arm's reach they are bound to throw themselves at each other.

As it happened, we did throw ourselves at each other. But not in the usual way.

One morning, when I was at the well drawing water for the animals, I saw her at her window. She had just risen and was washing herself. She was stark naked. I watched her and was rooted to the spot, as if she were a *houri* visiting earth. She saw me but did not cover up or withdraw.

Thereafter, every morning – except when she had her monthly flow – we trysted like that. I at the well; she at her window. I think she took pleasure in showing herself to me because I was the only person in the world who looked at her not as a hunchback or a hard worker but as a beautiful woman.

This went on for months. By then I was deeply in love with her and was thinking that in a year or so, when it would be my turn to seek a wife, I would marry her.

Then calamity struck …

Death has finished her tea. And she has stopped stroking my feet. Here I am talking about Leylâ – I haven't even got to her yet – when I should have been rattling away like Polonius, giving you some home truths …

What if I offered Death another cup? Do you think she might …? Yes, she says, she'd like one. And she'd like another cigarette, too … Good, I've got a bit more time.

All right. *Home truth one*: Turkishness. The real meaning. It's galaxies apart from the so-called Turkification that the so-called Kemalists are advocating. (Atatürk must rage in his grave every time he hears his name so misused and debased.) Let me tell you what Kemalism really means. It means building a nation on solid foundations like social justice, freedom of worship and equality for all, not least for women. It means the provision of health, education, wealth and happiness for *all* our citizens, whatever their race or creed! It does not mean separatism or elitism! It does not mean robbing Jews, Armenians and Greeks with outrageous taxes as we did in 1943! It does not mean persecuting Kurds, Lazes and our other minorities because they have different cultures and different languages! It does not mean embracing demented notions like this new pan-Turkism craze that seeks to ingather the Central Asian Turkic peoples and create an ethnically pure, ultra-nationalist, ultra-Islamist empire! True Turkishness means rejoicing in the infinite plurality of people as we rejoice in the infinite multiplicity of nature! It means rejecting all the 'isms' and 'nesses' – including Turkishness. It means renouncing single cultures, single flags, single countries, single gods and embracing – and preserving – every culture, every race, every faith, every flag, every country, every god for its difference and uniqueness. It means being both a Turk and a citizen of the world, both an individual and everybody!

You might say idealism has gone to my head. That the Ottomans had similar notions but failed. That so did Alexander the Great – and he also failed. You might be right. But what if you're not? What if *I* am right? What if, as you and I feel it in our bones, the potential for pluralism exists? Can we let it die just because we have doubts?

Death is smiling at me. So inviting, with her legs parted. I think I have to go now …

No, wait. She has poured herself another cup. And lit another cigarette. She says enough pedagogics. She says tell the child about Leylâ.

All right. Where was I? Oh, yes. When calamity struck …

It was a market day. We joined in the usual bustle: buying, selling, loading, unloading. Then, when it was time to go, no Zeynep. Eventually, we found her. In a field. Rolled up like a hedgehog. Badly beaten. And raped.

My father immediately guessed the identity of the rapist: the commander of the local garrison. It was common knowledge that he assaulted women. But we had no proof. Zeynep, insisting that her assailant had knocked her unconscious, refused to name the commander. That's another example of her thoughtfulness. If we had gone after the commander – and we would have done – we would all have been killed. Garrison commanders in those last years of the Ottoman empire were a law unto themselves.

Zeynep became pregnant.

Understandably, the rape had broken her. She never again showed herself to me. But because we could no longer entertain erotic thoughts, we became closer and attended to each other at every opportunity. However – and I should have realized this – she was marking time, waiting for her delivery. Often she would get me to promise that if she died, I would look after her daughter and cherish her – somehow she knew the baby would be a girl. Her daughter would be the proof that every calamity brings with it a blessing.

And so Leylâ was born.

And true to her word, Zeynep died immediately

after the birth. If you ask me, she just stopped living.

And true to my word, I cherished Leylâ as a blessing.

Then it was 1919. Atatürk landed in Samsun and summoned us to liberate our country. We fought one of the bitterest wars known to man. We died in our hundreds of thousands. Somehow I survived.

When I returned home, Leylâ, despite the near-famine that had prevailed, had grown into a beautiful child.

Again, I looked after her as the only person in my life that mattered to me.

Then I had to be off again. This time to higher education. Atatürk wanted me as one of his pioneer teachers. To introduce the Roman alphabet. To nurture the Turkish spirit. To revive the literary genius that we have always had. I undertook the task zealously. It was, I felt, the best I could do both in memory of my first teacher, Vartabed Uncuyan, and for the new generation, for Leylâ. I went here and there, even to Europe. Then I met my mentor, our beloved poet, Nâzım Hikmet. He took me in hand. And he shaped me.

Then when I finally settled in Istanbul, I sent for Leylâ. But my family refused to let her go. By then she was eighteen. I was over thirty. They wouldn't trust me with her.

So I went to fetch her. I found her forcibly married to some farmer who treated her like a slave. I returned to Istanbul a broken man. I wanted to kill myself. But though I had failed to protect Leylâ from marrying her brute of a husband, my promise to Zeynep still stood. I had to keep alive to look after Leylâ.

Within the year, Leylâ gave birth to a son. Having done her duty to her husband, she refused to have any more children. The husband, Rasim, threatened to kill her. My mother warned me. I rushed over to Amasya.

And this time, I abducted Leylâ and her son.

Rasim pursued us. But providence – Leylâ thought it was Zeynep's spirit – came to our aid. Rasim died of a heart attack as he was about to board the train we had taken.

Rasim's family swore vengeance. They would punish Leylâ; have her stoned like a common adulteress. I confronted them. I threatened to kill every one of them if they touched a strand of her hair. That scared them. Given that as a veteran of the War of Independence, a republican and one of Atatürk's most zealous reformers, I was a man of considerable influence, they thought I could do anything with impunity. So they offered to negotiate. They accepted some compensation for Rasim's death. But on the question of the custody of Leylâ's son, Abdullah, they would not budge. Sharia law, they claimed, gave custody of the boy to the father's family. And much as we pointed out that the sharia law no longer had any jurisdiction in the Turkish republic, they insisted on going to court. Turkey, they argued, was still a Muslim country, still a realm where the father's rights outweighed the mother's. However, Leylâ refused to go to court – despite my assurances that she would win her case. A drawn-out trial, she pleaded, would have an adverse effect on her son. Finally, through intermediaries, we reached a compromise. Leylâ would have custody of Abdullah, but she would never remarry – at least not until he came of age.

Thereafter, Leylâ and her son settled in Istanbul.

Inevitably, loving each other so much, we came to desire each other. But since she was Zeynep's daughter, I kept my distance. This angered Leylâ. One day she confronted me and asked me why I was spurning her. I tried to lie and said I was much older than she was. She laughed at that. I invented other excuses like too much work, infirmities due to war wounds and so on. She laughed at those, too.

Finally, I told her about Zeynep, about the platonic yet erotic relationship we had had. That shocked her. She avoided me for days.

Then, one evening when her son was staying with a friend, she came over to my house. No sooner had she walked in than she undressed. 'Do I have my mother's body?' she asked. I managed to nod. (Indeed, except for the hump, she did have Zeynep's body. Same roseate flesh, same luminosity of good soil.) Then she held my hand. 'When she showed herself to you, she was showing me. Showing you how I would look. And telling you to wait. You don't have to wait any more.'

And so we became lovers.

And when her son came of age, we married.

A word about her son, Abdullah. He's a good boy. Very much like you. A gifted artist. Keeps to himself. Abhors politics. But his canvases speak volumes against injustice. To this day, he thinks his natural father was a paragon. I mention that to show you how honourable a person Leylâ was.

Death stirs again, my child. Her portal is glistening with dew. What a glorious sight! Any minute now this *âşık*, this lover, will witness the Godhead.

She's letting me have one final cigarette. Time for last words.

Home truth two: Don't be fooled when people tell you their cultures and civilizations are superior to yours. Such paranoia afflicts much of Europe and the US. Just remember every culture, every civilization, every literature has its own splendour.

Home truth three: Remember you can neither change your roots nor transplant them. So be proud of them. Relish them.

Home truth four: Be a Loving Man. Always. And to everybody.

Home truth five: You went like water. Now come back like water.

The cigarette is finished. She is wrapping her legs around me …

Farewell, my child, my dear, dear child …

References

1. Veli, Orhan: *Bütün Şiirleri* (*Complete Poems*) – Varlık Yayınları, 1953)
2. Nâzım Hikmet: *Taranta Babu'ya Mektuplar* (*Letters to Taranta Babu*) – Adam Yayınları, vol.2, 1987)
3. Nâzım Hikmet: *Kuvâyi Milliye* (*Nationalist Forces*) – Adam Yayınları, vol.3, 1987)
4. Nâzım Hikmet – *Piraye İçin Yazılmış Şiirler* (*Poems written for Piraye* – Adam Yayınları, vol.3, 1987)

I have been greatly inspired by Saime Göksu Timms' masterpiece, *The Romantic Communist*. This biography is not only a superb account of Nâzım Hikmet's passionate and dolorous life, but also a most insightful study of his work.